PHILIP'S CHAIR

PHILIP'S CHAIR

A NOVEL BY DALE EUNSON

Mercury House, Incorporated
San Francisco

This is a work of fiction. Names, characters, places, and incidents either are the product of the author's imagination or are used fictitiously. Any resemblance to actual events, locales, or persons, living or dead, is entirely coincidental.

Published in the United States by
Mercury House
San Francisco, California

Distributed to the trade by
Kampmann & Company, Inc.
New York, New York

Mercury House and colophon are registered trademarks of
Mercury House, Incorporated

Manufactured in the United States of America

Library of Congress Cataloging-in-Publication Data

Eunson, Dale, 1904–
    Philip's chair : a novel / by Dale Eunson.
        p.   cm.
    ISBN 0–916515–48–6 : $18.95
    I. Title
PS3509.U5P47   1988
813'.52 – dc19   88-5332
                                                                          CIP

For Binks

PART I

Whenever and wherever the grayed (or dyed) remnants of the old crowd get together, we eventually find ourselves talking about Philip. Recollection is usually tinged with affection. The cruel things that were sometimes said have gentled. It is easier to live with him in memory than it was—as we used to put it—in the flesh. Someone will say, "Remember what a pall he could cast over a party?"

"Yes . . . but then after he'd had a few drinks . . ."

"Of course he might pull a blank on you next morning."

"We had an antique bergère chair in the kidney of the piano. We called it Philip's chair. He'd walk in and make for it like a buffalo to a water hole, then sit and glower at everybody, daring you to frustrate his gloom."

"Poor Philip."

"Why poor Philip? He was rich. He had talent. He could be delightful."

"But I used to have lunch with him and George at the Harvard Club occasionally. Stimulating as going on retreat."

"You read 'There but for Grace'?"

"Silly story. They all behave like fools."

"Grace is every boy's dream girl. I once asked Philip if he had ever known a Grace. He gave me that it's-none-of-your-business look and said, 'Please grant me at least a B for invention.'"

And remember the way he walked? As if he were wound up tight and the spring might fly out?

Oh, and the house he bought in the Hills of Beverly with the proceeds of his screenplay from that Astaire-Rogers musical what-was-its-name? How did that happen? Such bad casting. Philip Pearson writing a musical? Yes, and on the way down Coldwater after the housewarming Howard Greer said—and God knows the house needed warming—Howard Greer said, "The breeze you felt must have been Harold Grieve just leaving."

3

(Harold Grieve, who had decorated the house, was married to the silent film star Jetta Goudal.) I said, "You know why Philip chose Harold? So he could meet Jetta."

And Daisy. Were you with us that day she had hysterics at the Mission Belle on the way back from La Jolla?

No, tell.

Well, she had obviously planned to get him into the feathers during that Fourth of July weekend.

Who told you that?

Daisy did. Much later. Oh, she was mad for him there for a while. She got into her Magnin nightgown, saturated herself with Joy, dimmed the lights, unlocked the door, and popped into bed. And . . . no show. Poor Daisy.

I still say poor Philip. He was probably waiting for her in *his* room.

Maybe he should have been a priest. Father Philip.

I don't know. What about those weird dames? Like Whizzer Wilkens.

Yeah, what about her? Window dressing?

Maybe she beat him or chained him in the doghouse.

Oh, come on. Let's not fantasize.

How else do you explain him?

"John, you knew him longer than the rest of us."

"He was my oldest friend."

"Don't you know what made him tick?"

I ought to, but I don't, though I have spent long hours wondering, searching for the secret, if indeed there is a secret, a *clef*.

We went to school together, survived adolescence together, lived together for a year before I was married. He was best man at my wedding. Our lives crossed and recrossed in New York and California. When we were apart we kept in touch by letter, telephone, or wire.

He stood by for two days, hating every minute of it, while Liz was going through the agonies of childbirth. It was, he seemed to feel, not at all couth of her. A female should wander off into the fields by herself and whelp, not cause all this brouhaha, this nauseating, clinical discussion about two or three fingers of dilation and the relative risk of high over low forceps.

I have read what he labeled his Day Book, and shall quote from it occasionally, but I am afraid it is more significant for what it sidesteps than for what it reveals.

Bear with me. I must tell you about myself as well as Philip, if I tell it at all. But maybe if I set down everything I can remember about us, I will discover a few clues that have escaped me, and Philip Pearson will cease to haunt me.

1

Samuel Pearson was perfect casting for a banker: He looked solid, respectable, judicious, not fat but a little portly. His iron-gray hair tended to curl up at the back over his starched collar like William Jennings Bryan's. His brown suits never seemed new even the first time he wore them, and the gold chain that sagged across his belly, from a Waltham watch to a gold pocket-knife, was neither too heavy to be ostentatious nor too slim to be serviceable. You could trust a man like that. If you deposited your savings in the vaults of the First National Bank of Montana, of which he was vice president, you could rest easy about it.

I remember when Warren G. Harding was about to relieve the nation of Woodrow Wilson, who had not only not kept us out of war as he had promised to do, but had also clung tenaciously to the presidency long after being felled by a stroke. My father thought he was paying the Republican standard-bearer a compliment when he said that that fella Harding sort of favored Sam Pearson.

"Not at all," my mother countered with her stunning gift for the non sequitur. "Mr. Pearson is a Democrat." (She gave the word "Democrat" the denigrating inflection she gave "half-breed," which conjured up a slithery individual not to be trusted out of sight.) She turned to me at the supper table. "I happen to be privy to this information because when I worked at the polls in the primaries Mr. Pearson requested the Democratic ballot. But *that* is to go no further. Such information is sacrosanct." Mamma had been a schoolteacher and often used words like that even at the supper table.

"Nobody's perfect," Papa said. "Pearson's always been fair and square with me. We mighta been up shit crick when I asked for an extension on the loan, but he just said, 'Jim, old man, you're not the only son of a bitch got dried out last summer.'"

"Not precisely in those words, I presume."

" 'Pay up after the next harvest,' " Papa went on as if he had not heard her, as often he had not. "That's what he said. 'The bank don't want your land. If we was to foreclose on every poor bastard that can't settle up this fall we'd be up the crick with you.' "

"They're Irish, too," Mamma said. "And the combination — well!"

"The combination of what?" Papa asked.

"Catholic and Irish. Like Indians, where liquor is concerned."

"I never smelt liquor on Sam Pearson's breath," Papa said.

"Not during banking hours, of course. He'd be careful. But," and she raised her eyebrows, "I've heard that some years ago . . . you've got a music lesson tomorrow, Johnny. You'd better practice."

I went to the piano — I was paying for it ten dollars a month — and played "Clair de lune," which was mostly marked *pp*. Even so, I could not hear what happened to Mr. Pearson because Mamma's back was to me and her voice never carried unless she was mad. But Papa was facing my way, and I could hear the indignation in his retort, "Who'd repeat a thing like that?"

Whoever it was drew a snort from my father. "That fool woman ought to be horsewhipped is all I can say!"

I had never smelled alcohol on Mr. Pearson's breath and I figured I knew him better than Mamma did because his son Philip was my best friend. I spent a lot of time at the Pearson residence on Fifth Avenue three blocks north of Main. It was a big, two-story house — at any rate big to me who had lived only in ranch houses and the bungalows we rented in Cottonwood during the winter — with four bedrooms, one for Mr. and Mrs. Pearson, and separate rooms on the second floor for the three children, King (named for his maternal grandfather), Maureen, and Philip. (Most of the kids I knew had to double, sometimes triple, up but they did not have fathers who were vice presidents of banks.)

When I first met the Pearsons, King was already a freshman at Notre Dame. They could have used his bedroom for guests because there was a toilet upstairs, but they never seemed to have company. Except when King was home on holidays the curtains were always down.

There was a peculiar odor, sort of like punk, that lingered about the room for months after King went off to college. (Philip said it was incense King brought home from South Bend.) The room was sparsely furnished with a bureau, a ladder-back chair, and a single bed (with no pillow) covered with a popcorn-tufted spread. Nothing hung on the walls except a colored picture of a young woman and child over the metal bedstead. (There was one just like it in Philip's room, and for all I know probably one in Maureen's room too. I was never in there.)

"Is she some relation of yours?" I once asked Philip.

"Don't you know the Virgin Mary when you see her?" he asked.

"No. I never saw her. Who's the Virgin Mary?"

"She's the Holy Mother. Don't you have the Holy Mother in your church?"

"We have Mrs. Schilling, but she's old and she's got gray hair and she never had any kids," I told him. Mrs. Schilling was first reader and a Christian Science practitioner. Whenever Mamma had a migraine she would telephone Mrs. Schilling who would give her an absent treatment for two dollars.

King was studying for the priesthood, Mrs. Pearson confided when she showed me a class photograph he had sent home from South Bend. "He has already heeded the call," she said in a hushed voice. "I'm so proud, my firstborn being chosen." Philip resembled King around the eyes, but King was much better looking and didn't seem to have a chip on his shoulder. I thought he was about the handsomest young man I had ever seen. It was hard to picture him ever wearing a long skirt and a collar on backward.

Maureen had turned fifteen and was a junior at Cottonwood County High the fall of 1918. She had red hair like her mother — all three Pearson kids had red hair — and wore it in two large buns over her ears. "Cootie garages" we called them. Her face sometimes looked as if she had splattered red ink on it, especially right after school started in September. She wasn't very popular with boys until the freckles faded in November or December. Maureen once tried to hurry the process by bleaching them out, but the peroxide blistered her skin.

Maureen was torn between entering a convent and becoming an authoress like George Eliot when she grew up. For a while she evidently settled on the latter. Many evenings I would notice her at the Carnegie Library with her nose in a book that Miss Main, our straitlaced librarian, would not permit her to check out. They were mostly small books in fine print by foreigners like Balzac, Flaubert, and Tolstoy from stacks in Adults Only. (You could hide them inside Required Reading like *Alice of Old Vincennes, Silas Marner,* or *The Last of the Mohicans* in case Miss Main cast her eagle eye your way.)

★   ★   ★

In 1950 I took my wife back to Cottonwood to show her where I had grown up. Miss Main, looking exactly as I remembered her, was still the librarian. Lowering my voice to library level I introduced Liz and myself, and asked if by any chance she remembered me.

"Why, of course, Johnny," she said. "Though I suppose I must call you John now."

"Please don't."

"I have a special shelf for your works and Philip Pearson's."

"Miss Main, that's the nicest thing ever happened to me."

She showed us the shelf. There were our magazine stories, collected and annotated and bound in vellum, which I'm afraid few of them deserved, and all the novels we had written up to that time. And there stood Miss Main waiting for me to say something, as if anything I might choose to say would be a pearl worthy of her add-a-pearl necklace.

I could not help myself. I kissed her. She blushed and went all tiddly. "How—how is Philip?" she asked finally.

"He's—well, he's fine," I said, though "fine" was never precisely the word for Philip.

"You were such quiet boys," she said. "I guess I should have known. Expanding your minds with literature far beyond your years. Remember how you used to take down Adults Only and hide them inside big books so I wouldn't notice?"

"You mean you did notice?"

"But of course." She smiled. Twinkled, perhaps one should call it. "Well, it didn't seem to do your brains irreparable damage, did it?"

We talked for a little while, shying away from the subject of what happened to the elder Pearsons. Miss Main was eager to know how it was, working in Hollywood, and warned me not to stay out there too long. "Look what happened to poor Scott Fitzgerald."

"I don't think Hollywood can be blamed for Scott," I told her. "The seeds of self-destruction were planted in him long before he thought of Hollywood."

"And please, Miss Main," Liz put in, and meant it, "if you ever come west, plan to stay with us. We have a nice quiet guest room."

"I'm getting to be quite an old lady," Miss Main sighed. "Like old wine, I don't travel well anymore. But you are a dear to suggest it. It has been a great honor to have you stop by. Please tell Philip to come home and see us — while I can still see him. My eyes are not what they used to be. It's easier for the young people to fool me than it was in your day."

Outside on the steps I stopped and blinked at the golden dome of the Cottonwood County Courthouse across the street. The clock over the entrance had stopped either at high noon or at midnight. How long ago, I wondered? What year?

"She's a darling," Liz said.

"I used to think of her as a gorgon."

"Why are you crying?"

"Because it's all wrong for it to be an honor to Miss Main to have me stop by. She should be saying, 'Sssh, Johnny. Lower your voice.'"

★　★　★

Philip's room was always a mess. His mother had finally served notice that she was no longer going to pick up after him. At thirteen it was high time he learned to practice neatness about his quarters and person. "I should think you'd be ashamed to take Johnny up to that pigsty," she once said when he brought me home after school to show me his latest treasure — a personally autographed photo of Nazimova.

Movie star photos set you back twenty-five cents "to cover postage," but this one hadn't cost a penny. Philip's maiden aunt Grace lived in Los Angeles and had actually met Nazimova. At least she said she had, but it was hard to believe that anybody's maiden aunt could, or would, speak to a woman who danced half-naked with the head of John the Baptist on a platter. (Nazimova had been a favorite of Mamma's too, from *War Brides* through *Camille,* but *Salome* put the kibosh on her once and for all. You might expect Theda Bara or Louise Glaum to do a trick like that, but not Nazimova, and if people called that art, then art could get along without Mamma!)

Philip's bed was a duplicate of the one in King's room, but his walls were a crazy quilt of photographs of female and male movie stars clipped and trimmed from *Photoplay, Picture Play,* and *Motion Picture Classic. M. P. Classic* cost ten cents more than the other two, but we figured it was worth it because the portraits were reproduced in sepia.

In one corner of the room stood a dusty Ferris wheel that Philip had constructed from Meccano when he was only eight. On a table beside the door into the hall sat his portable Brunswick Talking Machine with a stack of records on a shelf under it. On the other side of the door hung a crucifix. Beneath it a library-sized dictionary lay open on its stand. There was no room for it downstairs in the parlor, and Philip and I spent many guilty hours looking up words like *penis* and *clitoris* and *vulva.*

On Philip's unmade bed lay his cotton flannel nightgown where he had dropped it this morning before breakfast, and beside the bed was Prince's old blanket. Prince was a very large and often smelly collie, especially smelly after it had rained, as it had done earlier that day. Above the headboard was pinned a

Harvard pennant. Harvard was where Philip was going to college because Mr. Pearson had gone there and graduated, Philip said, with a magna, whatever that was.

"Look here at this," Philip said proudly, removing the precious photograph from a large envelope. It was Nazimova herself, made up as the Brat. "To Philip, with every good wish, Nazimova," it was inscribed. We were both impressed by "with every good wish." Ordinary people write "yours truly" or "regards."

"Gosh!" I said. "Where are you going to hang her?" I glanced around the walls.

"I was thinking about there beside the crucifix, but Mother might think that was sacrilegious." The Pearson kids always called Mrs. Pearson "Mother," which seemed kind of funny to me, but classy too. Like rich kids in books. "What do you think?"

"I don't know about sacrilegious, but you got space there, and where else?"

Philip held Nazimova up next to the crucifix, shook his head no, tried crowding her in between Lillian Gish and May Allison, but decided it was a problem not to be disposed of lightly.

"What say we skate down to the Clef Music Store?" I asked. "Mr. Horowitz has got a new record of Galli-Curci's."

He thought about this. Philip's taste did not incline to the operatic. Besides, popular records cost only seventy-five cents while the big Red Seal twelve-inchers set you back two dollars. Now he shrugged, as if he were doing me a favor. "Okay. I'll make a deal. I go with you to the music store if you go with me to buy gym clothes. I've got to have them by tomorrow, and . . ."

He paused. "And what?" I asked him.

The skin between his freckles turned pink. "Well," he squirmed, "I don't know how to ask for — you know."

"No, I don't know. What?"

"That elastic gizmo you wear over your peter."

"Jockstrap."

"Yeah. But how do you ask for it?"

"You find a man clerk and tell him you want a jockstrap. That's easy. They only got Chad and Everett Fowler at the Male Mode."

"*You* ask for it."

"I will not. You got to get used to stuff like that. You're thirteen now."

"Mother," Philip called as we clattered down the stairs, "can I have some money for my gym clothes?"

"I haven't any cash," Mrs. Pearson said, coming out of the kitchen and wiping her hands on her apron. "Ask your father."

"The bank's already closed."

"Tap on the door and Mr. Tolson will hear you . . . I know what *you're* waiting for, Johnny." She disappeared into the kitchen for a minute and came back with a plate of fudge. I liked Mrs. Pearson. She was the best-looking mother in town. In fact she didn't look like a mother at all. She wasn't fat or lumpy, her voice was warm and husky, and she did not wear sensible shoes, even at home. She had blue eyes that seemed even bluer than they were on account of her flaming red hair, and a mole high on her left cheek. But it was her fudge that made her memorable to me. Stella Pearson made the best fudge I ever ate. It was smooth and creamy, not like the brittle, sugary stuff that my mother turned out once in a while.

I picked up a piece and bit into it. "Gee," I said, "you've done it again, Mrs. Pearson. I wish you'd tell Mamma how to do that."

Mrs. Pearson smiled. "I'm afraid your mother wouldn't appreciate that, Johnny." Meanwhile Philip was helping himself to a third piece. "Now, Philip, you know too much candy is bad for the skin at your age. Johnny, don't you ever — well, get hickies? I hate that word."

"Not so far," I said.

"Knock wood."

The weather had cleared up so it would be okay to roller-skate downtown. Mrs. Pearson watched us through the screen door while we fastened skates to our high-top shoes.

"Do I have to go to the bank?" Philip asked. "Why can't I just charge the stuff?"

"Because your father has conniptions about charge accounts."

My father did too, but he could not help himself. If it hadn't been for our charge account at the Sterling Mercantile Store there would have been long stretches when we wouldn't have had enough to eat.

There had already been a heavy frost, and the golden afternoon sun flamed the leaves on the aspen and cottonwood trees. We skated in silence for a block or two with Prince loping along at our heels. Then he gave up and went home. I was good on skates, but Philip took short, jerky strides as if he were afraid his feet would not keep up with him if he leaned forward. Consequently he fell often, and that afternoon he landed on his behind directly in front of St. Matthew's Church.

If I had been alone I would have crossed the street to pass the church on the opposite side. Priests and nuns scared me. They dressed up like witches and did not have homes or get married or have children, and their church was open all the time, not just on Sunday. What did they *do* in there, I wondered? I had never dared go inside, even when Philip once asked me to go along while he went to confession. "What have you got to confess?" I asked him.

"Well, the last time I sassed my mother, I contradicted my father, and I told a dirty story."

"What did the priest do to you?"

"Gave me three Hail Marys and asked me what the dirty story was."

"Did you tell him?"

"Think I'm crazy? I said I forgot."

A nun came out of the church entrance and scurried down the stone steps to where Philip was trying to get to his feet without removing his skates. "Poor little Philip," she said. "Are you hurt?"

"No, I'm okay, Sister Agatha. It's these darn wet leaves. My skate skidded."

"I did that when I was learning to skate," she said sympathetically.

A nun on roller skates? Sister Agatha must have noticed the expression on my face. She smiled. "That was before I became Sister Agatha."

Who was she *then,* I wondered? And who is she *now?* Does she have hair? Legs? Does she take a bath? Does she go to the toilet? Does she have birthdays?

"How is your dear mother?" she asked Philip as he brushed himself off.

"She's okay."

"We haven't seen her at mass recently. Father Gilpin was remarking on it just this morning."

"I guess she's been busy," Philip said.

"Well, remember me to Sam. And take care." She walked back up the steps and we skated off down the street, slower now.

"How come that — that lady calls your father Sam?"

"They're cousins," Philip said. "Least they were cousins. After you take the veil you're not related to anybody but God and you're the bride of Christ."

"I don't get it," I said.

We took off our skates in front of the First National. Philip rapped on the door. Directly it swung open and there stood Mr. Tolson, the old bookkeeper who wore an eyeshade and gray spats and had his sleeves rolled up so that the cuffs wouldn't get dirty. "Ah, the dashing banditti," he said. "*Entrez-vous.* You've come to rob the bank, I presume."

"Only my father," Philip said. He was used to Mr. Tolson's joshing.

"You got your six-shooters with you?"

"Sure. We never hold up a bank without them, do we, Johnny?"

I tried to laugh, but it came out hollow. Talk like that — robbing a bank — even if it was just a joke, made me nervous.

Mr. Tolson led us back to Mr. Pearson's office and opened the door. "Hands up, Sam," he said. "Here's the James brothers."

Mr. Pearson chuckled and raised his hands over his head, then lowered them and hugged Philip. You could see he was crazy about his family. There were photographs of all three kids and Mrs. Pearson on his desk. He held out his hand for me to shake. "How's your dad?" he asked.

"He's just fine," I said.

"I hear you all had a bumper crop."

"You bet," I said. "Finally the wheat went forty bushels to the acre."

"That's the ticket," Mr. Pearson said. "Crops like this year's make it simpler for all of us, don't it?" He turned back to Philip who was looking up at him with a frown on his face.

"Dad," he said, "shouldn't you say 'don't they'?"

"Got to watch my p's and q's around you young scholars, don't I?" He turned to me. "I'm afraid I let down my verbal bars after banking hours. Now, Philip my lad, what's the figure you hope to extract from your old man this afternoon?"

Philip explained about the gym clothes and track shoes and about what they could cost at the Mode.

A shadow crossed Mr. Pearson's face. "I'd rather you didn't go to the Mode," he said.

"Oh? Why?" Philip wanted to know.

"I'd just rather you didn't, that's all."

"But their stuff is regulation. That's what our gym teacher told us, didn't he, Johnny? Didn't Mr. Cram say that?"

I nodded, but I felt as if I might be getting into something that was none of my business. Maybe, with Papa still owing the bank till he sold off the wheat, I'd better not side with Philip against his father.

"I'm sure you can find something at Sterling's that's just as good. After all, how stylish can you be in a gym suit?"

Philip turned and kicked at the corner of his father's big mahogany desk. "Oh, shoot, *Sterling's,*" he said in disgust. "Why can't I go to the Mode? Johnny did, last year, didn't you?"

Again I nodded, but Mr. Pearson did not see me.

"What Johnny does is no concern of yours!" he said, his voice rising. "I don't want a son of mine going into the Mode. Do you hear, Philip?"

"Why? Do the Fowlers owe you money?" The Fowlers owned the Mode.

"The Fowlers don't owe me a goddamn thing!"

Mr. Pearson was breathing hard. He hit the desk with his fist and then looked at his hand as if he'd never seen it before. I turned away and glanced out the window. Mr. Cram, sporting a new short haircut, was coming out of the barbershop. He had been romancing Miss Pauling, our English teacher. She was only in her twenties and his hair was beginning to turn gray.

"*Finis!*" Mr. Pearson said. He removed his glasses and wiped off the moisture with his pen wiper. It left a streak of ink on one lens and getting it off took time. We stood and waited. Finally he put his glasses on again, reached in his breast pocket, took out his wallet, and handed Philip ten dollars. "There. This ought to take care of everything," he said.

"Thanks," Philip said, pocketing the bill. "But I still don't see why I can't . . ."

"Didn't you hear me say *finis,* Philip?"

"I heard you."

"Well," and he turned to include me, "I trust this little family contretemps will never be mentioned to anyone."

Philip nodded sullenly. I crossed my heart. That made Mr. Pearson smile. "Give my regards to your father," he said. "Tell him to drop by and see me, any time. Not just on . . . business matters."

It was only a block from the bank to the Clef Music Store so we didn't bother to put on our skates. Philip was mad, you could see that. I mean you could really *see* it. His eyes were squinted and his lips stuck out in a pout. He took short, stiff-legged steps and did not speak to Bones Kimble when we passed him coming out of Gates' Ice Cream Parlor. Bones was the fattest kid in Philip's freshman class, but you couldn't help liking him. He had a knack for making people laugh. We all thought Bones could be another Fatty Arbuckle if he ever wanted to.

A four-foot-high Victor dog with an ear cocked to His Master's Voice stood sentinel at the entrance to the Clef Music Store, which was owned by Moses Horowitz. Mr. Horowitz was the only Jew in Cottonwood, unless Lew Schwartz, the stationmaster, was passing, and was probably respected by everybody except my mother, who said Jews were money-grubbers and, besides, they had killed Christ. Papa said well, maybe so, he hadn't been there at the time and so far as he knew, neither had Mr.

Horowitz. Besides, Mr. Horowitz was a brother Mason. He belonged to the Blue Lodge of the Cottonwood Chapter, but he couldn't ever become a Shriner or anything like that because you had to be a Christian and swear some kind of solemn oath in order to go up further in the Masonic order.

Nevertheless, Papa said, Moses Horowitz was a better Christian than lots of Christians he'd encountered, one or two of them right in Mamma's own Christian Science church.

Mr. Horowitz greeted us just as cordially as if we were going to buy every Red Seal record in the joint, though he probably knew that we could not do anything except listen to one or two on the high-busted Victrola in the private booth.

"What can I tempt you with today, gentlemen?"

"I can't think of the name of it," I said, "but . . ."

" 'Whispering'? With 'The Japanese Sandman' on the other side?"

"No, Mr. Horowitz. It's classical. That new Galli-Curci."

"Think of that," Mr. Horowitz said, raising his eyebrows. "Galli-Curci already. Which one? 'The Bell Song'?"

"No, it's . . . it's . . ." Suddenly the name popped into my mind. " 'Caro Nome.' "

"Ah, that is very good. I am not enthusiastic about the high tessitura, but Galli-Curci is a musician as well as a trapeze artist. And pardon me, young man, but if you don't mind, it's 'Caro No-may.' That's Italian, not like Alaska. You don't mind if I should correct you?"

"No," I said, "I *want* to know how to say it. We've only got Latin and Greek in high school." We had had German, with Miss Trotter, but in 1917 they burned all the German textbooks and Miss Trotter had to go live with her sister in Menomonee Falls, Wisconsin.

"It means 'dear name,' " Mr. Horowitz explained. "*Caro* — dear, *no-may* — name. And I wish I could let you hear it this afternoon, but I'm sold out. Mrs. Kingman, you know Mrs. Kingman lives up back of the courthouse? She was in here not ten minutes ago and bought the very last one."

Mr. Kingman was a cattleman and Mrs. Kingman had come from back east somewhere, Minneapolis or St. Paul, I don't know which. Mrs. Kingman had once gone to Chicago to hear Mary Garden in *Thaïs* and never let anybody forget it. She was president of the Thursday Afternoon Club, which Mamma would have liked to join, but we were only farmers who rented houses in Cottonwood during a few of the winter months.

"You come back ten days from now and I'll have another shipment, let's hope," Mr. Horowitz said. "Meantime, how about the new Gigli? 'Your Tiny Hands Are Frozen,' from *La Bohème?* Sweeter to me than Caruso." He pronounced it Car-oo-zo. "Not that Caruso is not great, he is the greatest, but for Puccini, give me fat little Gigli. Ah, Puccini!"

He clasped his hands together, closed his eyes, and began to hum the opening bars.

"We got to hurry, Mr. Horowitz. We got to get down to Sterling's before it closes."

"Some other time then," Mr. Horowitz said. "Unless maybe you care to take Gigli out and bring him back if you don't like him? I don't know any other thirteen-year-old boys in Montana who ever heard of Galli-Curci, so I trust you."

"He's thirteen, I'm fourteen," I said.

"Good. Then I trust you more."

"Thanks, Mr. Horowitz, but I might scratch the record." I couldn't very well confess that we did not have a Victrola. If the price of wheat went up enough before we had to sell it, Papa had promised that we could have one.

It was three blocks from the Clef Music Store to Sterling's, so I went outside and leaned on the Victor dog while I fastened my skates. Philip stood beside me not doing anything but staring across the street. "Come on," I said, "you said we had to hurry."

He did not seem to hear. Instead, without looking right or left, he started across Main Street. Mr. Monroe's bakery wagon honked and Willie, the driver, had to brake so hard to keep from running him down that he killed his engine, but Philip kept right on going. He didn't even hear Willie yell, "Watch where you're going, you dumb bastard."

Philip walked straight into the door of the Male Mode.

A tailor's dummy, whose face looked a little like the movie star Wallace Reid, stood in the window and Mr. Chad Fowler, the younger of the Fowler brothers who owned the store, was tucking in its shirt. Mr. Fowler saw Philip and waved to him, but he went right on with the job of dressing the dummy in the latest Hart, Schaffner and Marx jacket.

I was tempted to stall for time. The post office was next door to the Clef Music Store. I could go in and get the mail — I was tall enough now to work the combination on Box 195 — and then see if Philip was still in the Mode. On the other hand, that did not seem like a best friend. Maybe he could not ask for a jockstrap and would need help. Of course he had promised his father that he wouldn't go to the Mode and I had heard him, so if I tagged along I'd be like an accessory or something.

I took off my skates once more, crossed the street, and entered the store. Mr. Fowler called out, "I'll take care of you young gents in just a minute. If I leave this character with his fly open he might get taken to the hoosegow."

Philip stood, his back to the entrance, looking at a pair of canvas track shoes. I walked up close beside him. "Gosh, you shouldn't be in here," I said very low.

"Nobody can tell me where I can buy clothes," he said.

"But he's not nobody. He's your father."

"He won't do anything. He never does."

Then Mr. Fowler was standing before us, smiling. He was a good ad for his store — tall and thin, his black hair Stacombed but still wavy and shiny, a heavy gold ring set with a diamond solitaire on the fourth finger of his left hand, the press of his dove-colored flannel pants razor sharp. Because we were avid movie fans, Philip and I had got into the habit of comparing people we knew to movie stars. My father looked kind of like Thomas Meighan, I thought. Philip thought his mother looked like Anita Stewart.

I took a look at Mr. Fowler and pegged him as Eugene O'Brien.

Mr. Fowler rubbed his hands together. "Now let me guess what you gents want. It's late September — about time for new gym clothes, not so?"

Philip was still staring at the track shoes, his lips in that pout. Apparently he was having second thoughts about defying his father.

"Well," I said, "I got a set last year, remember, Mr. Fowler?"

"As if it was yesterday. Let's see. Your name is . . ."

"Ewing. John Ewing."

"Ah *ha!* And now you've grown six inches — anybody can see that — and want another set."

"Well, no," I said. "Just an inch and a quarter, but . . ." I turned and nodded at Philip.

"It's me," he said, as if he were angry at something. "That is, I mean it is I."

Mr. Fowler laughed. "It is I, it is I, it is I," he said. "I try to remember that, but it sounds wrong when everybody else says 'It is me.' Tell me. This I never learned. What about 'than'? Does 'than' take 'me,' or 'I'?"

"We haven't come to 'than' with Miss Pauling yet," Philip said.

"Well, do me a favor and let me know when you and Miss Pauling come to it. I'll be on tenterhooks . . . And now, Mr. — ah — we haven't seen you in here before, have we?"

"Pearson," Philip said. "Philip Pearson."

"Sam Pearson's boy?" Mr. Fowler said.

Mr. Fowler stared at him for at least ten seconds before he said, "Well, whaddaya know? Young Phil Pearson. Let me look at you — for size."

Philip turned so that Mr. Fowler could see him square on. "I'm going on five foot one," he said.

"You favor your mother more than your father," Mr. Fowler said after a moment.

"All us kids do," Philip sounded less tense, more like Philip.

There was a funny look on Mr. Fowler's face. I'd seen Eugene O'Brien with that same look when he was sizing somebody up. "Your old man seems to have got pretty well wiped out."

"Wiped out? What do you mean by that, Mr. Fowler?" Philip asked.

"Just an expression. Now, let's see. You'll be needing?"

"Two undershirts, two gym pants, two pairs of socks, track shoes like these . . . and . . ." He took a deep breath and then came out with it very fast, "a jockstrap."

"Bravo!" Mr. Fowler said. "Some boys can't say that the first time out."

"I don't see why not," Philip said. "It's just—just something you need for athaletics."

"But you don't need it a hell of a lot when you're thirteen," Mr. Fowler laughed.

Fifteen minutes later we left the store. Philip carried his new gym outfit in the snappy brown paper sack stamped with the crowing-rooster trademark of the Male Mode. We walked along in silence for a block or two. Then I said, "You can throw the sack in Beaver Creek."

"But the wrapping paper's got the rooster on it too."

Another silence. Then, "Your father won't be home when you get there anyhow, will he?"

"No. But Mother'll notice. And she just might happen to tell him."

"Well, couldn't you ask your mother not to mention it?"

"Are you crazy?"

It was a problem, and the big brown sack began to burn Philip's hands. He said, "Come on. Let's go up and look at the billboard."

He meant the big advertising display that belonged to the Musselshell Theater up at Seventh and Clark. They usually pasted up new twenty-four sheets for big, important movies a week before they began advertising in the *Treasure State News,* and there was a rumor that Cecil B. DeMille's new picture, *Don't Change Your Husband,* with Gloria Swanson and Lew Cody, was in the offing. Philip and I had what Mamma called a crush on Gloria Swanson ever since *Male and Female* and we didn't want to miss anything she was in.

There was a new twenty-four sheet all right, but it advertised
Mary Pickford in *M'liss*. Mary Pitchfork, as all the kids called her.
We had outgrown her. We had become sophisticates.

"Look," Philip said. "I know what. We go down to Sterling's
and you walk in and ask for some of their wrapping paper, then
we'll go out in the alley and rewrap this junk."

"Why do *I* walk in?"

"You're my friend."

How could I tell even my best friend that we owed Sterling's
$260 for meat and groceries, and that the last time I'd gone in
there to buy supplies for the ranch, Mr. Sterling himself had
spied me and climbed down out of his cage on the second floor
to ask when we were going to settle up. I told him that we — Papa,
that is — he was waiting, hoping for wheat to go up to eighty-five
cents. Which was true, but that hadn't cut much ice with Mr.
Sterling. He scowled. "Well, tell him I can't keep charging
supplies till hell freezes over."

"Oh, he knows that, Mr. Sterling," I said. "And you'll be the
first debt he pays off."

I couldn't tell Philip that, and I didn't need to. It was none of
his beeswax. Besides, there was no reason he couldn't go into
Sterling's himself. Folks like the Pearsons wouldn't owe anybody
for more than a month, you could bet. Why, the vice president of
the First National probably had thousands of dollars in ready
money. "You go in yourself," I said. "I'll hold the gym junk."

"Well, if that's the way you feel," Philip said.

"That's the way I feel."

We were within half a block of Sterling's when suddenly we
saw Mr. Pearson step out of the Smoke Shop carrying a box of
White Owl Premiums. He stopped to light one, cupping the
match in the palm of his hand to keep the wind from blowing it
out. Philip said, "*Here. You* bought this," and thrust the
incriminating evidence into my hand. "Come on."

He started walking fast, right toward his father. Mr. Pearson
saw us coming. "Well, well," he said jovially, "we three meet
agayne in thunder, lightning, or in rain."

We both looked blank.

"Not a very good joke." Mr. Pearson smiled. "I never thought the three witches were Shakespeare's most sublime inspiration, but it just popped into my head." He looked down at the sack I was carrying. "You boys have been shopping, I see."

Neither one of us could speak. I wanted to help Philip out, but I couldn't lie. Maybe I could have if I hadn't been afraid Mr. Pearson would see through it. Then after what seemed like five minutes while we just stood there dumb, Philip took the package out of my hands.

"That's right," he said. "We've been shopping, for my gym clothes."

"And you went to the Mode."

"Yes," Philip said, in a so-what-are-you-going-to-do-about-it tone of voice.

"I . . . see." Mr. Pearson took the cigar out of his mouth and tapped off the ashes. Then he looked down at the sidewalk where part of the ashes still glowed. He made a point of stepping on the red spot. I had thought until that moment that parents were never at a loss for words. Mine never seemed to be.

"Who waited on you?" Mr. Pearson finally said.

"Mr. Fowler."

"Which one? Everett?"

"No, Mr. Chad Fowler."

"Ah," Mr. Pearson said, and seemed somehow relieved. Then he put his arm over Philip's shoulder. "Come on, son," he said, "your mother will have dinner waiting for us."

Philip turned and shot a look at me, as if to say, See? What did I tell you?

"You coming along, Johnny?" Mr. Pearson asked. "There's always room for one more."

"No, thanks just the same, Mr. Pearson. I go to work at six."

"To work? You mean schoolwork?"

"No. I've got a job from six to ten running the elevator at the Lewis and Clark Hotel."

"Aren't you a little young for that? I mean—an elevator in a traveling man's hotel?"

"It pays a dollar a night," I explained, "and there's not much activity that time of the evening, so I can do my homework."

"I know, but it seems to me . . . well, of course it's none of my business, is it?"

"You see," I went on, trying to justify my folks for letting me do it, "I can help out when times are bad. Anyhow, this way I don't need an allowance for movies and dates and — well, stuff like that."

Mr. Pearson frowned. "If you work every night," he said, "you don't need much money for movies and dates, do you?"

"Oh, I got Saturday and Sunday nights off."

He shook his head as if once more he did not know quite what to say. Then right out of the blue he said a funny thing: "Does your father know what a lucky man he is?"

"Oh, he's not very lucky, Mr. Pearson. At least not lately he hasn't been. Like last year when the hail cut a swath through our wheat and didn't even touch the section to the south of us. I guess Papa told you that."

"Yes, he told me," Mr. Pearson said.

from Philip Pearson's Day Book

Not to be opened prior to my death!

Oct. 4, 1918. My father cut my allowance to 50¢ a week until I make up the $9.50 I spent on gym clothes at the Male Mode. That would take me 19 weeks, but I told my mother and she said we'll see about that.

2

That fall my mother was not planning on moving into town before the middle of November, so I boarded with my sister, Evelyn, and her husband, Henry Peterson. Henry, who was thirty-two and ten years older than Evy, had escaped the draft because he had become father to a baby girl born on April 6, 1917, the very day, practically to the minute, that President Wilson had declared war on Germany. We were all relieved that Henry did not have to go off to Camp Lewis the way our hired man, Jim Sawyer, did, but, as my mother said with one of her sniffs, it kind of made you wonder. Maybe there was some truth in the old saying that God protects — well, never mind whom he protects. Whoever it was, I guess she figured Henry was included. She often said Henry did not have any get-up-and-go; he'd probably be a bookkeeper all his life.

"Evy could have done worse," Papa said. He was probably thinking of that German surveyor who took a shine to her one summer.

Because it was cheaper up there, the Petersons had rented a new, three-room bungalow on the prairie overlooking the valley where Cottonwood proper was pretty well shielded from the north winds. You'd walk out Main past the courthouse and it might be down around zero but you wouldn't notice it much. The snowflakes would be soft and drifting straight down. Then suddenly you'd make the top of the grade and the wind would be howling like a pack of wolves and turning the snow into needles of ice.

There were no trees up there. So far only five houses had been built, all of them exactly alike. There was a kitchen with the very latest improvement, a "breakfast nook" (which meant you didn't need a dining room), a bedroom where Evelyn and Henry slept, and a living room with a bed that pulled out from under a built-in, golden oak sideboard. I slept there with Henrietta who was a year and a half by then and no longer wet her pants at night. At least that's what my sister claimed. Anyhow, Henrietta was a good little kid as little kids go, and didn't keep me awake. Not much of anything could after a school day plus four hours on the Lewis and Clark elevator.

Of course the Peterson house was no place to invite Philip Pearson, or even my second best friend, Kim Sumner, whose father was in grain and feed. But it was always pleasant there. I liked Henry. Some men would have kicked at having a kid my age living with them and their wife and baby in a house that small, but he never said a word. Anything Evy wanted was hunky-dory with him. It was lucky I could do most of my studying at the hotel because Henry had to bring home a lot of bookkeeping from the Montana Power Company office where he worked, and he needed the breakfast nook table to spread out his papers.

Another thing. He'd worry about me if I was late, just like my father, but he'd make a joke out of it. Say it was eleven o'clock by the time I got home. (Sometimes they'd ask me to keep the elevator at the hotel running later than ten because there was a convention or something, and the Petersons couldn't afford a telephone so I couldn't let them know.) Henry wouldn't bawl me out. The light would still be burning in the breakfast nook and he'd be sitting there. I'd walk in the kitchen door — the front door was on the north side of the house and if you opened it, all of Henry's papers would fly galley west — and Henry would look up from where he was still ten dollars off getting his trial balance, and he'd smile and say, "Well, brother-in-law. How's the big man about town?"

On the night of the tenth of November I had to stay even later than usual, close to eleven-thirty, because the Knights of Columbus were having an installation of officers on the fourth floor. I didn't mind because for every hour, or part of an hour, past ten I would get twenty-five cents extra. But I didn't like to keep Henry up late, so I skated as fast as I could until I came to the foot of the hill, where I took off my skates and started to run.

We had had a light-powder snow late in October but it was long since gone. The night was crisp and crystal clear with the stars hung so close you felt as if you could sweep them in with a butterfly net. I guess I was staring up at them because I did not see Henry charging down the hill and ran smack into him. He grabbed me to keep me from falling.

"I'm sorry, Henry," I panted. "The Knights of Columbus wouldn't clear out, and . . ."

"It's okay, buddy. I wasn't coming after you. I just heard — Art Collwell came over to tell us somebody telephoned him — the war's over."

"No kidding!"

"That's what he said. I'm going down to the paper to see if it's true."

"Can I come with you?"

"Well . . ." He hesitated. "I guess it'll be okay with Evy. If the war's over there probably won't be any school tomorrow anyhow."

By the time we got there it seemed as though half the town had congregated in the street outside the office of the *Treasure State News,* but the door was closed, the shades were drawn, and there was no bulletin pasted on the window. So we all just sort of milled around and wondered to each other if it was true or not, and why didn't the Strongs (they owned the *Treasure State*) come out and let folks know one way or another?

Mayor Whitley was holding forth. He declared that since it was near onto midnight here in Cottonwood, Montana, it would be going on seven a.m. "over there." "And therefore," he went on, "it's probably just another false armistice. The Allies and the Boche are not likely to end the war until business hours."

"You got a point there, Mayor," somebody said. "I'm going to be damn mad if they got me out of bed at this time of night just to take a gander at the mayor's nightshirt sticking out from under his mackinaw."

Everybody laughed at that, everybody but the mayor. I felt a hand on my stocking cap and turned to look up into Mr. Pearson's face. "Aren't you up pretty late, Johnny, even for a confirmed night owl like yourself?" he asked.

"Henry said it would be okay, Mr. Pearson."

"I figured it would be something he could tell his grandchildren," Henry said.

I saw the two men looking at each other and realized they had never met. "Mr. Pearson," I said, "this is my brother-in-law, Henry Peterson."

They shook hands. "Peterson . . . Pearson," Mr. Pearson said, as if the similarity of names amused him. "Johnny here has told us about you. You work for Montana Power, isn't that so?"

"That's a fact," Henry said.

"You like it there?"

"*Comme ci, comme ca,*" Henry said.

"Ah. You *parlez-vous français.*" Mr. Pearson seemed impressed.

"*Un peu.* I had only two years at Minnesota."

A light came on inside the outer office of the *Treasure State News,* and the murmuring of voices, the stamping of feet, and the slapping of hands against thighs to keep the blood circulating all but stopped. Then the door opened and young Mr. Elwood Strong, Jr. — I guess it was too late for his father, who had heart trouble, to be up — came out holding a yellow dispatch in his hand. He was grinning from ear to ear, and when the sudden jumbled medley of voices asking "Is it true? . . . Has the armistice been signed? . . . Is the war really over?" quieted down, he read what was on the dispatch:

"November 11. Compiègne. The terms of an armistice were accepted and the document signed by the German delegates. The World War, the greatest conflagration in the history of man, will officially come to a close at eleven o'clock this morning, November 11, 1918."

Mr. Strong tried to read the rest of it, how it was at Compiègne (which he pronounced Com-pee-egg-nee) that the English captured Joan of Arc, and that in 1624 another treaty had been signed there between the Dutch and Richelieu, but nobody was listening. They were all yelling and pounding one another on the backs, and Mr. Peterson and Henry, who had only just met ten minutes ago, even threw their arms around each other. In the confusion I found Mr. Horowitz standing beside me. "Boys like you will never have to go to war," he said. "Such barbarism has been ended for all time."

Off to one side stood Mr. Greybull, the iceman. He wore a mackinaw with a black band around his sleeve. His nose was running and tears were leaking out of his eyes. He kept saying over and over, "Son of a bitch, goddamn son of a bitch." His boy, Donald, had been killed at St. Mihiel just two months before. Mr. Horowitz went up to him and put an arm across his shoulders. "Come on, Mr. Greybull," he said. "You need something to drink!"

Mr. Greybull tried to control himself. He wiped his nose and eyes with his fur mittens, and turned his head first this way and then that, as if ashamed that he could not look good news like this straight in the eye.

"Cry," Mr. Horowitz said. "Damn it all, you've got a right to cry."

"Don't anybody think I'm not glad it's over," he said. "It's just — why couldn't the sons of bitches have stopped it by the first of September, and then . . ."

"Mr. Greybull, I know where we can find some firewater," Mr. Horowitz said and led him away. We had had Prohibition in Montana since 1916.

The stimulus of the welcome news finally dried up, and then nobody seemed to know quite what to say except things like "Thank *God!*" and "Now our boys can get away from those mademoiselles and come home" and "We can get back to business as usual at last." A few men tried to get "Over There" going, but that was a war song and the war was over. It was hard to celebrate something that was happening six thousand miles away.

The spirit of the occasion picked up briefly when the final remnants of the Knights of Columbus staggered down the street, but they were beyond caring very much that a mere war was over. They were just killing time, trying to think of excuses to tell their wives why they hadn't come home by ten o'clock. After all, the installation of officers had begun at six.

When I found Henry again he was still talking to Mr. Pearson. They were getting along just fine. "Time you got home," Mr. Pearson said to me. He pointed at the illuminated clock over the courthouse entrance. "Ten past midnight. Now let's figure . . . eleven a.m. in France . . . the war will officially be over at four a.m. mountain time."

"How come Philip didn't come down with you tonight?" I asked him.

"Don't tell him I told you," Mr. Pearson said, lowering his voice, "but Philip was asleep long before I got the rumor. And once Philip gets to sleep only the crack of doom can wake him."

Then Mr. Pearson turned back to Henry. "Drop in one day soon, Henry," he said. *Henry*. Mr. Pearson was already calling him Henry.

"I'll do that . . . sir," Henry said.

"Now that this idiotic war is over," Mr. Pearson went on, "what I mean to say — it's been a good year, crops good, prices high enough to give farmers a breather, and if the livestock coats are any indication, we've got an open winter ahead. People are settling up their debts, paying on their mortgages and buying again. Banks will be healthier — for a while anyway. Tell you the truth, Henry, we at First National may expand a little. Of course I wouldn't want to take a good man away from my old friend Julius down at Montana Power." Mr. Pearson stopped to chuckle at that. "But if he's such a tightwad that he'll pay no more than twenty-five dollars a week to a solid family man like yourself . . . well, anyhow come in and see me soon . . ."

The upshot was that Henry went to work for the First National at thirty dollars a week.

On the fifteenth of the month Papa and Mamma moved into town for the rest of the winter, leaving Otis, our hired man, to batch it on the ranch, milk the cows, feed the hogs and the chickens, and gather the eggs before they froze. (Otis hadn't been drafted because he had asthma.) That winter we were lucky to get the Brown house to rent, though it was not lucky for the Browns. Mr. Ernest Brown was a young lawyer who had married the Harper girl. The Harpers were well fixed. It looked as if

Mr. Brown had the world—or anyhow the county—by the tail, and then he came down with consumption and had to go to a sanitarium in Arizona for the cure.

So Mamma, who took care of things like that, wangled practically a new house with all furnishings bought by the newlyweds only a year ago, including a bird's-eye maple bedroom set in one bedroom and a mahogany set in the other (that would be mine) for $22.50 a month.

When I told Philip about it he did not seem surprised because he did not really know what anything cost except candy and ice cream, movies, and his own clothes. That was the difference between country kids and city kids. When you lived on a farm you were exposed to the economic facts of life right along with hailstorms, hoof-and-mouth disease, and glanders.

But we were finally rich that fall of 1918. Papa held off as long as he could and got eighty cents a bushel for the wheat. We had had 320 acres planted that year, and it had gone forty bushels to the acre. (No hail, plenty of rain during the growing season, and none to rust it while it was ripening. Talk about miracles!) We had hauled 12,800 bushels of wheat to the elevator, and for a good ten minutes Papa had a check for $10,240 in his pocket. He brought it home so that Mamma and I could see it. "A goddamn fortune!" he said. "Take a quick look before—abracadabra—it's gone."

More than a third had to go for the mortgage. Then there were outstanding bills like the one at Sterling's. The binder and the tractor had been bought on time, and Dr. Condon had been waiting for his fee for taking out Mamma's gallstones last March. (They had not yielded to Mrs. Schilling's absent treatments.) Then, of course, you could not spend everything because like as not it would be two or three more years before there was another crop like this one. A farm kid had to take all those things into consideration before he had the nerve to ask for that bulky, green-and-yellow roll-neck sweater in Sterling's window.

But there was no doubt about it that winter. Everything was, Papa said, just jim-dandy. He even bought a new Buick touring car—the 1914 Tin Lizzie had come down with the pip—and when Christmas came around he managed to smuggle a big package under the Christmas tree. It was for me. A tabletop Victrola from the Clef Music Store.

There were three records already on the turntable when I lifted the fat lid: John McCormack singing "Mother Machree" (that was for Mamma, she loved McCormack), a jig called "The Irish Washerwoman" (for Papa himself), and "Caro Nome." Papa did not know Galli-Curci from a hole in the ground, so of course Mr. Horowitz must have blabbed about my coming in and listening to the record.

From then on I had a problem: how to divide my five dollars a week from the Lewis and Clark Hotel between movies and phonograph records. But that was a good problem. Not like the one the Pearson family came up with that winter.

★   ★   ★

It was a Saturday evening. We had had an eighteen-inch fall of snow the night before and the menfolks had not yet had a chance to shovel the sidewalks. When you walked you tried to fit your overshoes into bigger footprints somebody else had already made, and grownups had to carry their little kids or they would bog down. The wind that followed big snows was probably piling up ten-foot drifts around houses up on the prairie, but down here in the valley it was still and beautiful and as cold, the way Papa described it, as a bitch's tit.

Philip and I were going to see *A Tale of Two Cities,* which starred William Farnum. We didn't much want to because it was a costume picture and had been approved by both the history and English departments, a double-damning recommendation. But there was nothing else to do Saturday night. Mrs. Pearson had asked me to take supper with them before and to stay overnight with Philip after since our house was way uptown and theirs only three blocks from the Musselshell. When I asked Mamma she turned to Papa and said, "Do you think it's all right, Papa?"

Papa shrugged. "Why wouldn't it be?"

"I just wanted to make sure."

"What have you got against the Pearsons, Ella?"

"Nothing. Why would I have anything against the Pearsons?"

"It sounded like it, that's all."

"Well. I don't know where you'd get an idea like that."

This was, of course, years before I heard Mamma say that about Mr. Pearson's drinking, but she often had what she called "feelings" about people. Papa harrumphed and retreated into the *Saturday Evening Post* where he had been reading a story about Florian Slappey by Octavus Roy Cohen. Mamma could never see why he wasted his eyesight on one of these. What could there be funny about Negroes? In fact, she was as leery of Negroes as I was of nuns. Fortunately for her there was only one Negro family in Cottonwood. The father worked as a bootblack in the Lewis and Clark, and Mamma had warned me not to talk to him unless somebody else was around because you could never tell what one of *them* might do. I did not tell her, because it would have brought on a lecture, but I liked George. There were some things you'd better not mention to your parents, especially your mother.

"All right, Johnny. You'll need a nightshirt, a toothbrush, a towel, and a washrag," Mamma said.

"The Pearsons have got plenty of towels and washrags," I told her.

"I'm sure they have. Let *them* use them."

The first show would go on at seven with a newsreel and an installment of Pearl White's serial *Over the Top* before the feature, so Mrs. Pearson had dinner on the table promptly at six. Philip and I would just as soon miss Pearl White, but you had to be on time or you mightn't get in on Saturday nights. I sat next to Maureen at the table. She was looking much prettier now that she wasn't so plump and the freckles had faded. She even had a date with Pat Dempsey, who was coming by to take her to the movie at a quarter to seven.

"Such a nice young man," Mrs. Pearson said as she served a generous helping of chicken fricassee with dumplings as light as goose down. "Pat was a choirboy at St. Matthew's until last summer when he began to shoot up and his voice changed."

"Oh, Moth-er!" Maureen sighed.

Mrs. Pearson smiled. "Sam," she said, "do you sometimes get the impression that my name is Oh Mother these days?"

Mr. Pearson laughed and wiped a spot of gravy off his chest. "You must realize, Oh Mother, that the last thing a fifteen-year-old wants in a beau is a nice young ex-choirboy whose voice has just changed."

"He's no choirboy any longer," Philip volunteered.

"You shut up, Philip," Maureen said.

"What do you mean by that, Philip?" his father asked.

I knew what Philip was implying. He had seen Pat take a swig of rotgut from Wallis Ormonde's flask out behind the Guild Hall at the monthly high school dance. Everybody knew about Wallis. He was the Reverend Ormonde's son and a real hellion, but Philip was the only kid who had ever seen Pat skid off the straight and narrow.

Philip wished he had kept his mouth shut. "Nothing," he muttered.

"You must mean something. Tell us."

Philip jammed his chin down against his chest and lowered his eyes. "I just meant he doesn't sing in the choir any longer, that's all."

Mr. Pearson laid his napkin beside his plate in a determined manner and then turned his full stare on Philip. "Now, son, let's have it. What were you trying to say?"

"*Sam,*" Mrs. Pearson said

"Don't interfere, Stella!"

"But I *am* interfering," Mrs. Pearson said. "You will not take that tone with my son, do you understand?" And then she looked around the table, saw me, and the steel in her voice turned to honey. She smiled almost coquettishly. "Besides, we have a guest."

"So we have," Mr. Pearson said after a moment, and laid the napkin back on his lap. "I want to thank you, Johnny, for introducing me to your brother-in-law. He is becoming a valuable man to us."

"That's good," I said. Then there was a silence with nobody saying anything. Maureen and Philip stared at their plates as they ate. After a minute or two Mrs. Pearson got up and walked across to the big mirror that hung over the sideboard. She primped her hair and smiled at her own image. Then she turned back and took a funny kind of waltz step toward the table.

"Don't you think I'm beautiful, Johnny?" she asked me.

I wish I could describe the moment that followed that question. You could imagine maybe Lillian Gish saying something like that to Bobby Harron in a subtitle, but not your best friend's mother to a kid of fourteen right out loud. She had to be more than forty years old and she was wearing a kitchen apron. We all sat there as if lightning had struck somewhere near and we were counting off the seconds to tell how close it had hit.

Then, "*Stella,*" Mr. Pearson said very quietly. You could hardly hear him.

"Yes, Sam?" There was a lilt in Mrs. Pearson's voice as if she might start to sing. Or cry.

"I think you had better sit down."

She smiled that girlish smile again. "I will," she said teasingly, "as soon as Johnny tells me how beautiful I am."

"Well, yes, Mrs. Pearson," I managed to get out. "I think you're real pretty."

"But not beautiful? Aw . . . men used to tell me I was beautiful." Then she sat down again at the foot of the table as if nothing had happened. "Now then, we have pumpkin or mince pie for dessert. Which shall it be?"

We didn't talk much on the way to the theater, but it would have been hard to talk anyhow because the four of us — Pat, Maureen, Philip, and I — had to walk single file or else get snow in the tops of our overshoes. I had the feeling, though, that Maureen and Philip were glad we couldn't, at least that I couldn't say anything about the way their mother had acted. I wouldn't have anyhow, but of course they did not know that.

When we got to the Musselshell we were in for a surprise. A notice outside read, "We regret to announce that, because of the storm, the train bringing us the print of *A Tale of Two Cities* from Billings did not arrive today. Instead, we are showing at reduced prices the Dolly Sisters in *The Million Dollar Dollies*. We hope you will enjoy it and come back to see *A Tale of Two Cities* Monday or Tuesday."

Philip and I were informed enough to know that a theater always kept the print of a substitute movie in the projection booth in case of an emergency. A few of the grownups read the notice and walked away but we paid our quarters and went in.

When *The Million Dollar Dollies* had played the Musselshell six months previously our parents had said it was not suitable for young people. It might still be unsuitable for young people, but we could say we had forgotten about that, we had been told so long ago.

Actually it proved to be not very interesting. It was about two pretty blonde girls who wore mostly beads and feathers and transparent skirts and got caught in a harem. Annette Kellerman had been a lot nuder in *Queen of the Sea,* but it was all right for us to see her because she was a famous swimmer.

Maureen and Pat stopped at Gates' Ice Cream Parlor for a soda or banana split on the way home, but Philip and I thought it was too cold for ice cream. Besides, I had run out of cash. By the time we got back to the Pearsons', Philip's mother had already gone to bed, but we met Mr. Pearson coming up out of the basement where he had been banking the furnace. "How was Madame Defarge's knitting?" he asked.

Philip and I looked blank. "Who is she?" Philip asked cautiously, as if it were some kind of test question to trick him.

"She was in *A Tale of Two Cities* when last I read it. Did they amputate her in the movie?"

We had to explain about the Dolly Sisters, which struck Mr. Pearson as very funny. He laughed till he had tears in his eyes. "That's rich," he finally said. "Don't forget to mention it to Father Gilpin when you go to confession, Philip. He may give you a couple of Hail Marys, but I'm sure it was well worth it." He shook his head and laughed again. "What are their silly names? The Dollies, I mean."

"Yancsi and . . ." I couldn't remember the other one's name, or which one was which.

"Rozsika," Philip said.

"Well, I must say, you young blades are growing up. You set out to see *A Tale of Two Cities* and end up spending the evening with a couple of Dollies. Pleasant dreams. Don't talk all night."

Philip's room was tidied up, his bed made, the records and magazines neatly stacked. Nazimova hung at a respectful distance from the Virgin and Child, and Prince's bed was gone. (Prince had been run over by Dr. Condon's Franklin and had been put to sleep.) Philip noticed my look of surprise and reacted as if I suspected him guilty of turning over a new leaf. "Mother sneaked up and did all this this afternoon," he said derisively. "You use the bathroom first, okay?"

"Why?"

"Because you're a guest. There's a fresh towel and washcloth for you, and a new cake of soap."

I would have been ashamed to take the washrag and towel out of my sack, so I just got undressed, put on my nightgown, and went to the bathroom. There was no radiator in there so I didn't waste any time. When I got back Philip had not started to take his clothes off. He even had his cap on and he was bent over the dictionary.

"What're you looking up?"

"You know that word Mr. Cram used when he was giving us boys his pep talk in hygiene class?"

I could not remember many of his words because they had meant nothing to me, but what the lecture boiled down to was, treat girls respectfully like your sisters and don't jack off. No, you will not go blind, but it's bad for competition in athletics and, besides, a male has got just so many shots in him, so don't waste them before you get married. If the stress becomes too great nature will relieve it with nocturnal emissions. So boys, keep your hands off your guns. They can go off accidentally, ha ha.

"You mean masturbate?" I asked Philip.

"Of course not. I know that one. Orgy . . . orgy-ism, something like that."

"Oh. Orgasm," I said offhand. I had already looked it up at the Carnegie Library. Miss Main liked you to use the big dictionary right there in plain sight. If you looked up a word you would not forget it. I had not forgotten orgasm. "There it is, right there," I said, pointing. " 'The turgescence of any organ, the culmination of . . .' "

"I can read," Philip interrupted. "Only what does 'turgescence' mean?"

"Look it up," I said.

"And which organ?"

"Not the Wurlitzer at the Musselshell Theater."

It must have been near midnight when we finally got to sleep. We had talked about everybody in our class. (Philip was supposed to be very bright; anyhow they were letting him take sophomore English.) About how could you explain a homely girl like Geraldine (Gerry) Malnick getting to be so popular, big nose and all? We speculated about what teachers did for fun out of school, or were they always serious, and what made Miss Cadwell smell like a salted mackerel? I asked Philip if a guy like King, who was going to be a priest, ever went out with girls and he said, "Certainly not. He has other things to think about." I didn't ask what. There was a big pause and then Philip asked if I knew what went on in that big white mansion out east of Cottonwood, which they said was a house of ill-fame. I said very loftily that ill-fame was just another word for a whorehouse, but I'm glad he did not ask me what went on in a whorehouse because I didn't know. Then we talked about what it would be like when we left home for good and could stay out all night if we wanted to.

Philip, of course, was going to Harvard, but that was still three years in the future, and I did not know whether we could afford to send me to college anywhere ever. Next summer, or the summer after that, Philip was going to visit his aunt Grace in Los Angeles, and she had promised to take him through one of the movie studios.

"My father wants me to be a lawyer," I said, "but I think I'd rather be an actor." I had never thought of it until that minute, but with Philip being so high and mighty about going through a movie studio I couldn't help saying it.

"Your nose turns up," Philip said.

"My mother says it'll straighten out when I get through adolescing."

"You haven't even begun yet," Philip said.

"A lot you know."

"You mean you have? How can you tell?"

"Stuff has started to grow."

"What stuff?"

"Well, for one thing . . ." I said mysteriously, and raised my arm so that he could see the fuzz in the armpit.

Philip seemed impressed. "Anywhere else?"

"That's a *private matter*," I said.

He thought about that for a while. And then he said, "I may be a writer."

"Yeah, writer!" I scoffed. "What have you got to write about?"

"You'd be surprised," he said.

"You've got to go to Europe and meet fascinating people and see stuff like the Pyramids before you can be a writer," I informed him loftily. "Nothing ever happens in a place like Cottonwood."

"Something might," Philip said, "now we've got airplanes. Say you and I are lying here in bed like now, and suddenly an airplane crashes right in that window."

"Airplanes don't fly at night."

"Oh." This set back the embryonic writer for a second or two, but he was not daunted. "It's not you and me, it's my mother and — and a friend, and it's daytime. And now this airplane . . ."

Maybe the creaking of the house as it cooled off woke me. For a minute or two I just lay there and stared at the window. The lace curtain shimmered in the bright moonlight. There was not a sound. I remember thinking, *lace curtain. The Pearsons are Irish. Does that make them lace-curtain Irish? Why doesn't anybody say lace-curtain Dutch? Or Scotch?* Then there came a distant and feeble cry, or not so much a cry as a wail, like a sound you could imagine a ghost making if a ghost could make a sound, or the scratchy descending glissando of a kid practicing on a fiddle.

I sat up and looked down at Philip. He was fast asleep. I

remembered Mr. Pearson saying that once Philip got to sleep not even the crack of doom would wake him.

Then I heard footsteps coming up the stairs, light, as if whoever was making them was barefooted or wearing carpet slippers. They went down the hall, running, past the door to Philip's room, past Maureen's, turned the corner toward King's room, and then I couldn't hear them anymore. Then there were heavier footsteps climbing the stairs. They stopped outside our door, and the door opened cautiously. The moonlight was so bright I could make out Mr. Pearson's face. His hair was tousled the way it would be if he hadn't yet combed it when he got up in the morning. He was wearing pajamas and a flannel bathrobe tied with a cord with tassels on the ends.

"Mrs. Pearson has been sleepwalking," he said quietly. "I thought she might be in here."

I shook my head. "I heard somebody go down the hall."

"Go back to sleep," he said, and closed the door. I did not go back to sleep but sat there in bed, pulling the blankets up to keep warm. Philip turned over and muttered something in a dream. Then I heard Mrs. Pearson's voice, fierce and angry.

"Don't touch me! Let me go!"

There was the sound of a window being jerked up and shutters knocking against the outside of the house. I crept out of bed and looked out the window. Catercornered from ours was the window to King's room. The shutters were flapping in the wind, and with her back to the window, Mrs. Pearson stood holding a candlestick with a lighted candle in it. I could see only the tassels on Mr. Pearson's bathrobe. Mrs. Pearson seemed to be holding the candlestick between them so that he could not touch her, and she didn't have anything on, not anything at all. Then Mr. Pearson grabbed the candle and it went out. I could not see either of them for a second, but suddenly she was leaning out the open window as if she would do anything, even jump, to get away from him. Mr. Pearson grabbed hold of her, wrestled her back into the room, and jammed the window down again, and once more came that ghost-cry echoing through the walls.

After a long while the footsteps passed our door once more and started down the stairs.

I still sat there, shivering and unable to move. Then there was a knock on the door. Maureen tiptoed in. She looked as if she were about to cry. "I'm scared," she whispered.

"It's all right, I guess," I said. "Your father said your mother was sleepwalking, that's all."

Philip finally woke up. "What's the matter? Why'd you wake me up?"

"Mother's been sleepwalking again," Maureen told him.

They looked at each other. It was a private look. Then we heard the front door slam.

Philip got out of bed and we all went with him to the window. The moonlight was so bright it made shadows of the bare trees and telephone poles on the snow, which sparkled as if it had been sprinkled with diamonds. Suddenly a figure darted down the walk to the street. It was Mrs. Pearson, and she still did not have anything on, not even her shoes. Right behind her came Mr. Pearson. She could not run very fast, but zigzagged like a jackrabbit trying to escape a hound, cutting this way, then that. When Mr. Pearson would grab for her she wouldn't be there. But finally she bogged down in the high snow beside the path, and fell. She lay very still, her long red hair fanned out across the glistening snow. It was as if she were dead and could not feel the cold.

Mr. Pearson picked her up in his arms and carried her back toward the house.

We heard the front door close and then there was no sound except for the sharp crack of a beam in the attic. I looked from Maureen to Philip. Their eyes were turned away, not even glancing at each other. Then Maureen shuddered, said, "It's cold," pulled her robe tight around her, and walked out of the room.

I thought Philip might want to talk, but he did not. Maureen had forgotten to close the door, so he closed it, got back into bed, and lay there staring at Nazimova. I lay down and turned on my side and stared at Dorothy Dalton as "The Flame of the Yukon." Of course it was too dark really to see either of these exotic ladies very well, but if Philip didn't want to say anything about what had happened, then neither did I.

Looking back, I just now realize that Philip and I, who knew each other longer and better than anybody else either of us ever knew, seldom talked about anything that was very important to either of us. At that time, back in February of 1919, neither of us knew how to open up our secret, sensitive, and sometimes dark passages either by probing or by voluntary confession. It was fear, of course, fear of accidentally hitting a boil and not knowing how to cope with it if we did. Later we were too glib, too quick with the good-natured (or sometimes ill-natured) insult technique, the wisecrack or the whimsical circumlocutions demanded by our crowd in the twenties and thirties. We could congratulate each other on a success — "So it's money you want!" and "Promise you won't change, promise you'll stay the same sweet son of a bitch you always were!" — and even briefly mention a failure — "Sorry Brooks Atkinson clobbered your play. What does he know?"

I could ask advice of other close friends, even spill my guts to them when I was troubled, but between Philip and me I sensed an invisible wall. He must have felt the same way toward me, but then he never spilled to anybody that I know of.

In spite of the chilling episode with his mother, I was about to fall asleep once more when Philip said something. I turned over.

"What?"

"Which one is which?" he asked.

"What are you talking about?"

"Yancsi and Rozsika. Which one is which?"

"Search me. One's fatter than the other. That's all I noticed."

from Philip Pearson's Day Book

Feb. 16, 1919. Last night John and I saw *The Million Dollar Dollies* at the Musselshell. It was okay with my father. Mother had a headache today.

3

Mrs. Pearson left town for about six weeks. Philip told me she was visiting her mother back in Iowa. For the first few days Maureen was absent from school. She had to cook and take care of the house until Aunt Grace had time to get there from Los Angeles. I told Mamma that I wanted to invite Philip to supper because Maureen could not cook much of anything except goulash (that was as far as her class had got in domestic science) and Philip hated it.

"Any evening," Mamma said. "But how odd that poor Philip's mother would traipse off to Iowa in the middle of winter."

"Her mother's sick," I heard myself say.

"Oh. You never told me that."

I had not told her that because so far as I knew, Mrs. Pearson's mother was in good shape. I just did not want Mamma to get hold of anything queer about the Pearsons. She could turn a kitten into a tiger and have a mountain lion left over.

"What seems to be the matter with the old lady?" Mamma went on. When I did not answer immediately her voice assumed an ominous note. "Johnny, I asked you a question."

"She had a nervous breakdown," I said.

"Well. That explains a lot."

When I asked Philip to supper I had to confess what I had said about his grandmother, in case Mamma mentioned it.

"Why did you go and say that?" Philip asked.

"Did you want me to say your mother was sick?"

"You'd better not, because there's nothing wrong with my mother at all." He sounded as if he were about to cry.

"Maybe not, but . . ."

"How would you like it if I said *your* grandmother was loony? You never even met my grandmother."

"I never said your grandmother was loony, I just said . . ."

45

"And don't worry. I'm not coming to supper—ever—so you needn't bother to make up lies about my family."

I did not speak to Philip all the time his aunt Grace was in Cottonwood.

For a while Kim Sumner and I got chummy. Kim's mother had once heard Rudyard Kipling lecture, which made her runner-up at the Thursday Afternoon Club to Mrs. Kingman, who had heard Mary Garden in *Thaïs*. Fortunately Mrs. Kingman never had a daughter, or she would have been saddled with the name Thaïs Kingman. Kim Sumner, even prenatally, had been referred to as Kim. Had he been a girl, Kim would have served quite as well.

Kim was kind of a lummox. He was overweight, he had warts, and he stuttered. When anybody asked him his name he would say "Ku Ku Ku Kim," so that was what kids called him, even to his face. Not that he minded; he seemed grateful that anybody noticed him. Kim's father was in grain and feed so they weren't poor, but Mr. Sumner had worked for his spending money when he was a kid, so Kim had to have a job too.

He had the same hours as I did, six to ten as a messenger boy. The Postal Telegraph office was adjacent to the Lewis and Clark, and there was a swinging door between for the convenience of hotel guests. Usually things quieted down at Postal as well as at L. and C. late in the evening, so Kim would mosey over and hang around the hotel lobby. If Alyce, who held down the cigar counter, was not playing a fish on her flashy line, she would deign to talk to us. Her place of business was directly beneath a life-size oil painting of Sacajawea pointing out the Gates of the upper Missouri River to a grateful Meriwether Lewis and an astounded Lt. William Clark.

Alyce (yes, that was how she spelled it) had more blonde curls than Mary Pickford. On America's Sweetheart they were cute, but on Alyce they were a come-on. They bounced and jiggled when she walked, and she walked with a gait all her own. She took short, mincing steps, held her head high, her shoulders forward, and her arms tight against her sides so they wouldn't swing. You couldn't help noticing Alyce, and of course, that was what she had in mind. She somehow managed to look as if she knew everything there was to know and only wished she could tell it to you but it was too risqué (risqué was very big in those days) for your ears. When not otherwise occupied, she always had her hair, her lips, or her nails to fall back on. She could repair these and talk to Kim and me at the same time, and even what was not too risqué for our ears often held us in thrall.

She would hint—with a toss of the curls and a "Don't you wish you knew!"—the most outrageous things about the most respectable citizens in town, naming names. The jeweler, Mr. Cadwallader, for instance, was sixty-five and a deacon of the Methodist Church. "There's life in the old boy yet," Alyce would giggle. "Take it from one who knows as shouldn't."

We did not know what "life in the old boy" meant, but whatever it was it apparently had no business being there at his time of life.

Then one evening she said, "Whatever happened between you and little Philip Pearson? I haven't seen him around lately."

"Oh, nothing much," I said. "He's been studying nights, I reckon. I see him at school."

"I'm glad of that. I thought it might have something to do with Mrs. P."

"Wha wha wha do you mean by that?" Kim asked, his eyes bugging out.

Alyce dug her compact out of her bag, opened it carefully so as not to wreck her still-tacky nails, focused the tiny mirror on her lips and, though it was almost time to close up shop for the night, went to work on them with her lipstick.

"Oh, one hears things, Ku Ku Ku Kim," she said around the lipstick. She tried out Mae Murray's bee-stung-lip expression in her mirror, but was not satisfied with it.

I looked at Kim who stood there grinning like an idiot. "There's nothing to hear," I said.

"I heard," Alyce went on, rubbing off the red paint and starting all over again, "I mean to say, one *hears* things, doesn't one? For instance, that Mrs. P. was taking a marital vacation—

isn't that a cute expression? Marital vacation? Sounds almost as good as Waikiki. *Who with* I leave to the imagination."

"That's — that's silly!" I said, louder than I meant to.

Alyce smiled patronizingly. "Of course, a fourteen-year-old boy would know all about that."

Two weeks went by. Maureen was back in school making up the time she had lost. She even asked me if I wouldn't come over Saturday night for supper. Aunt Grace had learned how to make chili con carne from a Mexican restaurant in Los Angeles and it would take the top of your head right off. Apparently Maureen did not know that Philip and I were not speaking. I said thank you, but not that Saturday. I had a date.

By this time I was not sure whether I had insulted Philip or he had insulted me. At any rate I was bored with the feud. We could avoid each other's eyes in geometry, but it was something else in gym where you moved around a lot, and in manual training especially. We had been assigned adjoining benches and had to share the big tools like jointers and ripsaws.

Philip, who had very little manual dexterity, had managed, after a number of false starts, to complete a pencil box during the first semester. Now he was struggling with a coat hanger. He had split two when he tried to insert the hooks, but hoped to have another ready as a surprise for his mother's forty-fifth birthday, which was in April. I noticed that in March he was still working on it, so I figured Mrs. Pearson was expected back in April.

I had embarked on a much more ambitious project and was afraid I had bitten off more than I could chew: a piano bench. As soon as I got to making my own money I was going to buy a new piano: a Lyon and Healy baby grand, price $550. I had seen one at the Clef Music Store. It was wired for small lamps with pink shades so you could read music without lighting up the whole room. Mr. Horowitz claimed it was next best to a Steinway or a Mason and Hamlin. He would let me buy it on time and pay off the debt ten dollars a month. But of course he had to demand a hundred dollars down.

Papa did not see why the old upright, which had been moved from Wisconsin to the homestead, to town, to the wheat ranch, to town, to the cattle ranch, and back to town, was not good enough for a kid. So it had a high E-flat that stuck in rainy weather. That was just one key out of eighty-eight, wasn't it? So practice on the other eighty-seven.

I was preparing for the momentous day when I would own a baby grand by having a piano bench ready for it, one that I was making with my own hands at no cost whatever except two semesters of Friday afternoons between three and four. During the first semester I had managed to complete the end pieces, two slabs of oak stained and polished to a fare-thee-well, and decorated with carved-out designs of a Grecian lyre. They were less than perfect—one lyre looked lopsided—but who noticed the ends of a piano bench? Mr. Gleason, our manual training teacher, a fair man I had to admit, had given me a B-minus on the project so far. That hurt, because otherwise I had three A's, one A-minus, and one B-plus, but the sting of the B-minus had been soothed somewhat by Philip's C. (The top of his pencil box stuck when you tried to slide it out of its grooves.)

Now I was bogged down with the top of the bench, which had to be perfect. There had been no single slab of that smooth, hard golden oak more than twelve inches wide in the shop supply cupboard. What I would have to do was match two nine-inch planks for grain, and then cut those eighteen inches down to sixteen. "Better saw each one of them down only a half-inch at first," Mr. Gleason advised. "That'll make seventeen inches, and then take the final inch off with plane and sandpaper."

"Why can't I leave one the way it is and sand the other one down to eight?" I asked. That would mean only one cut.

"You want the seam in the middle, don't you?"

I had not thought of that, and I hadn't thought why it might be necessary to leave myself so much leeway until I laid the two eight-and-a-half-inch planks beside each other. Then I got the point: The connecting seam had waves in it that no amount of glue could fill up, let alone conceal.

And so began hours, weeks, months of planing, sanding, planing and sanding, repairing one groove only to create another, until the top—if it were glued together—measured sixteen inches, then fifteen and three-quarters (who'd notice a quarter of an inch?), then only fifteen and a half. There was no doubt, it was beginning to look narrower than any piano bench I had ever seen. At that point I called Mr. Gleason over to inspect it and try to persuade him that the present imperfection was scarcely noticeable — I would be sitting on it anyhow — and didn't he think it was ready for the stinking glue pot and the clamps?

He stared at it and shook his head. "You wouldn't want me to let it go this way," he said. (Oh, yes I would, I thought.) And then, "You're making this for yourself, you tell me?"

"That's right," I said. And I confessed that I was planning on buying a piano to go with it one of these days.

"Well, you'd better sand off a little more," he said. "Fortunately you've got a small butt. Another inch won't matter."

It did not help that Philip was standing there watching. There was only one small consolation. Mr. Gleason stopped beside Philip's bench after he left mine and looked down at his work-in-progress: the third coat hanger. Mr. Gleason sighed, shook his head, and said, "If at first we don't succeed, try, try again, eh, Philip?"

I had a strange sensation, which I guess added up to feeling sorry for Philip. I said, "Can I help, Philip?"

"When I want your help I'll ask for it," he said.

We did not speak again for several days.

Presently it was April and my brother-in-law, Henry, reported that Mrs. Pearson had come home. The *Farmer's Almanac* pronounced it spring, but the fellow who wrote it had pretty obviously never been in Montana where it might snow again any minute. But storm windows were coming off and heading for the basement, buds were swelling on trees and shrubs (hold your breath — they could get nipped by a frost), mothers were spring cleaning and fathers grouching over having to beat the Axminster (and an occasional oriental) rug, which had not been off the floor since last September.

And there was another symptom of spring. Girls looked prettier than they had during fall and winter, and did not sound as silly when they congregated at the water fountain. The boys took more pains with their hair and a few even cleaned their nails. There was more note passing in class, more couples holding secret confabs under the trees outside, and monthly grades were down as much as five to ten percent.

Apparently it was not only the students who were victims of spring. Mr. Cram, our gym and biology teacher, had bought a secondhand Winton-Six. He was the only teacher who owned a car, and we all suspected he had gone in debt to buy it in order to impress Miss Pauling.

It never occurred to any of us that Miss Pauling might be a beauty. She was "nice looking," she was "pretty," my mother even admitted that she was "attractive, I suppose." "Certain men like that type," Mamma added. But nobody we personally encountered five days a week could be a beauty. Katherine MacDonald, billed as the "American Beauty," was entitled to the term, so was Alma Rubens, but Mona Pauling could not be in that category or she would not be a schoolteacher, would she?

However, she had—well, *something*. Not only for Mr. Cram, but even for Mr. Jensen, our principal, who spent more time visiting Miss Pauling's classes than he did those of older, plainer teachers. (I noticed that he practically never showed up in horse-faced Miss Draper's civics class.) You would be answering a question about irregular verbs, or reading a theme aloud. You would hear the door open and glance back over your shoulder, and Mr. Jensen would be standing there staring at Miss Pauling through his gold-rimmed glasses. It was funny, too, because Mr. Jensen was married.

If it had been anybody else, Mr. Cram might have taken a poke at him, but Mr. Jensen was boss of the school and could get teachers fired. Oh, I guess Mr. Cram knew Mr. Jensen was just looking, but it made him nervous.

So he bought the Winton to take Miss Pauling home after school and—on Tuesdays and Thursdays—he cheated on our three o'clock gym class. He would work us out hard on the crossbars, the ropes, and the horses for half an hour. He'd get the sweat pouring off us and then he'd say, "Okay, that's it for today. Now you boys run down to the brewery and back. Running is one of the best and most complete exercises ever devised." Mr. Cram was sixty years ahead of his time.

Then he would hurry out and cross the yard to the main building, and disappear into Miss Pauling's classroom. She had a free period from three to four on Tuesdays and Thursdays.

Philip and I, being smaller than the others, usually returned from this boring jaunt at the tail end of a gang of thirty-five or forty, depending on how many had colds and got excused from gym. This had not mattered much to either of us; being unable to compete in athletics with any great success, we said, Who cares? We were great snobs and had more important things to think about.

That is, neither of us had cared last year, but in April of 1919 who came in last and who came in next-to-last from that round-trip to the brewery became more important than an A in Latin or being old enough to see Louise Glaum in *Sex*.

The brewery, which had been closed since 1916, was crumbling into decay roughly a mile and a half from school. On the way out, you'd go eight blocks down Seventh, right on Yellowstone to Beaver Creek, then follow the old horse-trail along Beaver to the brewery hitching post. Kick the hitching post for luck and start back. The pack usually jogged along together in no particular pattern on the way out. You'd even have enough breath to talk a little. It was on the return trip, around the time we turned off Yellowstone onto the straightaway of Seventh, that the spirit of competition inevitably raised its head in the leaders — Oliver Schultz, George Wilson, and Buckie Bristol.

They would be trotting along, maybe horsing around a little, trying to trip each other, and then you'd see Oliver begin to lengthen his stride and ease past one or two kids up there in the vanguard. George and Buckie would notice him, of course, and start to spring. Soon the three of them would pull away from the pack, which would also pick up speed. We all knew that Oliver, George, and Buckie would come in one, two, and three. That was a fact of life you could do nothing about. (Maybe they took Mr. Cram seriously and never masturbated.) So. Granted that the best anybody else could come in was fourth, fourth was practically as good as first.

By that time this afternoon, as always, there was no spring left in the pack. We could do no better than grunt harder, try to lift each foot a little higher, and just hope we would not get a side ache to double us up.

And then it began to rain. One of those heavy, straight-down April pelters with an occasional rattle of thunder caroming off the mountain to the east. Not that it mattered much except we would have to take our soggy gym clothes home to be washed sooner than usual. Mr. Cram had assured us that as long as we kept running we would never catch cold, but he had never said anything about sleet, and that's what the shower suddenly turned into. Sleet mixed with hail the size of beebee shot.

The sting of hail on our heads and bare shoulders spurred a last desperate surge from the pack. We ran as we had never run before, silent except for the squish of track shoes in the mud. I was aware that the pack was pulling ahead of me. Me and someone else. I glanced to my left and there was Philip, puffing, his mouth open, his face red, his eyes boring straight ahead.

He had begun to grow this spring. I had not realized that before, but he was already an inch or two taller than I. It seemed as if he were muscle-bound though, or it had never occurred to him that his legs could take longer strides. He still ran like a small boy, all drive and no direction.

I could not catch up with the pack, but I could damn sure beat Philip Pearson. I had to beat Philip Pearson.

There was the school, up the hill two blocks ahead of us. Oliver, George, and Buckie were running—oh, God, they could still sprint up the hill, even up the steps to the gym! Between them and us was the pack, with Norm Fowler, Everett Fowler's boy, leading.

My side began to ache. I leaned forward, lifted one foot ahead of the other—each weighed a ton—and pulled ahead of Philip. Not much, maybe a couple of yards. I didn't dare look back, it would slow me down.

Then I heard his breath right behind me, and he grabbed the tail of my undershirt, which had come out of my gym shorts. I tried to wrench it away from his hand, but he had broken my stride, if you could call it that, and he hung on.

I turned and faced him, glaring at him, hating him, and gave him a shove that sent him sprawling. He never let go and pulled me down after him. Neither of us had ever got into a fight with anybody before, but, sprawling there in the mud, the sleet and hail pelting us, we pummeled each other like two groggy prizefighters until he finally hit me in the mouth.

I wiped my mouth with the back of my hand, then stared at my wrist where blood was spreading like red ink on a blotter. I became aware then that Philip was not taking this opportunity to hit me again.

"I didn't knock your tooth out, did I?" I heard him say.

I felt my front teeth. They were all there. I shook my head. "Naw. Just cut my lip a little when I fell."

Philip was getting to his feet, trying to brush off the mud. He offered me his hand. I looked at it a minute, then took it.

"Are we speaking?" I asked him.

"I guess so."

I stood up and sucked on my lip. It was beginning to swell.

"That wasn't fair, grabbing my shirttail."

"Yeah, but you were ahead of me. I had to."

I looked at him straight on for the first time. Water was running out of his eyes. Maybe it was tears, maybe it was just rain.

We both turned and looked off to where the gym was inhaling the rest of the pack.

"You care who gets in last?" he asked me. "If you do, you go in ahead. I don't care."

"I don't care either," I said.

"Then what say we go in together?"

"Okay. But I'd have been next-to-last if you hadn't grabbed hold of me."

Philip grinned. "That's why I grabbed you." And he started to run. It caught me by surprise and it took me a few strides to catch him and grab his shirttail. "I was just kidding," he said.

"Like fun."

We walked the rest of the way side by side. Just before we went in the door he said, "I got a new autographed picture of Dorothy Phillips. Want to stop by and see it?"

"Not unless you come to my house first," I said.

"Okay, if that's the way you feel."

from Philip Pearson's Day Book

April 11, 1919. Mother came home from Great Falls yesterday. King sent me a rosary from Marshall Fields. He was visiting the Reillys in Chicago over the weekend.

The first time I went to Philip's house after his mother came home I was afraid to look at her for fear she would be different. Maybe not look different, but act different. After all, what I had seen her do that night was crazy, wasn't it? Screaming, keening, running around naked in the snow, that had to be crazy. If she would behave like that, what wouldn't she do?

But Mrs. Pearson was just the same. "Why, Johnny, where you been keeping yourself? It's been a long, long time, hasn't it?"

Indeed it had been, and where had *she* been, what had *she* been doing in the meantime? "It's nice to see you again, Mrs. Pearson."

She held me off and sized me up. "I think you've grown."

"It's about time."

"Here. This will stretch the inches." She handed me a plate of that irresistible, incomparable chocolate fudge.

"Come on," Philip said. "I got Dorothy Phillips upstairs."

Mrs. Pearson laughed. "Philip, darling, some folks might misunderstand that."

She was the same as ever, just as friendly, just as easygoing. Maybe I hadn't seen what I had seen. Maybe that was a nightmare, and she had really gone off to visit her mother in Iowa.

That summer was not much different from other summers. We moved back out to the ranch. It was hot and dry. I helped shock the wheat. The crop was not nearly as good as last year's, but at least we would not have to borrow more from the bank to see us through to 1920. We would need to tighten our belts, though. Papa began to talk about diversifying again. Putting all his eggs in one basket—wheat—was too damn risky. If he had a herd of cattle to fatten up when wheat was off because of hail or drought, that would hasten the day when he could sell out, be rich, and go back to God's Country. God's Country was Wisconsin, where we had come from when I was six.

"We'll see, Jim," Mamma would say when this topic came up.

"What do you mean, we'll see, Ella?"

"Just—we'll see. There are other things to be considered."

"Yes? Such as?"

"Such as Johnny for one thing. There's his college."

"He can go down to Madison," Papa said. "That's a good school."

"We'll see," Mamma said and winked at me as if we were in cahoots. And maybe for once we were. Mamma had her heart set on going to California if we could ever leave Montana, and I wouldn't have minded that at all. (A gypsy fortune-teller had once told Mamma that she would live and die "beside the sea." California was beside the sea, and Hollywood was in California.)

Philip spent a month with his aunt Grace in Hollywood that summer of 1919. Well, not precisely in Hollywood, as I was to discover when we finally went to California, but Genesee Street south of Melrose was close. Philip could not resist saying, as he brushed an imaginary speck off his lapel, "I spent the month of August in the cinema capital." It sounded so debonair, so Adolphe Menjou. Never mind that the voice speaking it was changing.

He came back to Montana in early September as red as a tomato, and proud of the patches of parchment that peeled from his shoulders. "Most of the time I was at my ahnt's beach club," he boasted. Where he had picked up "ahnt" I don't know. He had called her Ant Grace in the spring. Maybe from Mary Miles Minter, because Philip had met her. They were not formally introduced, but he had climbed over the wall of the Paramount Studios at Sunset and Vine, and while he was sneaking around looking for Gloria Swanson (who, curse the luck, was actually

seen at Ahnt Grace's beach club that very day), he had run into
Miss Minter.

"How—how come you got to speak to her?" I asked.

"Easy. I just said I was from Montana and the *Treasure State
News* wanted an interview."

"Did she give you one?

"No," Philip had the decency to admit. "She called a studio
cop and had me . . ." He started to say "thrown out," but that
would sound too common. Tramps got thrown out. Philip
Pearson got "ejected."

Nevertheless, thrown out or ejected, he had actually been in
the divine presence of, even spoken to, one of the luminaries of
the Hollywood firmament. So she was a lesser luminary.
Nobody else in Cottonwood had ever even spoken to Ben
Turpin.

"But wait till I tell you what happened to *me* this summer!" I
said breathlessly. For a couple of minutes I had not been able to
wedge a word into his monologue.

"All right," he sighed wearily. "What happened to you this
summer? I can spare you five minutes."

"*I* own a grand piano."

"So you own a grand piano."

"What do you mean, 'So you own a grand piano'? Does any
other kid you know own a grand piano?"

"I just mean to say, is that in a class with Mary Miles Minter?"

"You can go to hell!" I said.

And thus began another week in which we were not speaking,
because the unexpected gift of the piano was the greatest thing
that had ever happened to me.

My birthday had been on August 15. We were out on the ranch
in the foothills twenty miles from Cottonwood. It was the
second and last day of thrashing time. The big red machine that
sacked the grain and blew the chaff out of its long elephant snout
onto bright yellow straw piles had arrived at six a.m. the day
before. I had been driving one of our three teams—Papa and
Otis, our hired man, drove the other two—delivering the sheaves
from the distant rows of shocks to the thrasher. It was my

birthday, and nobody but me had remembered it. I could not blame Mamma—with the help of Mrs. Bacon, our neighbor's wife, she had fed twenty men three whopping meals each day—and I did not expect Papa to remember. He never remembered any dates except Christmas, the Fourth of July, and the dread day when the mortgage fell due.

But finally came quitting time of the day, which had begun with the alarm set for four. When I came in from separating the milk, I found Mamma collapsed in the wicker rocker in the kitchen. I thought she was asleep and was about to go to bed myself when she stirred.

"I didn't forget, Johnny. There just hasn't been time to . . ."

Her voice trailed off with fatigue. "That's okay," I told her.

"Come here." I went to her. She pulled my face down and kissed me. "Hand me my sewing basket, will you?"

She opened it and took out a small slip of paper. She handed it to me, but it was too dark to read anything except the letterhead: Clef Music Store.

"Light the lamp," she said.

I lit it. The big round translucent globe that housed the chimney was splashed with red roses. (Whenever I remember that evening, as I often do, I still see those hideous roses on that lamp.)

"Happy birthday," Mamma said.

"Received," I read aloud, "the sum of one hundred dollars as down payment on . . ." And then my voice went. I could not speak the last words aloud. ". . . on a Lyon and Healy baby grand piano, to be delivered October 15, 1919 . . ."

"Well?" Mamma said after a moment. "Aren't you surprised?"

I still could not say anything. I fell into her lap as I had not done for years, and we hugged each other. Then I said, "But we can't afford it this year. You shouldn't have."

"Now don't you start telling me what I shouldn't do. One man in the family doing that is enough. It's not just people like the Pearsons who can do for their children."

She had a little windfall, she went on to tell me. "Remember my great-uncle Gary? You never met him—I hardly knew him myself. He *drank,* my mother told me. Anyhow, he had no direct heirs, and I was one of several distant second-generation nieces and nephews. Each of us got a hundred dollars."

"Why didn't you tell me?"

"It wouldn't have been a surprise then, would it?"

There were times when I thought my mother was not in a class with other boys' mothers. There were times when I wished she were not my mother at all. This was not one of those times.

"Of course," she went on, "you'll have to keep up the payments. We can't ask Papa to do that, not with the crop what it is this year."

"Don't you worry," I cried. "Ten dollars a month'll be a breeze."

"Well, just so's you understand."

"They promised me my job back at the Lewis and Clark this fall."

Their promise was no good. The manager apologized but he had already hired Mr. Blakely who could work all year. And perhaps a grown man around the lobby of a hotel was more fitting. (I suspect what he was implying was that a boy my age might inhibit the risqué repartee of Alyce and her traveling men.) Curiously enough, Mr. Blakely had been fired from the bank shortly after my brother-in-law, Henry Peterson, went to work for Mr. Pearson. Herman Blakely had saved his money and did not really need a job, but he was bored. He confided to me that he had not realized how it would be with no job to keep him out of the house. "Now you take Mrs. Blakely, well, she's a good woman, I'm not saying anything aginst her, but she goes on and on. So much damn talky-talk. Know what I mean?"

"I guess."

"I wouldn't mind if she had anything to say, but it's just so much mouth-flap. I'm sorry if I took your job."

"Oh, that's okay."

It was, too. I walked right across the street and got a job delivering the *Treasure State News.* It would mean setting the alarm for four every morning, seven days a week, come rain or blizzard, but I would have my evenings free — for practice, for movies, for study, for the library.

Oh, now that I was fifteen there were countless things to occupy my evenings. Even girls. Or rather, one particular girl.

4

Gerry Malnick came to Cottonwood that first year with the cards stacked against her. First of all, that name: *Malnick*. What was it? Some kind of bohunk anyhow. Nobody had ever seen her parents. They must have done their shopping in Springer, which was a whistle-stop on the CB&Q out near their sheep ranch, and probably bought their clothes out of mail-order catalogues.

Gerry was more substantially built than her peers, her torso sturdy and practical, meant for following a team of horses and a harrow, or having babies. Her legs and feet were no mere decorative appendages; they were strong and muscular, and when she tried to emulate the mincing gait of her classmates — as she did before she learned better — you couldn't help laughing.

Her hair was not really blonde, it was cornsilk yellow, and could have been radiant swinging loose in an abundant mane or in a braid shining like warm taffy. But by the time she teased and frizzed it into cootie garages over her ears (one of them too often bigger than the other) she looked like Olive Oyl in *Popeye*.

Then, of course, there was her nose. It was not in a class with Cyrano's, but it was memorable, especially when there was a healthy shine on it, which Gerry seldom bothered to powder. She used to say — after she got the courage to play the clown — "Funny I never hear anything bad about myself. Must be because everybody knows I'm coming before I turn the corner."

She roomed and boarded at the girls' dorm. Some twenty girls like Gerry (though I should not say that; there were no girls like her) lived there, and the widowed matron, Mrs. Gossett, rode herd like an ill-tempered swan on her noisy, silly cygnets. In her eyes, anything in pants — even short pants, which Philip and I wore until we were juniors — was a potential despoiler of her virgins. Her police tactics did not make for popularity in the average country girl, though one of them did somehow manage to escape her and get knocked up and expelled from school.

During our freshman year I scarcely noticed Gerry Malnick, though I must have met her. I find now that I was standing beside her in the class picture in our 1919 *Annual*. Two rows behind us stands Philip Pearson, obviously wishing he was somewhere else. My face is in profile; I probably thought I looked older from that angle. And looking straight into the camera is Gerry, her big mouth under that big nose grinning from ear to ear. Not smiling, mind you — you could never call it a smile — grinning, as if the world were almost too wonderful to be borne, and saying, Look at me! I'm Gerry Malnick, and I'm to be part of it!

She did not come on strong. Not at first, at any rate. Had she done that, she would have received the cold shoulder from those who considered themselves her betters. She was merely always *there*. When you turned her way she would look up and grin at you, and it made you feel good. The grin was not a come-on for the boys; there was nothing remotely sexual or flirtatious about it. It merely said, I like you and hope you like me.

Somehow, by the time we had finished our sophomore year, Gerry was the most popular girl in the class. Not so far as dates with boys were concerned, but just the "most liked" by both boys and girls. Oh, there were one or two of the pretty young things who resented her popularity and could not understand it. I doubt that Gerry understood it herself, but presently she realized she had it and, having it, could use it to escape a future on a sheep ranch.

Gerry was not a very good student. Perhaps she could have been if she had not been so involved with the extracurricula of Cottonwood High. She loved Cottonwood County High and the student body gave the love right back. Getting A's and B's was small potatoes compared to that.

By the time we were juniors she was president of the class. She was cheerleader and could stir us to a frenzy of enthusiasm for a sadly mediocre team. "Give 'em the ax, the ax, the ax! Give 'em the ax! *Where?* Right in the neck, the neck, the neck, right in the neck, *there!*" She was chairman of the Cottonwood Beavers, a booster club. She had the lead in the class play, *The Neighbors,* by Zona Gale. She played the farmer's wife; I was the hired man. I don't know whether she could act or not—who cared?—but she could make you laugh by merely making a face when she forgot a line. She hawked tickets to every student event and was junior representative on the staff of the *Annual*. By the time we were seniors she was business manager (I was her assistant) and, by acclamation, student-body president. Oh, we had our seasonal football and basketball stars, but there was only one Gerry Malnick. She was School Spirit.

I don't know whether I was in love with her or not, probably no more so than almost everybody else was at Cottonwood County High. I merely wanted to be around her, to spot her coming down the hall, and to hear her call out, "Hiya, friend!" Funny, big-nosed Gerry Malnick, with only two "Monkey Ward" dresses to her name, was an irresistible phenomenon.

Philip was one of the few who could resist her. It was not snobbery on his part, though he could be snobbish. He simply could not understand what I saw in her. "She's just a homely, loud country girl," he once said. "She's not classy."

Being classy was very important to Philip in those days. Perhaps it was all his life, and maybe that was one of his troubles. Very few girls could measure up to his definition of "classy." In later years he dropped the *y* and a girl, or woman, merely had class. But the meaning remained about the same.

Philip's conception of classy at that time was Thelma Darlington. You might not like her—she was stuck-up and had no school spirit—but you could not deny that Thelma was beautiful. She was born with a face so geometrically perfect that it was unfair to girls who were merely pretty. Neither too tall nor too short, she was not too anything. One could not imagine an adolescent pimple daring to stain the warm ivory of her cheeks. Her raven-black hair was bobbed à la Irene Castle. (Thelma's hairdo was a first in Cottonwood High. No other girl could even muster the courage to copy Thelma for two or three years.) Her Swiss-chocolate eyes seemed always to focus on someone coming right behind you. (Perhaps they were not focused at all; she merely needed glasses and was too vain to wear them.) On anyone less beautiful her nose might have been described as "turned up," but Thelma's, of course, was retroussé. Her lips were parted in an almost perpetual smile, she held her head high and slightly tilted, and her neck — even severely framed by middy blouse and tie — was as the lily among thorns.

Thelma was a senior when we were merely sophomores, so she was far too old and worldly for the likes of us. Still, Philip could worship from afar and, observing her with her peers, endow her gratuitously with transcendental cerebrations and her soft voice with brittle Wildean aphorisms. (We had discovered *The Picture of Dorian Gray* in the murky Adults Only section of the library.)

Thelma was graduated and already a freshman at Missoula by the time Gerry Malnick scrambled to her throne at Cottonwood, but it offended Philip's sense of the proprieties for Gerry to command such popularity while the memory of his goddess, Thelma, was still warm.

A theme on this subject was responsible for Philip's trip to Helena to compete in a statewide contest.

Miss Pauling had suggested that we write a thousand-word paper on a subject of our own choosing, so long as it was inspired by an actual incident. It need not be the whole truth, she said, but when an author (we were going to be *authors?* Wow!) sets out with a basic truth, the fiction borne of it more often retains the essence of reality. Such talk was far over our heads, but Miss Pauling always made us stretch a little.

Gerry wrote about the death of her pet lamb caught in a wolf trap. It was purely factual, and stilted. ("Very nice, Geraldine," Miss Pauling commented.) I wrote about driving our hired man to the hospital after he was thrown from a horse and broke his leg. It too was purely factual.

"John," Miss Pauling said, "wouldn't it be more effective if we knew what was going on in the poor fellow's head? Not merely what occurred? What happens in a story is only interesting as it affects the characters."

"But I don't know what was going on in his head," I said.

She smiled. "Nobody will arrest you for inventing, for fictionizing, so long as it *might* be true. For instance, there are some grownups who don't like to be beholden to young people. They feel that it belittles them. Such an emotion might have been coloring your *Otis*'s gratitude to you."

Yes, that would make it a better story. Otis was probably ashamed to have a kid help him. Why hadn't I thought of that?

Meanwhile Miss Pauling was saying, "Philip, this is — quite remarkable, quite . . ." She frowned, unable to find the word. "Please stay after class, will you? I'd like to discuss your theme with you."

Philip let me read his theme next day. He had not actually called his characters Gerry and Thelma, of course — they were Gilda and Mélisande — but he might as well have. There was the brash and vulgar Gilda and there was the exquisite, sensitive, glorious, radiant, and several other adjectives Queen Mélisande, who had never truly been understood or appreciated by her middle-class subjects. (I'm afraid he actually labeled them the Rabble, a term which we had recently learned from studying the French Revolution. Though embarrassing in retrospect, I daresay, it was a portent of things to come. We no sooner learned a word than we vied with each other to try it out, sometimes to the consternation and amusement of our families. I shall never forget the look on my father's face when I asked him if one of our cows was *enceinte*. God knows where I picked that up; we had no French teacher.)

The queen spoke faultless English, never said "ain't," dressed in perfect taste, had black hair, a retroussé nose, a swanlike neck, and tried futilely to make the Rabble appreciate the finer aspects of life such as etchings, Shakespeare, crepes suzette, and Mozart. (Philip himself did not "appreciate" Mozart, but he had read that appreciating Mozart was a hallmark of the intelligentsia, and one day he vowed he would. At that stage he was no further along in music appreciation than Massenet's "Elegy.") So, "discouraged and sick at heart," the queen abdicated in favor of her younger sister, the loud, brash, and pushy creature with the oh-so-common touch who spoke the language of the people. The Rabble got what they rightly deserved, a reign of vulgarity that even they finally came to despise. So they overthrew Gilda and humbly petitioned the return of Queen Mélisande.

"Philip," Miss Pauling told him after class, "you bit off more than you could chew, but I like that. You have a feeling for words. Do you think your family would mind if I recommend to Mr. Jensen that you represent us in the state contest this spring? It would mean your going to Helena."

"They wouldn't mind," Philip said.

"I can guess the starting point, the spark, for this story," she said, glancing at the pages lying on her desk. "I usually read the best paper or two aloud to the class. But you can understand why not this time, can't you?"

"That's okay," Philip said.

"Strange." Miss Pauling shook her head in what might have been admiration, or possibly mere confusion. "I don't agree with your point of view, but I would not want to discourage what may develop into a genuine talent after you — well — mature. But if you do go to Helena — may I suggest something?"

"Sure."

"Write about something simpler and closer to home. Don't try for — for transliteration, if you know what I mean. I'm not sure that's the exact term for it."

Philip could only guess. "You mean write about the people as they are, not disguise them as somebody else?"

"Yes. *Yes,*" Miss Pauling said. "And — another thing. Try to empathize with all the characters, not just the one or two you like best."

Philip frowned. "Empathize?"

"Put yourself in the place of. I felt here that you did not really understand, what did you call her?"

"Gilda."

"Yes. Gilda. Well, if the people liked her, she must have had something about her to like, mustn't she?" Miss Pauling turned and glanced about the room as if to make sure she was not being overheard. "Now, regard your model. She may have her faults, but she is a very courageous and admirable young woman.

The— 'the people,' if you will, love her. There's got to be a reason."

"I don't know what it could be."

"You're fifteen years old, Philip. One day you will."

Philip went to Helena. While he was gone an extraordinary thing happened. I would never have known anything about it except that Gerry had to tell somebody, so she told me and swore me to secrecy.

She had forgotten her English composition textbook and thought she must have left it in Miss Pauling's classroom. Gerry was about to enter just as another hand reached for the door. It was attached to Mr. Cram, who was hurrying over from the gym after sending us off on our brewery jaunt. (That day, with Philip gone, last place would be mine unchallenged.) "Beauty before age," Mr. Cram laughed.

Gerry giggled. "Some beauty. If you like a mud fence."

"I rise to take exception," Mr. Cram said. "Mud fences are invariably brunettes."

They solved the contretemps by sashaying in together and then stood immobilized by a most improbable sight: Miss Pauling struggling with our principal, Mr. Jensen, who was bending her over her desk and trying to kiss her. Mr. Cram bounded across the room, grabbed Mr. Jensen by the arm, yanked him around, and punched him in the nose. As he had probably been wanting to do for months.

Blood spurted and dripped in Mr. Jensen's hand. In a reflex Miss Pauling handed him her handkerchief. Mr. Jensen held it to his nostrils and glared at Mr. Cram, who just stood galvanized by a surge of adrenalin. Nobody said anything.

After what seemed like an hour Mr. Jensen started for the door. Only then did he notice Gerry standing with her big mouth hanging open in shock. He paused and frowned, then brushed past her.

Gerry looked at Miss Pauling and Mr. Cram who were standing beside each other like store-window dummies. They stared at her. Still no one said anything. Finally Gerry said, "I—I thought maybe I left my English comp. book in here," and pretended to look about for it. Then Miss Pauling and Mr. Cram began to help her, and it was Mr. Cram who presently said, "Is this it?"

He handed it to Gerry, who made a great fuss about opening it and finding her name in it, and then said, "Yeah, gee, thanks. This is it. I sure wouldn't want to lose it, would I?" And then she said, "I'm sorry," which could have meant that she was sorry she had left the book, that she was sorry Mr. Jensen had attacked Miss Pauling and Mr. Cram had to sock him, or that she was sorry she had been a witness to it.

"These things happen," Mr. Cram said uneasily.

"And, Gerry," Miss Pauling said, "we're sorry too, aren't we, Mr. Cram?"

"That's a fact," Mr. Cram said.

"We're sorry for a lot of things," Miss Pauling went on, "but most of them are too trivial to mention afterward, aren't they?"

"I'm not sure I know what you mean, Miss Pauling."

"Well, I mean — like forgetting one's books and trying to find them and coming upon certain — situations we do not understand. Unless we know what they are about they are not worth mentioning, don't you agree?"

"Oh," Gerry said. "I won't mention a word. Cross my heart and hope to die."

She started to turn away, but it did not seem right to exit on such a note. She sensed the need for some casual conversational blotter to absorb the ugliness of what had taken place.

"By the way, Miss Pauling," she asked, "have you heard anything about how Philip is making out in the theme contest?"

Miss Pauling's hands were clenched in white-knuckle knots, and her lips were stiff and dry. "Not yet," she managed to say.

"I just wondered," Gerry said.

Miss Pauling gasped for breath. "Go! For God's sake, go, Gerry, before I . . ."

Gerry turned and bolted from the room. As she closed the door she heard Miss Pauling break into hysterical sobs.

Something had to happen. Mr. Cram, or Miss Pauling, perhaps both of them, must resign and leave town. Or Mr. Jensen would tie the can on Mr. Cram for attacking him, then Miss Pauling would quit and marry him. Wanting vengeance, they would tell the whole story to the *Treasure State News* and the scandal would be headlined in the paper. Then Mr. Jensen would resign and leave town because of the stench. If he hesitated, his faculty would hand in their resignations en masse. Of course the school board would not accept such wholesale resignations — the school would have to close and that would be a national disgrace — and that august body would wait upon Mr. Jensen and force him out. The newlyweds might be persuaded to return, and possibly the new Mrs. Cram would be chosen to become the first woman principal of Cottonwood County High.

Or if this fanciful scenario was pure wishful thinking, then Mr. Jensen would surely resign because it would be too embarrassing for him to face Miss Pauling and Mr. Cram in faculty meetings. "He could go 'because of ill-health,'" Gerry suggested.

"Or sometimes it says, 'For family reasons,'" I added hopefully. We fully expected Mr. Jensen to announce his resignation during assembly the following Monday morning. He did not. He wasn't even there. Well, maybe Wednesday . . .

We waited. Nothing happened. Not a thing. Nobody resigned. There was no scandalous headline in the *Treasure State News*. But there was a small item on page five. Mrs. Victor Jensen had been delivered on Monday of a seven-pound baby boy, to be named Victor, Jr. Mother and son were doing well. That was why Mr. Jensen had not shown up on Monday. Gerry and I felt as if we had been sitting on a time bomb and the fuse had sputtered out. Actually it had not. It was merely an exceptionally long fuse.

from Philip Pearson's Day Book

May 8, 1920. I won second prize in the theme contest. I would have won first but I spelled superfluous "superfulous."

"Philip Pearson, son of Mr. and Mrs. Samuel Pearson of this city, has been awarded one hundred dollars as second prize in the statewide writing contest held in Helena last week," the *Treasure State News* announced. (I read it at four-thirty in the morning on the first leg of my delivery route. Since it was May there were already fingers of light in the eastern sky over the Dakotas.) "Young Philip, a fifteen-year-old student at Cottonwood County High School, wrote a two-thousand-word paper titled 'Marianne.' His teacher, Miss Mona Pauling, head of the English Department at Cottonwood, informs us that Philip is a youngster of bright promise and she predicts a future for him in the literary field if he applies himself. So our advice to you is: Apply yourself, young man. Meanwhile, congratulations on climbing this first rung of the literary ladder."

"Philip," Miss Pauling said in class that afternoon, "we are all very proud of you." Everyone applauded. Miss Pauling beamed and Philip turned red and glared angrily at his inkwell. "Stand up, Philip. Take your bow. You must learn to accept accolades gracefully."

Philip got to his feet, looked at nobody, ducked his head like a nervous blue jay, muttered "Thanks," and sat down again.

"Philip is modest about his honor, but we like him for that, don't we? His achievement is all the more praiseworthy for a young person his age because the writer sits there all alone during his travail. No one is cheering him on. There is no basket to be shot, no goal line to carry the football across, no time record to break. A writer merely delves into his own psyche and sets down what he finds there."

This was not going down too well with members of our athletic teams who had expanded their muscles, strained their lungs to bursting, cut out banana splits, and got to bed at ten for the honor and the cheers of old Cottonwood.

"Oh, I am not belittling the athletic hero. He too has his place, his day in the sun." She smiled. "But being your English teacher rather than your coach, I am allowed my little prejudice. Perhaps Mr. Cram may feel differently." There was a ripple at her mention of Mr. Cram. Everyone knew about their attachment. Gerry and I glanced at each other; we knew more than anybody else. "But you see," Miss Pauling went on, "I have always felt discipline of the mind to be even more difficult than discipline of the body, and creative writing is the ultimate discipline.

"And now let me make a confession. You see, I had the temerity to suggest to Philip that he write about something quite simple, something within his own ken, his field of experience, that is. And did he take my advice? Not at all! He wrote a fantasy. It is all about the daydreams of a girl—a girl, mind you, not even a boy—who cannot believe that her parents are really her parents. Marianne feels herself far too extraordinary to have sprung from such very ordinary stock, and fantasizes herself as a foundling, perhaps the child of a famous actress and the governor of the state, whose career will be jeopardized if he admits he is the father. It is not the first time that this theme has been explored, of course, nor perhaps will it be the last. Still . . . we would honestly like to know where you got the idea, Philip. Would you deign to tell us?"

Philip was beginning to glow under all this praise. He waited for a moment as if trying to think, then shook his head. "I don't know. I guess I just thought it up."

"Ah," said Miss Pauling, as if this were the only proper answer to her question. "Of course. You just—thought it up. You see," she turned to the class, "most of the time the author does not know where his inspiration comes from. I can well imagine that in the long, long ago, a citizen of Stratford-upon-Avon might have asked his old friend Will Shakespeare where he got the idea for *Romeo and Juliet,* and Will probably would have replied, 'I just thought it up.' Come to think of it, that's not a bad definition of inspiration, is it? Congratulations, Philip."

Being bracketed with the Bard, however incidentally, must have been flattering to Philip's ego, but one could sense that most of Miss Pauling's students thought she was laying it on with a trowel. And that word "inspiration." *Poets* were *inspired.* But how could a pimply-faced, redheaded kid who lived right down the block be inspired? What Philip needed, and would very shortly get (like right after the bell rang) was to be shaken down a peg or two, probably by Pete Greybull, who was taking English

Comp. II for the second time and could not play center on our basketball team next fall unless he got his grades up.

But Philip was saved this well-deserved embarrassment by the arrival of Mr. Jensen himself. He entered so quietly through the door at the rear of the classroom that none of us knew he was there until we saw Miss Pauling stiffen, raise her glance over our heads, and say, cold as ice, "Yes, Mr. Jensen? There was something you wanted?"

Mr. Jensen cleared his throat. "Yes. I must speak to Philip Pearson."

"Very well, Philip. You are excused."

Philip rose and followed Mr. Jensen, leaving us wondering if perhaps even more formal praise was not about to be dished out by the principal himself. George Whitley, the mayor's son, raised his hand.

"Yes, George?" Miss Pauling said.

"I just was thinking. Did Shakespeare have acne?" He looked around the classroom for approbation. There were a few snickers, but nobody dared to laugh out loud.

Miss Pauling clamped on her set smile. "I really wouldn't know," she said. "I doubt that anything so trivial, so totally inconsequential, was ever recorded by any biographer. And George," she went on, "I suggest that over the weekend you memorize a speech from *Macbeth,* Act Five. Begin with 'To-morrow, and to-morrow, and to-morrow,' and end with 'a tale told by an idiot, full of sound and fury, signifying nothing.' Have it ready for Monday."

George groaned.

I stopped by the Pearson house on my way home from school to tell Philip how George had got his comeuppance, and also to find out what Mr. Jensen had had to say that was so important. I went to the kitchen door because Mrs. Pearson would probably be preparing supper and would not want to traipse through the house to answer the door bell. I knocked and waited. There was no answer. Well, Philip probably hadn't come home yet, and his mother was upstairs. I started back down the walk when I heard the door open. I turned around. Standing in the doorway was

Sister Agatha, fussing with her beads, as my mother called the Catholics' rosary. She said nothing, just stood there passing one bead after another through her fingers. Cautiously I retraced my steps toward the door.

"I just wondered if Philip was home."

Sister Agatha nodded, her lips moving in silent prayer.

"I can come back if he's . . ." If he's what? Doing an errand? Writing another theme?

Finally she seemed to see me. The automatic fidget of her fingers ceased. At the same moment I heard a wailing sound that took me back to the night Mrs. Pearson ran out into the snow.

"You're Philip's friend?" Sister Agatha asked. I nodded. I noticed then that her eyes were red. She fumbled for a handkerchief from some hidden pocket in her voluminous black skirt, and blew her nose.

"There has been a—an accident," she said at last. "King . . . the Lord has chosen to call him to His side. We must try to understand." Her fingers began to move again.

"You mean—you don't mean King's dead?" I gasped.

She nodded almost imperceptibly. "He has been granted life everlasting," she said. "Hail Mary full of grace the Lord is with thee blessed art thou amongst women and blessed is the fruit of thy womb Jesus Hail Mary full of grace . . ." Once more I heard the sound of sobbing. Sister Agatha closed the door softly.

The story, or all that I was ever to know for sure, was in the *Treasure State News* next morning. I read it at four-thirty a.m. under a street lamp outside the courthouse as I set out on my paper route.

"King Pearson, son of Mr. and Mrs. Samuel Pearson of this community, was killed instantly when the motorcycle he was driving skidded and struck a streetcar yesterday morning. Riding with him, and also deceased, was a young woman whose name is not known and whose body has not been claimed.

"The twenty-one-year-old King Pearson was a graduate of Cottonwood County High School. An extremely well-favored youth, well-liked by all of his classmates and admired by everyone who knew him, King was in his last year at Notre Dame and was preparing, his family informs us, to take instruction in the priesthood.

"The remains will be returned to Cottonwood for interment. Services at St. Matthew's will be private. The sympathy of their many friends goes out to the bereaved Pearson family."

A good many years later Philip wrote a story about a young man whose mother, to appease her own guilt over an unnamed mortal sin, had bullied him into giving his life to the church. As a last expression of his carnality before taking the vow of celibacy, he had smuggled a little tramp (Philip's fictional girls were either tramps or virgins) into his dormitory room for a final night of fleshly delights. He was taking her home next morning when he and the girl were killed. Whether this approximated the truth or was as fictitious as Philip's tale of Gilda and Queen Mélisande I don't know. The story was never published. I suspect it was not submitted to anyone for publication. I found it amongst his various pitiful lares and penates along with the curious Day Book, which I have been quoting occasionally, not so much for what it tells us as for what it chooses not to tell. For instance, of that event:

May 12, 1920. King's funeral. John Barrymore is starring in *Dr. Jekyll and Mr. Hyde* at the Musselshell. My folks wouldn't let me go.

5

We should not have moved back into town that fall of 1920, the start of my senior year at Cottonwood. I should have boarded with Evy and Henry once more as they halfheartedly suggested, but it did not take much persuasion for me to agree with Mamma that it would be too cramped at the Petersons' now that Henrietta was a toddler.

During May and June the wheat flourished. Long green waves of grain that would soon turn to gold in the bank rolled across the bountiful land as far as the eye could see. It was going to be another bumper crop, Papa said, and this time there would be no nonsense about it. We would pack up our duds and go back to Wisconsin. Mamma winked at me. Her mouth formed the silent word "California."

Then when the wheat began to head out the rains stopped. Papa said it was as if the Man Upstairs had turned off his goddamn sprinkler. A clear blue Montana sky without even a memory of a cloud invited the sun each morning, and temperatures soared into the high and dry nineties. Grasshoppers sent up their scouts from Wyoming, and soon followed in a sticky avalanche. You could not walk outside without feeling and hearing that sickening crunch under your feet.

When the wheat was finally ripe you'd rub the withered heads between the palms of your hands and only a few shrunken kernels would fall out.

Wisconsin (or California) receded once more, and Papa met the postponement of his hopes with his stoical "That's the way the wind blows." We'd have to stay in Cottonwood for another year anyhow, he reasoned, because it wouldn't a been fair to take Johnny away for his last year of high school, so what the hell? Sam Pearson and the bank would see us through. They'd have to, by God. Too bad about that son of his being killed.

I was sixteen that August. I had reached the dizzy height of five feet seven and was even shaving and dusting powder on my face to conceal the fact that there was nothing much to conceal. I was not the most popular kid in high school — neither was Philip — but I got by and was invited to lots of parties, probably because I could play the piano for impromptu dancing of the fox-trot and the hesitation waltz. I did not have pimples and I was far from tongue-tied. I could drive the family Buick and compete with Oliver Schultz and his dad's Jordan, when I had enough cash left over from payments on the piano to buy twenty cents' worth of gas.

Gerry became my girl. Well, sort of. At least she went to Guild Hall dances and the movies with me once in a while. Sometimes we held hands, but usually we had too much to talk about to remember that teenagers were supposed to hold hands. (I was Gerry's assistant manager on the *Cottonwood,* a four-page paper that we put together once a month with Miss Pauling as supervisor, all working up to the climax of the 1921 *Annual* come spring. Gerry and I had to canvass the town merchants for ads.)

When I thought about it I sometimes wished Gerry were prettier, but I did not think of it very often. I liked her too much to wish that she was anything but just the way she was. If she were pretty she wouldn't be Gerry. I entertained no daydreams of walking with her into some future sunset or even — not *even,* especially — night dreams of taking her to bed. If there was any taking-to-bed to be done at that time, a girl would have had to be a pretty good tackler. I was fascinated by sex, but scared of it. It seemed, from all the movies I had seen, to be something that any villain worth his salt tried to inflict upon the heroine, and the hero tried to protect her from.

Philip was half a year behind us, a super-junior. Which merely meant that he would be graduated in February of '22 rather than June of '22. Most of his small class of twelve boys and ten girls were the not-so-bright fallbacks from the class of '21, not the jump-aheads from '22, which he was. Then he was still having trouble with acne and his feet had outgrown his body. He had reached his final height—five feet nine—and wore a number eleven shoe.

I did not see as much of Philip as I had in other years. For one thing, he wore a black band around his coat sleeve. Then, of course, the whole Pearson family being in mourning, I was not invited to "drop in any time you're passing by." I did once, but Mrs. Pearson came to the kitchen door and did not invite me in because, she said, "Father Gilpin has come to tea."

It came as something of a surprise to me that priests took tea with ladies, or with anyone for that matter. One of my peers, in a moment of confidence, had told me that someone had told him—and this person was in a position to know because he had been to Rome—that priests drank some bitter concoction that their brothers, the Benedictine monks, brewed so they wouldn't wake up in the night with a hard-on.

★   ★   ★

It was a Saturday night, the night of the opening blast of a deadly parade of blizzards that roared across Montana that winter, paralyzing the state and shifting the patterns of many of our lives. At around five o'clock the telephone rang. I picked it up— Mamma was taking a nap after one of her migraines—to hear the voice of Mrs. Sumner, Kim's mother. Kim, she said, seemed to be coming down with something. "We hope not the flu but we never can tell, can we?"

"No, Mrs. Sumner. I'm sorry."

"Oh, are you, Johnny? That's so very nice of you." I could hear her turn to Kim and say, "Johnny says he's sorry. Isn't that nice of him?"

"Well, anahoo, Johnny, what I wondered was, since you're such buddies, you two, would it be an imposition to ask you to do Kim a teeny favor?"

(*Oh, Mom, I can do it, for gosh sake,* I could hear Kim say, and his mother answer, *No, you can't, dear, because mother won't hear of it. Just feel your forehead.*)

"Are you there, Johnny?"

"I'm here, Mrs. Sumner. And you want to know will I take Kim's job at Postal this evening."

"Why, how ever did you guess? You must be psychic. Some people are, you know. I read just the other day . . ."

"Yes, Mrs. Sumner. I will if I can. I'll call you back in five minutes."

"Well, we'll all hold the thought and trust the answer will be in the affirmative," she went on. "And how is your mother?"

"She's fine."

"I am not fine," I heard Mamma call from the bedroom. "My head is killing me. Will you get off the telephone so I can call Mrs. Schilling?"

"In a minute," I called back.

"What was that?" Mrs. Sumner wanted to know.

"Nothing. Nothing at all."

"Well, please remember me to your mother."

"I will. Good-bye."

I tiptoed to the bedroom door. Mamma had gone back to sleep. I'd have to make two quick calls, one to Mr. Murdock, the boss and telegrapher at Postal, to ask him if I could get off from work at nine instead of at ten. And then, if this was possible, I'd have to ask Philip to meet me at the Musselshell at nine for the second show instead of at seven for the first as we had planned. The movie was a German picture called *Passion,* all about Madame Du Barry, and it had a new Polish star called Pola Negri. According to Cal York in *Photoplay* magazine, "Miss Negri pulls out all the stops and runs the gamut of emotions from A to Z. A never-to-be-forgotten experience in the art of the cinema. Don't miss it!"

It all worked out. Mr. Murdock said Saturday nights were always slow and there probably wouldn't be more than two or three telegrams to deliver anyhow, and none after nine. If one seemed important he'd telephone it to the recipient.

The change in time was okay with Philip. He said he would come down to Postal and meet me there instead of in front of the Musselshell because snow was already coming down and the wind blowing like Billy-be-damned. The outdoor lobby of the Musselshell would be about as cozy as the Cave of the Winds.

Mr. Murdock was right. There were only three telegrams waiting for me and I was back from delivering them by seven with nothing to do from then on. I strolled through the door into the Lewis and Clark to say hello to Alyce. She looked different somehow, not quite so many curls.

"How do you like my bangs?" she asked. Oh. *That* was it. Bangs.

"They're pretty," I told her.

"My! Haven't we grown since last we met in days of yore," she said, making a moue with her lips as if somehow growing was a risqué thing for me to have been doing.

"I'm five-seven," I said.

"And going to make some little miss mighty, mighty happy one of these days, I'll bet!" She giggled.

"I wouldn't know about that," I said.

"One of these days," she sang, "and if you need any pointers you know where to come."

Philip, having nothing to do, came in at about eight-fifteen. He had a library book along in case I was busy, and even though I was not he sat down on the Postal waiting bench and opened it. It was a new book he'd found in Adults Only, but Miss Main let him take it out when he told her it was for his mother, who had forgotten to give him her card. I looked over his shoulder at the title. *This Side of Paradise,* by F. Scott Fitzgerald.

"I never heard of him," I said.

"He's from Minnesota," Philip said, "and it's all about Minnesota and Princeton. I may change my mind and go there. It's about the Jazz Age too."

"What's the Jazz Age?"

"I don't know why I associate with such ignorant dumb ignoramuses." Philip grinned and shrugged elaborately. "The Jazz Age. That's what we're living in right here right now, in case you're interested. And girls are not girls, they're flappers."

"Sez you."

"Sez me. You want to know why?"

"Not much."

"No intellectual curiosity," Philip said, shaking his head. "They're called flappers because they don't buckle their galoshes so they flap when they walk."

"Thanks. And you spelled superfluous 'superfulous,'" I shot back.

Philip gave me what passed for a dirty look, and said, "'A friend should bear his friend's infirmities.'" We had been studying *Julius Caesar,* and Miss Pauling had made us memorize long swatches of it.

I thought for a long moment and then said, "'All his faults observed, set in a notebook, and conn'd by rote.'"

"'Et tu, Brute!'" Philip intoned.

"What the hell's going on over there?" Mr. Murdock wanted to know. He got to his feet, stretched, and took off his green eyeshade. It left a dark crease across his forehead, cutting into the wrinkles. He had worn the eyeshade for so many years that the crease was permanent.

"We're just quoting Shakespeare," I apologized.

Mr. Murdock peered out the window at the swirling snow. "A lot of good the Bard is going to do you when you're shoveling yourself out of six feet of that miserable white shit tomorrow. Here. This just came in. It goes down Main four blocks. Better wait and see if the lady wants to answer. If she don't, don't bother to come back."

I looked at the name and address on the envelope. *Miss Fern Walbrook. 117 North Main Street.*

"There's got to be a mistake," I said. "One-seventeen is the Wholesome Bakery."

"I do not make mistakes," Mr. Murdock said. "There's a rooming house upstairs, smart ass. Entrance is the alley beside the bakery."

"You want to come along or meet me at the Musselshell?" I asked Philip.

He got up, buttoned his mackinaw, and yanked his stocking cap down over his ears. "Oh, I'll tag along with the working classes," he sighed wearily.

We walked down Main Street but could barely see the displays in the windows it was snowing so hard. We met nobody. Only fools and children would come out on such a night, and we were a little of both. We could probably have any seat we wanted at the Musselshell and hang our legs over the seatbacks ahead of us. We were held up by a long freight where the tracks crossed the street, and I glanced up at the street sign. The words Main Street were all but obliterated by the snow. "That's the name of a new book," I shouted at Philip, pointing at the sign.

"I'll bet," he yelled back over the rumble of the train.

"No. Cross my heart. Miss Main let me take it out."

"What's it about?"

"What do you think it's about? It's about people like us in a little Minnesota town like Cottonwood only it's called Gopher Prairie."

"Ho hum," Philip said, touching his mitten elegantly to his mouth.

The train rumbled off through the snow, the red lights of the caboose fast fading. It was the last train that would get through for a week. We braced into the wind and made it to the bakery where we hid in the entrance to get our breath. Sure enough, just beyond the entrance to the bakery was the alley and in the alley a steep flight of iron-grill stairs so icy you had to hang onto the railing. At the top a metal door chattered on its frame. The howling wind blew the doorknob out of my hand when I released the catch. It took both of us, leaning our weight against it, to close it again.

One dim light hung like an inverted, fly-specked lily from the scabrous ceiling of a long dark hallway. We stood there a minute getting used to the gloom, glancing at several doors in what was otherwise a blank wall covered with dark brown paper, the pattern barely visible. Something moved on the floor and Philip jumped. "Haven't you ever seen a rat?" I laughed. He had not.

I knocked on the nearest door and waited. The fragrance of warm bread, yeast, and cinnamon sifting up from below made me hungry. "Does your mother ever buy baker's bread?" I asked.

"She says she wouldn't be caught dead."

"Mine neither. It smells good."

There was no answer so I tried the next door down the hall where it was darker. Some name was written on the door but I couldn't read it. I knocked and waited, then knocked again.

"I'm busy fa Kris' sake," came a voice, a girl's voice it sounded like.

"I'm sorry to bother you," I called, "but are you Miss Fern Walbrook?"

"That's me," came the reply. "What's it to you?"

"I'm the Postal Telegraph boy. I've got a telegram for you."

The woman, the girl, whatever she was, did not answer, but I could hear her mumbling something to somebody, and then I heard a man's voice.

"Wait till I get something on," the girl said presently.

We waited, it seemed a long time. Philip asked, right out of the blue, "Who wrote this book, this *Main Street* you're so crazy about?"

"Sinclair Lewis. He's been in the *Post*. He's from Minnesota too."

"What do you mean 'too'?"

"Like F. Scott Fitzgerald."

The door opened halfway. She was a girl, no doubt about it, and in that dim light she was pretty. She wore a pink wrapper and fuzzy slippers and her blonde hair was bobbed. A musky odor drifted past her and mingled with the fragrance from the bakery below. "Here's the telegram," I said.

"Who'd be sending *me* a telegram?" she said, glaring at it. And then, seeing us standing there, "It ain't collect, is it, because if it is . . ."

"No, ma'am, it's paid for all right, but Mr. Murdock thought if you wanted to answer it I could take it back to the office for you."

"Okay," she sighed, and opened the door wide. "Come in and squattyvoo where it's light enough to read."

I walked in, but Philip hesitated in the doorway. "Come in, come on in, Red," she said. "The more the merrier as the fella said."

It was a bedroom and so small that a person could get into the bed from one side only. There was someone in it now, lying on his back up next to the wall. I looked at him and then wished I hadn't. The man was a towhead and when he took a drag on his cigarette I recognized him in the glow. He was Otis, our hired man who came to town every couple of weeks on Saturday nights and drove back to the ranch in time to do the chores Sunday morning. He always said he stayed over with friends. He had once rescued me from a charging bull when I was little, and I had written that theme about his breaking his leg.

"Hello, Otis," I said.

"Howdy," Otis said, swallowing a couple of times. "Long time no see."

"That's right."

"How's school coming along?"

"I'll graduate, I guess."

"You better or your dad'll whup you. You've met Fern here, looks like."

"We've met," I said.

"He's my boss's son. Jim Ewing's kid," he explained to Fern, who stood there with the opened telegram in her hand.

"Glad to meet you," she said. "Listen. Would you read this here to me? I—I don't rightly know where my glasses got to . . ."

"Fern can't read very good," Otis said.

"You keep your trap shut, you horny bastard," Fern said, handing me the telegram.

Philip looked as if he were about to bolt but did not have the strength. I took the telegram, held it under the light, and read it: "DEAR DAUGHTER YOUR MA PASSED AWAY THIS MORNING COME HOME AND KEEP HOUSE FOR ME YOUR LOVING FATHER SIDNEY WALBROOK."

I tried to put myself in her place, tried to imagine what it would be like to get a telegram saying Mamma was dead. That must have been what Miss Pauling meant by empathy. After a moment Fern said, "Loving father my tokus!" Her face was red and angry, and she was turning slowly round and round, not seeing anything but something ugly back there in the past.

"Do you want to send an answer?" I asked finally.

"Answer?" She began to shiver and mew like a kitten.

"Come back to bed, Fern," Otis said. "You'll catch your death out there in the cold."

Hunched over, moving her head from side to side, wiping her nose with her clenched fist, she crept back toward the bed. Otis held the covers up for her, and you could see that he was naked. A tattooed snake crawled around his belly button. Fern crawled in beside him and covered the snake with her shaking body. Otis put his arms around her. "There, there, Fernie," he whispered. "We all gotta go sooner or later."

"Yeah, but that son of a bitch, if he thinks I'm ever coming back after what he did . . ."

Otis looked up and saw me still standing there. "I reckon there won't be no answer," he said quietly, and with a kind of strange dignity. "You better go . . . and oh, John, you won't let on to your pa where you seen me, okay?"

"Scout's honor," I said.

Philip got out ahead of me. We stood in the hall for a minute under the fly-specked lily and breathed very hard. The smell of the room was gone, leaving nothing but the warm incense of bread, yeast, and cinnamon.

"That — that lady is a whore, isn't she?" Philip asked.

"You know as much about it as I do," I said. "Come on, or we'll be late for *Passion*."

There were only eleven customers for the second showing of *Passion* that evening, and none of us had ever seen anything like it before. Pola Negri as Du Barry did indeed run the gamut from A to Z. Our own American idols, including Gloria Swanson and Nazimova (who was supposed to be Russian, but who knew for sure?), paled by comparison.

Philip and I sat there breathing hard. I was glad I had not brought a girl because I wouldn't have known what to say to her afterward. You couldn't very well watch Du Barry bouncing around in bed and then take your girl to Gates' Ice Cream Parlor for a chocolate malt, could you? So Philip and I never moved, half-expecting some grownup like Mr. Jensen to come down the aisle, grab us by the necks, march us out, and have Mr. Thaxter, the owner of the Musselshell, arrested for contributing to the delinquency of minors.

And then, just as Pola, fighting mad and screaming, her clothes being ripped off, was tumbled into the tumbril for her rough ride to the guillotine, the screen went dark. Obviously the film had broken as it far too often did. (By the time a picture reached Cottonwood it had already been spliced any number of times, and sometimes large chunks were left out.) Then we noticed that not only was the screen dark. So were the auditorium exit signs. So was the lobby behind us.

After about half a minute Mr. Thaxter himself hurried down the aisle. He was carrying a foot-long flashlight. There had been a power failure, he announced, on account of the storm, probably, and there was no knowing how long it would last. Telephones had gone out too, more than an hour ago. If we would stop on our way out our money would be refunded, or we would be given tickets for another night.

Philip and I took the money. Philip said that if the priest found out what kind of a picture it was he wouldn't be allowed to go again, and we had probably seen the most risqué parts of it anyhow. It did not occur to either of us that Du Barry and Fern Walbrook were in the same business.

It was the worst winter anybody could remember. Oh, there were two or three old-timers (one of them had known Charlie Russell. *He drawed pictures on the looking glass over the bar of Chandler's saloon right here in Cottonwood* — it used to sit where Sterling's is now — *to pay for his drinks*) who claimed the blizzard of '88 was worse. "Why, even the mountain cricks froze solid. You'd go to cut yourself slabs of ice for your icehouse, and dad-blamed if there weren't speckled trout all through 'em. That's the God's truth!"

That first storm dropped two feet of snow in twenty-four hours. We were just getting shoveled out from under it when another eighteen inches fell, driven by an arctic wind that piled up ten-foot drifts. Then the sun came out just long enough to thaw the surface and a sudden drop to forty-five degrees below laid a glaze of ice on top.

Though we were fairly comfortable in town — we had coal in the basement to last us, and staples could still be found at Sterling's — stories of hardship began to circulate. Five hundred head of steer on their way to market in Chicago froze to death in their boxcars on a siding. A farm woman's body was found three days after she left her house to go to the privy. (They wouldn't be able to bury her until spring.)

I had to break my word and tell my father about where I had seen Otis. If he had been unable to make it back out to the ranch, our fifteen cattle, six horses, four hogs, and various dogs, chickens, ducks, and geese would be starving.

Papa did not seem angry or even surprised. I had been afraid that he would fire Otis, but he only shrugged. "Glad you told me," he said. "You got to find out about that side o' life sooner or later. Nobody can expect a buck like Otis to be cooped up all winter with no outlet. It's different in summer. Then a man can work it off . . . Don't mention this to your mother."

"I've got enough sense not to do that."

"I'll make up some excuse to go out there to the ranch in the morning . . ."

He told Mamma that he'd met a neighbor downtown and this neighbor had told him Otis was sick. The roads were already impassable for automobiles — besides, our Buick was drained and up on jacks for the winter — so next morning Papa left at daybreak. It was one of the few days when the sun broke through. He walked twenty miles to the ranch. It took him six hours. Otis was there, of course, and had everything under control. "Hell, Jim," he told Papa, "I'd 'a' let you folks know if I couldn't make it home."

"Unless you was froze stiff as that dang pecker of your'n."

"Sorry about the kid walkin' in on me and that chippie. I'd 'a' hid my face if I'd 'a' knowed it was him."

"He's sixteen going on seventeen," Papa said.

He walked back to town the next day just as another blizzard began to howl.

It was more rugged for the kids who delivered the *Treasure State News* than for anybody, even the milkmen we sometimes passed on our routes. They at least could climb into their wagons and get out of the wind between stops. Four a.m. always found it colder or the wind blowing harder than at any other time of day or night. You could pile on two union suits, four pairs of socks under your boots and overshoes, two sweaters beneath your mackinaw, pull your stocking cap down over your eyes and nostrils, button up your rabbit-fur mittens, and the blood in your veins still felt like ice water.

And then, your subscription list always kept changing, new names added, old ones dropped. In summer we could carry slips of paper with lists of these changes, but in winter it was always pitch dark, and who could read anything anyhow with eyes and nose streaming? We tried to memorize these changes last thing before we set out each morning with the packs on our backs, but the cold numbed the brain as well as the fingers and toes, and there were many complaints about "those damn kids that keep skipping us." Not that it mattered much. The *Treasure State News* would have had trouble replacing us at five dollars a week.

It was like my mother to suggest that I quit. "Why do you have to get up every morning in the middle of the night and go traipsing out in this awful weather?"

"You know, Mama."

"Yes, but something terrible could happen. You could come down with pneumonia. Besides, you don't get enough sleep."

"It was you who told me I'd have to keep up payments on the piano. I'm not complaining."

"I know, but in weather like this! It wouldn't matter if you missed a morning or two."

"I've missed two already."

"And they didn't fire you now, did they?"

"They didn't pay me either."

"Well, I've got a feeling in my bones," Mamma went on, "that come March fourth the weather—and I don't mean just the *weather* — everything's going to get better. With Warren G. Harding in the White House there'll be good times again and our ship will come in."

Harding was inaugurated, and the storms continued. (Our ship was nowhere on the horizon.) And then suddenly on the first of April, like the worst kind of April Fool's joke, the Chinook blew down from the Rockies. The snow and ice began to melt and water to trickle, then gush, through the fields seeded to winter wheat. Meandering streams became rivers, flat plains were flooded, and the seed rotted — what was not washed away — before it could sprout. Farmers watched and waited helplessly for a cold snap that never snapped, until there was no snow in sight except on the distant peaks.

When the waters finally began to recede there was a stampede on the banks to borrow money for spring wheat seed to take the place of the winter wheat, which by then must have been approaching St. Louis, riding the rampaging Missouri, fed by the Yellowstone and the muddy Musselshell.

"You farmers have got us where the hair is short," Sam Pearson told Papa. "There's nothing we can do but lend you more dough — as long as it lasts."

"You know I don't want to borrow," Papa told him ruefully.

"Who does?" Mr. Pearson replied.

Gerry and I were finding it harder and harder to get ads for the *Annual*. A few old reliables came through — the banks, Montana Power, the creamery, institutions like that — but the economy of Cottonwood was at the mercy of agriculture, and farmers were not paying their bills. "Got to wait until fall, nothin' else we can do . . . You expect to get blood out of a turnip? . . . Okay. Force me into bankruptcy, then you'll never get your dough."

We had just been refused an ad by Gates' Ice Cream Parlor. "Sorry. Our profit margin's too small." Mrs. Gates laughed, or tried to. (They had had to let their clerk go and she was helping out.) "What do I mean profit? I mean we're trying to cut our losses, so we got to skip you young folks this spring. Have to wait till our ship comes in."

"That's what my folks say," Gerry said as we crossed the street to tackle Mr. Horowitz. (I felt pretty sure Mr. Horowitz would divvy up. I had my ten-dollar monthly payment in my pocket. I would hand it to him and then Gerry would hit him for the ad.)

"Your folks say that too?"

"It's about all they can say."

I had never seen Gerry so serious. "You folks didn't lose your wheat this spring, did you?" I asked.

"No. Our crop died during the blizzards. Twelve hundred sheep. Every last one of them."

Our ploy worked with Mr. Horowitz. He still had my ten-dollar bill in his hand as I introduced him to Gerry. "Mr. Horowitz," she said, "please don't put that away."

"Why not? I should stand here waving this around to show off I'm a millionaire?"

"I was just thinking," Gerry hurried on, "if you add fifteen dollars to that ten spot, Johnny and I can let you have a full-page ad in the *Annual*."

"Is that a fact!" Mr. Horowitz said.

"Yes. We just happen to have a vacant page directly opposite the Male Mode."

Mr. Horowitz shook his head in admiration. "The old one-two — that I should fall for it at my age." He jabbed a key on his cash register, the bell rang, the drawer flew open. Mr. Horowitz reached in, grabbed another ten and a five, and shoved them — along with my original ten — at Gerry.

"Maybe I could hire you two robbers to collect some of the bills owing to me."

It was hard to do business with a man like Mr. Horowitz, but I tried. "Now what do you want to say on your page?"

"Just say Moses Horowitz is a sucker for kids and should have his head examined."

We were on our way to tackle Mr. Thaxter at the Musselshell Theater when Gerry ran up to a squat, white-haired little man wearing bib overalls, threw her arms around him, and kissed him. "Oh, Pa," she cried, "I didn't know you were coming to town."

"Had to," Mr. Malnick said. "Had to see Sam Pearson."

"How'd it go?" Gerry asked him.

"You're not to worry, you got enough on your mind with your school and graduating." He spoke with a slight accent that I could not identify. It was not German or Scandinavian, those I could spot.

"But, Pa, if you've got problems . . ."

"Who does not have problems? Not you, my girl, I hope."

"No. Everything's fine. Fine," Gerry told him.

"You sure it's all right at the dormitory?"

Gerry shot me a nervous look. "Oh, all right. Yes, it's all right. They don't mind at all."

"You told them your Pa would pay up as soon as . . ."

I could not hear the rest of that, but Gerry nodded very fast. "Pa," she said, "this is Johnny—Johnny Ewing. I've told you and Ma about him."

"Glad to meet you, Mr. Malnick," I said. "I'm sorry about the sheep."

"Yeah . . . well . . . got to wait till our ship comes in, unless we sink first." He laughed as if he had made a joke. He turned back to Gerry. "You're a good girl?" he asked.

She smiled. "Yes, Pa. I'm a good girl."

"You sure?"

"Sure."

"Stay that way."

"Oh, Pa, don't worry about *that*."

"Gerry's just about the best girl there is in Cottonwood High," I said.

"I like to hear that," Mr. Malnick said. "That is music a father can dance to." He turned back to Gerry and hugged her once more. "I got to go now," he said. "Train time."

"You take care, Pa. And give Ma my love."

He walked off toward the depot. We watched him until he turned the corner and then we tackled Mr. Thaxter. He bought a half-page for fifteen dollars.

from Philip Pearson's Day Book

May 9, 1921. Gerry Malnick has disappeared. Rumor hath it that she was expelled. I asked John. He says he doesn't know.

It was a day or two before we missed Gerry, and when we did we just thought she had a cold and was confined to the dorm. Then I met Edwina Hall at the drinking fountain. Edwina, a chubby girl who wore ribbed stockings and hand-me-down button shoes (she was the youngest of ten), was Gerry's roommate. She was a grind, never asked to dances, and must have fumed inside over Gerry's popularity.

"How's Gerry?" I asked.

"I wouldn't know," Edwina said. "She's gone home."

"When will she be back?"

Edwina shrugged. "Search me, as the pickpocket said."

"But—but—" I spluttered, "we're right in the middle of the ad campaign for the *Annual*. She wouldn't just go off and not . . ."

"Look. Don't blame me. I'm just her roommate."

I hurried into Miss Pauling's room. She was alone, grading themes. Gerry would certainly have told her how long she would be away.

"Miss Pauling, excuse me, but do you know when Gerry will be back?"

"Shut the door, John, will you?"

Something about her voice was different. It was usually young and full of enthusiasm, often spilling over into laughter. I closed the door and advanced slowly toward her desk. "Is anything the matter?"

"I'm afraid there is," she said. "I know how you feel about Gerry—we all feel that way—and I wish there were some way I could avoid telling you, but you'll find out sooner or later. Everybody will, they always do, that's what is so—so . . ."

I sank into the desk seat directly before Miss Pauling's big desk. She turned and stared out the window where the returning sparrows were lisping as they played hide-and-seek among the pale young leaves of the old cottonwood.

"Gerry had to go home. Let's just say that."

"For how long?"

"For—I was going to say for good, but it's anything but good, I'm afraid." She turned back and looked at me. "Gerry is not coming back." Her voice was flat and hard.

I felt as if I had been kicked in the gut. "No, Miss Pauling. You don't—you can't mean that."

She nodded. "Some of the money that she—and some that you had collected and handed over to her—Gerry did not deposit in the special account at the bank. She spent it."

"Gerry wouldn't do a thing like that!" I cried. The things you say at emotional moments when you're young.

"But she did," Miss Pauling said. "She told me herself."

We sat and stared at each other. Then I said, "You mean they're not going to let Gerry graduate?"

"Mr. Jensen says he could not possibly award a diploma to such a person. Mr. Jensen expelled her."

"I hate Mr. Jensen!" I cried.

"We must all try to understand and not to judge."

"He judged! He's just trying to fix her because she walked in here with Mr. Cram that day and . . ." I saw a look of pain in Miss Pauling's eyes. She laid the back of her hand on her open mouth. "Oh, Gerry never told anybody but me, and I never said a word," I said.

She rose and came forward to place her hand on my shoulder. "Thank you, John," she said. "But I don't think we can blame that unfortunate episode for . . . After all, Gerry did spend money that did not belong to her. A sum of $235. I wouldn't have told you except that it is going to be up to you and me to check with all the advertisers to find out who actually paid up and who did not."

"Did she tell you why she did it?" I asked.

Miss Pauling sighed and walked back to her desk. "The Malnicks lost all their sheep this past winter. They had no cash and could borrow only enough to keep them alive. She couldn't face the ignominy of dropping out of school—you know what a big shot Gerry has become here at Cottonwood. Gerry Malnick *had* to graduate or else. So she told her father that she had talked to Mrs. Gossett at the dorm, and that Mrs. Gossett told her the bill for room and board could be paid later. Unfortunately she never mentioned that her family was strapped for cash. I guess she was intimidated by Mrs. Gossett. I can't say I blame her—I would have been too at her age. Youthful pride—she couldn't let it down. Oh, tomorrow would come, but not *tomorrow*. Not until she graduated. Gerry Malnick was flying so high everybody had to look up to see her. Gerry Malnick could not have such a mundane problem as lack of money. And I'm afraid she didn't spend it merely on room and board. She bought a yellow dress for the senior prom."

"How did anybody find out?"

"I asked her to let me see the deposit book." Miss Pauling threw her head back and cried out, "God, oh, God, why didn't I do that sooner, while it was still only thirty-five, fifty, seventy-five dollars instead of two hundred and thirty-five!" She swallowed hard. "So, I had to face the problem and take it to—to Mr. Jensen. Frankly it never occurred to me that—that something could not be done to smooth things over. If I had had the cash I would have . . ." She paused and seemed to look inside herself. "Would I? I wonder? Yes. Yes, I think I would have, if I had known he was going to . . ."

"Gerry's not a thief," I said. "She just . . ."

"It was *there*—too handy when she needed it so badly. We all thought she was much stronger than she was."

I found the tears beginning to come. "We've got to do something."

"I wish I knew what," Miss Pauling said.

I blew my nose. "I'm glad I'm not coming back here next year," I said.

"If it means anything to you, John, neither am I. And neither is Mr. Cram."

"Good!" I said vindictively. I could have asked questions, were they going to get married, where were they going, and things like that, but that did not seem important.

"And John," Miss Pauling said, "let's not mention this, shall we?"

"It's making me sick at the stomach to talk about it."

She put away the themes she had been grading and closed the drawer to her desk. "That theme of yours about building the piano bench in manual training. I like it. I couldn't help wondering how wide it was when you finally glued it together."

"Not quite fourteen inches," I confessed.

"And did you get the piano to go with it?"

"It's sitting right in front of the piano bench," I said.

"Are you going to be a pianist?"

"I don't think so. I just like music."

"Well, you may be a writer someday. You're different from Philip Pearson, but . . ." She walked with me to the door. "About telling what I told you. I suppose it doesn't matter much. We can't bottle up the truth, no matter how hard we try."

After she walked down the hall I stood for a minute trying to get used to the label Gerry Malnick would wear as surely as Hester Prynne wore her scarlet "A." *Thief* did not seem quite right. I walked back into Miss Pauling's room and opened the big dictionary to the *T*'s. "Thief. One who steals, esp. stealthily or secretly." No, there had to be another word. Gerry had not done what she had done either stealthily or secretly. She had just done it. How about *embezzler?* I flipped the pages back to the *E*'s. "Embezzle. To appropriate fraudulently to one's own use, as property entrusted to one's care."

That was it. Gerry was an embezzler, she had embezzled $235 entrusted to her care. An honest person should not feel sorry for an embezzler. It was a crime. But I could not help wondering what had happened when she went home and told her parents she embezzled the *Annual* funds to pay her room and board. That nice, white-haired little man I had met, the one in bib overalls who had wanted to know if she was a good girl, would he still think she was a good girl?

And what about her mother, whatever she was like. Did Gerry show her the yellow dress that would never be worn to the senior prom? . . .

"What are you doing in here?" It was Philip's voice. I turned away from the dictionary and saw him standing in the doorway.

"Looking up some dirty words."

"Listen," he said. "I just heard Gerry Malnick got expelled."

"Who told you?"

"It's all over. Do you know why?"

"I don't know, I don't *know*," I said and tried to walk past him. I guess he must have seen that my eyes were red.

"Gosh, I'm sorry," he said, gruffly, as if it were hard for him to get the words out.

"You didn't even like her," I said.

"No. But you did."

It was the nicest thing he had ever said to me. I could put up with a lot from anybody who understood, without my telling him, what was going on inside me.

"I don't want to talk about it."

"Okay." We walked out of the room together and closed the door behind us. "What I was looking for you for, do you want to go see *Way Down East* tonight? We could take in the first show and maybe stay around for the second — it's Friday — if it's as good as *Photoplay* says."

6

The graduation ceremony for our class of '21 was *Midsummer Night's Dream* without Puck, Barnum and Bailey's circus without Jumbo. There was not a mention of Gerry Malnick. It was as if she were dead, or, rather, had never been alive.

Yet her spirit haunted every one of us as Mr. Jensen platitudinously intoned his farewell. This sunny day in our Treasure State was not an end but, "permit me to say, a commencement." (How many times had he and others like him said that, how many more times would they repeat it?) We would never forget our years at dear old Cottonwood High or the friends we had made there. Those precious memories would live with us ad infinitum. If there had been a few unpleasant experiences — and how could one savor the *sweet* unless he had sipped of the *bitter?* — we would in time turn from them, as the carpenter turns from his lathe, to distill their beauty and discover their true meaning. (Was this a veiled reference to Gerry, or merely his annual excrescence?) We were no longer children but young adults now, our shining faces focused on the exciting world of the twenties, the thirties, the challenging world of tomorrow. We would not be graduated today unless we had achieved a certain standard of scholarship, but the basic moralities as taught by Our Savior, honesty, decency, and consideration for the rights of others, so beautifully and simply expressed in those immortal words, "Do unto others as ye would have them do unto you," these moralities he chose to believe had been reinforced in us during the past four years.

Period. The four long years that had become a way of life were suddenly, finally over. Now what?

My family did not know the direction of the future. They would not know it for sure until the summer was over and the wheat harvested. But again it began to look as if, no matter how bumper the crop might prove to be, it could do little more than get us out of the hole and pay up the debts incurred during the last two slim years. My father no longer spoke of settling up and going back to God's Country. However, California was right there around the corner for Mamma. "Now that Johnny is finished with high school, what's to prevent our going? Luna"— she was Mamma's older sister—"will help find us a house and Johnny can go to the University of Southern California."

Papa did not bother to reply. What was to prevent us was, short of a miracle, no wherewithal.

So where was I to go to college? Was I going to college at all? Philip had another semester of high school, and his application to Harvard had already been accepted. But I had to mark time in uneasy limbo.

During my senior year I had required but two more units to complete the sixteen necessary for graduation. To round out my schedule I had taken, at the advice of Miss Pauling, a stenographic and typing course. She had said, "If you are going to be a writer, you'll want to know how to type, and the ability to take shorthand notes never comes amiss. Secretarial work pays well, and I have a feeling that you'd have no trouble getting a job. There are certain situations in which employers—bosses, if you will—prefer men to women. When it is necessary to travel, for instance, it would be unseemly for a man to take a young lady along with him."

(Whatever happened to *unseemly?*)

"Another thing. I know nothing of your family's financial situation, but many young men pay their college tuition by doing part-time work, and typing pays much better than raking leaves or mowing lawns."

Rather than go out to the farm with my parents while we awaited, once more, the fate of the wheat (and the Ewings), I remained in town, boarded with Evy and Henry and Henrietta, now a noisy five-year-old, and looked for a job. Miss Pauling had been right. I landed one on the second day of my search. A lawyer named Horace W. Claymore had recently lost a secretary who had left him, he said, to get married. (That's as may be. I rather suspect there was another reason.) Besides, he would prefer a male secretary. Some of his clients were rather rough characters.

Mr. Claymore was a fine figure of a man. (He reminded Philip and me — yes, we were still doing it — of Milton Sills, who always played high-class gentlemen.) Tall and ramrod-straight, the sheen of his dark hair dramatized by a streak of white rising from the left temple, Claymore was "aristocratic looking." He spoke precisely in complete and meticulously crafted sentences, and in an accent I had never heard before. He said "Bahston" instead of Boston, was formally courteous, and called me Mr. Ewing.

Mr. Claymore did not have many clients, rough characters or otherwise, and there were days when he did not appear at the office at all. Sometimes he would let me know, sometimes not. When he did I would telephone Philip and ask him to come down to the office if he wasn't doing anything. I had found that there was fascinating material in Mr. Claymore's private law library. Philip and I spent many hours devouring case histories of aberrant characters such as we never knew existed. They made our Mr. Jensen's attack on Miss Pauling seem like a mere holiday afternoon's hoopla.

There was only one thing wrong with Mr. Claymore. He sometimes forgot to give me my twenty dollars on Saturday afternoon. Once when he did not forget, the check was returned, marked Insufficient Funds. When I told him about it he apologized. "How stupid of me. It slipped my mind that I have just transferred my office account to another bank." He wrote another check on another bank. When that too came back he was understandably distressed. (So was I. I wanted to have the piano paid for so that we could move it with us if we left for California.) Mr. Claymore blamed it on the absurd complexities of modern-day bookkeeping, making it necessary for money to be deposited for a certain length of time before the depositor could draw upon it. How could anyone keep up with these tiresome technicalities? He wrote another check, advising me to delay cashing it for two or three days, just in case. When I finally cashed it, it did not bounce.

I confided the incident of the bouncing check to Philip. He mentioned it to his father. "Dad wants to talk to you some noon hour," Philip told me.

"This is in strictest confidence, my boy," Mr. Pearson told me, "but you ought to know for your own protection. Mr. Claymore is very possibly the most brilliant attorney in Cottonwood. He comes from a fine old New England family, and he has a lovely wife. Close friend of Mrs. Pearson, I may add. Charming woman. But I regret to say that Horace is undependable. If he were, let's use the word 'stable,' he could be one of the most prosperous trial lawyers in the state, with a clientele that would require four competent legal secretaries instead of one youngster just out of high school. I don't mean to demean you, John."

"I understand," I said.

"There have been occasions when he had a case on the docket and he simply did not appear in court."

"But—why didn't he?"

Mr. Pearson lowered his voice. "I'm afraid that poor Mr. Claymore is an alcoholic. If I were you, I'd begin to look around for another situation." He smiled. "And now you've had what they call 'experience' it should not be too difficult."

An alcoholic . . . I had never heard the term. Oh, I knew about drunks—you couldn't escape a few staggering along Main Street on Saturday nights, even since Prohibition, but common drunks, reeking and red-nosed, bore no resemblance to the impeccable Mr. Horace W. Claymore who never smelled of anything but Lavoris and Lilac Vegetal water. I came to the conclusion that it must be a matter of one's rung on the social ladder. If you were a day laborer and you drank more than you could hold, you were a drunk. If you were well educated, a professional man, came from a fine old New England family, and had a lovely, charming wife, you would hold your liquor much better and be labeled an alcoholic.

★　★　★

I began to look around for another job during my noon hours, but very few employers were in the market for seventeen-year-old male stenographers just out of high school. My six weeks with Mr. Claymore did not qualify as valid experience. Then I stopped looking, because the last two salary checks were prompt and did not bounce. Besides, this job was merely a stopgap, wasn't it? Maybe I could stretch it out till we moved.

Mr. Claymore came in unexpectedly one afternoon while Philip was there. We had been reading an account of a wife who sued her husband for divorce because of his insistence upon oral sex (which we figured must mean talking while having intercourse), and had not heard Mr. Claymore's footsteps. Seeing Philip, he paused for a moment, inclined his head graciously in greeting, then walked stiffly across to his inner office and closed the door.

There was something unusual about him, and for a moment I could not place it. Then I realized what it was. The elegant member of the old New England family, the most brilliant attorney in Cottonwood, had not bothered to shave this morning!

We quickly replaced the weighty volume on its shelf, and Philip hurried out.

I sat down at my desk and stared at the Underwood, which had been silent for days. I dusted it, then for something to do put a piece of the heavily embossed stationery with the tasteful letterhead, Horace W. Claymore, Attorney at Law, in the machine. What a funny term that was — Attorney at Law. Could you be an attorney at anything else? Banking? Poultry raising? The door to the inner office opened and Mr. Claymore stood there, his hand braced against the door frame.

"Would you care to step inside, Mr. Ewing?" he said politely.

"Of course," I said, thinking here it comes. He's going to can me because he caught Philip here while he was away. I could hear him saying, "Mr. Ewing, this office is not a social forum." I walked past him and stood beside his massive carved mahogany desk with the gold pen-and-pencil set, the rocking-horse blotter and day book, and the photograph of the lovely lady who was Mrs. Horace W. Claymore.

"Sit ye doon, sit ye doon," he said affably as he returned to his desk. When he sat, his rump did not quite jibe with the swivel chair seat but slid off the arm, and it almost threw him. "Excuse me," he said. "Just a slip of the old Claymore gluteus. No permanent damage, I'm happy to say."

He pretended to realign the desk set with the photograph, then sat back and smiled. "My beautiful wife," he said. "She has her problems, no doubt, as I have mine . . . Now."

He turned to me and frowned, as if he wondered what I was doing there. "Oh, yes," he said finally. "That was young Philip Pearson out there, was it not?"

"Yes, Mr. Claymore. He just happened to drop by to — to tell me about going to college next year. He wasn't going to stay or . . ."

Mr. Claymore raised his hand to stem the tide of excuses. "I have no objection to your entertaining guests when I am absent. Of course if you were taking advantage of my absence to forni-cate with a young lady, I trust you would bolt the door."

"Oh, Mr. Claymore," I said, "you don't think . . ."

"Why not? Good exercise. Well, no matter. Nice-looking chap, Philip."

Taking a key out of his pocket, he slowly, meticulously insert-ed it into the key slot of the top drawer of his desk, lifted a pint bottle of bourbon out of it, unscrewed the top, put the bottle to his lips, and took a long swig. "Ah," he said. "Mother's milk." Then he screwed the top back, replaced the bottle in the drawer, closed the drawer once more, and locked it. Finally he looked back across the desk at me.

"We were discussing torts?" he asked matter-of-factly.

"You said Philip Pearson was a nice-looking chap, sir," I said nervously.

"Ah, yes. So I did. Doesn't look much like old Sam, does he?"

"No," I said. "He seems to favor his mother."

"And his father, Wilma and I have always thought."

"But didn't you just say he doesn't look much like Mr. Pearson?"

"That is what I said, and that is precisely what I meant," Mr. Claymore said. There was a look of impish mischief in his expression. "I never say anything I do not mean." He paused, turned, and looked out the window at the mountains in the distance.

I waited for him to go on. Presently he said, "I happened to run into my friend Jason Bartlett at the club last night. Jason mentioned in passing that my secretary had been in his office at the Chamber of Commerce applying for a post. He said afore-mentioned secretary had mentioned Sam Pearson as a reference. Then Jason said that a 'not-to-be-named' person had told him Sam had suggested that he (the 'not-to-be-named' person) look for another position. Now I can't help but wonder, is this person you?"

I swallowed hard. Oh, Lord, oh, Lord, I should never have started looking for another job. Now I'll be without one altogether. I'd been a fool.

"I'm sorry, Mr. Claymore, but . . ."

"No need for tears." He nodded several times slowly. "Stands to reason Sam Pearson would feel the way he does. I'm one of only three or four persons who know that Sam is impotent, and he knows that I know, I suspect. Mrs. Claymore"—he bowed formally to the lady in the photograph—"that is, Mrs. Claymore's intimate friend, Stella Pearson, confided in her."

"Impotent?" I repeated. I had only the vaguest suspicion of the difference between impotent and sterile.

"Well, not precisely," Mr. Claymore went on in the same reasonable tone. "Interesting physiological phenomenon. As I understand it, he has no problem with erectile tissue. It is merely the fact that an opening at the base of the penis ejects the semen before it can enter the vagina. I have read that this is one reason George Washington was the father of his country, and merely the stepfather of Martha's two Custis children."

I must have gone quite white. At any rate I could not move.

"Poor old Sam. He must accept the cigars for three offspring he knows damn well did not spring off his loins. That's why, when each of them was born, he would get drunk and take off to his cabin in the mountains for several days. Then he would come back, see the baby, and the father instinct would have its way with him . . . Now this should go no further," Mr. Claymore went on, "but you ought to realize that Sam Pearson's advice to you to get another job was not purest altruism. He is a good, honest, dependable man, but few men can resist punishing others for being privy to such an embarrassing clinical datum."

Mr. Claymore sounded as if he were completely sober, but maybe when you were an alcoholic you were not necessarily drunk when you had too much to drink. You merely told, or invented, stories that you should not. We sat in silence for a long time. I did not quite know how to get up and go out. It would seem ridiculous, after what had occurred, for me simply to rise and ask, "Will that be all?"

At last Mr. Claymore said, "Next time you're in the Male Mode shopping for a tie — you need a new one, by the way, and I detest dots — take a good look at Mr. Everett Fowler. See if you do not note a striking resemblance to Philip Pearson. As for Maureen and the late, lamented King — wonderful young man, I understand — I have no notion who their sires might have been. Poor Stella . . . she *would* have children. And being of the Catholic faith, divorce from Sam was *de toute impossibilité*."

When finally I could I rose to my feet. "You'll be wanting me to leave, won't you?"

"Why, dear boy, certainly not. You have done nothing to offend me."

He started to rise, did not quite make it to the perpendicular, and sank back into his chair. Then as if saying first to himself, "Stand up!" he heaved his body upward and steadied his strangely disjointed and inarticulate torso by touching his long, spatulate fingers to the desktop. He smiled, pleased at his accomplishment, smothered a yawn, and said, "Well, Mr. Ewing, if you have nothing further on the calendar . . ."

"There *is* something, Mr. Claymore," I said nervously, "but if you haven't got the time . . ."

"Time," he repeated. "I used to have it but I have mislaid it. Perhaps it's at the club — in the bar." This seemed to delight him.

"As Marcus Aurelius said, 'Time is a sort of river of passing events, and strong is its current.' I suppose if you lose time, then it must follow as the night the day, you also lose the passing events . . . You were saying?"

His voice was not slurred. His eyes were focused squarely upon mine. I had to go on.

"It's about my father," I said. "He needs to talk to a lawyer about — about bankruptcy."

"Whose bankruptcy?"

"His own, I'm afraid."

"Ah," he said, and there was genuine sympathy in his tone. "A regrettable — but a passing shadow on that river. Well, no attorney gets rich undertaking bankruptcy proceedings on a contingency basis, but — set up an appointment at our mutual convenience and we'll talk. Perhaps there is another way out. And now I think I shall take one of those ways myself and adjourn to the club. I somehow feel the need of . . ."

His voice did not taper off. It ceased abruptly as if a needle had been lifted from a record, and he collapsed like a ventriloquist's dummy tossed carelessly on the floor.

I was growing up fast.

★ ★ ★

The 1921 wheat crop was a disaster. There had been no rain from May 20 to July 30, and when it finally came hail preceded it and pounded what little ripening grain there was into the earth. Mamma would not have to cook for the threshing crew this summer.

My father staggered under this final blow to his faltering hopes as surely as Georges Carpentier did when he was walloped in the solar plexus by Jack Dempsey back in Jersey City that same July. This time there would be no bell to save us and permit us to catch our breath for another round of harrowing, planting, waiting, growing, ripening, waiting, harvesting, and threshing. There was only one way out.

Bankruptcy was a shameful word to Papa. Crooks and swindlers went bankrupt. Men of mean character who ran up

bills they never intended to pay chose that cheap way out, but not
James Ewing. James Ewing paid his honest debts, he always had
and he always would, by God!

"There's nothing else for you to do, Dad," my brother-in-law,
Henry Peterson, argued. "I shouldn't be telling you this, but the
First National has already instituted foreclosure on a lot of farms
mortgaged like yours. Pearson and the other officers, they don't
want to, but they have no choice."

"I thought once we got a Republican in the White House
again, money would be easier," Papa said.

"Harding can't control the weather, I'm afraid. Look at it this
way, Dad. Bankruptcy is no disgrace when it's used as a last
resort. The law is there to protect folks like you from being
thrown in jail when they can't pay their debts."

Papa shut his eyes. His head sank low onto his chest. After a
long moment he said slowly, "Henry, you figure if I went to Sam
Pearson and laid my cards on the table . . ."

"He knows what's in your hand. There's nothing he can do
this time. The bank is overextended. It's got to liquidate all the
property it can get its hands on in order to pull through."

I made the appointment for Papa with Mr. Claymore.
Claymore, sober, kept the appointment. He was as courteous, as
tactful as he might have been with a rich client planning to sue
for a million dollars' damages. A highly regrettable combination
of circumstances had forced such a course of action upon my
father, he said. He understood Papa's reluctance to resort to it,
but there was nothing shameful about it. He named several
famous persons who had gone bankrupt and revived, because of
it, to earn the respect and admiration of their peers.

Papa listened. His mind believed it, but his spirit wilted. It
never quite recovered.

Mamma, on the other hand, began to glow. Although it had
been her idea to come to Montana in the first place, she had
never liked it. She had always felt superior to her farm neighbors,
but being labeled a farmer's wife had restricted her social ambi-
tions in the town of Cottonwood. Now we would be moving
on — to California, of course, because my father, a proud man,

could not return to Wisconsin a bankrupt. "Wherever you want to go to, Ella," he said, "if we can get there. But what am I going to do after we get there?"

"There'll be *something,*" Mamma said, "if God means us to go. Sister Luna says there are all kinds of jobs waiting for able-bodied men at the chair factory in Inglewood where Eugene works. The Ransimers are just dying to have us come." I had never met Eugene Ransimer. When Aunt Luna had come to visit us once she had come alone, and Papa had confided to me that he was just as pleased.

I could see my father weighing the pros and cons of going to work in a factory at his time of life. He was sixty-one. There was no light in his eyes. "That's all very well, Ella," he said, "but how the hell are we going to get there?"

"Oh, ye of little faith!" Mamma cried.

"Railroads don't run on faith," Papa said.

"James Ewing, that is sacrilegious and I will not listen to it!"

"Very well," Papa said, starting for the door. "When Mary Baker Eddy delivers the railroad fare, let me know. Meantime I've applied for a job as cook out at the mining camp."

Mamma's face turned brick red. She had to fan it with her apron to keep from fainting. "What will people say?" she gasped. "Why—why—why—how can I hold my head up if people know you're a cook?"

"Keep your head down," Papa said. "Anyhow, with what little I can bring in, and with Johnny to help out, we'll be eating, which some aren't."

I doubt that anyone, except the poor coal miners subjected to my father's grub, ever knew or cared what he was doing. In November Cottonwood awoke one morning to an event on that passing river of time that shook the town and the countryside to their foundations.

from Philip Pearson's Day Book

Nov. 21, 1921. We were going to get a new collie, but now we can't because my father's bank has failed and father is ill. Maureen has come home from the university at Missoula to help Mother.

My mother brightened when I came home that afternoon and told her. "That's wonderful!" she said. My face must have betrayed my inability to translate the failure of the First National Bank to "wonderful."

"Don't you see," she said conspiratorially, "now it's all right for us to be broke. The *bank's* to blame! I'll write and tell Luna and Eugene."

"You haven't told them about our bankruptcy?"

"Of course not. I *knew* something like this would happen. I can write and say our savings went down with the bank, and they'll send us money to get to California. God has found a way!"

Mamma, as was her wont, had leapt to a conclusion with total disregard for any hurdle that might trip her along the way. It had not occurred to her — and it should have, because Papa used to mutter that Eugene Ransimer never let go of a nickel until he'd rubbed the buffalo off of it — that money for train fare would not be dispatched, or telegraphed, the very same day Aunt Luna received the distressing news about the loss of our life savings.

When the reply finally arrived (ten days later) it indicated sororal concern for the plight of sister Ella's family, but added, "You know poor Gene. He's worked and slaved all his life to lay aside a nest egg for a 'rainy day.' I'll have to choose the right moment to bring up what you suggest. Now, just before the holidays, I know what he would say: Jim and Ella were crazy to go out there to Montana in the first place, and now they expect me to bail them out. I'm not saying he won't eventually come around, but it's going to take time. All is well here. We have a new Ford touring car, and plan to drive to Pasadena on January first for the Tournament of Roses parade. Love from your sister Luna."

Mamma took to her bed for three days with a sick headache.

Meanwhile the Petersons were packing up to leave for Casper, Wyoming, where Henry's brother had found him a job as bookkeeper for a big oil-rig outfit. Henry said that after they got there he'd look around for something for Dad Ewing to do. "Don't bother," Mamma said airily. "We'll be leaving for California any day now."

"Mamma," Evy said timorously (she was always a little scared of our mother), "I hope you're not putting all your eggs in one basket."

"I have no idea what you mean by that," Mamma said.

"Well — that is — expecting the Ransimers to . . ."

"I am expecting the Ransimers to do nothing. Our future — as is everyone's — lies in God's bountiful basket, and God is Love."

"Knock on wood," Henry said quietly, and knocked on the lid of the portable Victrola.

"When *we* get to California we will find something for *you* to do, Henry, so we can all be together again."

It was late spring before the letter from Aunt Luna arrived with a promissory note for $500 to be signed by my father. "Just a formality," Aunt Luna wrote, "in case something should happen to any of us." The formality also stipulated that the loan was to be paid off no later than a year from date of signature. Meanwhile it would draw five percent interest, which was two percent more than the Ransimers could earn from any reputable bank.

"It's usury," Papa said, "but we're up the creek."

Mamma burst into tears of relief. That was one of the few human reactions I ever witnessed from her. All others were triggered by her trust in God, Who was, however, inclined to be a forgetful old party devoting far too much of His time to His sparrows, and needed reminding (via Mrs. Schilling, the practitioner, when our straits were desperate) that Mamma was His Perfect Child, and that there was no life, truth, substance, or intelligence in the disturbing mortal error surrounding her. Dogged trust in God, and false pride, these were her hallmarks.

The date of our leave-taking was fast approaching. The streets, the friends, the sounds and smells of Cottonwood, which I had so long taken for granted as eternal fixtures of existence, took on new dimensions as I realized they would soon be left behind. I found myself thinking, I may never see Main and Fifth again, never enjoy another movie at the Musselshell, smell the aroma of the soda fountain at Gates', never hear the courthouse clock chime, never again hide behind the stacks at the Carnegie Library so that Miss Main would not catch me with a copy of *Bel-Ami,* never see the Victor dog outside the Clef Music Store . . .

Which reminded me. I still owed Mr. Horowitz $240 on the Lyon and Healy piano. Would I have a legal right to ship it out of the state before it was paid for?

I asked Mr. Claymore's advice. (He was behind two weeks in my salary.) I told him the circumstances of its purchase. "Since you are a minor, and your mother paid a hundred dollars down, she must have signed a contract. Have her look into the matter."

Mamma had mislaid her copy of the contract and had no intention of "looking into the matter." Mr. Horowitz was a Jew and a Jew would demand his pound of flesh. (I had read *The Merchant of Venice,* hadn't I?) Translate pound of flesh into seizure of piano. He would never consider giving back her hundred-dollar deposit or the $210 I had paid, adding up to $310 in all. So we would say nothing, and the next thing Mr. Shylock Horowitz knew, we — and the piano — would be way out there in a California bungalow watching the waves of the Pacific Ocean roll in out of an everlasting sunset. I could pay what I still owed if I wanted to, at my convenience, and what could he do?

"Mr. Horowitz," I said later that day, "my family and I are moving to Los Angeles."

"My congratulations," he said. "Go to the Philharmonic, you'll hear Galli-Curci, you'll hear Kreisler, you'll hear Caruso and Rachmaninoff and Levine. Ah, I envy you."

"What I wanted to talk to you about was the piano."

"You want me to buy it back, is that it?"

"Oh, no. No. I want to take it along, but — well — you know it's not paid for yet and . . ."

"And I would have trouble suing you way out there in California. That's what you're thinking?"

"You won't have to sue anybody, Mr. Horowitz. I'll keep on paying every month, but I thought maybe . . ."

"You're a good boy," he said, patting my shoulder. "A real *goniff* I would be if I did not trust a boy who buys grand pianos when he is fifteen years old. *Mazel tov*."

The day before we were to leave I rang the front door bell at the Pearsons' house. The kitchen entrance would do for "Is Philip at home?" but this was good-bye, maybe forever, to the Pearson family.

Maureen came to the door. I had not seen her for a year and she was different. Taller, thinner, her blue eyes larger and a little troubled. When she saw who it was she smiled. "Come in, Johnny. Or are you John now?"

"To your family I'll always be Johnny, but I'm going to try to — to phase that out with new people."

"Philip tells us you folks are going to California."

"That's right. Los Angeles. My mother has a sister in Inglewood. That's a suburb."

"Are you going to college there?"

"We'll have to see about that," I said. We walked down the hall toward the parlor. (Mrs. Pearson must have run through here naked that night, I thought.) "Dad, Johnny Ewing has come to tell us good-bye," Maureen said.

The shades were drawn to keep out the heat of the afternoon. Mr. Pearson, wearing bedroom slippers and a madras silk bathrobe over his pajamas, sat in his big brown leather chair, doing something with his hands that at first I could not make out. Perhaps the diffused light, or possibly the patent absurdity of his doing such a thing, kept me from immediately interpreting the movement of his fingers. He looked up and smiled. "I'd get up," Mr. Pearson said, "but I'm afraid I might drop a stitch."

There was no doubt about it: He was knitting. Apparently it was going to be some sort of scarf; it already trailed off on the waxed floor. "There," he said putting it down. "Gives one something to do with the hands and keeps the hounds of the mind at bay."

"I just came by to say good-bye to you all," I said.

"Ah, yes. My boy tells me you people are moving to California."

"That's right. At least I hope it's right."

"We never know," he said. "We do what we think is best for the greatest number at the time, don't we?"

"I guess."

"And sometimes that backfires, and we find ourselves — as I've heard your father say — up shit creek."

I had never heard Mr. Pearson use an expression like that, and I could see Maureen blush. "Well," I said, "I guess I'd better be going."

"When you get out there to sunny California, be sure to pay your respects to my sister Grace."

"Oh, Dad," Maureen said, "Johnny will have other things to do besides calling on old folks."

"I daresay," Mr. Pearson sighed. Then he smiled. "Well, that being the case, say hello to the Dolly Sisters for me."

"The Dolly Sisters?" I repeated, puzzled.

"Remember? You and Philip spent the night with them when you were supposed to be at *A Tale of Two Cities.*" He chuckled.

"You never forget anything, do you, Mr. Pearson?"

"No, and sometimes I wish I could."

Mrs. Pearson was seated at the kitchen table polishing a silver tureen. "Mother, it's Johnny," Maureen said. Mrs. Pearson looked up and squinted at me. I guess she was beginning to need glasses. "You've been neglecting us," she said.

"I've been busy," I said, "working for Mr. Claymore."

"So I heard. I know Mrs. Claymore. Philip's working too this spring. Messenger boy. Nothing as high-toned as a legal secretary, but then he wasn't foresighted enough to know that he might not be going off straightaway to Boston."

"You mean Philip's not going to Harvard?" He had not mentioned this possibility.

"It depends upon so many things," Mrs. Pearson said. "Hard times for all of us, aren't they? Maureen had to come home from school."

"Oh, Mother," Maureen said, "as if that mattered as long as you and Dad are all right."

Mrs. Pearson crossed herself. "And you're going to California. Philip will be envious. You keep in touch with us, you hear?"

"I hear," I said. "I'll never forget you folks, you can depend on that."

"You better not." I started out of the kitchen door. "Wait." I turned back. Mrs. Pearson reached into the icebox and took out a small brown paper sack ornamented with the crowing rooster of the Male Mode. (Who had been in there and bought what in that proscribed shop?) "It was the only thing I could find," Mrs. Pearson apologized, "but it's not the sack that matters to you, I'm sure, it's what's in it."

I opened the sack. There must have been at least two pounds of Mrs. Pearson's fudge in it. I kissed her. She did not smell like my mother or any other mother I had ever been near.

Walking down the street I ran into Philip who was out delivering a telegram. He turned without a word and walked along beside me. "You want some of your mother's fudge?" I asked after a little while.

"No, thanks. Dr. Condon says maybe it causes this." He indicated a hickey on his chin. "Remember the night I went along with you when you delivered a telegram to the whore?"

I smiled, and suddenly felt very sad. We passed St. Matthew's. "Remember how you fell on your ass that day and the nun came out and picked you up?"

"She did not!" Philip said.

"Like fun!"

Another silence. Then Philip said, "Lots of stuff has happened since then."

"It sure has." Neither of us identified any of the stuff.

"I'll write once in a while and tell you about doing the shimmy with Gilda Grey."

Philip jabbed me on the arm and blinked several times. "Goddamn," he said angrily. "I got something in my eye. Take a look, will you?"

"Since when are you goddamning?"

He got down on his knees and I rolled his eyelid back and peered into the eye. There was nothing in it, but it was red. I diagnosed it as conjunctivitis, which seemed to satisfy both of us. "Lot of it going around," he said.

We were within a block of the last house we ever rented in Cottonwood. "Lookit," I said, "you better get that thing delivered or you'll get the sack."

"Yeah, I better."

We stopped and avoided looking at each other. "Maybe you'll come out and visit your aunt Grace sometime," I said.

"I don't know. She's got cats."

"So she's got cats."

"They make me sneeze a lot."

"Oh. I was just thinking . . . maybe you could stay with her and go to college out there."

"I was supposed to go to Harvard this September."

"I know . . . it's nobody's fault."

He turned away and frowned, his lips protruding in that familiar, unattractive pucker, as if he were about to spit. "If a lot of folks like yours hadn't of gone bankrupt my father's bank wouldn't have closed its doors, and . . ."

"You go to hell!" I said. I turned and walked away from him, vowing one more time, but not the last time, never to speak to my best friend again.

PART II

7

Genesee, like a majority of streets and those others arbitrarily labeled lanes, drives, or avenues, was lined with California bungalows, some larger, more ornate than others, but all loosely cut from the same pattern and set cheek by jowl on narrow lots, leaving scant space for a driveway to the garage at the rear. Nothing except shrubs (roses and geraniums) and trees (pepper, a few palms, an occasional eucalyptus), the color of the paint job, and the number on the door served to inform a householder of his own private demesne. He needed no key because no one ever locked a door. (I once took a pal of mine — he was drunk but still ambulatory — home and put him to bed in the wrong house.)

There was usually a small porch at the front, sometimes covered, sometimes not. The door opened directly onto the living room, which was set apart from the dining area by a built-in divider that might display family knickknacks, keepsakes, a radio, or books if you were the bookish sort. Between dining room and kitchen was the mirrored sideboard, also built-in. (Built-ins might lack the style and cachet of furniture, but they were cheaper and occupied less space.)

The kitchen held not only gas stove, refrigerator, and cupboards, but also a breakfast nook, just like the one in Henry and Evy's house on the prairie. To the right (or left) of living and dining rooms was a narrow hallway giving onto two (or sometimes three) bedrooms and one bath, complete with tub and shower head. The rubberized, flowered shower curtain, which, when in use, draped inside the tub, permitted the lady of the house to flaunt her personal taste. Seldom, however, did it succeed in keeping water from puddling the linoleum floor of the bathroom.

We rented such a house (two bedrooms, a pepper tree, $22.50 a month) in Inglewood, a suburb on the Yellow Car Line ten miles from Grauman's Million Dollar Theater in downtown Los

117

Angeles. Grace Pearson, Philip's aunt, lived in an almost identical house on Genesee south of Melrose (a dusty palm, hydrangea bushes, their snowball bouquets tinted blue by the addition of rusty iron scouring pads to the soil around the roots). Miss Grace had to pay twenty-five dollars a month because she was within walking distance of the A & P, which was important since she had never learned to drive. She had another use for the garage at the rear.

It was her sewing room. In it were not only the implements of her trade—the latest Singer sewing machine, ironing boards, sewing boxes—but three dress forms labeled Alla, Mae, and Betty, and a fourth whose size and appellation altered with the change of Miss Grace's clients. She preferred "to serve," as she put it, no more than four at a time.

Miss Grace, as she was known to a good many, and some not so good, luminaries of Hollywood, had never had an original conception in her life, but she could copy anything. Show her a photograph of a Lanvin, a Molyneux, or a Lady Duff-Gordon in Harper's *Bazaar* or *Vanity Fair,* and she would faithfully (and privately) reproduce it to the ultimate, intimate invisible seam, rolled hem, and hand-stitched buttonhole. Most of the stars zealously maintained images of wild extravagance by scattering their bounty on mansions, mink, or lovers whose attractions were obvious (and photographable). But there were a few who did not mind saving a buck on their wardrobe if they could acquire reasonable facsimiles of originals at a fraction of the cost.

Which was why one might often spot a Lancia, Pierce-Arrow, or Rolls-Royce in the shade of Miss Grace's fraying palm before her bungalow on Genesee, its uniformed chauffeur passing the time by reading *Captain Billy's WhizBang.* And, like as not, in the garage at the back, Miss Grace pinning up the skirt of Alla Nazimova, Mae Busch, or Betty Blythe.

Philip had told me that his aunt Grace knew Nazimova. This was not a lie, only a half-truth. To have explained that she knew the great Russian tragedienne because she copied clothes for her would have denigrated both Nazimova and Aunt Grace. Nor did Grace Pearson own a membership in the beach club frequented by Gloria Swanson. Philip had cultivated that burn on a bath towel in the backyard beside the garage-sewing room. He confessed the truth when he came out to California that fall of 1922.

Quite obviously, though Philip never elaborated on it, Sam Pearson had possessed neither the foresight nor the fortitude, or perhaps had been too downright honest, to withdraw his own funds from his bank when he saw, as he must have seen, the approach of doomsday. Consequently there was no money for tuition at Harvard, but, by boarding with Aunt Grace and occupying her spare bedroom, Philip could become a California resident and attend UC Southern Branch down on Vermont tuition free. Southern Branch was seldom mentioned, because it was such a comedown from Harvard.

In spite of the fact that we had parted, as my mother would put it, bad friends, I was glad when Philip appeared on the scene. Southern California had been a bewildering experience. I felt like an actor secure in his lines in one play who had gone to sleep and awakened in another whose lines, plot, and mise-en-scène were unfamiliar and whose characters spoke Hindustani.

"You wrote me that you were going to USC this fall," Philip said accusingly, "and now you're an office boy at Goldwyn's. How come?"

I had been eager to confide in somebody, but had been unable to tell even my father because maybe I had been wrong, maybe there was nothing to it. I had merely told Papa that Dr. Copley's former secretary had returned.

Not long after we got settled in the Inglewood bungalow I had taken the E-car down to USC and gone to the bursar's office. I explained that I wanted to go to USC, I showed my credentials from Cottonwood High, and then I confessed that I had no money for tuition and would have to work my way through. However, I could type sixty words a minute and take shorthand.

The bursar took a long look at me, then picked up the telephone and said, "Raymond, I think I've found a lad for you."

"Raymond" was Dr. Raymond Copley, head of the French Department, who had told the bursar to be on the lookout for a young man with my qualifications. The girl who had acted as his secretary was dropping out of college because she was pregnant and getting married — in that order. "It will probably be a matter of personality," the bursar explained. "Ray's finicky, but *I* see nothing wrong with you. If you hit it off, you can start work immediately, and begin classes this fall." Dr. Copley was teaching a three-day-a-week course in summer school.

Dr. Copley was in his early forties, I guessed. A good-looking, deeply tanned, well-built man with a firm, warm handshake and a deep baritone voice, he had a trick of smiling and looking you straight in the eye without blinking, as if to say, See how warm and simple I am. I liked him, and he apparently liked me. I went to work that same day and enrolled in his elementary French class for the summer months. (A very tall football player was making up a credit in the same class. He could, and often did, peer over my shoulder. It was the first thing that made me feel at home since coming to California.)

The Ewing family was, as Papa expressed it, sitting pretty. For the moment at least. One thing was sure: Papa had a job at the chair factory at five dollars a day. He had told the management that he was a steam engineer and they had believed him. True, he had worked with steam forty years earlier on a donkey engine for the Great Northern in North Dakota, but now he needed glasses to read the gauges, and half the time he forgot them. We were always worried that he might blow himself and the whole plant to kingdom come.

Mamma, euphoric over having levitated us to California, had no doubt whatever that she was on the brink of a fortune at selling real estate. As long as my job would pay my tuition, we would be rolling. She would keep up the payments on the piano. No problem.

"So get on with it," Philip said impatiently. "You and the French prof were like peas in a pod. What happened?"

I had been working for him for three weeks when he asked me for dinner at his home in Alhambra. He lived there with his mother — no, he had never married, "Who would put up with me?" — and had told her, he said, about "the good-looking young cowboy from Montana." She had insisted that he bring me home to dinner. She was such a *chère maman* and liked to flirt with good-looking young men. "After all, she's had to put up with me for all these years." "Why, you're not so bad looking," I protested, quite seriously I'm afraid.

So how about next Tuesday? That would give *Maman* plenty of time to prepare her *spécialité, Crêpes Roulées et Farcies.* I did like *Crêpes Roulées et Farcies, n'est-ce pas?* I took a deep breath and said *"Oui,"* hoping to God that they weren't made with liver or raw oysters.

"I can guess what happened," Philip said. "You used the wrong fork."

Crêpes Roulées et Farcies turned out to be nothing more sinister than French pancakes stuffed with chicken in a white sauce, and Mrs. Copley, the *chère maman,* only a rather plump, jolly, discursive woman from St. Louis who doted on her son and addressed him as Bud, or Buddy. Buddy was, she told me while he donned an apron and washed the dishes after dinner, the best son God ever made, no two ways about that! Fatherless since he was sixteen — and maybe that was a blessing in disguise, Mr. Copley, rest his soul, being the kind of man he was — Buddy worked his way through college while supporting his mother, mind you! Now she lived in this gorgeous home plunk down in the middle of an orange grove, and Buddy gave her anything and everything a mother's heart could desire. And — would you believe it? — he always remembered to telephone if he was going to be late or if something unexpected came up. She never had a moment's worry.

She was relieved that I was Buddy's new secretary because, "just between you and me and the gatepost," she had got the feeling that Miss Culpepper, the young woman I had replaced, had set her cap for Buddy, and she would never have been right for him, no, not in a million years! Not that Buddy could not see through such a conniving chit if he was a mind to, but all the same, the dear boy was only a babe in the woods where women were concerned. (Miss Culpepper couldn't even boil an egg!) A dear sweet innocent like Buddy needed protection.

It had been a hot day, but around ten o'clock the fog rolled in and cooled things off. "I'm pooped," sighed the *chère maman,* finally. "If you boys want to burn the midnight oil you have my permission to stay up as long as the oil lasts," she laughed. "But as for me, I'm going to hit the Simmons."

"Well, it's time for me to be going home," I said, getting to my feet.

"But I thought you were staying over tonight," Dr. Copley protested.

"Of course," Mrs. Copley joined in. "The boys always stay over with Buddy. He's got the most swank quarters out there in that little cabin in the grove. No call for you to take that long streetcar ride to Inglewood tonight."

"Didn't I mention it?" Dr. Copley asked.

"No," I said, "but — well, I'd have to call my folks . . ."

"*Do* that!" he said, smiling and turning on that sincere look with his eyes wide open so that the whites glistened. "Tell your mother it was all my fault. I'll talk to her and explain, if you want me to."

"No, no. It's all right. I'm not a kid. I just don't want them to worry."

"A boy after my own heart," said Mrs. Copley. "Isn't he a dear, Buddy?"

"If you say so," Dr. Copley said, humoring her.

I made the telephone call and explained. Of course it was all right with my parents, though I had awakened them, but my mother reminded me of something I had not thought of. "You've got no pajamas with you."

"I guess it'll be okay if I sleep in my BVDs for once," I told her.

"There's no need for that," Dr. Copley said, loud enough for her to hear. "I've got scads of spares."

The cabin in the grove was screened on two sides from floor to ceiling. The crickets were hard at their frictional mating calls, and the night air hung heavy with the almost palpable scent of orange blossoms. We undressed in the dark — "So as not to disturb the night peepers," Dr. Copley said — and he found a pair of pajamas for me in the wardrobe.

"Gosh, Dr. Copley," I protested. "You shouldn't give me these. They're silk."

"And not a speck too good for you," he said. "And while I think of it, I wish you'd call me Ray. Not at the office, of course, but I feel awfully formal getting into bed with somebody who calls me Doctor."

I had thought there would be twin beds, but there was only one, and it did not look very large to me. Ah, well . . . The silk pajamas had no warmth, and I guess I shivered.

"If you're cold," Dr. Copley — that is, *Ray* — said, "come over and snuggle. I'm used to sleeping out in the open."

"I'll be okay in a minute," I told him, trying to keep my teeth from chattering.

There was a long silence. I could hear a church bell and he explained that it hung in the San Gabriel Mission. Someday soon he would take me to see the Mission Play.

"I think we can be great friends," he said into the darkness after a little while. "I detect the glimmerings of intellectual curiosity, but your youth, your western background, and your parents, from what you tell me, have not given you much opportunity to exercise it. Not that they are not fine people, understand, but unworldly, unable to lead you into a stimulating area of existence they know nothing of. You need a mentor. Will you let me open some doors and lead you through?"

I was no longer cold, but talk like that made me nervous. "Sure," I said, "but I don't know why you'd bother with a person like me."

"Because I *like* you," he said, and while I could not see the expression on his face, I could tell by his voice that he was smiling. Then he reached over and patted me on the cheek. "Goodnight, John. Sweet dreams."

★   ★   ★

"I couldn't get to sleep," I said to Philip. "And I got to thinking, except for my baby niece and you when we were kids, I never slept with anybody. I was afraid I might snore and wake him up, or pull the sheet off him, or turn in my sleep and bang into him. Then I got to mulling over what he'd said about our — well — our relationship. He wanted us to be friends, but he was in his forties, and we could never be friends like — like you and me, for instance. So what would we *be?*"

★   ★   ★

But finally I did go to sleep. For how long I slept I don't know. Something woke me. Maybe it was the rumble of a Santa Fe freight on the tracks a mile or so to the south. Or maybe it was his snoring, though when I first woke up he did not seem to be doing that. The snoring started about a minute later.

I was lying on my back and presently I became conscious of a warm weight on my privates. The moon had come through the fog and illumined the cabin. I turned my head carefully and looked across at Dr. Copley. He was lying on his side, facing me, snoring now, his eyes closed. In turning he had apparently flopped over in his sleep and dropped his hand on me where it still lay, his fingers loosely cupping my penis through the silk pajamas.

★   ★   ★

Philip and I had been sitting on the edge of the pool at Bimini Baths while I told the story. It had been hard for me to get it out. It would be one thing to say *the* privates, *the* penis. That was like anatomy. But substitute "my" for "the" and it was, as Evelyn Waugh put it in *Decline and Fall,* shy-making. I had not been looking at Philip, but now I turned. His face was brick red and he was taking quick, catch breaths. "What's the matter?" I asked.

"Nothing. Did you — did you get a — a hard-on?" he asked, so low that it was little more than a whisper.

"Of course not!"

"What did you do?"

"I just moved, very carefully, so I wouldn't wake him up — *if* he was asleep — and turned over on my stomach."

"Do you think he was awake — or asleep?"

"That's what's been bothering me ever since."

"If he was awake, that'd make him a — a pervert, wouldn't it?"

"I don't know what makes a pervert. All I know is, I didn't like it, whatever it was."

"So what did you do then?"

★ ★ ★

We got up early next morning. Dr. Copley wanted to know how I slept and I said, "Never better."

"Nothing like good old shut-eye in the great open spaces," he baritoned, took a deep breath, and dropped to the floor to do fifteen push-ups. Mrs. Copley fried ham and eggs, with no French accent, for breakfast. Dr. Copley drove us down to USC where I took dictation and typed several letters for him to sign. Then I boarded the streetcar and went home to touch firm base in Inglewood.

I never saw him again.

★ ★ ★

"You know something?" Philip said. "I think you made it all up. You read something like that in one of Mr. Claymore's law books and you're trying it out on the dog."

I grabbed him by the arm and twisted it up behind his back until he said he was sorry. He slipped into the water, swam across the pool and back, splashed water in my face, then climbed out and settled down beside me once more.

"If you couldn't earn your tuition at USC why didn't you settle for Southern Branch where you could go for nothing?"

"Because it would take two hours each way from Inglewood," I said.

"Is that all?"

"That's all." It wasn't, but if Philip would not answer my questions, I could give him some of his own medicine. So I said nothing about the puncture of my mother's real estate balloon.

She had actually sold one house for four thousand dollars and, as soon as escrow closed, would be handed a commission of a hundred dollars. (She worked through Dependable Real Estate, Inc., and split the five percent commission with the office.) Money, Mamma said euphorically, might not grow on trees in California, but it grew on houses, and it would be a good idea for Papa to quit his job and the two of them open an office of their own, then they wouldn't have to split commissions. Papa fortunately demurred. While she waited for this hundred-dollar curtain to rise on her grand opera, she bought — on time — a dining room table and four chairs for $125. Then the buyer's check for the binder bounced and the deal never cleared escrow. If Dr. Copley's questionable advances had not already convinced me to abandon thoughts of college, I now had a practical reason to do so.

"Has your aunt Grace told you about how she helped get me the job at Goldwyn?" I asked Philip. By that time we were getting dressed in the locker room of Bimini Baths. It was lined with tile and our voices bounced back and forth from one wall to another endlessly.

"Stop mumbling," Philip said.

"Did your aunt Grace tell you about me and Mae Busch!" I shouted.

MaeBuschMaeBuschMaeBusch the walls reverberated. Philip got his mouth close to my ear and whispered, "You can tell me about it in the car on the way home — if you insist."

It was half an hour later. We sat in the old sleeve-valved Willys-Knight (twenty-five dollars down, ten dollars a month for ten months) beneath the palm standing shaggy sentinel before the little bungalow on Genesee. I had not spoken to him since that "if you insist" crack.

"Well," I said with great dignity, I thought, "you are at home now. You can get out. In fact, I insist."

"Okay," Philip said with mock weariness. "I apologize, if that will make you happy."

Mr. Pearson had suggested that I pay my respects to his sister Grace when we got to California. I had no intention of doing it—I suspected he was merely being polite—but one warm afternoon in August I found myself in her neighborhood. I had come across a help-wanted ad for a typist at a fan-mail answering service on Santa Monica Boulevard, which I could reach by streetcar. The job had been filled. The lucky employee would work at home on his own typewriter—I didn't have one—and would be paid three cents per letter, plus postage, of course. ("Dear [fill in fan's name]. How sweet of you to write to tell me of your admiration for me and my last picture. It is devoted friends like you who give meaning to my efforts on the Silver Screen. My next picture is going to be just super, they tell me. It is called [fill in name of movie], and I trust that you will urge your friends to see it at the earliest opportunity when it comes to [fill in name of fan's town or city]. With sincere good wishes from your friend—[stamp in Anita Stewart, Madge Bellamy, Priscilla Dean, etc.]")

I had found Grace Pearson's address in the telephone book and presently stood on the porch of the Genesee house and rang the bell. (A Marmon roadster was parked under the palm that day.) After a long wait, a rather befuddled little woman wearing a sewing apron and carrying a pincushion appeared around the corner of the house. "What do you want?" she said angrily. It was hard to understand her because she had a pin in her mouth.

"Are you Miss Grace Pearson?"

"Yes, I am, and I wouldn't have bothered to answer the ring if I hadn't been afraid it might be Betty and I wouldn't want her to run into Mae. I'd make her wait in the house until I got rid of Mae. They don't want each other to know that I create their Worths and Pacquins. If you're selling something, just shoo!"

This was, as Shakespeare said, Greek to me, but it seemed to make sense to Miss Grace. "My name's John Ewing," I explained, "and your brother Sam suggested that I come by and call on you. I'm from Cottonwood, Montana."

She smiled. The pin dropped out of her mouth. She stooped

and picked it up. "Oh, of course. You're Philip's friend. Come along, we mustn't keep Mae waiting. She's got a temper."

I followed Miss Grace into the garage-sewing room. Mae Busch—I recognized her from *Foolish Wives*—stood immobilized and boiling mad on the stool where Miss Grace had left her, the hem of her bugle-beaded, hobble-skirt evening gown only partially pinned up.

"God damn your soul, Grace Pearson," Mae Busch yelled, "how dare you leave me standing on this fucking stool!"

"Now Mae dear," Miss Grace said calmly, getting on her knees before her, "just hold your horses. I'm saving you six hundred and ninety-eight dollars. If you can't behave like a lady, I'll charge you fifty dollars more next time."

"Who says there'll be a next time?" Miss Busch fumed. "And what's that stupid jerk doing here? Get him the hell out!"

"Pay no attention to Mae," Miss Grace told me, going on with her hem pinning, "she's really a dear, all bluster and profanity, but underneath she's hiding a heart of gold!"

"The hell I am!" Miss Busch said.

I had never heard a woman, and very few men, talk like that. I could feel myself blushing.

"Okay, kid," she said. "Pop your eyes back in your head, move your ass, and hand me a cup of that foul brew Miss Grace peddles as coffee."

I threaded my way between the cats—a Persian, a Siamese, and a purebred shorthair—to the percolator on the electric warmer, poured a cup of coffee—"Just black," Miss Busch called, "so I can keep awake"—and handed it to the dazzler on the pedestal. "Thanks, dahling," she said, and then, "Who are you?"

"He's a friend of my brother's family from Montana," Miss Grace answered.

"Well, you can go back and tell 'em you met Mae Busch. That should shake them to their arch supports."

"I would," I said, "but I'm not going back."

"Then write 'em. And be sure to make that Mae with an *e*."

"Oh, I know how to spell your name. I saw you in *The Devil's Passkey*."

"And wasn't I a pisser?"

"Oh, yes. Wonderful."

"More wonderful than Maude George?"

"Much more."

"Talk like that will get you everywhere in this town. You're learning fast."

"But I mean it, Miss Busch."

"You know something? I think you do. If you're not going back to Wyoming . . ."

"Pardon me," I interrupted. "But it's Montana."

"*Vive la différence,*" she said. "Anyhow, as I was saying when I was so rudely interrupted, if you're not going back to Montana, what are your plans? And Grace, if you don't mind, you are pinning that hem to my goddamn stocking *and my leg is bleeding!*"

"Mae, stop fussing," Miss Grace said.

★   ★   ★

So I found myself telling Mae Busch—*Mae Busch*—that I was looking for a job and that I had certain qualifications: I could type sixty words a minute and take shorthand.

"You've sold me, dahling," she said with a stagy wave of her hand. "I was afraid you wanted to be an actor, God forbid. You could be, with your looks, but you're a little short. Of course there's always Ramon Novarro, but he's a queer." She laughed, a deep throaty sound. "There's a non sequitur loose around here. Swat it if you happen to see it, will you?"

I had no idea what she was talking about, but I loved the music it made as it came from her throat.

"You're not a queer, are you?" she asked after a moment.

"I don't know what you mean, Miss Busch."

"Then I guess you're not. Now, if you can wait until Lady Duff-Gordon here"—she patted Miss Grace on the head—"finishes mutilating me, we'll *motah* out to the Goldwyn Studios in Madame's new Marmon, and I'll put the screws on Joe Jackson. Let's see. I'll tell him unless he puts you to work immediately I shall refuse to play the lead in *The Christian*. Okay with you?"

Was it ever okay with me! I did not know, or care, who Joe Jackson was, or what job he might have for me. I had fallen in love.

8

March 23, 1923. John took me out to the set where Erich
von Stroheim was directing *Greed*. I saw the most beautiful
woman in the world. Barbara La Marr. She smiled!

It was not much of a job, but I was actually inside the Goldwyn
Studio in Culver City, a long dream's jump from the Musselshell
Theater in Cottonwood, Montana. My salary was eighteen dollars a week, even less than Mr. Claymore had paid me a year ago,
but there was a nice difference: I collected it at the cashier's office
every Saturday noon and the check did not bounce.

I had the right to say, and sometimes said when asked, "I'm in
the movies." I breathed the same air and ate the same food at the
same commissary as John Gilbert, Aileen Pringle, Eleanor
Boardman, Ramon Novarro (a queer? I soon learned what that
meant), Conrad Nagel, Mae Busch, and Carmel Myers. And
maybe, just maybe, some director would one day notice me and
say, "You've got a photogenic face. Let's make a test." (Nobody
ever said it.)

Meanwhile there could be a less glamorous future for me. I
would probably advance from office boy, where most of the day
was spent typing captions (e.g., "Mabel Ballin and George Walsh
in a dramatic scene from *Vanity Fair*" or "Beryl Mercer, Mae
Busch, and Richard Dix in a scene from *The Christian,* the
famous novel by Hall Caine") and pasting them on production
stills, to secretary (twenty-five to thirty-five dollars per week),
and eventually, if I could learn to write, to publicist (sixty to
seventy-five dollars per week!).

Joe Jackson was not only Mae Busch's friend, he was the friend
and confidant of everybody fortunate enough to know him. A
former newspaper reporter, Joe had worked on the Louisville
Courier-Journal before coming to California at the invitation of
Samuel Goldwyn to head his publicity department.

When I asked if I might bring my friend Philip Pearson out on the lot some Saturday morning, Joe said, "Why, co'se you can, boy." And as he scribbled a studio pass, "If I was you, though, I'd tend my p's and q's on Von's set. Von's a genius they tell me, an' geniuses're scarcer'n vestal virgins in Culver City, so we best humah him. You splain so your chum'll undahstan', yuh heah?"

That was Joe. Apologizing to his office boy for having to keep his guest back of the sight lines on Stroheim's set.

★ ★ ★

Philip arrived promptly at ten o'clock. I had told him that if I got to the studio early and worked hard I could finish my stills by then. I met him under the columns at the front gate on Washington Boulevard and passed him through. He had got himself up in his best suit, shined his shoes, doused himself in Old Spice, powdered his freckles, and conquered his unruly red hair with Stacomb. He kept clearing his throat, and, as we passed the commissary, his self-conscious steps grew shorter and shorter. He stayed close by me, glancing furtively from side to side.

"Nobody's going to arrest you," I told him. "You didn't jump over the fence this time."

"I need to go to the toilet," he whispered. "They have one here, don't they?"

"Even Lillian Gish has to pee, they tell me," I said. My cynical worldliness knew no bounds.

"You have gone Hollywood," he said reproachfully.

I took him up to the publicity department can and waited while he relieved himself and slicked down his hair and tightened his tie so that his neck bulged over his collar.

"Do I look all right?" he wanted to know.

"You're not here for a screen test."

There were two companies on the call sheet that morning: Rupert Hughes directing *Souls for Sale* on Stage 4 (that would be the big ballroom scene with 150 extras), and then there was Stroheim and *Greed* on Stage 2. Stroheim had shot most of his picture on location in San Francisco, but there were still a few pickup shots needed at the studio. Zasu Pitts and Gibson Gowland had been called for this one, a scene in McTeague's bedroom.

"You don't want to see that, do you?" I said hopefully after Philip had examined the call sheet.

"What makes you think I don't?" he said. He had gained courage now that his bladder was empty.

There was always a no-nonsense atmosphere on a Rupert Hughes set, where I took him first. Being the author of hundreds of short stories, novels, and plays, Hughes believed in "story" rather than the so-called art of the cinema in which many less talented directors indulged. Hughes had been signed by Samuel Goldwyn during his first roundup of what he labeled Eminent Authors. There were Mary Roberts Rinehart, Rex Beach, Gouverneur Morris, Maurice Maeterlinck (of all people), Rupert Hughes, and one or two more. Hughes was the only one who survived.

Philip and I had both read *Souls for Sale* when it appeared in *Redbook* back in 1921. Now, miracle of miracles, here we were on the set watching the author himself direct his own movie version of his novel about the movies. Right there before the camera, with hot kliegs and cool Cooper Hewitts blazing on them as we entered the stage, were Barbara La Marr, Aileen Pringle, Eleanor Boardman, and my new friend, Mae Busch, all preening like exotic jungle fowls with ostrich-feather headdresses and gowns spangled by the French designer Erté. (I doubted that Aunt Grace could have copied any of them.) Barbara La Marr's black velvet gown sported a fifty-pound beaded train that would have made a peacock fold its tail in envy.

It was a scene purporting to be an elegant party in a Hollywood-that-never-was. Rupert Hughes, his tongue firmly planted in cheek, was out to show Cecil B. DeMille a thing or two, by God! He loved beautiful women and loved to see them dressed to the nines. What he, Erté, and Cedric Gibbons, the art director, had achieved was pure, tinsel Hollywood as dreamed by Peoria — or Cottonwood.

"Camera," Hughes called. "And ladies, remember you are all *ladies*. Let the action begin."

It was a long shot. Philip watched the action unfold with eyes wide and mouth agape. His expression seemed to say, This is life the way it ought to be, the way I want it to be, the way I'm going to make it when I'm grown up; there'll be no ugly people, no pimples, no garbage, no bank failures. His eyes, I noticed, began to follow Barbara La Marr to the exclusion of everyone else as she glided through the scene. I could scarcely blame him. Her beauty was too perfect, too serene to have been sculptured in mortal flesh and bone.

When the action finished she stood not five feet from Philip. She looked our way and smiled. Maybe it was at Philip, maybe someone behind him. At any rate it made a lasting impression on him for he seems not even to have mentioned Mae Busch or Aileen Pringle in his Day Book, yet he actually met and talked with them that day. Mae saw me and said to Aileen Pringle, "Pringle, you ought to know Johnny Ewing. He's in publicity now, and if you want any stills he'll steal them out of the files for you."

"Miss Busch, please," I said, my love for her cooling.

"Well, you'd better. Who's your redheaded friend?"

"Philip Pearson," I said. "We went to school together."

"You should still be there," Aileen Pringle said, and grabbed my ear and looked behind it. "See," she said to Mae Busch. "Still wet back there."

"Pleased to know you," Philip said.

"What's this ridiculous conclave?" Rupert Hughes wanted to know. He was somewhat deaf.

Mae Busch introduced us to Hughes who recognized our western accent. "Keep it," he said. "I came from Keokuk a long while ago and I've never quite lost mine."

"Well, actually," Philip said, finally finding his voice, "I was born in Iowa too. Algona."

"That's no crime," Hughes said, laughing, because Philip looked guilty at having dared say anything so inconsequential in this rarefied company.

"And you?" Hughes said, turning to me. "There's an underlay of the Midwest there, it seems to me."

"Remind me to be underlaid sometime," Miss Pringle said.

"Wisconsin, and then Montana," I said.

"And what are you doing here in Babylon?"

"I'm working in Publicity."

"But he can take Gregg and type sixty words a minute, if you can believe a word the little bastard tells you," Mae Busch put in.

Hughes laughed. "How much commission do you pay this bedizened, foul-mouthed wench whom I adore to distraction?"

I did not know how to respond to that kind of banter. "Rupert," Aileen Pringle said, "you're making that boy blush."

"An achievement not to be discounted in this vale of tears," he said. "There may be a market for it . . . All right, ladies. Places."

So Philip presently, and reluctantly, allowed himself to be wrenched away from the Woman Who Was Too Beautiful and confronted with the Man You Love to Hate, and on that Saturday morning, Stroheim lived up to the absurd sobriquet his press agent, Fritz Bailey, had saddled him with.

Stroheim was a bullet-headed Prussian who made his reputation playing villainous Huns in World War I movies, hence the Man You Love to Hate. When he turned to directing he cultivated an aloof, irascible manner in order to intimidate the businessmen he was forced to deal with. Otherwise, he would never have been permitted to launch into a project like Frank Norris's *McTeague,* a realistic, somber tragedy about sad and not very bright people that ran counter to what any sane exhibitor would think of as box office. It was said, and perhaps it was true, that Stroheim wrote a more or less conventional scenario, sold it to the studio executives, then threw it away and simply shot the book itself, page for page. The scene, which Philip and I could barely see because the set was small and banked with lights, was the squalid bedroom of the McTeagues, played by Gibson Gowland and Zasu Pitts. McTeague was drunk, thought his wife was hiding money for more booze from him, lurched into the bedroom, woke her up, yanked her out of bed, and began to cuff her around.

There was not a sound except Stroheim's voice, prompting, urging, stroking the silent actors through the action. "Now you see him, Zasu, you realize he is drunk. Gowland, grab her now, yank her up, shake her, strike her. Cut. You did not strike her hard enough, Gowland. You hate her. You vant to hurt her. Ve shoot once more, no?"

Philip could hear Stroheim but could not see the actors. During the interval between takes he began to inch forward. I grabbed his arm, shook my head, and held him back. It was obviously a difficult scene, and I could tell from the camera clipboard, this next would be take twenty-one. The actors, as well as the director, were on edge.

"Quiet! Roll 'em! Action." Stroheim called, and once more the degrading scene began. Philip and I squatted on our heels so that we could peer beneath a bank of Cooper Hewitts. And suddenly another squalid scene flashed before my eyes — a nude woman was standing at a window, a man grabbing her to keep her from jumping out. What movie was that in? But it couldn't have been a movie, could it? I had never seen a nude woman in a movie. Then, as Gibson Gowland cuffed poor Zasu and she screamed, I remembered. It was Philip's mother and the man he thought was his father.

"Cut. Zasu. A little more *erschrecken* — how do you say it? — terrify of sis drunken monster."

"I'm afraid it will look funny and people will laugh," Miss Pitts said.

"I am sa judge of zat. One more time, please."

And so they began once more, and this time it was right. You could tell from the excitement in Stroheim's voice that this, the twenty-third take, was exactly what he wanted. Zasu Pitts was terrified, not too much, not too little, and Gibson Gowland was about to let her have it.

And then Philip sneezed. It was a gargantuan explosion that caught him unprepared and, since he was already squatting, knocked him over onto his butt. The sound itself would not have mattered because, of course, *Greed* was a silent picture, but it made both Zasu Pitts and Gibson Gowland flinch.

"Jesus Christus!" Stroheim yelled, leapt to his feet, turned, and looked squarely at Philip sitting there on his ass. Stroheim was not a large man, but as he stalked forward he was monumental in rage, his face livid, fists clenched, the cords of his neck exaggerated as Grey might have drawn them in his *Anatomy*.

"What — why — who let these sodomites on my set!" he screamed. Sodomite was his favorite term of contempt.

"I'm sorry," I said, pulling Philip onto his feet once more. "It was an accident. He couldn't help it."

And then, backing away from Prussian outrage verging on apoplexy, Philip uttered what was probably the most ill-timed compliment ever heard. "Mr. Stroheim, sir, I thought you were wonderful in *Foolish Wives*."

"Out!" Stroheim screamed. "Out, before I order you both to be castrated!"

We turned and ran off the stage. Afterward — long afterward — Philip could laugh about it and say, "Touch me. I'm the fellow who ruined that great scene in *Greed*."

★   ★   ★

After our pulses slowed we proceeded in silence toward the back lot, threading a path through a heterogeneous agglomeration of carpenters, electricians, technicians, bewigged actors, worried writers, five-dollar-a-day extras, trucks hauling lights, cameras, and walls of sets, a bevy of squealing nautch dancers, the dog star Strongheart frisking with his trainer, Claire Windsor (until recently Ola Cronk from Kansas), in hoop skirts and eating a strawberry ice cream cone, and even Ramon Novarro wearing nothing much but a loin cloth and dark brown makeup. He had been testing for the native boy in *Where the Pavement Ends*. Ramon was not much older than I. I knew it must be wrong to be whatever they said he was in the sex department, but he was not queer in any other way so far as I could tell, and I could not help liking him.

"I'm sorry," Philip said abruptly. "I guess that's what you want me to say, isn't it?"

"I don't want you to say anything. You couldn't help it."

"But what if you get canned?" There seemed to be genuine concern about that in his tone. I began to thaw.

"I won't. Stroheim's tempers are famous but they don't last. Even if he gets around to complaining to my boss, Mr. Jackson will understand. He knows Von."

"Well, I just want to say," Philip said, pouting his lips and turning to look away from me, "I hope you don't get in a jam."

I touched him on the shoulder in lieu of thanks.

We were relaxed. "Come on," I said, "nobody else is working, but as long as you're here you might as well look at the set for *In the Palace of the King!*"

"Lead on, Macduffer."

The set was the exterior and courtyard of the king's palace and remarkable for its size, second only to "Griffith's gigantic erection," as the wags called his *Intolerance* set, which still stood east of Vermont in Hollywood. Very few kings could have afforded such a residence as this one, and none would have been impractical enough to build the unbanistered stair that climbed, like a bullish Dow Jones chart, the entire facade of a sixty-foot-high wall.

"Would anybody mind if we climbed it?" Philip asked.

"I guess not. But why? There's nothing much to see from up there."

"Does there have to be a reason for everything?"

Hugging the wall itself, we climbed almost to the top before acrophobia slowed me down. I spread-eagled my body against the wall.

"What's the matter?" Philip asked.

"It's okay. I'll get used to it. If you want to go up the rest of the way, be my guest."

Philip panned his gaze eastward across the rooftops of the studio stages. There were the bare backs of numberless sets in the foreground, then the glass-walled stages and the imposing electric sign facing east that read "snoitcudorP nywdloG" and *sitrA aitarG srA* from our angle, and to the left of that the spire of the new Catholic church. Washington Boulevard ribboned past the pie-shaped Culver City Hotel, the Thomas Ince (which in Cottonwood we had pronounced "Inky") and Hal Roach (no trouble with that one) studios. Beyond to the left was the base of the mammoth coliseum being constructed for *Ben Hur* in the middle of a bean field, and beyond that the boulevard was finally swallowed like a thread in the crumpled outskirts of Los Angeles, its hem raveling westward toward the sea. Far to the north rose the Hollywood hills, and to the southeast, oil derricks sprouted like asparagus on the bare Baldwin Hills.

"It's all ugly," Philip commented. "Let's go down where we can't see it."

We sprawled on the steps some twenty feet from the ground. The March sun was unseasonably warm and we were safe within the gleaming ramparts of Cedric Gibbons's dream palace. If you listened carefully you could almost hear the sound of trumpets and the hoofbeats of the king's courtiers returning victorious from the hunt.

"Are you in a hurry?" Philip asked after a long moment.

"No."

"Is it okay to smoke?"

"It sure as hell is not! If a fire ever got started the whole shooting match would go up in five minutes."

"I just thought I'd ask."

"Since when have you been smoking?"

"Most writers smoke while they're writing."

"Maybe, but I don't think that's what makes them writers."

"The trouble is," Philip said after a moment, "I can't think of anything to write about. Got any ideas?"

"Look," I said. "They say you should write about what you know, what you've been through. You've been through stuff."

"I don't know what you mean."

"Well, how about your own family? The bank failure, partly because your father was too decent a man, because he couldn't let people lose their property and starve. And then what it did to him — and you, you're going to UC Southern Branch instead of Harvard. And Maureen, well, I don't know about Maureen. You never told me."

"She's going to business college in Des Moines. So she can get a job as a secretary, if she doesn't get married." It was the first time I could remember that Philip had ever volunteered any information about his family.

"Does she mind? Is she disappointed?"

"I never asked her."

"Well, ask her," I said. "Or — if you want to write about her — imagine how she feels. It must be kind of like the way you feel. Boys and girls can't be all that different."

He thought about that, then shook his head. "A thing like that happens and my family just moves back to Iowa. What kind of drama, what kind of ending is that? They're just — well — people. They're not characters."

"You never told me they'd left Cottonwood," I said.

"You never asked."

"And if I had you'd have resented it."

"Maybe," Philip admitted.

We had never had such a bars-down, intimate conversation. "Have you told your father how you feel about not going to Harvard?"

"Oh, sure. He knows I hate it here, and he hates it too, but what can he do? He's had to move into my grandmother's house back in Algona. Not even *his* mother's, my mother's mother's."

"I should think that was a story. How does an independent man like your father feel having to do that? And then," I went on without stopping to think, "there's your mother's story."

He stiffened slightly. "I don't know what you mean."

Having started I could not stop. "Remember that night, the night when we woke up and she was tearing through the house with your father trying to keep her from jumping out the window?"

Philip merely looked puzzled and a little amused, but said nothing. I went on doggedly. "Then she ran out of the house" — I did not say "naked" or "bare-assed," you'd never say that to a friend about his mother — "and fell into the snow and your father picked her up and brought her back inside? Of course I can understand you could never ask either of them what that was all about, but you could invent some kind of mystery. She — that is, the woman, was crazed on dope — the way Wallace Reid was before he died, or — or — well, you could think of something," I ended lamely.

Philip began to laugh.

"I don't see anything funny about that," I said.

"You must have had a nightmare," he said.

"No, I didn't," I persisted. "Don't you remember, you finally woke up? Maureen came into the bedroom too, she was scared, and we all went to the window and looked out. You've got to remember that."

"I can't remember your nightmares," he said. "I have enough trouble remembering my own. Come on. Let's go."

We walked back to the studio where things were quieting down because it was lunchtime. "I'll pick up my check," I said.

While we stood in line in front of the cashier's office a priest passed us. Philip said, "Good morning, Father," and the priest, making a sign of the cross in the air, said, "Bless you, my son."

I could see from Philip's expression that this pleased him. If anything had been troubling him, he now had absolution for the sin of thinking about it. The "priest," having blessed Philip, winked at me. He was Cecil Holland, makeup artist and character man, playing a small role in *The Christian*.

9

When I got home that afternoon my mother met me with the news that Philip had telephoned. He had tried to reach me at the studio, but I had already gone. "He said he wanted to come out and spend the night," Mamma said, "so I said fine, come ahead."

"You didn't ask him for supper—that is, dinner—did you?" I had recently discovered that "supper" in Montana was "dinner" in California, and "dinner" was "lunch."

"Why, that's only good manners. You've eaten at the Pearsons plenty of times."

"I know, it's just . . ." My mother, if not the worst cook in the United States, would undoubtedly have been a runner-up in any regional finals. It was not until I began to be invited out for meals that I discovered one did not necessarily need surgical instruments to slice a pork chop.

"Philip—why, *any* of your friends is always welcome to whatever we have."

"Yes, I know."

"Your mother may not be the fanciest cook this side of the Rockies, but . . ."

"You're a very good cook," I lied, to cover my shame at wishing I could have taken the call and suggested that Philip and I meet downtown. We could have had something to eat at Boos Brothers Cafeteria, perhaps, where a string quartet, stationed on the balcony, drowned out the clatter of cutlery with schmaltzy renditions of Victor Herbert and Johann Strauss the Younger.

"Then why didn't you want me to ask Philip to supper?" Mamma persisted.

"I just thought if we met downtown we'd have time to go to Grauman's afterward and see Rudolph Valentino in *Blood and Sand*. Philip's crazy about Nita Naldi."

"She's vulgar," Mamma said, "but you can still go after supper,

142

if you insist. Save you both money. We're having your favorite —
pork chops."

Where she got that idea I don't know, but once such a thought
was implanted in her mind it remained as indestructible as the
Pyramids. "That's nice," I said.

"And we're not eating in the breakfast nook. I don't know why
I bother — he's just a boyhood chum — but somehow I felt like
setting the dining room table with the 1847 Rogers and Aunt
Millicent's Haviland. We haven't had anybody for supper in so
long."

Well, that was something. "There's just one thing," I said.
"Would you please not ask Philip about his folks?"

"Why ever not?"

"I'd just rather nobody did." It was hard to explain. Anyhow,
Mamma's interest in anyone usually sounded like prying.

"Well, of course, if you don't think I'm good enough to
mention the Pearsons and the — the whatever *her* family name
was, if any, I'll have you know — " she was angry and beginning to
cloud up, "I'll have you know that the Romaines don't take a
backseat to any — "

"It's not that, Mamma. It's not that at all."

"Then what, pray, is it?"

"Well . . . Philip is . . . he's sensitive about his mother and
father, that's all."

"Ashamed of his own parents? I've always liked Philip, I never
would have thought — "

"Mamma," I interrupted. "Listen. Mr. Pearson lost his job, he
can't get another one, they don't have much money, they've had
to go back to Iowa to live with his mother."

"That's nothing to be ashamed of," Mamma said.

"Anyhow," I said, "Philip would rather not talk about it."

"Well!" Mamma wiped a tear from her eye with her apron. "In
that case I will not say a word. Not one word."

"Oh, Mamma, for heaven's sake!"

"And thank you for reminding your mother how to behave."
She started toward the kitchen.

I was sorry I had brought it up. I could hear her heaving deep, tragic sighs audible enough to penetrate the sideboard between kitchen and dining room. I would have to apologize, or she would have a migraine.

I walked into the kitchen silently and stood behind her. Her shoulders were rising and falling with each sigh, still meant for me where she had left me, in the dining room. Then still unaware of me, she opened the refrigerator door and stared at its contents with distaste.

"I'm sorry, Mamma," I said.

She started, turned, threw her arms around me dramatically, and clutched me to her ample bosom in a smothering embrace while she let down the floodgates. My arms were pinned to my sides, but I finally managed to pat her back and pleaded, "Please don't cry, please don't cry." A loving son should have been moved by his mother's tears. I felt nothing but a hard knot in my stomach.

Finally she let me go and blew her nose. "It's all my fault," she said. "I forget you're just a little boy."

"I am not just a little boy. I am almost nineteen years old."

"You'll always be mother's little boy to me," she said.

Fortunately my father came in the backdoor from work at that moment, and interrupted whatever unfortunate thing I might have been going to retort. While Mamma's eyes were still red (Papa would not notice without his glasses), she turned on a smile for him.

"Jim," she cried happily, "get out of those overalls and put on your suit and shirt and tie."

"Why? I'm pissed," Papa said.

"We're having company!"

"I wouldn't change clothes for the Prince of Wales tonight," Papa said. "Who's coming?"

"Philip," Mamma said, and when Papa looked blank, I explained, "Philip Pearson — from Cottonwood. You remember."

"Oh, sure," Papa said. "Nice kid. Sam Pearson's boy."

"But we're not supposed to mention his folks to Philip,"

Mamma said, lowering her voice confidentially, and giving me a knowing wink.

"Why?" Papa asked. "Is he keeping them a secret?"

Oh, God, how I wished I had never brought it up.

"It makes the poor boy sad," Mamma said with great sympathy, "after everything that's happened. You know, Sam's bank failure, his disgrace."

"Oh," Papa said.

I never did have time to wonder why Philip wanted to come out to see me because at that moment the door bell rang.

"There he is now!" Mamma cried, and clutched at her bosom as if she were about to faint. "Jim! Get out of those dirty clothes!"

"Oh, all right," Papa said, knowing when he was licked.

Dinner was not as bad as it might have been. Mamma's mashed potatoes contained the minimum of lumps and the pork chops were less formidable than usual. "I hope you like pork chops as much as Johnny does," Mamma said to Philip as we sat down at the table. "Personally I prefer beefsteak, but Johnny is so partial to pork I can't bear to disappoint him."

"I like pork chops," Philip said.

Those four words were almost the only ones he spoke after saying his how-do-you-do's. He looked as if he wore a straitjacket under his shirt and coat. Aside from the atmosphere created by his frigid reserve there was only one uncomfortable moment during the meal. Papa got started on the Teapot Dome scandal, and how it was all to be blamed on Albert B. Fall, the secretary of the interior, and "that crooked Irishman" Harry M. Daugherty, the attorney general.

"Jim," Mamma put in, raising her eyebrows, "we have a guest who is Irish."

"Who's that?"

"Philip Pearson."

"That's okay with me," Papa said. "I've got nothing against the Irish, but you take that Daugherty, I wouldn't trust him as far as I could throw him. And look at the mess he's got the president into. None of it's Harding's fault, he just trusts his friends too far." He turned to Philip. "I don't know's you ever noticed it, young man, but I always thought there was a resemblance between Warren G. Harding and your dad."

"Jim," Mamma said.

"And come to think of it," Papa went right on, "it's not just physical. Your dad trusted folks too, and their troubles got to be his troubles. I always figured that's the reason the bank—"

"*Jim,*" Mamma interrupted, staring at Papa as if trying to hypnotize him.

"What?"

"Remember what we were talking about just before supper?"

For the first time Philip was showing some interest in what was going on. He looked from Mamma to Papa and then at me. I shut my eyes and wished I were dead.

"What was that?" Papa said, frowning.

"Never you mind," Mamma sighed. "Let's not talk politics at the supper table. Philip, how about another chop?"

"Thanks, Mrs. Ewing," Philip said.

"It does my heart good to see boys eat."

"You want to go to the movies?" I asked Philip later. "*Scaramouche* is playing up at the Regent."

"I've seen it," Philip said. "Let's take a walk."

A mild Santa Ana was blowing and the night was even warmer than the day had been. We strolled out Queen Street and soon came to the open fields west of Inglewood. To the north, searchlights scissored lazily across the sky, every once in a while pausing to flirt with a lone cloud riding the warm wind off the desert. I had forgotten; tonight was the premiere of *The Covered Wagon* at the Egyptian. That's what the searchlights were for.

Finally I said, "Well, what's eating you?"

"It's disgusting, it's filthy," Philip said. "I don't want to talk about it."

"Suit yourself."

We walked on for another minute or two, then he stopped and stared at the searchlights. "But I've got to talk about it to somebody," he said.

"Meaning if you knew anybody else in Los Angeles you wouldn't talk to *me* about it."

"That isn't what I meant and you know it."

"That's what it sounded like, and you know it."

I walked on and then realized Philip was not with me. I stopped and turned. He was standing where I had left him, rubbing his fist into his eyes like a child. I went back and touched his arm. "I'm sorry," I said.

"It's . . . it's . . . Aunt . . . Grace," he finally said.

I waited. And waited. "Has something happened to your aunt?" I finally asked.

"Yes . . . no . . . it's just—she's a mistress!" he hissed.

There were schoolmistresses, there were mistresses of art and science and mistresses of great estates who went about with dozens of keys clanking on chains fastened to their belts. There was also Mistress Dorothy who was Doll Tearsheet, but Aunt Grace bore no relation to her. I waited for him to go on, and presently—with long pauses—it came out.

By the time he had got back to Genesee Street from the studio it was midafternoon. He walked around the house and went in the backdoor to the kitchen. Everything was silent and he figured Aunt Grace was either working out in the garage or taking a nap. He was thirsty and Aunt Grace usually kept a bottle of Welch's grape juice and one of freshly squeezed orange juice side by side in the refrigerator. He was standing there beside the breakfast nook sipping his orange juice when a man he had never seen before came in from the living room. He was carrying an empty glass in his left hand. The man was at least sixty years old and had gray hair on his head and chest, and his stomach bulged in a noticeable paunch. He was sweating and breathing hard, and was wearing nothing but a pair of black socks.

Boy and man stood staring at each other, neither able to move or speak. Then the man covered his genitals with his right hand and said, "Grace—that is, Miss Pearson—wanted some grape juice."

"Who are you?" Philip managed to gasp.

"My name's Parks. Fred Parks." The man made as if to shake hands with Philip but realized the immodesty such a gesture would compound, and said, "Excuse me, I better get some clothes on," and walked back into the living room.

"What have you done to my aunt!" Philip called.

"She's okay," the man said.

Philip followed and discovered the man about to go through the door into the bedroom hall. "Don't you go in there without any clothes on!" he shouted.

"I got to. That's where my clothes are."

At that moment Aunt Grace, clutching a flowered wrapper about her, came through the hall door.

"I thought I heard voices," she said inanely, and then, looking up into the man's face, "Oh, Fred, Fred. This is awful."

"It sure is," the man said.

"Get dressed."

"Jesus, Grace," the man said, "I wouldn't have had this happen."

"I thought he'd be gone all day."

Then the man turned to Philip, "I'm sorry to have met you under such conditions, but don't think ill of your aunt. She's a wonderful woman." And he scurried into Aunt Grace's bedroom.

Philip went into the bathroom and vomited. When he finally came out Aunt Grace was still there waiting for him. "Sit down, Philip," she said.

"No, thank you," Philip said. "I'd rather stand." (I wonder if he remembered that pompous statement when he got to writing screen dialogue? It would never have played.)

"I can only tell you how it happened," Aunt Grace said, "and then judge me however you may want to."

She had known Fred Parks and his wife for twenty years. They lived only a few doors down Genesee, but in a bigger house. Mr. Parks was in the fertilizer business and had made a pretty good thing of it. His wife contracted TB five years ago and had been a semi-invalid in and out of sanitariums ever since. Fred was a healthy man, a good man who cared deeply for his wife, but he needed what a healthy woman could give him.

"You mean *sex*," Philip spat out the dirty word.

"Not the way you say it."

So . . . it happened, how and exactly when did not matter.

"I'm sorry you had to find out in such a—a shocking, I suppose that's the word, manner, but in a way I'm relieved. You couldn't live with me for long and not learn about us, unless I changed my way of life. And that I'm not prepared to do."

"Aren't you ashamed?" Philip asked her.

She shook her head. "No. Maybe I should be, but I'm not."

"But you're—you're committing adultery."

"Oh, I see. The woman taken in adultery. Yes, I suppose I am, but we're hurting nobody."

"What about his wife?"

"She's ill, don't you understand? She's been ill for years. Fred is not giving me anything that he could give her."

"But," Philip persisted, staring at her, wondering why this— this fornicator—did not look any different from the Aunt Grace he had admired until a few minutes ago, "but you're my aunt, you're my father's sister. What do you think he would say if he knew all this time you've been acting like a—"

"A whore?" Aunt Grace finished for him. "Why should he ever know, unless you tell him? Besides I'm not *that*. A whore sells herself. I give myself to a man who needs me and who fulfills the same need in me."

"But you couldn't be in love with a man like that?"

"I see. Yes, that would make a difference, wouldn't it? If we were both young and beautiful it would be tragically romantic, and you could forgive that. But people our age fall in love too, Philip."

Aunt Grace reached out to touch him, but he shrank away from her. "Where are you going?" she asked.

"I don't know," he cried, and bolted out of the house. He walked the neighborhood streets for a couple of hours and then went into a telephone booth at a gas station and rang our number.

A silent interval longer than the others seemed to indicate that Philip's pathetic recital was finished. I looked about and realized we had come back into town and walked right past our house. We were almost in the center of Inglewood. The second show of *Scaramouche* at the Regent was already under way. We stopped and stared at the one-sheets in the lobby. You'd certainly never know that Ramon Novarro was a queer, I thought. Or that he was all that short. He probably wore lifts.

"Do you like Alice Terry?" I asked, for something to say. In a blonde wig, she was playing opposite Novarro.

"She's okay," Philip said.

The streets were almost deserted. Directly ahead of us on the right was This Side of Paradise, the local pancake and waffle house open all night.

I said, "Gosh, Philip, I don't know what to say."

"I didn't ask you to say anything," he muttered.

"How about a snack?"

"If you want one."

We went inside and sat down at a window booth. A kid outside was hawking the bulldog edition of the *Examiner*. A headline screamed, "Ax Murderess Convicted!" I ordered a strawberry waffle with whipped cream. Philip said he was tempted but he guessed he'd better not. Strawberries sometimes made him break out. Still. Something to do with being a redhead, he thought. Maureen couldn't eat strawberries either. So he settled for half boysenberry and half chocolate.

We had almost finished our snacks before either of us spoke again. Then I followed Philip's gaze in the direction of the blonde waitress who was making time with a motorcycle cop having a stack of wheats and sausages at the counter. She looked a little like Alyce, who ran the cigar counter at the Lewis and Clark Hotel in Cottonwood.

"It wouldn't have been so disgusting," Philip said, "but they must've just done it."

I was confused. "Who had just done what?"

"My aunt—and that man."

"Oh, *that*. Yes. I see what you mean."

Our mere presence on earth made it fairly obvious that our parents had had intercourse, but it was something we would rather not think about because it seemed so silly. One's parents had to sleep in the same bed, unless they were rich and had twin beds (or separate rooms, as they sometimes had in DeMille movies), but when they went into their bedroom they closed the door, and it was pleasanter to assume that they went to sleep, or maybe read for a while if they couldn't sleep.

What went on we knew, of course, in a general way, but, never having experienced sex, its mechanics repelled almost as much as they kindled the imagination. At least mine. I cannot vouch for Philip's.

"What are you going to do?" I asked presently.

There was no anger in this direct question, for a change. "I'd like to go home," he said. But if he went home he would have to tell his father and mother why, and they would be horrified.

"She's a Catholic like your folks, isn't she?" I asked.

"Some Catholic!" Philip said. "And they think she's a saint." They could always call on Aunt Grace when they needed her, they often said, and next thing you knew the door bell would ring and they'd open the door and she would be standing there. (I remembered that she had come when Mrs. Pearson went wherever it was she went that time.) "Some saint!"

"It's funny," I said.

"I don't see anything funny," Philip said.

"I mean," I said, impressed at the depth of my philosophical irony, "here we are living in the Jazz Age. Our parents are supposed to be scandalized at the way we're behaving—getting drunk on bootleg hootch, driving fast cars, staying out all night, necking. I feel cheated. We've got to be missing something. You and me, we're doing nothing. We're still virgins. I drive a sedate old high-busted Willys-Knight and share it with my folks. I pay ten bucks a month on it, and buy no more than three gallons of gas at a time because I don't have more than seventy-five cents left to spend, and I still call up my folks if I'm going to be out late. I haven't had a drink of anything but some lousy beer Papa brewed in the cellar in Cottonwood. And here I am working in a movie studio! And you—you're so innocent you start to foam at the mouth because you catch your maiden aunt humping her next-door neighbor. Maybe we should get into the act."

I had heard that word "humping" at the studio, but had never uttered it before. It seemed so—well—like dogs.

For a minute I thought Philip might throw what was left of his waffle in my face. But then he snorted, the prelude to a laugh that finally shook him until he cried, and made even the cop and the waitress turn to stare at us.

When he finished I asked, "Why were you laughing?"

"You got any better suggestions?"

We got up and started toward the cashier, but as we approached Philip edged me out of his way. "My treat," he said. "Buy a gallon of gas."

Outside I walked to the corner and started to turn down Queen Street again, but Philip stopped. We could hear the clanging of the L.A.-bound streetcar approaching Manchester a couple of blocks to the south.

"What's the matter?" I asked.

"I better go back to Genesee," he said.

"You're welcome to stay with us."

"Thanks, but—I guess not. I'd have to go back sometime. It might as well be tonight."

"It'll take you two hours."

"I know, but she'll be worried if I don't show up."

"I thought you wouldn't care about that."

"I thought so too," Philip said, and grinned. "When you said that about humping—well—I don't know why, but all of a sudden it was like a movie—like that scene with Zasu Pitts and Gibson Gowland—and it was silly, and I was the worst actor in it, and von Stroheim was saying, 'Cut. Let's try it one more time.' And I got to laughing, and—"

"There's the streetcar," I warned. It was grinding to a halt for the Queen Street crossing.

"Thanks. Thanks for listening," Philip said, sprinted across the street and swung onto the E-car as it moved off into the darkness.

10

Lunch at the commissary was the high point of my day at the studio. There was an art department table presided over by the elegant clotheshorse Cedric Gibbons, a scenario writers' table, a directors' table, and a publicity table. Actors did not flock together at lunch. The big stars, with handkerchiefs around their necks to keep makeup off their costumes, were loners. They might invite guests, relatives, or magazine interviewers to lunch, or have lunch catered in their dressing rooms where they could relax, study their scripts in privacy, take a nap, or make love.

I was permitted to join the ribald scriveners at the publicity table soon after the *Examiner,* on a day when it was hard up for murder, adultery, or rape, actually published a handout (totally fabricated) that I had written and handed to Joe Jackson for approval. As I remember—and such prose is not easily forgotten—it ran, "Carmel Myers, Goldwyn star and film favorite in India, has been invited, along with the Prince of Wales, to be an honored guest of the Maharajah of Jaipur on his annual tiger hunt. Regretfully, Miss Myers has been forced to cable regrets because of her allergy to cats. Besides, she will be occupied for a year in playing the siren Iras in the forthcoming Goldwyn production of *Ben Hur,* to be directed by Fred Niblo. Better luck next time, Maharajah."

Mr. Jackson blue-penciled the last line as flippant and gratuitous, and handed it to his secretary to send to mimeo. After it was published I waited for the ax to fall. If Carmel Myers saw it she would raise hell, demand to know who had written such nonsense, and get me fired. I did not know actors very well. They would stand still for anything in print so long as it did not involve them in scandal.

I could not, however, resist taking credit for my anonymous debut as a writer. I showed the squib to Fritz Bailey and said, modestly, "I wrote that, Mr. Bailey."

Fritz was, I thought, the epitome of worldliness, sophistication, and wit. He had recently arrived from Gotham (which was
what he called New York), where he had "covered the theater
beat" (theater beat, what a magic term) for the *Daily Telegraph*
and *Variety*. He had done publicity for Paul Whiteman, palled
around the Village with Gene O'Neill, and knew everybody on
the Big Street from Jimmy Walker and Babe Ruth to Louella
Parsons, whom he could refer to as "My friend Lolly." It was this
last connection that got him his job at Goldwyn because his
friend Lolly, who chronicled the intimate details of Hollywood
luminaries, could make or break a star. At least that was the
persona she had managed to establish, and the town both
respected and feared it.

Fritz had other fascinations for me. In a community where
physical perfection was the norm, he was not only excessively,
almost aggressively, ugly in appearance, but a hunchback. His
back had been broken, he claimed, in attempting to rescue his
buddy John Barrymore. "Jack," Fritz confided, "contrary to
published reports, was giving a—ah—strictly private performance at a Chinese *maison de plaisir* on the Barbary Coast when
the San Francisco earthquake struck." Fritz paused to chuckle.
"Fact is, Jack claims to have set the damn thing off. Fortunately I
was being plaisired, shall we say, in an adjoining cubicle. I heard
Jack yelling for help. As I carried him down the stairs the
balustrade gave way and we both tumbled. My back cushioned
his fall. Otherwise Broadway might never have witnessed his
Hamlet." Knowing nothing of the facts of the matter, I had no
reason to disbelieve Fritz's story.

"Well," Fritz said, chuckling wickedly, "welcome to the
Society of Literary Whores. Keats may not deem it obligatory to
smash his Grecian urn out of envy—the dear boy would never
have written *regretfully* and *regrets* in one sentence—but you sure
as hell got in all the credits. We ought to break a magnum of
Veuve Clicquot over your *jeune* brow, but for lack of such civilized accoutrements in these benighted times in this miserable
asshole of the Western Hemisphere, pray join me at the publicity

table for some luke-cool imitation chili con carne. Ugh!" He grimaced, belched, and took my arm to lead me (and support himself) down the stairs from my cubicle in the publicity building. Such conversation was heady stuff to an eighteen-year-old less than a year out of Montana. I hoped that one day I too could command the English language to sit up and beg the way Fritz could.

Personal anecdotes were, if not strictly forbidden at the publicity table, at least frowned upon and restricted to a maximum length of two minutes. If anyone launched into a story that smelled of anecdotage, Tom Reed would raise his wrist so that all could see his watch, and begin a countdown. If this did not discourage the narrator, Tom would cry "Cut!" at the end of the prescribed time, or sooner if he could get away with it. Mostly there were awards (a near beer) for the best crack of invention of the day, friendly insults, Rabelaisian banter, double entendres, topics of intellectual interest such as the alleged thirty-six positions for intercourse, and salacious innuendo about the members of our own stock company.

There was, for instance, our French leading lady whom I shall call Marie Devereaux because that was not her name. Marie, Bill Conselman averred, had pubic hair that hung to her kneecaps, and it was said not only to inhibit her more fastidious admirers, but occasionally to make the dismounting a tricky exercise in ballistics.

Bill was by acclamation awarded the daily bottle of near beer for this colorful invention, but he refused to accept it. Why? Because it was true. And how did he know? Everybody know, he said, Mademoiselle Devereaux was a dyed-in-the-wool nymphomaniac.

"Nymphomaniacs, man's best friend!" Fritz Bailey said.

But, Bill went on, if Marie became a star her quaint little excesses could prove to be a problem to our industry. What if Will Hays got wind of it?

Brows were knitted while this exigency was pondered. Then Jack Neville came up with a solution. Granted, it was a desperate one, but desperate problems demanded desperate remedies. It would therefore be incumbent upon the male members of the department to service the young woman and keep her from going public. Every able-bodied man must put his shoulder or whatever to the wheel.

There was a chorus of amens, though Tom Reed said he refused to give up his Sundays, unless it rained. He played tennis at Westside. "All day?" Fritz asked.

"No, but afterward I'm not at my best."

This seemed to present problems. Then Fritz looked at me, and directly everyone else followed the direction of his gaze. I had not said a word.

"Gentlemen," Fritz said. (The two ladies of the department had not honored us that day.) "I think I see a light at the end of the tunnel. This young man must prove himself in order to join our hallowed ranks. True, he is no longer a virgin, having been published by Hearst, but I suspect he needs — if I may be permitted a descent to the vulgate — someone to take it away from him."

There were cries of "Hear, hear!" and then Jack Neville frowned. "There's the danger," he said, "that she might eat him alive," and Fritz chuckled, "not to be confused with a fate worse than death. All in favor raise your right hands."

Every hand at the table went up except mine. I stared down at my plate of chili. Tom reached in his pocket and handed me a little tin box with the word *Trojan* on the cover.

"I presume you were a boy scout?" he said.

"Well — when I was a kid."

"But you still remember the motto — Be Prepared?"

"Meeting adjourned sine die," Fritz said.

Philip and I were at that stage of late adolescence when gonadal ferment is at its height. At least I assume he was having the same problem, though this was a phenomenon I would not even have discussed with a doctor. For me the painfully pleasant tumescence in the groin was difficult enough to tame (cold showers and sprints around the block at bedtime) without the stimulation of the steamy climate at the studio. There, sex was not only a salable commodity (if you could get it past the Hays office) along with comedy, drama, and melodrama, but a standard topic of conversation. It was a mark of your mental and physical health and maturity (after all, it was 1923) to recount sexual encounters in candid (make that *ugly*) terms. "That homely blonde in Wardrobe puts out." "You know that girl retoucher? She's one hell of a good lay." "I had a tasty piece of tail last night."

It was early in May. The weather had turned balmy. Lazy fingers of the ocean breezes drifting in from Santa Monica were aphrodisiacal. In a few months I would be nineteen, a shameful age to be a virgin, but I was primed for the great moment with that box of Trojans, thanks to Tom Reed. Yet there were certain things one could not ask, even in such a permissive atmosphere. Like, when do you put one of the damn things on? First, or after you get things going? If the latter, do you have to say "Wait just a minute, until . . ." Won't that be embarrassing? Won't a girl start laughing? Won't I?

Yes, I was primed, and whenever I looked at a girl I wondered, could she be the one, would she let me make love to her? How do you ask a girl that? Or don't you? Does she want to be pushed over? Do you have to say "I love you"? Won't she maybe expect you to marry her if you mention love?

Jillian Watson, the girl retoucher who was said to be the good lay, was a new friend of mine. She was twenty-three, pretty in a wholesome way, five feet six in her flats, serious, wore glasses, and was hell-bent on becoming an intellectual. Unable to go to college (her father was a mailman in Albuquerque), she took a course in retouching. She designed her own clothes, she confessed, and she found Wagner's Ring cycle an emotional orgasm. (She said that word right out loud!) She read French novels "in the original." I once found her with Daudet's *Sapho* propped open in front of her tuna salad at lunch. She was also deeply involved with the modern Germans, having recently completed all of Suderman's plays (unfortunately in translation, and she was sure they lost much leaping that hurdle), and was plodding relentlessly — twenty pages a night — through the first volume of Wasserman's *World's Illusion*.

Yet they said this girl was a good lay . . . Well, you could never tell a book by its cover, could you?

"John," she said that Saturday noon when I stopped beside her at the commissary counter, "are you doing anything this evening?" (She had been reading *Madame Bovary* and eating a salami sandwich.)

"Not exactly," I hedged. "A friend of mine and I . . ." I paused, wondering how I could get out of that awkward locution without bruises, and started again. "I have a friend. We thought we might go down to the Mason and see Margaret Anglin in *A Woman of No Importance*. He likes Oscar Wilde."

"Oh. I saw her last Monday. She's very good—a little mature for the role, perhaps."

"But it's Saturday night . . . maybe we can't get tickets."

"Your friend is a man?"

"Well, Philip's eighteen." (He was actually eighteen years and two days old.) "We went to high school together."

"Now isn't that a coincidence!" Jillian said. "It just so happens that I have an old school chum visiting me. A lovely girl who needs cheering up. Winifred Streeter. I'd thought we could have a little supper, just potluck, and listen to some Wagner on my new Orthophonic, and if it's not too foggy, walk on the beach. They say the grunion should be running tonight."

I looked at her sharply and found myself blushing. Was she sending up smoke signals, or didn't she know that an invitation to watch the running of the grunion was just as good as inviting you to bed? Larry Barbier had told me that.

"That should be—interesting," I said, doing my best to raise an eyebrow after the fashion of Adolphe Menjou in *A Woman of Paris*.

"You know about grunion, don't you?" she went on. "They come in on certain tides, burrow into the sand with their tails, and lay their eggs. Then they wash out on the next wave."

"I've heard about grunion, but I've never met one," I said, lowering the eyebrow. "I'll telephone Philip."

Retouchers made good money. With forty dollars a week Jillian could afford a bungalow of her own two blocks from the beach in Venice. It was actually not much more than a shack, both damp and musty, but she had a knack with furnishing and decorating that transformed the place, in my estimation, into a Greenwich Village hideaway. There was an old sofa, several peeling wicker chairs rescued from Goodwill, a Buddha won at the nearby Ocean Park pier ("Strictly a conversation piece," Jillian explained), low-wattage table lamps set on the floor, monk's-cloth draperies, throw rugs, enormous pillows, and generous swatches of dizzily splashed batik carefully strewn to conceal frayed or soiled spots. This, I thought when we walked in that evening, is sure as hell *la vie de bohème*. Bring on Mimi and Musetta!

"What kind of girls are these?" Philip had asked with a studied oh-by-the-way manner when I picked him up to drive to the beach.

"They're not girls, they're women," I said. "At least the one I know is. She's twenty-three and the other one went to school with her in Albuquerque, so she's probably twenty-three too."

"Oh." That *Oh* had a ring of relief about it. They had once been high school girls; *we* had known high school girls. Albuquerque and Cottonwood were both small towns, so they were just small-town people. Still, something nagged him.

"If they're so old, what do they want with us?"

"Jillian said Winifred needed cheering up. I think I can guess what she meant by that."

I reached into my pocket, took out the box of Trojans, opened it, and handed him one. Philip stared. "Is that what I think it is?"

"Not if you think it's a toy balloon."

"I don't think I want this thing," he said slowly.

"You might catch cold without it."

He said nothing for at least a minute. "If you don't want to go," I said finally, "I can drop you right here at the car stop, and you can be home safe with auntie in twenty minutes. I'll tell them," I could not resist adding, "that my friend petered out."

That cheap remark won the comment it deserved — a blowout that sounded like a raspberry. It took us half an hour to jack up the old Willys, wrestle off the right rear tire, patch the inner tube, put it back on, and pump it up to sixty pounds once more. We did not speak a word except an occasional "Damn!" I finally got back behind the wheel, but Philip was watching the approach of the big red streetcar. It slowed, stopped to pick up two passengers. Philip was not one of them.

He climbed into the front seat beside me. Either he had lost the Trojan in the shuffle over the tire, or it was in the pocket of his jacket.

Jillian had not lied about her friend. Winifred was more than pretty. She just missed beauty by a pug nose. Winifred spoke very little and that little in a barely audible register. I had just read *The Man of Property* at Jillian's prompting and, unable to resist showing off, said, "You remind me of Irene."

"Irene who?" Winifred asked. She reclined on the floor, an elbow propped amongst the palms that crowded one of the big pillows. She wore sandals and a loose-fitting gray housecoat. (Irene seldom wore anything but gray.)

"Galsworthy's femme fatale. Soames's unhappy wife." (I wished Miss Pauling could have heard me. She would have been proud of such literary allusion from one of her recent pupils. As the twig is bent . . .)

"What's that?" Winifred said flatly.

"Don't pay any attention to him," Philip said, staring at her. "They're the only French words he knows."

"Well, I didn't know you could speak, you darling redheaded boy," Jillian said, pouring applejack into porcelain cups. "How about a splash?" she went on, handing cups to Winifred and Philip who had eased down beside her. "Or are you afraid of breaking the law?"

"I'm not afraid of anything," Philip blurted out, sticking out his lips in that self-conscious pout.

"I'll bet you're afraid of this," Winifred said, and without warning kissed those pouting lips.

Jillian pretended not to notice. "I couldn't come by anything but apple," she said, handing me a glass. "My friendly bootlegger is in the tank. Of course he'll be sprung by Monday, but meanwhile . . ."

"Meanwhile give me apple any time," I said, with panache. I had tasted the stuff once at Fritz Bailey's house, and hated it.

Winifred let go of Philip and sprawled back amongst the palms, smiling knowingly up into his startled face. "Would you call that a brown study?" she said, turning to Jillian.

"Now, Winnie, don't be a tease," Jillian said, and raised her glass. "Here's to the annual running of the grunion."

Yes, she knew what her invitation meant.

Perhaps after three cups of applejack anything would have tasted good, but the salad and stew, both heavily laced with garlic, seemed delicious to me. (My mother thought that garlic was merely something that "wops" and "those little brown people from south of the border" stank of, and would not tolerate a single clove of it in her kitchen.) The Orthophonic was blasting out the "Prelude" and "Liebestod" from *Tristan und Isolde,* so there was little need or opportunity for conversation except during intervals when Jillian, or I, would rise, sway across the room, and flip the platter. She explained that "Liebestod" literally translated as "love death," but that was so inadequate. Wagner had not meant it to be the death of love but rather that divine oblivion while making love. During another pause I heard Winifred say to Philip, "You know something? You won't need these on the beach," and she began to take off his shoes and socks. He looked as scared as a cornered cottontail, but gamely tried to grin as if to say, Oh, this happens every night. It was the last thing I observed for quite a while.

I must have gone to sleep. Presently I was aware of the absence of music and, opening my eyes, discovered that I was alone in the room. I rose carefully because the floor was tipping, and walked toward the kitchen and the sound of running water. Jillian stood at the sink, her eyes closed in ecstasy. She was humming—with dazzling disregard for the key—the opening bars of Tristan's "Prelude." Da-da-da-da—da-da-dum . . . Had her eyes been open she could have seen, not eight feet distant, her next-door neighbor gargling with Lavoris in his bathroom.

"Where's everybody?" I asked, steadying myself laconically against the doorjamb.

"It was grunion-running time in Holland," Jillian sang gaily. "I thought it was the better part of discretion if we let the lovebirds hunt alone."

"It's not too foggy?"

"Just enough . . . there. They're all finished," she said, and wiped her hands on the dish towel. "Besides," she went on in the same matter-of-fact tone, "*les anglaises sont arrivées* ahead of schedule, so . . . I'm sorry, John. I was looking forward to it too."

She passed me in the door, strolled back into the living room, and lit a cigarette.

"I'm sorry I went to sleep," I said.

"You poor darling, you passed out. I hadn't realized how young you are."

"It was a wonderful dinner."

"I love to cook. I guess I'm greedy for all the goodies — food, music, books, travel, and, yes, sex. I can't afford to travel yet, but I can cook, I can buy records, and sex — well . . . too bad. But, as I say, the English sometimes cross the channel at the most inopportune moments."

I gathered my courage together. "Jillian, what does that mean?"

"The curse. How would you like the 'Good Friday Spell' as a substitute? We can play it low so the neighbors won't complain."

I was beginning to feel better. I would not have to prove anything tonight. The room had steadied down. "Tell me about your friend," Jillian said, squatting on the floor before the Orthophonic.

I told her what I could, which wasn't much, how he had been scheduled to go to Harvard but his father's bank had failed and they'd lost their money, so he was attending Southern Branch and living with his aunt who was a dressmaker. And then she told me about her friend Winifred. Winnie, she said, had got married when she was still a junior in high school in order to get away from home. Her mother and father fought like tigers. But Winnie had leapt, as Jillian, ever classical in her references, put it, from Scylla to Charybdis.

"Jess Streeter, who has a Harley Davidson agency in Santa Fe, is a no good jealous son of a bitch," Jillian explained. Or, maybe, she went on in a more philosophical vein, that was not quite fair. He had an aberration and could be interpreted from a Freudian point of view, but that made him no easier to live with. "Have you ever read Freud's autobiography?"

I shook my head.

"Well, you have time. I'll lend it to you . . . What were we talking about?"

"About Winifred's husband," I said, relieved to come back to a live, though admittedly pretty queer, American character.

"Oh, yes, Jess. Or better I should say, oh, *no*, Jess. According to Winnie the only time he was ever sexually aroused was when he was jealous. Then he was a bull. So she tried to cater to his deviation. She would invent some little episode and give a few imaginary details. That satisfied him in the beginning, but lately he had begun to demand places and names. So Winnie picked Gallup as a place and foolishly said the man was a Buick dealer. What was his name, Jess demanded? 'Joe Smith,' Winnie said, the first name that popped into her head, and what difference would it make? Gallup was so far from Santa Fe that Jess would never follow up. Besides—Joe Smith. How many thousands of Joe Smiths were there in this country? Well . . . Jess straddled his Harley Davidson and drove it straight to Gallup and, would you believe it, there actually was a Buick dealer named Joe Smith. Jess marched into his office and beat up on him. That's when Winnie came to visit me for a few days. She's trying to decide whether to divorce Jess when he gets out of the pokey or go back to him. Would you turn over the record, dear? The best part's just coming up."

Either the bewildering anecdote, or time, was having its effect. I could cross to the Orthophonic and flop the record with no trouble at all. And, as Jillian swooned to the "Good Friday Spell," I thought, and now Winnie is out watching the grunion run with my best friend, eighteen-year-old Philip Pearson, and I got him into it.

The screen door opened and Winifred, lugging a sandy Navajo blanket, came puffing in. Her damp hair dangled like weeds over her shoulders and her bare feet were speckled with sand. She stamped them hard, then stood on one foot and lifted the other to get a look at the sole. It was blotched with tar.

"Never mind," Jillian said, "that stuff won't spot. You can scrape it off later. There's a can of kerosene out back."

"I need a drink," Winifred said.

"Help yourself."

Winifred poured herself a slug, then went back to the door and held it open. "Come in, Mr. Montague," she called.

After a long wait Philip sidled in past her, without looking at her or any of us.

"How ran the grunion?" Jillian asked.

"What grunion?"

"I think they're a myth."

"Howsomever," Winifred said. She spread her legs and bent forward at the waist so that her mane of hair almost reached the floor. Then she waggled it back and forth like a horse brushing off flies. "You know something?" she said, or I think this is what she said, "Grunion are not the only living things that lay eggs in the sand, eh, Philip?"

I looked at him. The corners of his mouth were twitching. He was trying to smile but couldn't.

"You want to take a shower?" Jillian asked.

Philip shook his head. "Might as well anyhow," Winifred said, scratching her flanks. She had to pass him as she left the room, and patted his cheek. "You know something?" Winifred could not make any statement, it seemed, without that hook. "You're kinda cute — I don't care what people say. Like it says in Sophie Tucker's song." She began to sing, "One of these days . . ." (Shades of Alyce, the cigar girl, who had once said that to me!) She turned and gave Jillian a secret, knowing look.

"Winnie, that's not very amusing," Jillian called after her, then turned to Philip. "She's got a macabre sense of humor." She followed Winifred into the bedroom where we could hear but not understand what they were saying. Winifred would laugh and her voice would rise, then we could hear Jillian giggle and shush her.

Philip had not spoken. He was staring angrily at the Buddha whose eternal candle had flickered out. Suddenly he seemed to make up his mind about something, glanced around the room, spotted his shoes and socks, and proceeded to put them on.

"Take a shower before you do that, or you'll scratch all the way home," I said.

He did not hear me. When his shoes were on he started for the door.

"Hey, you can't go off like that."

"Who says?"

"You won't get far. I've got the car keys."

"I'll wait." He slammed out of the house. After a moment Jillian returned from the bedroom.

"What happened to Big Red?"

"He's — he's waiting out in the car."

"Something wrong?"

"He's not feeling so good," I told her. "I'd better take him home."

"That's too bad. Tell him there's nothing to feel bad about. Maybe it was the applejack and the garlic stew."

"Maybe. Well, thanks for everything, Jillian. And say good-night to Winifred for us."

"Will do."

"See you Monday."

I turned to go but she stopped me with a "Wait." She hurried over to the bookshelves, grabbed a book, and brought it to me. "It's time you knew about old Sigmund," she said, and kissed me on the cheek.

The windshield kept fogging over. I tried leaning out the side window but that made my eyes tear. Finally I stopped, got out, and rubbed the windshield with the raw potato you always kept under the front seat if you lived near the beach. Philip sat there like a dummy. I decided that if he had nothing to say neither did I. But as usual I grew bored with the silence first, and broke it.

"Well, you'll have plenty to confess tomorrow morning, won't you? Father, forgive me for I have sinned. I sassed my mother, I told lies, and I screwed a girl."

"Ve-ry fun-nee," he muttered. At least the dummy was alive. I drove on. The fog began to lift and I could make out the pie-shaped Culver City Hotel where the studio had temporarily installed a new contractee named Lucille LeSueur until she could find an apartment. I turned left and followed the zigzag road across the fields toward west Hollywood. Suddenly the last scrim of fog lifted and the night turned brilliant.

"She was making fun of me, wasn't she?" Philip said at last.

"You're a very funny fellow." That was no answer, but it kept the conversation going. "We're both pretty humorous. I pass out and you . . . Move over, Robert Benchley."

Nothing more was said until we turned east on Melrose. Then I said, "Look. I'm sorry. What more can I say?"

"What are you sorry about?"

"That I got you into this."

"It's not your fault."

I guess we were talking about two different things. I let it go for a minute or two, then I said, "I didn't know she was married."

"Who's married?"

"Winifred. Didn't she tell you?"

He shook his head.

"Yes. She's got a husband named Jess back in Santa Fe, but he's in jail. That's who she meant when she said that about telling you-know-who about — well, Venice and stuff."

Philip let out a breath that he seemed to have been holding for a long while. "Then maybe it's just as well," he said.

I decided not to ask what was "just as well." If I did, he would probably clam up. Presently he continued, "I mean, that would have been adultery."

"You mean — if you had done it?"

He nodded.

"It would have been adultery?"

Again he nodded.

"I don't think so," I said. "It would have been for her, but not for you."

"You sure?"

"That's what it says in the dictionary. The one who's married commits adultery. The other's just a fornicator."

Philip frowned. "I'm not so sure about *us*."

"Meaning you Romans?"

"Yeah. I think the single person, the like you say fornicator, is just as guilty as the married one in the eyes of the Lord, and to Him it's a mortal sin."

"But you didn't commit it. So what's the big deal?"

"I wanted to. I tried to. That's just as bad, isn't it?" He sounded as if he were close to tears, as if he wanted me to convince him that the impulse was less sinful than the act would have been. All I could say was, "If that's the rule, then everybody I know— including me—is a mortal sinner. Feel better?"

He obviously did not.

We dropped this freighted topic.

★   ★   ★

Ten years later, but before he broke into the *Post* with "There but for Grace," Philip wrote a story called "Episode of the Grunion," which was published in one of the small-circulation, so-called literary magazines. He was paid seventy-five dollars for it. In it he employed a device that he often used later: a first-person narrative told by a female. The "I" was a spinster named Emily, an attractive woman who wrote historical novels. At forty-five Emily was remembering, in the rational tranquility of her middle years, a night on a moon-drenched beach long, long ago, and her gentle, skillful seduction by a handsome, poetry-quoting stranger whom she had just met at a party in Laguna. His name was Winfield, but his friends called him Winnie.

It was all in the nature of an idyll, the male and female sex drives delicately limned in literary pastels, with no heavy breathing, no stimulation below the belt. At the finish, the tone turned gently melancholic. When Winfield escorted Emily home (she lived with her very ordinary parents in a stucco bungalow in South Pasadena), he confessed brokenheartedly that he was married, and his wife was a Catholic.

Emily never saw Winnie again, but she could never quite forget him. Or, she mused in an epilogue, had the episode ever really happened? Was it perhaps merely a spinster's hallucination? She toyed with the notion of consulting a psychiatrist, but discarded it. A psychiatrist would try to deprive her of her dream, and dreams were truer than truth, Winfield more real than flesh-and-blood man, and her own self only a fool's fancy without them.

★ ★ ★

We changed the subject, and stopped at an open-all-night drive-in for hamburgers and malteds, one chocolate, one strawberry.

Philip said he had written to his folks that he was going to quit school at the end of the spring term. Southern Branch was teaching him nothing that he wanted to know. He had been taking a course in original composition, but the instructor was living back in the Dark Ages. He wanted you to write like Joseph Conrad or George Meredith.

If Philip could find a job he would rent a quiet room away from Aunt Grace, her prattle, her bargain-hunting movie stars, and her pot-bellied lover. He needed a place where he could be alone and write. He had a lot of ideas now. Did I think he might get a job at Goldwyn this summer? I said I would snoop around and let him know if I heard of anything.

It must have been almost three o'clock Sunday morning when I braked the old Willys in front of the bungalow on Genesee Street. Lights were on inside the house, and by the time I cut the motor (Philip and I had not quite finished talking; I had not had time to tell him that Rupert Hughes needed a secretary and had asked me if I would be interested in leaving Publicity), the door banged open and Aunt Grace came running toward us. She was followed by the man I had never seen before — Fred Parks.

"Oh, Philip, Philip, where have you been?" she cried.

"I told you. I was going to a party."

"But I didn't know where and — and — and I tried everywhere. I tried your folks, John, and they didn't know, and I was so — so — " She began to cry.

By this time Mr. Parks had come up beside her and was trying to calm her. "Now, Grace, take it easy, take it easy. Maybe you'd better let me tell him."

"No," Grace said, "he's my brother — I mean, he was my brother. Oh," she howled, "how can I say *was* about my only brother? Oh, Philip, you poor fatherless boy."

By this time Philip was out of the car. His aunt threw her arms around him and hung on his neck for support while she sobbed. I didn't know whether to get out of the car or not, so I sat in it, my feet dangling out of the open door.

"It's your father," Mr. Parks said.

"He's dead," Aunt Grace cried. "My brother Sam is dead."

"Apparently there was an accident — with a hunting rifle," Mr. Parks explained.

"Or — or that's what they'll give out," Aunt Grace said when she could control the sobbing. "But how was I to know?"

Philip put his hand against the open door of the Willys for support, and looked from his aunt to Fred Parks, his face under the white streetlight an amalgam of pain, bewilderment, and frustration. I laid my hand on his arm. Finally he said, "Please, somebody tell me what happened."

"He telephoned," Aunt Grace gulped. "Sam telephoned. He wanted to speak to you. Right after you and John left for wherever you were going."

"The beach," I said.

"A party at the beach," Philip amplified.

"And I said I didn't know where you were or how long you'd be gone, and he finally said, 'Grace,' he said, 'Grace' — I'll never forget as long as I live but I didn't know what he meant at the time — "

"For God's sake," Philip cried, "tell me what Father said!"

"I'm trying to, Philip. He said, 'Tell my boy everything's going to be all right. There'll be plenty for him — and Stella — and

Maureen, too, to do anything they want to do.' So I said, 'Sam, what does that mean?' and he said — the way he used to when we were children and I'd pester him — 'Sis, ask me no questions and I'll tell you no lies. Good-bye.' Just like that. And it wasn't more'n two hours later when Stella called me and told me . . .''

Philip's lips were moving, but he made almost no sound. His chest rose and fell like that of a man in coma, his eyes clamped shut in pain, and the fingers of his hand on the door splayed like a starfish. He was whispering something. I was never quite sure what it was, but I think he was saying, "Jesus, forgive me," over and over.

Philip went to Harvard that September.

11

When you are young males emerging from adolescence, when a continent separates you and totally disparate styles of life absorb your interest and demand your attention, the fierce flame of boyhood friendship is wont to flicker, then gutter, and survive only in the moldy memorabilia of memory.

Philip's and my relationship was about to fall into this category when I received a letter from his mother. Mrs. Pearson sometimes felt that I had taken the place in her heart of the son she had lost long ago, she wrote. She wanted to "keep in touch." So how was I getting along at the studio? (I had left the studio by then and was working for Rupert Hughes.) Philip had told her how kind I had been during those months he spent with his aunt Grace, how often I took him with me in my car, and how I had been with him the night he got the news that his father passed away. She had never thanked me. Now she wanted to. And did I ever hear from Philip? He did not write to her or Maureen very often — Maureen was working in Chicago as a secretary — and she worried about him. He seemed so alone back there in Cambridge and never mentioned any friends. Maybe he had them but Philip was a very private young man. It was just his way, but not a very satisfactory way for his mother. However, if he ever wrote to me and mentioned anything like — well — something he needed or that was bothering him, would I let her know?

I felt a little guilty. I had not written Philip, or heard from him, in more than a year. I found the letter I wrote him that day when I was going through his effects. I don't know why he kept it all those years. It was written during my *humorous* phase at its most repulsive.

Dear Philip:

In case you have forgotten auld lang syne and all that stuff, my name is John Ewing and we used to know each other back in the dear dead days of Cottonwood High where you wore a tulip and I wore a red, red rose, etc. Rumor hath it — why doth rumor alwayth have to hath it? — that you are now treading the halls onceth trod by the Adams gang and weird kids like Emerson, Holmes, and Thoreau, and that when you get your sheepskin you run the risk of becoming president of these United States. Well, lots of Harvard grads do; why should you hold out for emperor?

The way I figure it, you are twenty now and ought to be a junior, barring accident. Seriously, how goes it with you? Do you like Harvard and Cambridge as much as you thought you would? Do you have a steady? If so, give name, age, color, shoe size, etc. Do you still want to be a writer? Will you go to New York when you are graduated? (I have just learned that one does not graduate, one is graduated, but I suppose Harvard has already taught you that.) Do you plan to starve in a garret in Greenwich Village, or let a rich dame keep you? If you have a choice, may I suggest the latter.

And now about me. I'll bet you can hardly wait! You went to Hahvahd, doncha know, and I went to Rupert Hughes, and I am writing this witty letter on his witty typewriter at his gorgeous house at 4751 Los Feliz Blvd., L.A. *Our* library and workroom is forty feet long and twenty feet high and is stacked with books. There may be no such thing as a Hughes B.A., but there ought to be because I should be paying him for what I'm learning about — well — everything. He is brilliant, erudite, gentle, and kind, and besides, I am madly in love with his wife, Pat, though she doesn't know it and I hope I can keep it a secret from her. She's only twenty-four and he's fifty-three. Dunt esk me to explain. She's southern and has red hair. Maybe you saw her in *Tol'able David* with Dick Barthelmess. Her name was Patterson Dial.

I work part of the time at the studio and part of the time here at Los Feliz. Mr. Hughes is still directing an occasional movie, but he has begun work on a biography of George Washington (who did *not* go to Harvard, incidentally, so you don't actually have to, to be president) as well as writing two serials a year for *Redbook* and *Cosmopolitan,* at least one short story a month, and a weekly column for *American Weekly*. You say you want to be a writer?

I think I made the right move in getting out of publicity, much as I like the people there. I just wasn't very good at the job, and right when I'm beginning to worry about getting the sack, along comes Rupert Hughes and offers me fifty dollars a week to become his secretary. *Fifty dollars*. And a promise of a ten-dollar raise every year! Touch me. And sometime this winter or next spring I'll be coming to New York. (Only a cheapskate would travel without a secretary.)

Well, Old Paint, it has been more than a year since you heard from me and I promise not to write again unless you reply within three months. I will take it to mean that east is east and west is west and never the twain shall meet.

Just on the off chance I may let you know when we go to New York. Maybe you could come down for a weekend. I could put you up at the Elysee.

Ave as well as *Vale,*

John

PS Have you read any good books or screwed any bad girls lately?

Though his style loosened up considerably later, there was always something formal about Philip's letters. They read as if he felt he might have to turn them in for grading by an instructor, or that possibly one day they would be published. (I wonder?) There were never any erasures, no XXX-outs. Every sentence was precisely furnished with subject and predicate, no carelessly dangling clauses or sidetracking of topics, few by-the-ways. (It was not until we shared an apartment later than I found out why: He wrote a first rough draft and kept it in his files.)

My letter brought an instant response — I think his mother was right; he was lonely — and thus began a correspondence that

persisted intermittently for the rest of his life in spite of the
convenience of picking up the telephone when we were
separated.

As usual (I was to discover), his letters devoted themselves first
to answering questions (or avoiding them), then to commenting
somewhat patronizingly on what you had written, and finally — if
you were lucky — to making a few pompous observations about
himself and his world.

Dear John:

I answer your rather impertinent personal queries herewith.
How goes it with me, as you put it? It goes fine.

Do I like Harvard and Cambridge, et cetera, et cetera? Yes, with
reservations.

Do I have a steady? A steady what? "Steady" is an adjective.

Do I still want to be a writer? Yes. My tutor is encouraging. He
doubts that I will ever be a popular writer, like your Rupert
Hughes. He holds out Henry James as a model. In case you
have never read James, start with *The Bostonians*. That one
requires less black coffee to cross the *finis* line.

Do I plan to starve in a garret or let a "rich dame" keep me?
Are those the only alternatives for a man of — forgive the
expression — letters?

I am glad you have struck it rich. (*You* could keep me and save
me from a "fate worse than death.")

I may take you up on coming to New York when, and if, you
get there. Mr. Chandler, my tutor, has suggested that I meet
one of the editors of the *Unicorn*. They went to school together
in Vermont. I wrote a short story that Chandler thinks might
be worth showing to someone, for criticism if nothing else.
Not that it will not be nice to get together with you again, but
I might as well kill two birds with the price of one ticket if
possible. I am not making fifty dollars a week. Let me know
when you are coming.

Let's see. Is there anything else that an ignorant, unprincipled dropout like yourself would be interested in? Could I tempt you to crack T. S. Eliot, for instance? They tell me that I am occupying the quarters he did when he was an undergraduate.

I think Eliot is the single most pervasive influence on English poetry, possibly the English language, in our time. You may quote me. Read "The Waste Land."

"Seriously," I liked hearing from you, John.

It's not easy to make friends when one is bucking for a magna.

As ever,

Philip

PS What was the name of that French prof who made a pass at you at USC? I ask because there is a Dr. Raymond Copley teaching French here this semester. The name rings a bell.

PPS In re. your PS. In Boston the past tense of screw is scrod.

So Philip was still planning to be a writer, and was aiming at the *Unicorn*. Well, after observing the perks and the lifestyle of Rupert Hughes the thought of writing had also crossed my mind.

12

Pat Hughes, in ankle-length black mink and John Frederic hat, carrying Jinka, her ill-tempered Pekingese (he had ridden from California in their drawing room), was striding along beside her husband. Rupert Hughes, wearing a three-hundred-dollar vicuña suit and trailing ashes from a dollar cigar (his own brand, shipped from Havana), was parrying questions from two reporters hurrying along beside him. They wanted to know what he had to say to the Daughters of the American Revolution whose bowels were inflamed (the reporters said) because he had dared to reveal that Parson Weems had invented the story of George Washington and the cherry tree.

Behind them came three redcaps trolleying eleven pieces of Vuitton luggage. And behind them came I, checking to make sure nothing was mislaid or stolen, and wondering why everyone was in such a hurry. Suddenly we were compressed into the gate and then expanded and spewed out into the ritual pandemonium of Grand Central, where at least two thousand commuters with as many destinations were charging through a mad quadrille without benefit of a caller.

Miraculously we survived and found ourselves on Vanderbilt Avenue where a parade of checkered taxis jockeyed for position. For the first time I looked up into the fantasy of steel and concrete that echoed the rattle and roar and eternal rumble of New York.

Presently I was in a taxi, the eleven pieces of luggage stacked around and over me. "Hotel Elysee," I managed to say to the driver whom I could not see, and then settled back, hoping that if I fainted I would come to by the time we reached 60 East Fifty-fourth Street.

It seemed as if everyone in New York was rich except the nameless poor who, I gathered, lived in segregated districts like Hell's Kitchen and Hester Street, and seldom made it up to our

176

posh part of town even to beg. They were said to be quaint and happy, rather like the musical comedy peasants of Austria and Hungary — only less colorfully dressed — and well worth a visit, if one had the time. But they were not on my agenda during this first short trip. They could not compete with Carnegie Hall, the Metropolitan Museum, or the Metropolitan Opera, where Maria Jeritza, the reigning Tosca, was bringing the old house down by warbling "Vissi d'arte" while lying flat on her stomach.

Take the subway, and somehow it was acceptable for the rich to use the subway to go *way down there,* where old Trinity Church marked Period to the Exclamation Point of Wall Street. Up Wall and note the imposing pile of the Stock Market where, in 1925, the bulls were rampant and the bears biting the dust. And while you're downtown don't miss Fraunces Tavern where our forefathers lifted a mug or two and raised revolutionary young voices in bibulous psalms to liberty.

Then stroll back up to the village where not even artists starved in those days and love was said to be free. And, if it was a nice day, meander up to Thirty-fourth and Fifth and drop in for tea at Peacock Alley in the Waldorf and mingle with the *nouveau* or *ancien riche,* scions of aristocracy with their wives or mistresses, and a smattering of theatrical celebrities. And possibly Peggy Hopkins Joyce (that somewhat different virgin, as Alexander Woollcott described her) might be on the prowl, displaying on her fingers and around her neck the lovely wages of sin, and, if you were lucky, catch a glimpse of Jimmy Walker, that equally different mayor.

Your heart beating a little faster — did something magical happen to ordinary air as it crossed the Hudson? — hurry on up Fifth, pause before the Library lions (which were said even then to roar whenever a virgin passed), then give Delmonico's the go-by unless you were with a very rich friend who could pick up the tab, pass Saks, and pause to gawk at St. Patrick's. (I would wait to enter the latter edifice until Philip arrived. Then I could follow his moves and not run the danger of being pounced upon and whisked off to some dank dungeon because I worked for Rupert Hughes, who had once been quoted as saying humorously that he felt guilty every time he passed a Catholic church without setting fire to it.)

And at night there was, of course, Times Square and Broadway, that cheap, garish, and frabjous street of playwrights' dreams. I fell in love with it that very first night, and no wonder. Mr. Hughes's ticket broker had got him three seats in the second row at the Liberty Theatre for *Lady, Be Good!*, a new musical that featured a couple of hoofers named Adele and Fred Astaire. The Gershwins had composed it in a jaunty, new musical idiom that needed no translation for young people of my generation.

No one could have had a more joyful introduction to the theater. One day, I vowed, I would be a part of it. Rupert Hughes had been, not many years earlier; he had had three comedies running simultaneously. All you had to do was put one amusing word after another on blank paper. And perhaps know a few of the right people. Well, I knew one of them already. *Give my regards to old Broadway, and tell 'em I'll be there!*

★ ★ ★

From the train Philip would go, he had written me, straight to the editorial office of the *Unicorn* on Forty-third Street, and afterward come up to the Elysee where I had a single room and bath. He would be high if the appointment had gone well, low if they had said get lost. In any case, dinner and a drink at a speakeasy would be in order — four courses for $1.25 and fifty cents for an Orange Blossom — and tickets afterward to Katharine Cornell in *The Green Hat*. The tickets cost $3.30 each, but what the hell? I was now earning sixty dollars a week, and I had not seen Philip in a long while so I was liking him without reservation. If he thought he was the only person who had become a man about town during the last three years, he had another think coming. And yes, I must admit that it would not be displeasing to impress him with my largesse. The Ewings had once been in debt to the Pearsons, hadn't they? Well, that evening I would turn the tables.

Philip was late. It was almost four-thirty, and the train from Boston had been due at two-fifteen. He should have been at the editorial office by two-thirty, and no self-respecting editor was going to waste more than fifteen minutes on a Harvard senior, was he? Or maybe he had been busy and kept Philip waiting . . .

I walked to the window. The wind was blowing hard, swirling dirt and detritus from the new skyscraper piling up across the street. At this stage it looked as rickety as Philip's old Meccano Ferris wheel.

Through my closed window jackhammers sounded like insane woodpeckers. A steel girder suspended on its cable above Fifty-fourth Street threatened a spindly hard hat waiting to guide it into place. It would soon support an office. What might happen in that office? Would a doctor heal the sick? (The sick would have to be damned rich if their doctor could afford a suite in this neighborhood.) Would a rotten business tycoon try to buy a governor? Or would a great attorney (who paid his secretary regularly every Friday) discuss the merits of plea bargaining with his guilty client? Right in that still empty space?

There was a knock on the door.

Philip wore a tan raincoat and muffler, and a Dobbs hat that was too small for him, as hats usually were. He mistakenly believed that hats with small brims made his large, craggy head look smaller. I reached for his hand, but he was using it to shield his right eye. "I got something in my eye," he muttered.

"Let me take a look," I said.

I laid my arm across his shoulders and guided him toward the bathroom where the light over the washstand would be bright.

"I'll do it," he said. "I can't stand anyone fussing with my eyes."

"I wasn't going to fuss with your eyes," I said.

He sounded cross. Maybe the appointment had not gone well. He peered into the glass, pulling down his lower eyelid with his forefinger and turning his head from side to side. "It happened right downstairs. Feels like a hot rivet. Ouch! Damn! Okay, take a look if you want to."

"It's not that I *want* to."

"What's the matter? You mad about something?"

"Shut up and let me look."

I held the upper and lower lids open with thumb and fore-finger, and suddenly I was back in Cottonwood and we were about to say good-bye that day I left for California. Philip's eyes were red — both of them — and I was telling him that it was probably conjunctivitis.

"Are you thinking what I'm thinking?" Philip asked.

"Depends on what you're thinking."

"*Deja vu,* as the French say. Only that time it was con-junctivitis."

"You were shedding tears because your old friend was going off into the sunset."

"The hell I was!"

I stepped away from him. "You've got that eye so inflamed from rubbing it that I can't see anything but the inflammation."

"Sure, sure. It's all my fault." He raised his voice and called, "Is there a doctor in the house?"

We both laughed. "Not that I know of," I said, "but Pat Hughes is good at this. She got part of my windshield out of my eye a few months ago."

"Maybe it'll go away," he said, hanging back.

"And maybe you'll lose your eye. If Mrs. Hughes can't get it out, they'll know a doctor."

It became quite the biggest production Philip had been involved in since that day he had sneezed on von Stroheim's set. Mr. and Mrs. Hughes were entertaining the Wodehouses and Tibbetts at cocktails when I led him into their living room. I tried to back out without having to explain what the trouble was, but Mrs. Hughes could see that something was wrong and I had to tell her. She sat Philip on the floor with his back to her and his head in her lap while Mr. Hughes produced the small magnify-ing glass he always carried in his vest pocket. Philip, staring up with his good eye into the interested faces of P. G. Wodehouse and his wife, Lawrence Tibbett and his wife, and Rupert Hughes and me, all gathered round and peering down at him, obviously wished he were dead.

"Plummy," Mr. Hughes said, "this would make a good scene, wouldn't it? Young man nobody knows comes into party with cinder in his eye. Everything stops while beautiful young woman gets it out."

"Right-O!" Wodehouse said. "Only of course in my story Jeeves would be removing the clinker."

"And the eye that contained offending clinker would belong to Stinker Pinker," Mr. Hughes said, "sole heir to the Pink-Nottle fortune, who would hence try to lure Jeeves away from Bertie Wooster in case a similar contingency arose."

"Good plotting," Wodehouse laughed, and turned to his wife. "Ethel, jot that down, there's a good girl."

"Ring the welkin, sing out the glad tidings!" Mrs. Hughes cried. Lawrence Tibbett, who had just signed his first contract with the Met, hit a ringing high G that shook the chandelier, and Mrs. Hughes exhibited a tiny black speck on a rolled point of her handkerchief.

"I'm sorry," Philip said, staring up into her face as if she were Mélisande and he Pelléas.

"What is your name, young man?" she asked.

"Philip. Philip Pearson."

"And I'll bet no one calls you Phil," she said. How could she know that?

"You can get up now, Philip Pearson," Mr. Hughes laughed, and took his hand to help him to his feet.

"I've told you about him," I said. "Philip and I went to high school together." I did not remind him that he had met Philip once before, on the set of *Souls for Sale*.

"Of course. You're the young man who was coming down to interview an editor of the Eunuch's Horn, aren't you?"

"The what?" Philip said.

"The *Unicorn*. Psychic slip."

"Oh. Yes. Yes, I am."

"Well, how did it go?"

Philip swallowed several times. "It looks as if I'll be joining the staff after I finish Harvard in June."

"Congratulations," Mr. Hughes said. "I suspect Plummy and I should be plying you with champagne and caviar. You'll soon be in a position to send us rejection slips."

"Consider yourself plied," Wodehouse agreed.

"And what do you and Mr. E. plan to do to celebrate?" Mrs. Hughes wanted to know.

Philip turned questioningly toward me. "I've got tickets to *The Green Hat,*" I said.

★ ★ ★

"You want to know something?" Philip said. "I'm glad I got that damn rock in my eye."

"Why?"

"I don't know, but . . . it just — well — everything seemed so — so easy and natural. I didn't know people like that could let their hair down and enjoy themselves."

"What did you think they did?"

"Oh, I don't know. Maybe talk about the abominable taste of the middle clahses, the stuffy moralities of the boobwazies."

"These are pretty exceptional people," I said.

"Gosh!" Philip said, lifting his glass. "P. G. Wodehouse. Why, he's a legend in his own time."

It was midnight. We sat at the bar of Tony's (at least half the speaks were called Tony's, but this one was on East Fifty-fourth Street). We had had dinner there too, after sickeningly sweet Orange Blossoms that had had no effect, but that was four hours ago when we had still been postulants and were seated at a cramped table, in what, in case of a raid, could easily pass muster as a tearoom. Then my key to admittance had been "Otto over at the Elysee sent me. I'm stopping there." (Otto was the doorman.) Now I carried a card in my wallet — the nest egg for dozens that would join it during Prohibition — identifying me as a member of Antonio's Exclusive Club, and we had been ushered into an ill-lighted back room with smoke so dense that our own reflections in the mirror behind the bar were blue phantoms.

"What'll it be, gents?" the voice belonging to the barely visible bartender asked.

I waited for Philip; he waited for me. Finally I said in what I hoped was Michael Arlen's most Mayfair-weary manner, "Make mine a dry martini. *Very* dry, with just a twist of lemon."

"A martini at this time of night?"

"That's what I said, sir." That would put him in his place.

"Call me Mac. 'Sir' gets me all goose bumps."

Philip closed his throat. "A martini for me too — Mac."

(Many years later *Redbook* published a story of mine called "Martinis at Midnight." Philip telephoned from the opposite coast when he read it and maintained that he had had first dibs on that title, but said he wouldn't sue me if I sent him fifty percent of the take.)

The martinis arrived. We lifted our glasses and sipped carefully. I was glad Philip could not see the face that I made. Neither of us said anything for a minute or two, then I said, "It's a hell of a long ways from Cottonwood, isn't it?"

"I knew you were going to say that," Philip said.

"Because you were thinking it too."

"Could be. But I wouldn't have said it. I don't say everything that pops into my mind."

"Or much of anything else some of the time."

"If you're trying to be insulting," Philip said, "try harder."

Another silence. Another sip of gin and vermouth.

"You wrote me about Dr. Raymond Copley being at Cambridge. Did you ever run across him?"

"I take French from him. He never made a pass at me. Maybe I'm not his type. I'll give him your regards."

"Don't bother."

Another silence. Another sip. Then Philip said, and his voice was strangely warm, "You know, this tastes good after you get used to it. I may have another."

"Two more martinis, Mac," I said.

Either the pauses in our dialogue ceased or we were no longer conscious of them. Philip remarked that he thought Katharine Cornell had an androgynous quality, and I, not knowing what that meant, agreed heartily. (It must be a word he learned at

Harvard, I thought. I'd look it up.) And what did he think of her leading man?

"Leslie Howard is the penultimate sophisticate," Philip stated. "And speaking of sophistication, what about your Mrs. Hughes?"

"I never thought of her as sophisticated."

"She's one of the most beautiful women I've ever seen."

"It's because she's a redhead. Like goes for like."

"That is not true," Philip flared. He began to enunciate his words carefully. "She — she's from some other world."

"People in the know call that Virginia."

"That's not what I mean. I know there's a trace of the South in her accent, but there's something about her face, her voice, the way she moves."

"You should write that down and send it to Irving Berlin," I said. "Something about her face, her voice, the way she moves. You've caught a bad case of brain damage."

"Oh, shut up," he snapped. "I feel totally impersonal toward the woman, the way I'd feel toward a magnificent sculpture, a painting. I do not have to — to — to — "

"Take it to bed?" I supplied.

He sat up straight and spoke slowly. "You are the sort who could rationalize the Lord's Supper as a Freudian sublimation of sexual gratification."

"Wow!" I said. "I hadn't thought of that, but I'll work on it."

He picked up his martini glass and stared at it. "But I still don't see how a woman like that could marry an old man of fifty-three."

"I can assure you he does not feel toward her as if she were a sculpture, a painting."

"But how could *she* love *him?*"

"In the first place he is a fine man," I said. "And in the second, little boys from Cottonwood, Montana, are not supposed to know the answer to questions like that. But how about this one? Could we use another of these martinis to promote this impersonal colloquy?"

"Good question, old boy," Philip said, matching my Leslie Howard delivery. "After mature deliberation, I suspect the answer to be in the affirmative." He could not help laughing. "Come to think of it, the other side of the street is just across the street but the night is dark and the wind carries a bitter chill so 'tis well to be prepared."

"Well put," I said. "What a piece of work is man, how noble in reason."

"You are too kind," Philip said, bowed to the accolade, and all but fell off his stool. I grabbed him by the arm and helped right him.

"Mac," I said, "two more for the road, and what say you make them doubles since they must insulate us from chill November's surly blasts?"

"You know best," Mac said, "but we don't carry folks out of this speak. We sweep the remains under the bar."

"Johnny?" Philip said. He had not called me Johnny since we were kids. "I like our dialogue better than Michael Arlen's. We ought to write a play sometime."

"I hadn't thought of you as a collaborator, but if you play your cards right I might consider you. What'll we call it?"

"Right away you present problems. Still, mustn't write a play without a title. How about— 'Martinis at Midnight'?"

"Well — if you like alliteration. Let's see . . . Katharine Cornell in 'Martinis at Midnight.' How's that sound?"

"Not so good as Ina Claire. For me, Ina Claire in anything. Say! I can see the marquee. Opening tonight, Ina Claire in 'Anything.' "

"Now," I said, "you are being ridiculous—no, make that silly—and our friend Mac here will be the first to give us a bad notice. I think it is time we explored the possibility of wending our weary way across Fifth-fourth Street."

"I do not propose to wend my weary way across the street. I am disappointed in you, my cliché-ridden small-town friend."

"I beg your forgiveness."

We bowed toward each other.

"But I will be in no condition to depart until this lady on the adjacent stool removes her hand from my pocket," Philip explained with great dignity. He turned to her. "Madame, if you are temporarily out of funds, perhaps I could—"

"It's not your money she's after," Mac interposed. "Flora, how many times do I tell you, keep your mitts off the customers. Go peddle your tail elsewhere, okay. The young gentleman is not interested." He turned to address us. "Two kinds of women I can't stand, drunks and gropers, and Flora here's both of 'em."

Wending our weary way across Fifty-fourth Street had its hazards. Philip paused to relieve himself in the shadow of a moving-van, and then we staggered off toward Park instead of Madison. By the time we reversed course and finally found ourselves leaning against the door of the Elysee, it was locked and we had to buzz the night clerk.

The clock in the lobby said two-thirty. The never-ending mutter of Manhattan was muted, and the wind had slacked off, leaving in its wake a clutch of stars strewn carelessly across the black slice of sky above Fifty-fourth Street, with Venus in the west luring them to their death across the Hudson. It had been a great evening. I did not want it to end.

I looked at Philip. He was leaning against the door, eyes closed, a silly grin on his face. I said the first thing that came into my head. "Philip, are you still a virgin?"

He opened his eyes. "That's a hell of a question."

"I'll tell you. I'm not."

"I'm very happy for you," he snapped.

"It's no good saving it for a rainy day."

"What I am is none of your business," Philip said. It was pure Cottonwoodese, with no embellishment from Michael Arlen.

"Oh, come off it," I said. "Sex is the coming thing. You ought to get in on it while the price is right."

The night clerk unlocked the door and we rolled in.

★ ★ ★

It must have been around five a.m. when I woke to the sound of retching. I looked across at Philip's bed; it was empty. Then I heard the sound again—from the bathroom. I thought, if Philip's sick, I should be too. I had as much to drink as he did, but I felt all right. I turned over and tried to go back to sleep, but kept waiting for him to come back to bed.

After a minute or two I got up, crossed to the bathroom, and opened the door carefully. The light was offensively bright and the air sour with vomit. Philip was sitting on the floor, leaning against the toilet bowl. "You all right?" I asked.

"I'm fine," he said, trying to focus his eyes on me. "Cheer-o, old chap."

"You don't look fine."

"I did not ask for criticism. The show is still trying out in New Haven. I'll let you know when we open on Broadway."

"You'll catch cold. Better get up and come back to bed."

"How practical of you," he said. "I'd never have thought of that."

He tried to rise to his feet. I gave him a hand to speed the process and then steered him toward his bed. He began to giggle. "You have turned this room into a yacht," he said. "You needn't have gone to so much trouble. I'd have understood."

"Nothing's too good."

He flopped onto the bed and sat there looking up at me impishly.

"Be dead dog, dead dog," I said. "Lie down, Rover."

"Better not. I'll just hang onto the rail till the pitching stops, thank you, Captain."

"Suit yourself."

I got back into bed and closed my eyes. "How are your folks?" he said conversationally, no games.

Oh, God, I thought. First he wakes me up by getting sick, now he wants to talk. "My folks are fine," I said wearily. "How're yours?" The words came out automatically.

"My mother is living in Iowa," he said. "She is a widow because my father was killed in a shooting accident. Lucky accident, they say."

I sat up in bed, jolted wide awake. "Jesus, Philip, I'm sorry. I wasn't thinking. You know how, if somebody says, 'How're your folks?' you say, 'They're fine, how're yours?'"

"Quite all right, old man," he said, snapping out the words.

"Cut it out, Philip. I said I was sorry. Nobody ever said it was a — a lucky accident."

"Really? How stupid of them, because that's what it was," he went on grimly. "If it hadn't happened, if Sam Pearson hadn't made it happen, I would not be graduating from Harvard with a magna and going to work next June on the staff of the *Unicorn* at the magnificent salary of forty dollars per week."

"You're drunk. You're still drunk and babbling. Go to sleep."

"Just as you say, my gracious host." He lay back on his pillow. Morning light began to filter through the window shades along with the groaning of trucks delivering the day's dairy produce from Long Island. Presently Philip said, "Funny what people die for."

"Oh, knock it off," I said. "Let's get some sleep."

"You take Boy Fenwick," he went on as if he had not heard me. "He died for purity." (Boy Fenwick in *The Green Hat* had committed suicide on his wedding night because he discovered he had contracted a venereal disease and did not want to infect his bride.) "And my father? Well, my father died for me. Stupid of him, wasn't it?" He made a strangling sound and, after he caught his breath, cried out, "Oh, God, and I didn't even like him very much. I sometimes used to wish somebody else was my father!" He began to whimper. "Why did he have to do it to me?" He doubled up his fists, jammed them into his eyes, and began to sob.

I crossed to his bed, sat down beside him, and pulled the blankets up around him. "It'll be all right in the morning," I said. "Go to sleep." I could not help thinking, How would you feel, Philip, if you knew that Sam Pearson was not your father, but he had loved you so much that he gave his life to give you what you wanted?

★　★　★

I was dressing next morning. Wearing shorts and undershirt, Philip came out of the bathroom. He had taken a shower and was toweling his hair. He was heavier than he had been three years ago. A little flabby. The summer freckles on his shoulders had all but disappeared.

"It smells as if somebody had thrown up in there," he said cautiously.

"It's got a right to," I said.

"Were you sick?"

"Not me."

There was a pause. "Me?" I nodded. "Sorry," he said. "I don't remember."

"I'm just glad you made it to the bathroom. You okay now?"

"Never felt better."

"I've got a headache," I said. "I should have got rid of it the way you did."

"How many martinis did we have?" he asked.

"Three, four, five. Who counts?"

"Live and learn," he said. He returned to the bathroom. I finished tying my tie, then went to the bathroom door. Philip was applying a dab of Stacomb to his hair.

"You never told me about your interview with *Unicorn*," I said.

"Not much to tell. A fellow named Grainger. Elwood Grainger. Teddibly cosmopolitan, teddibly lit'ry."

"I thought you wanted to be a writer."

"One needs food," and he went on in the same affected manner. "One hopes that while one is earning enough by editing to pay the rent one can spin a few yarns."

"Are they going to publish the story your prof sent them?"

"No. Grainger says it's a little papier-mâché, a trifle Fitzgerald. An original idea, but I'm not old enough to grapple with it yet. I should put it aside and pick it up again in a few years."

"What's it about?"

"Oh . . . a girl."

"Wow!" I said. "Isn't that a little controversial?"

"A very special girl, I hope." He paused and his eyes lost their focus. "Have you got some aftershave gunk?"

I opened the cabinet behind the mirror. "Help yourself."
He doused himself from the bottle of Old Spice.

"What do you call this story?"

"'The Day Before Tomorrow,'" he said.

"I don't know what it means, but I like it," I told him. "How'd you think of it?"

"I don't know . . . I guess I was thinking about how you live just today, it's always today, but tomorrow is always ahead of you with God knows what, and it shades — and lots of time spoils — what you do today."

I was much impressed. "I see what your Elwood Grainger meant."

"How's that?"

"Lay it down and pick it up after you've lived a little."

"Maybe."

It was a good moment between us. We were becoming adults, I thought. We could really talk about life and stuff without getting in jabs at each other. "Philip," I asked, only a little wary about revealing my ignorance to him, a Harvard man, "what is the meaning of androgynous?"

"Both male and female," he said, loftily. "Greek *andro* — man, *gyne* — woman. Why do you want to know, child?"

"Last night you said Katharine Cornell was androgynous, that's all."

"I did?" He was quite pleased with himself. He finished combing his hair, then peered into the mirror. There was a red spot under his left nostril, but it was scarcely noticeable. "Even in his cups," he said, as if quoting from an interview, "Pearson was always literate. He could never descend to the vulgate."

"But he could sure piss in the street," I said.

He stared at me in the mirror. "What do you mean by that?"

"You. You took a leak behind a moving-van. Remember?"

"I did not!"

I began quoting from the same imaginary interview. "Philip Pearson, promising writer and editor, was once charged with exhibitionism. However, the incident only served to humanize him in the eyes of his adoring public."

He stared at me. His face had turned beet red and when he spit out the words, his voice was shaking: "Why are you doing this to me?"

"Look, Philip," I said. "I'm not doing anything to you. You peed in the street. You had to. So what?"

He brushed me aside and went into the bathroom where he began to dress. In his anger he jammed both legs in the right leg of his trousers, and almost fell. He caught my look of amusement and that made him madder. I finally said, "Look at it this way. Horses do it all the time. Of course," I went on foolishly, hoping to kid him out of his ridiculous temper, "horses are exhibitionists, but if you had that much equipment to exhibit who could blame you?"

"Are you accusing me of being an exhibitionist?"

"Oh, for Christ's sake, Philip, what's eating you?"

"Nothing. Not a thing."

"Because if anything is, get it off your chest."

He did not answer. I stood there watching him finish dressing, tie his tie, get the knot too high, rip it off, retie it the same way, then gather up his pajamas and robe and slippers, and stuff them into his overnight case.

"I thought we had a good time last night," I said. "It was a swell show, too many drinks, but a lot of laughs. Our first time together in Gotham. So you got sloshed—so did I—and you relieved yourself in the street. A lot worse crimes are committed out there every night."

He walked slowly over to the window. His shoulders sagged. "What else did I do?"

"Not a thing. You were fine. As you said of Leslie Howard, you were the penultimate sophisticate."

He raised his eyes heavenward. "I may have peed in Fifty-fourth Street, but I could never have said *that*." He threw himself on his bed and covered his eyes from the shame of it.

"So help me God," I said.

He giggled. "I'm sorry you had to hear such a thing. You're too young."

He sat up on the bed, and when he spoke it was in a voice with no affectation, no attempt at humor. "I'm sorry. I don't know what got into me. I'm just a bastard, I guess."

"That explains everything," I said in relief, and went into the interview routine. "When asked to name his greatest virtue, the author stated with becoming modesty, 'I'm just a bastard, I guess.'"

One thing still bothered me. Had he forgotten what he had said about his father early this morning? I determined to test it. "I was meaning to ask before you went into epilepsy just now, how is your mother?"

"Fine, the last I heard," he said casually. "Had a little cold in the sinuses, but nothing serious."

"And Maureen?"

"She seldom writes, but she's thinking about coming to New York. If you ask me, she should get married. And how are your mother and father?"

"They're fine," I said.

So he remembered nothing. Fine! "Okay, let's go over to Child's and slip into some butter cakes and coffee."

from Philip Pearson's Day Book

Nov. 14, 1925. New York. I am here interviewing Elwood Grainger, staying at the Elysee with John. Have promise of job, beginning as reader. Met P. G. Wodehouse through Rupert and Pat Hughes. Mrs. H. took cinder out of my eye. Went to speakeasy, and whore tried to pick me up.

Nov. 16, 1925. Boston. Dinner at the Bartletts'. Jeanne and Christopher announced their engagement. Damn, damn, damn!

Who were Jeanne and Christopher? What had they meant to Philip to justify those three damns and an exclamation point? I wish I had known about them while he was still alive so that I could have asked him. Or could I have? Probably not.

13

Philip and I saw each other about once a year, whenever I went to New York with the Hugheses. After he was graduated from Harvard — he made it cum but the magna eluded him — he spent a couple of weeks with Mrs. Pearson in Iowa before settling down to a staff job on the *Unicorn*. Maureen, bored with Chicago she said (I later learned that her beau there had got married), had gone to New York ahead of Philip and found a job as secretary to an advertising account executive at BBD&O. She rented a two-room, fourth-floor walk-up over a kosher deli on Waverly Place in the village. It cost fifty-five dollars a month, so Philip moved in with her to save them both money.

Philip slept on the daybed in the living room, which was furnished with odds and ends of whatever was available and cheap. Maureen, as finances permitted, slowly modulated its jazzy draperies and substituted chairs (mostly second-hand, but she was an expert with a paintbrush) for the stacks of shaggy pillows, and Mrs. Pearson shipped the big brown leather armchair that had stood in the Pearson parlor back in Cottonwood a long while, another life, ago. "You remember this old Morris chair?" Maureen asked, the first time I climbed up to the apartment. "Of course," I said. Sam Pearson was sitting in it the last time I saw him. He had been knitting — a scarf, whatever. "Gives one something to do with the hands and keeps the hounds of the mind at bay," he had said.

"It's a man's chair, and it takes up a lot of space," Maureen said fondly, smiling down at it as she laid her hand on the back, no doubt seeing her father in it too. "Mother had it recovered and sent it along, mostly for Philip, I guess, but he never sits in it, I don't know why."

It was a convenient arrangement for Philip. They split expenses down the middle and Maureen did all the household work—the shopping, cooking, and cleaning. "Your kid brother's got it made," I told her.

"Oh, I don't mind," she said. "Philip needs his spare time for writing. And once in a while he takes me out to dinner, or the theater. It all evens out."

From what I observed it did not even out at all, but that was their business. Maureen was obviously devoted to him and very much impressed by what she called "his gift." She wanted to do anything within her means to nurture it, including typing and retyping his stories.

"He ought to pay you for *that*," I said.

"Pay me? Why, I wouldn't let him. It makes me feel—well—part of it." Yes. That was it. It gave her a sense of Sharing in Creation. She did not use the word *genius*—a sale or two would be needed to confirm her conviction that her brother was a budding genius—but it was implicit in the reverence in her voice when she talked about him.

Philip had not sold anything as yet, Maureen confided, but he seldom any longer received mere rejection slips. "Of course, he'd never mention this to you," she said, "but he's getting a great many encouraging letters." Editors were writing little notes like "Sorry, this is not for the *Journal,* but it shows promise," or "This isn't up *Collier's* alley, but we'd like to see your next. Why not try a young love or sports story?"

He had to submit everything he wrote to the *Unicorn* first. There he had the questionable advantage of the personal criticism and advice of Elwood Grainger, who had given Philip his job. A man in his fifties, Grainger could say of himself with a smirk of self-approval, "Being an intellectual, I daresay I'm a trifle captious." He smoked a pipe—his tobacco redolent of maple—wore rumpled gray tweeds and spats, affected an umbrella rain or shine, and quoted extensively from Swinburne, whose nineteenth-century purple passions were now safely entombed. Grainger was not only a nit-picker, but secretly disapproved both content and characters in fiction dealing realistically with the age we lived in. "I should feel more at home," I once heard him say, "with Edith Wharton and Henry James as next-door neighbors than your monosyllabic Hemingway."

I had been receiving nothing but rejection slips. I had written three or four short stories that Rupert Hughes had ripped to shreds. "People don't talk that way," he had said about the dialogue of one. "Keep your ears open as well as your eyes. Don't merely observe. *Listen*." And about another, "I see it, but I don't feel it. I'm not *in* that wagon box with that kid. Put me there beside him. Freeze my fingers to the old mare's lines, sting my face with the sleet."

"How do I do that?"

He shrugged his shoulders. "It's your story. You're the writer. Sometimes one word will do it, one sentence changed. Hunt for it. Agonize a little more."

Agonize? I hadn't realized agony was involved. I was beginning to grow discouraged about writing as a career — besides, it seemed relatively unimportant; I was leading a rich emotional life. Then I read of a shocking incident in the local papers. A young man had been killed during a hazing episode at USC. He had been a bright youngster, it was reported, and had had a promising future in music. He had not wanted much to join a fraternity, but his father was a Greek letter man and put on pressure, so he allowed himself to be pledged. One night, after various other humiliating indignities, he was paddled unmercifully, suffered cardiac arrest, and died. The story touched me more than it otherwise might have because I knew the background, had walked past the frat house where it had happened, and had speculated on whether I might be tapped if I stayed on at USC.

I wrote the story and showed it to Mr. Hughes. "This, now, this is damn good!" he said. "But the ending. It's soft, it tapers off. It should build — from shock to shock."

"But that's the way it happened," I said.

He laughed. "Please," he said. "You start with what happened, and then you make it interesting enough to read about."

"What would you do?" I asked him.

"What would I do?" He turned and walked abstractedly across the library-study and workroom, moved past the ten-foot table stacked with George Washington research, stopped to stare out the window at the pool. "I shouldn't tell you this, I've made it a rule never to tell anybody *how* — but I'm pretty sure if you do it, you'll make a sale. It feels like *American Mercury* to me. I'll send it to Henry Mencken. Now let me see the manuscript again . . . Right *here*. Right after they discover that the boy is dead . . ." And he told me what to do.

I did not agree or disagree with him. I was eyeless in Gaza and he had lived there for so long that he knew the lingo and every turn in the road.

He showed me the letter that he chose to send along in his own handwriting:

Dear Henry:

I regret to say that I have not been able to indulge myself in the luxury of writing the yarn we discussed when last I saw you in New York. Deadlines, deadlines, deadlines always hanging over my head like that old Sword of D., and the hair that holds it showing signs of stress.

However, I am sending along a short story I wish I *had* written. It's the maiden voyage of my young secretary, John Ewing, who is hell-bent on becoming a writer in spite of the awful example he sees before him. I hope you and George agree with me that "Autumn Idyll" belongs in the *American Mercury,* long may it wave.

As always,
Rupert

"How much do you think they'll pay?" I asked.
"With the *Mercury* it's not the cash, it's the credit," he said. "There's a certain cachet about being published in that little green magazine. Frankly, and just between us, I'm not at all sure why. But there it is. Of course they pay something — as little as they can get away with. Two or three hundred dollars."

My mother would be disappointed. As soon as I told her that Mr. Hughes had liked my story she began to plan to move into a fancier section of town. "A writer should have a better address," she said. But I was quite content. Two or three hundred dollars for words *I* had strung together? That was a form of magic. I would write to Philip and tell him, when I received the official acceptance. Or, I might even telephone him.

Two weeks later, along with the household bills and routine correspondence, I found a letter in the mailbox from *American Mercury*. I stared at it for a long while, then laid it unopened on Mr. Hughes's desk. He had worked all night and it was one o'clock before he and Pat came down, dressed to go to the Montmartre for lunch. "Come along with us, Mr. E.," Pat said. At least I think she said that, but I'm not sure because I was watching Mr. Hughes glance at the mail to see if anything needed his immediate attention.

He came to the letter from the *Mercury,* looked up at me over his glasses, then tore the envelope open. His face brightened as he started to read it (they like it!), then he frowned (no, they hate it), and then he burst into laughter (what could that mean?).

"Never take anybody's advice," he said, and handed me the letter.

Dear Rupert:

I like your young man's story. It is a little muscle-bound in the writing, but he handles his theme with sensitivity and vitality. Until the ending. Following the discovery of the boy's death, it goes to the devil in a cascade of moralistic fireworks written in a style totally divorced from what has preceded it. A story of this genre should end "not with a bang but a whimper," and he should instinctively have known that. George and I feel that we ought not to reward young Mr. Ewing for his lapse by publishing "Autumn Idyll." Perhaps this will l'arn him. Tell the kid to come in and talk to us old farts when he's in New York.

Best regards,

Henry.

PS I am returning the manuscript of "Autumn Idyll" under separate cover.

Mr. Hughes laid his arm across my shoulders and hugged me. "Forgive me," he said. "I thought . . . well, never mind what I thought. I made a rule and I broke it. I should write 'One man's meat is another man's corn' a hundred times on the blackboard."

When we got back from lunch (which I do not remember very well) the afternoon mail had already been delivered. In it was the monthly copy of the *Unicorn*. I picked it up and opened it to the masthead to see if Philip's name had been added to the list of associates. It had not been. So he was still only a reader. Why, I wondered, did that make me feel a little better? Was I envious of Philip?

In laying the *Unicorn* aside I glanced at the table of contents on the cover, which had been badly mutilated in its passage across the continent. There were stories by Faulkner, Glenway Wescott, .Morley Callaghan, and several others whose names were becoming household words, and at the very bottom, "The Fur Mittens" by Phi —; the rest of the page had been ripped off. I opened the magazine again and leafed through it. There it was. "The Fur Mittens" by Philip Pearson.

I sat down hard. Why, the son of a bitch! He hadn't told me a thing about it, just let me come across it as if . . . as if he were Somerset Maugham or Hemingway or Shakespeare and sold one every day of the week. He might have let me know. Why? Why, so I could congratulate him and tell him I was happy for him, of course. Why else?

I was suddenly aware that Mr. Hughes was standing beside me, looking down at the magazine opened to Philip's story. "So your friend broke into the *Unicorn*," he commented. "I'm delighted for him."

"So am I," I said. "Yes, so am I."

Mr. Hughes patted me on the shoulder as if I had suffered a death in the family. "I know how you feel. There's only one thing worse than a bad break. That's a good one for a friendly rival at about the same time. Never mind, you'll make it soon."

I read the story. I had to admit that it was good, though more an evocation of a mood than a story and faintly reminiscent of Galsworthy's "Indian Summer of a Forsyte." An old lady about to die entertains fleeting and poignant memories of a winter afternoon sixty-five years ago when she and a handsome young man — or was he handsome only in her memory? — went skating on a lonely pond in the forest. A buck watched them from the underbrush for a while, then followed a doe off into the tall whispering pines. The girl learned to skate backward. She fell and sprained her ankle and the boy carried her home. He wore fur mittens. It was the first time she had inhaled the musky odor of a male (or perhaps it was only the mittens) and she fell in love with him. He never called her afterward. She married, had six children, and lived with her husband whom she loved devotedly until he died ten years ago. But now, as death creeps upon her, she looks up and sees not her husband or any of her offspring, but that handsome young man, smelling a little like a wild animal, standing there beside her bed and offering her his hands on which he wears the fur mittens.

I telephoned Philip that evening. The connection was bad and that did not help my heavy-handed ragging. I said I'd happened on a copy of the *Unicorn,* and there was a story, obviously by John Galsworthy, but signed Philip Pearson because, apparently, Galsworthy chose to disclaim credit for it. (Philip began to chuckle.) I said I thought Philip had a lawsuit and should get himself a lawyer. He thanked me, and asked for the lawyer's name. I said I thought Clarence Darrow was a comer and would probably take it on contingency. Philip said he appreciated my thought, and that it was generous of me to call him long distance, and did I know that Elwood Grainger had sent an advance copy of "The Fur Mittens" to O'Brien, who had just let him know today that it would be included in his 1929 *Best Short Stories.* I said, ah, well, that just proved O'Brien was for sale like everybody else and what else was new? Well, he said, not that it made much difference — Philip Galsworthy would still be tied to the same desk and receive a raise of only ten dollars per week. He would still tolerate old friends like me. And oh, by the way, his name would be on the masthead of the *Unicorn* next month under Junior Editors. I told him he had my deepest sympathy but that it was no disgrace, and Time the Great Healer would soon make such indecent exposure easier to bear.

★   ★   ★

Liz Bartlett was a young fan-magazine writer who could not drive a car. Something to do with depth perception, she claimed. Since her job on *Photoplay* magazine demanded extensive travel about the sprawling city — interviewing celebrities at their homes, reporting studio activities, and covering sneak previews at far-flung communities like Riverside and Santa Barbara, she had a problem. She solved it by being perpetually engaged to some young man — preferably unemployed and available at a moment's notice — with an automobile. Felix had a Chrysler roadster, Donald a Buick, and Doug a wheezing old Pierce-Arrow.

I met her when she came to interview Rupert Hughes during his last days as a director. She was not quite a beauty, though you would remember her face long after you forgot perfection. She had enormous black eyes, flawless alabaster skin, and wore her straight jet-black hair in bangs like Louise Brooks. Her mouth was large, she outlined it with scarlet, and her nose was — well — a problem. More than retroussé, it definitely turned up, but as she said, "What the hell?"

Beneath the patina of sophistication that she achieved out of sheer bravado, the jargon of the Fourth Estate, and the ultra-fashionable wardrobe (some of it copied out of fashion magazines, I discovered, by — of all people — Philip's Aunt Grace) lay the defenseless and easily bruised spirit of a Victorian maiden. That sensitive core she chose to ignore, and each morning charged off to fight quixotic battles for the underdog. She was a socialist, of course. That went without saying, though nothing much ever went without saying by Liz.

Having come from the South, she was laden — but never bowed down by — guilt about the blacks, and took it upon herself to Right the Wrong. To begin with she addressed bootblacks, elevator men, and porters as Mister, often to their confusion, and once declared that she was seriously contemplating the adoption of a black baby whose mother had stabbed its father to death in a drunken brawl. I don't know what changed her mind; she probably realized in time that it would prove impractical. However, the vision of stark-white Liz Bartlett in four-inch French heels, skirt at the knees, and deep cloche hat all but hiding her eyes, arriving at a preview in Pomona with a black baby in tow must have been all but irresistible to her.

When she discovered that Jews were not merely patriarchal figures out of the Old Testament (there had been none in her little southern town) but were actually all around us and had been persecuted ever since biblical times, she adopted them all, singly and collectively. Being Jewish was Donald's principal attraction, I believe, because he was certainly less than personable. While she was "engaged" to him, she insisted that he take her to his family high holy-day feasts (he did not much care for his mother, which in itself, Liz told him, was a disgrace to his religion, his forebears, and his ancient tradition) and learned, in Hebrew, the ritual of Passover.

That was Liz Bartlett. I liked her. I liked her vitality, her enthusiasms, her hates, her highs and lows, and that current of boundless energy that drove, and sometimes drained, her.

She telephoned me one afternoon. There was to be a preview in Long Beach of *The Glorious Betsy,* the first all-talking picture. A turning point in Hollywood history! Cataclysmic, no less. She had to be there to review it and Robin's Chevy had cracked a rib or something. She was utterly *desperate.* Would it be at all possible, would it be asking too much? . . .

"Not at all," I said.

Something pretty cataclysmic had happened to me that day too. It would be a turning point in *my* life and I was bursting to tell someone besides my parents, who had taken the news in stride. (I had telephoned Philip but he was inconsiderate enough to be at a fifth reunion of his Harvard class.)

I had mailed off at least ten short stories and they had come winging back. Introductions to editor cronies of Rupert Hughes like Rex Short, Horace Lorimer, and Edwin Balmer had not turned the trick: "Shows promise . . ." and "Let us see your next story . . ." and "Not quite up our alley." To make matters worse Philip had sold another short story to the *Bookman,* which was a notch above the *Unicorn* and paid him $250. "That's great," I wrote him. "Now you can afford to put leather patches on the elbows of that tattered tweed jacket."

I wrote another story and mailed it on my own to *Woman's Home Companion.* (I was embarrassed to accept any more special treatment.) Two weeks later the reply arrived in the mail:

Dear Mr. Ewing:

We are delighted to inform you that we like your story "Sun Dog" very much, and plan to schedule it in our February issue with illustrations by Harold von Schmidt. Herewith our check for $500 for all serial rights. We trust that you will give us first look at your next effort.

Sincerely yours,

Gertrude Lane, Editor

PS Do you have an agent? Living at that distance you will need one. We do not usually suggest agents but we do not like to see our contributors in the wrong hands, and so I mention Harold Ober, a reliable gentleman who represents such contemporary writers as F. Scott Fitzgerald, Faith Baldwin, Philip Wylie.

That letter had arrived in the morning mail. While I was still reeling, Rupert Hughes came home from a lunch with his guest Rex Short, the editor of *International,* which published one serial per year by Hughes. I had been introduced to Mr. Short earlier that morning. He had returned from lunch at the Montmartre "to discuss the upcoming serial," I assumed. Instead, Mr. Hughes summoned me from my little cubicle and asked how I would like to go to New York. Rex Short was promoting his present secretary to an associate editorship (that sort of thing could happen) and was in the market for a replacement. He needed a man because he traveled a lot. Short had liked my appearance. Hughes had plugged my capabilities and said he would not stand in the way of my advancement. It could be the beginning of whatever I or Fate might choose to make it. A writer needed experience — experiences — new worlds to observe and absorb. I had had Hollywood for the present. If I were his son he'd say it was time for a change. Hell, he would say it anyhow.

"Of course you realize I'm merely trying to get rid of you." He laughed, put his arm around me, and gave me a hug.

★ ★ ★

"A fine thing," Liz said when I had finished telling her the news on the way to Long Beach. "I like you, I like your car, and you don't drive like a maniac the way Robin does. Here I am on the brink of announcing our engagement and you spring this on me! Stop the car."

I braked to a stop near the summit of Signal Hill. God was experimenting with His limitless battery of special effects: A full moon sifting through the Long Beach fog translated into stark poetry the dismal derricks, their oil pumps nodding like grasshoppers.

"Something on your mind?" I asked.

"Yes," Liz said. "I'd like to kiss you — just to prove no hard feelings." She kissed me. It was not altogether unpleasant. "I envy you," she said, after a long moment. "A short story sale and New York all on one day. Remember this moment. You may use it. Don't they always say it couldn't happen to a nicer guy? Of course I don't know you very well, but — "

"But you like my car."

"I guess that's it. But somehow I get the feeling that I'd rather have been engaged to you than to your car. Lousy timing."

I don't remember much about *The Glorious Betsy* except that for some reason the star, Conrad Nagel, lisped, which didn't help the love scenes.

from Philip Pearson's Day Book

Sept. 14, 1929. I found a new apt. on E. 44th. $75.

Can walk to office. Hate subways. Hope it works out living with John.

Try for a while. Not much space for privacy. Maybe he's beginning to grow up.

PART III

14

Philip had left a key with the superintendent. My first impression, after opening the door to apartment 7B, was that there had been a mistake. I had got into an unoccupied apartment. Then I saw Sam Pearson's Morris chair in a corner and a few incidental pieces lined against the walls. It reminded me of a farmer's living room ready for a square dance.

I set down my bags and slowly turned a full 360 degrees. The room had possibilities. It was spacious enough — fifteen by twenty — and there was a large window overlooking the backs of similar apartments on Forty-third Street. (You could see the Chrysler spire, but you had to put your neck in a sling to do so.) The walls were painted a commercial beige and every corner was hospital clean. ("It'll take a while for the friendly roaches to find us," Philip said later.) There were cork floors, which ought to deaden the click of heels, and twin beds pulled down from one of the twenty-foot-long walls. When up, as they were that morning, you would hardly know they were there.

There was a large closet, the conventional combination bath-shower and toilet, a tiny kitchen with two-burner stove and a refrigerator with nothing in it but milk and orange juice and peanut butter.

It would do, but it needed clutter. There were no pictures, no ashtrays or knickknacks on the glass-topped coffee table, no bookshelves, and only three lamps, two standing like totems at either end of the modern love seat, the other near the window.

Maureen, I found out later, had done what she could to counter Philip's leanings toward monastic simplicity, but had succeeded only with the window, which was framed by a splashy Dorothy Draper palm-tree print. ("Philip," she had said, "you can't live in that room without some color. It's a cell.")

We all change, I thought. The changes sneak up on us while we're looking the other way, doing the other thing. What had happened to, what had become of, the boy I used to know, the kid with the junky bedroom that his mother said was a pigsty? Where were the glossy eight-by-tens of Nazimova, Gish, and Allison, the Harvard pennants, the Virgin Mary, the dog's bed, and the old Brunswick? Where were his books? He was going to be a writer. He must have books.

Ah, *there,* piled on the window ledge behind the Draper palms. His Oxford dictionary, his Roget, a biography of Emerson, fiction of Fitzgerald, Dreiser, Wharton, James, *The Oxford Book of English Verse,* "The Waste Land," and an autographed copy of George Weller's *Not to Eat, Not for Love.* Philip and George had been classmates at Harvard.

His clothes, two identical Brooks Brothers suits — one brown, one gray — hung in the closet beside a pair of blue slacks, a tweed jacket thin at the elbows, and a Burberry raincoat. On the floor, lined up as if for military inspection, were two pairs of wingtip shoes, one black, one cordovan, and a pair of rubbers. In the corner stood an umbrella, neatly buttoned down. There would be plenty of room for my stuff.

After I had unpacked and showered, I telephoned the *Unicorn.* Philip had been expecting my call, but his voice sounded clipped and noncommittal, as if he thought he might be monitored. "Hello? . . . Oh, yes, John. Glad you made it . . . How about lunch at the Harvard Club? . . . Good. Meet me there at twelve-fifteen . . . No, inside. I'll tell the doorman to let you in."

Well, that's not exactly a wild, ticker-tape reception, I thought, so screw you, buster. And then the timbre of his voice changed. Instead of hanging up, he asked, "You haven't checked in at *International,* have you?"

"No. I thought maybe I'd mosey up this afternoon and get the lay of the land, if you'll pardon the expression. I'm not supposed to start work till Monday. Oh, by the way. I suppose there's been nothing in the papers about my selling a story to *Woman's Home,* has there?"

"You did?" he said, as if somehow that took a weight off his mind. "That ought to hold you for a while, oughtn't it?"

"I don't need holding. I'm going to be making eighty dollars a week which, as Shakespeare said, ain't peanuts."

"We'll talk about it at lunch."

It was a bright, cool, windy day. I walked over to the Lexington entrance of Grand Central, strolled through and out onto Vanderbilt, and then on west to the Harvard Club. "I'm a little early," I said to the doorman, "but Philip Pearson is expecting me."

"Ah, yes, Mr. Ewing. Go right on in, sir."

I sat facing the entrance. Promptly at twelve-fifteen Philip entered. He did not glance at the doorman or pause to check his hat, but kept his eyes straight ahead, as if he were afraid someone might speak to him. Halfway across the lobby he realized that he had not removed his hat, flipped it off, and in so doing dropped the rolled-up newspaper he was carrying under his arm, stooped to pick it up, and seemed relieved that nobody was laughing at him. It was, somehow, a comic, an almost Chaplinesque, performance.

"Philip," I said, "goddamn, it's good to see you." I grabbed his hand and pounded him on the back with my free fist. He frowned, obviously hoping that none of his peers had noticed this unseemly exhibition.

"Ah, yes, well," he said. "Let's sit down out here for a minute or two, while I . . ."

We sat opposite each other, a small coffee table with a Harvard Club ashtray between us. He did not speak. Finally I said, "Nice little place you've got here."

"Yes," he said, as if I had really meant what I said, "it's convenient. Inexpensive too, for lunch . . . You have a nice trip?"

"Except when the Navajos surrounded us at Holbrook," I said. He did not smile. "I wrote another short story on the way."

"Good. I hope you sell it. You like the apartment?"

He could write "digs," but not say it, apparently.

"It's not the Ritz, but it has its humble charm."

Then we sat as if there were nothing more to say. A minute or two passed. "What's the matter, Philip? Are you trying to tell me you wish I'd stayed in California?"

"Oh, no, no," he said quickly, and his face turned red. "It's not that at all."

"Then what the hell is it?"

"You haven't seen the papers this morning, have you?" he said, and looked down anxiously at the *Herald Tribune* rolled up in his hand.

"No," I said, "but my taxi driver said something about a panic on Wall Street. You didn't have your patrimony tied up in the market, did you?" (Oh, God, why did I say patrimony?)

"Very funny. But—here. Take a look at this."

He unrolled the *Herald Tribune* and pointed at a two-column head near the bottom of page one.

"Editor Apparent Suicide," read the banner, and the subhead went on, "Rex Short, Editor of *International Magazine,* Succumbs, Victim of Gun Shot."

I looked up at Philip, who was brushing something off his jacket, then I read the story. Short, complaining of a headache, had gone home from his office yesterday afternoon, greeted his wife, and told her he thought he would take a nap. He went into his bedroom, locked the door, and—five minutes later—Mrs. Short heard a gunshot. Unable to open the door, she had summoned the building superintendent who produced a duplicate key. Together they had found Short lying on his bed, a bullet hole in the roof of his mouth and the weapon, a revolver, in his hand. Rex Short was fifty-three years old, had been born in Sandusky, Ohio, married Valerie Tweed, also of Sandusky, in 1898. There were no surviving children. A son, Rex Short, Jr., had been killed in France in 1918.

I had met the man only once and had neither particularly liked nor disliked him. Of medium height, he tried to disguise a pot belly with corset-fitting vests and, I suspect, a support girdle, which made him look like a pouter pigeon. He had impressed me as pompous, prone to pronunciamentos concerning publishing, claiming infallible information on what would sell a magazine and what would not. Rupert Hughes said that Rex Short's secret was the very *common* common denominator of his own personal taste. He never tried to outguess the public. He bought what he himself liked.

"Well," I said, "Happy New Year."

"They wouldn't bring you all the way from California and then send you back, would they? Or would they?"

"Look at it this way. Where Rex Short has gone he's not going to need an executive secretary."

Philip was biting his nails. "It's rotten luck," he said. "I wish there was something I could do."

"Thanks, but I can always go back to Rupert Hughes."

"I don't want you to do that," Philip said, with genuine concern in his voice. I suddenly realized that it was only the second time in our lives that he had ever seemed to care how I might feel about anything.

He cleared his throat. "Look," he said trying to sound gruff, "you can't leave me holding the sack on the apartment. I'll sue you if you welch out on it."

"Oh, ho," I said, matching his change of mood. "Now it comes out. That's why I've got to stay in New York."

"Why else? Come on, let's get something to eat." He got to his feet. "The popovers aren't bad. You need strength."

Philip introduced me to two of his former classmates as we moved down the buffet counter, with an explanatory addendum, "John's from Hollywood." Their only comments were a lightly contemptuous "I've never been west of the Roxy" and a self-conscious stab at humor with "Perhaps you ought to spend a little time in our decompression chamber."

"What are you going to do this afternoon?" Philip asked, after we were seated.

"Go up to *International* and see how the wind blows."

"Maybe you should wait until Monday. They're probably all in shock — or jockeying for position."

"Then I'd better jockey with them," I said. "I want to get it over with. Yes or no."

We went on eating for a few minutes. Then he said, "Maureen wants us down in the village tonight. She's having a small party."

"What for?"

"You, you fool. She likes you — God knows why."

After lunch I walked up Fifth Avenue and turned west on Fifty-fifth Street. It began to sprinkle. I had no umbrella, so I darted under Robert's stylish awning, and shared the dry spot with the French doorman. The shower gave me an excuse to delay what I was about to do, and more time to formulate its execution.

I knew the name of no one at *International* except Rex Short himself, and the remains of Rex Short now lay in a box at Campbell's Funeral Parlor. Whom should I talk to? Who knew anything about me? Whoever it was, what would I say to him? Or perhaps it was a her? Should I pretend I didn't know what had happened? No, that would be stupid. Nobody would want an executive secretary who did not read the papers.

"La pluie est finie," said the doorman.

Something was obviously finished. "What?" I asked.

"The rain has stopped," he deigned to translate.

"Oh. *Merci,"* I said.

At the newsstand in the lobby of the International Tower I bought a copy of the November issue of the magazine. It had occurred to me that Mr. Short's immediate subordinate might be the one to ask for. I found his name and title: Jordan Bell, Associate Editor, on the masthead.

On the fifteenth floor, which housed the editorial offices, I finally got the attention of the receptionist, a woman of indeterminate years who was totally absorbed in painting her lips with a pointed brush. "Yiss?" she finally said in annoyance at the interruption. She had an accent all her own, something that derived from her singular notion of ultrarefinement plus the fact that she could barely part her lips lest the paint job crack.

I told her that I would like to see Mr. Bell. Mr. Jordan Bell. Did I have an appointment? No. Then to what was it in reference to, please?

"Well," I said, "it's rather difficult to explain, but perhaps if Mr. Bell knew that John Ewing of California was in the reception room, he might know who I am, and what it's about."

"Oh, *yiss,*" she said. "Mr. John Ewing. I have your name right here." She glanced down at the pad before her. "You are to report directly to Mr. Tweed's office. He is one flight up."

"Would you mind telling me who Mr. Tweed is?"

"Who our Mr. Tweed is?" she repeated incredulously, as if I might have asked who Al Smith is. "Mr. Tweed," she said, "happens to be our publisher, that is all."

G. W. (for George Washington) Tweed not only admitted to, but boasted of, his seventy-nine years, and wore them well. Six feet one and straight as an Indian, his hair sprang in a startling white pompadour from a wide forehead. That, plus a high-bridged nose and fierce blue eyes made me think of a condor about to take wing and soar over the rooftops of mid-Manhattan.

"Frankly," he was saying, "I was unaware that you existed. Rex seldom bothered to share details with me. Were you a friend of his?"

"Friend? No. I met him only once. With Rupert Hughes. I was shocked, of course, and sorry to learn that—"

"Ah," he said, sounding relieved. "It's no secret—you'll hear it around—I was not very fond of my son-in-law, but I respected him as an editor. Howsomeever . . ."

(So Mrs. Short was G. W. Tweed's daughter. There were little wheels within big wheels.)

"Might I ask how you knew who I was, and that I was coming into the office, sir?"

"Rupert Hughes telephoned me when he read the news about Rex. Knowing Rex, he suspected that you might—under the grim circumstances—be stepping into a vacuum here. He seems to have a high regard for you. Tells me you're going to be a writer."

"I hope to. I've sold a story to *Woman's Home,* and—"

"If my friend Gertrude Lane likes your work, then . . . but you want an editorial job. Why?"

"Because I've written a lot of stories that did not sell, and I've got to help support my parents at home." I was ashamed to use my parents, but Tweed looked like the kind of man who might be swayed by such corn.

He returned to his enormous mahogany desk, sat down, and lit a cigar. "Tell you what, young man," he said with the gravity of a commander deciding to negotiate rather than blow his enemy out of the water, "I'll let you in on my plan, but don't mention it till you see it in the press."

"I won't."

"We're going to give Jordan Bell a crack at the editor's desk. He's got a secretary already, so he won't be needing another."

(Then how do I fit in? Or don't I?)

"We are running into troublous times, I predict," he said, as if he alone were privy to such information, "and this is no time to be adding employees to our payroll. You can understand that?"

"I do, Mr. Tweed."

"And loose promises made by the late Rex Short are no obligation of mine."

(Okay, then let the ax fall.)

"Howsomeever, Rupert Hughes is one of our most valued contributors. Did you know that when we start a serial of his, circulation jumps fifty thousand?" I shook my head. Tweed cocked his chin at a roguish angle and continued. "Now we would not want to offer his next serial to the competition, would we? Besides, I like you."

I smiled foolishly.

"So I suspect we'll put you on the staff as a reader. How much did you say Rex said he'd pay you?"

"Eighty a week, Mr. Tweed."

"Good-bye. That's more'n we pay readers. We'll have to shave that a little, my boy."

"I couldn't afford to stay in New York for less." I got to my feet. "It's been nice meeting you, Mr. Tweed."

"Sit down, sit down. I said I like you, and I like the way you got on your horse and started out. I've done that myself in my time. You may make a wheeler-dealer one of these days. Okay. Eighty it is."

He rose and offered his hand. "Drop up and see us once in a

while," he said confidentially. "Let us mere practical folks up here who pay the bills know what's going on amongst the intelligentsia down on the fifteenth floor. I'll be keeping my eyes on you."

15

Maureen's party for me would have been long forgotten were it not that I met the supporting players in a new cast of characters who were to become fast friends for the last two acts of Philip's and my own fragmented human comedy.

There was, of course, Maureen herself, dear, good, competent, responsible, and slightly harried Maureen, who always worried lest things would not "go." She and Philip had seen *Serena Blandish* the week before and she had cut her red hair short and slicked it back like Ruth Gordon's. That had been a mistake and she kept telling everybody how awful she looked. She did not look awful, but the style was too severe for her gentle, round, freckled face. What she looked like was the ingenue's understudy suddenly called on to play the vamp.

There was Esme Jones, an extremely tall, formidable young woman who had gone to Vassar and now, only four years unlinked from the Daisy Chain, was an assistant to Harold Ober. (Ober, I had found out earlier, was already Philip's literary agent and he had turned Philip over to Esme to handle.) She looked as if she belonged on the prow of a ship where she could shrug off the waves without batting an eyelash, rather than in an office on Forty-eighth Street reading manuscripts. When Philip pointed her out I wondered if I could ever hope to cope with such a female.

"Why haven't you been in to see us?" she asked me, taking my hand and crushing it. "Harold had a note from Gertrude Lane about your first short story."

"I only got here this morning." I was pleased that she had already heard of me, but cowed by her proportions.

"We'll be expecting you." She turned to indicate the man beside her. "Mr. Ewing, this is Daniel Mobridge. Daniel is from the South, and he's a chemist who does some important and mysterious things that often produce very bad smells."

He was as tall as Esme but did not look it because he was softer and looser jointed, and seemed more vulnerable. He would be no good up there beside Esme on the prow of a ship. "I didn't get your name," he said, smiling. The southern accent was there, but on a tight leash.

"John," I said.

"Mine's Dan. I hate Daniel. And don't let this amazon intimidate you. She's not bad once you get to know her."

Being a chemist, Dan had access to grain alcohol. That night he had brought as a house present a gallon of the stuff that, with the addition of an equal amount of water and a few vari-colored drops acquired at the cordial shop around the corner, Maureen had translated into eight quarts of instant scotch, bourbon, gin, and rum.

"It's lethal, but not deadly," Dan explained, "and you're guaranteed not to go blind. Perhaps impotent for a few days, but that will pass."

Being helpful with the drinks was Joe Tyler. Joe was about my age, I thought, a little shorter, eager to please, and both as likeable and as annoying as an overgrown pup. He thought he could win your approval by barraging you with stories and double entendres (which he strove for desperately upon any occasion). He held down a copywriter's desk at BBD&O and was bucking hard for the Elizabeth Arden account, but Maureen said privately that that was years in the future, if at all. "Poor Joe tries too hard," she said. She liked him, and said he was a handy man to have around — but he was not her beau. Somehow it was important that I know this.

"Have you heard the marvelous story about the taxi rider going up Fifth Avenue?" he asked eagerly, during one of those unexplained lapses in general conversation.

"No, we haven't, Joe," said Cornelia Chase with a saccharine smile. (I'll get to Cornelia in a minute.) "I don't think we have, that is. Have any of the rest of us heard the marvelous story about the taxi rider going up Fifth Avenue?"

There were embarrassed headshakes and murmurs of no.

"I *thought* I was right," Cornelia went on merrily. "Tell us, Joe, what about the taxi rider going up Fifth Avenue?"

She had already taken what wind there was out of poor Joe's sails, leaving him floundering in the Sargasso Sea along with thousands of others who have unfortunately launched their anecdotes with "Have you heard the *marvelous* one about . . ."

Joe swallowed hard, and took a deep breath. "Well, it seems," he began, spilled part of his drink in his nervousness and had to wipe it up and start again, "It seems I — I wish I was dead. No, not really. Look, there's this guy riding in a cab up Fifth and the cab makes a left on Fifty-seventh Street and runs over that traffic button in the middle of the street, you know? So the cabbie turns and cries to his fare, 'My God, we've killed Nita Naldi!'"

All of us, except Cornelia, had wanted the story to be good so that an explosion of laughter would put Cornelia in her place, but there was only a snicker or two and Cornelia said, as if confused, "Yes, I suppose it's marvelous, but not funny. Was it supposed to be funny too?"

"Well," Joe frowned, "you see, Naldi has these great big . . ." He gestured toward his chest.

"Tits. We all know that word, I'm sure. What was good enough for Ben Jonson is good enough for little ole me . . . oh, I see." Cornelia brightened. "So when the taxi driver hits the big button he thinks . . ."

"Exactly!" Maureen said angrily. "And now let's talk about something else. Cornelia, you need a fresh one. What'll it be?"

"Surprise me," Cornelia said.

"Don't tempt me," Maureen muttered.

Cornelia Chase and Lucille (Lucy) Franklin were Cliffies whom Philip had encountered while at Harvard. They had come to New York upon graduation and taken an apartment in a new development on West Twenty-third Street. Cornelia had a job as proofreader at Harcourt Brace, and Lucy, who could get by on a minimal allowance from her father — her mother was dead — wanted to be an illustrator and made the daily rounds with her portfolio of samples. Lucy's candor about herself was touching. "I'm not terribly good, but I'm persistent," she said. "But I'm also better than a lot of the crap I see in the slicks. Maybe I should start being nice to you. You may be running *International* one of these years."

I asked Lucy that evening if she was engaged — or anything. "Not engaged," she said. "But as for *anything* . . ." She looked across the room at Philip, who had found a lone chair under the lamp in the corner and, amidst all the hubbub, was reading the *Atlantic*. "Just look at that redheaded bastard," she said. "He's all alone."

"He's always been that way, ever since I knew him," I told her.

"Really? Then what makes him so — so tempting?"

"Tell me about Cornelia Chase. What's with that dame?"

"Ask me sometime when I don't want to kill her," Lucy said. But then went on, "No. I'll tell you — if this is it, and who knows? She's bright, brighter than anybody I know; she got straight A's at Radcliffe. She's an only child and her parents worship her and never once said, 'Now, now, Neely, that's not a very nice thing to say.' Dorothy Parker is her model. Mrs. Parker can get away with murder because she makes her victims laugh. Neely's victims seldom laugh."

"And you live with this alligator?"

"Oh, one-on-one she can be a darling. It's when she's got an audience — like now. Come over here, Neely," Lucy called. "John thinks you're some kind of alligator."

Cornelia laughed merrily. "You're not very observant, young man. Note the square snout. Pure crocodile. Now see here. I've got some questions. For starters, tell me everything you know about Philip Pearson. You have five minutes."

"Ask Maureen. She knows him far better than I ever will. And she loves him."

"Meaning you don't?" Cornelia asked.

I had never thought about that. Yes, maybe in a way I did not quite understand, I loved Philip. What he did, and what he did not do, mattered more to me than it would have had we merely been old friends. I wanted his approval and I wanted my approval — or disapproval — of him to mean something to him.

I looked across the room. Esme and her Daniel were swaying together — there was scarcely room to dance — to Rudy Vallee's version of "Do do do what you done done done before, baby." Beyond them sat Philip, staring off into space. He picked up his glass of diluted alcohol, took a big swig, set it down, and began to bite the nail of his right forefinger, with the persistence of a dog scratching at a flea. I thought, how can I get him to stop that? And then, why do I care? Directly he became aware of my scrutiny and came back from wherever he had been, glanced up, first at me and then at Lucy beside me. Suddenly he sprang from his chair, crossed the room at a bound, barely missing Esme, stood in front of Lucy, and snapped out, "Let's dance." It sounded boorish, but he was smiling down at her and the smile turned the boor into a cavalier.

Without a word she went into his arms and they moved off, skillfully avoiding feet and chairs and ashtrays and the other two dancers. They were beautiful and exciting together, like two soloists who alone would scarcely be noticed, but as a team blend into a sensual showstopper. I had never seen Philip dance before. Where had he learned? Who had taught him?

Cornelia and I watched them for a long moment. Then Cornelia said, "You know something? Unless Philip is dancing he always moves as if his drawers pinched, but when he dances he's in the nude. Remember, when you write about him, I want credit for that crack."

"What makes you think anybody will ever write about him?"

"Bound to," she said, and suddenly she was very, very young and earnest. "It's my opinion that what makes a person fascinating is not what you know about him, but what you don't. As soon as you know you say to yourself, oh, is that all? Well, maybe it's intentional, maybe it's not, but Philip always holds something in reserve. I don't want to know what it is. Leave me my mysteries." She looked at me. "Of course I don't know *you* as yet, but I feel as if I will in ten minutes."

"You couldn't make that fifteen?"

"Twelve, and not a minute more," she laughed.

There were eight or ten more guests who remain a little foggy in memory. There was Jinna somebody who wrote blank and what she described as "tough" verse — rhyming and meter were already becoming passé — and Barney, the bearded man she lived with who was trying to look like Trotsky. They had brought along their two male dachshunds, Bach and Mozart, who kept mounting each other while the would-be communist tried to convert a five-foot-ten and very nearsighted *Vogue* model to the hammer and sickle. There was an off-duty cop who came in around midnight bearing a bottle of genuine confiscated Irish whiskey.

Late in the evening I found Lucy and Philip standing beside me. Lucy tugged at my elbow and whispered, "What has Hollywood got that we don't?"

"I've got to work tomorrow," Philip said. "Stay if you want to. You have your key."

So I had, and I felt a tingle all over my body at the thought of it. Philip Pearson and John Ewing, late of Cottonwood, Montana, now New Yorkers, shared a pad on East Forty-fourth Street, within hailing distance of Broadway, the Met, Carnegie Hall, the Empire State. They were a little drunk on homemade hooch and were at a party in Greenwich Village. They held down editorial jobs on national magazines. They were writers (well, John had sold one short story, had another one in the hopper, and Philip had sold at least two), they would share a literary agent with the likes of F. Scott Fitzgerald and Agatha Christie, and John was only twenty-five and Philip was twenty-four.

"What are you grinning about?" Philip asked, frowning.

"Us," I said. "And what have you got to scowl about? We are very rich."

Philip put his forefinger to his lips as if to keep me from telling a secret. "I know," he said, lowering his voice, "but it's vulgar to boast. Keep it low key."

"I knew you'd say that. I'm afraid you're going to be angry."

"What have you done now?"

"I bought that Rolls this afternoon. I couldn't help myself."

Philip pretended horror. "You didn't drive it off the floor, did you?"

"Yes. Yes, I did."

"Oh, my God. What will people say?"

"Look at it this way," I said. "You've got to be terribly secure to drive your own Rolls-Royce."

"Touché, dear boy. Glad you thought of that." His voice was growing more and more British. "Of course we must humor James and let him motor us to the theatah for rehearsals. You know what an old crosspatch he is."

"Speaking of theatahs. Do you think the Music Box will do? Or is it too — too —"

"Garish? Exactly what I was thinking! Frankly I prefer the Booth. Doesn't intrude on the play, and better acoustics for the *intime* drawing room comedy they've come to expect from us, don't you know."

"Anything to make you and Ina happy, chum."

Lucy and Cornelia were watching us, wondering who would first let the ball get past him. They had obviously never seen Philip in this mood, and were delighted. Philip had the bit firmly in his teeth and was enjoying it, basking in the girls' admiration and the silence that had descended upon the others in the room.

"Speaking of Ina, I had a tête-à-tête with Miss C. last even'," he said. "She has mixed emotions. She is mad to do the play, but loves it so much she is afraid she might let us down. It's a little too real for her, she feels, too flesh and blood."

"Pity," I said, "but admirable. Did she have any suggestions?"

"She mentioned Lynnie, but of course we'd have to build 'Cedric' up a wee bit for Alfred. Would your artistic integrity permit that?"

"I'm tempted, but perhaps we should go with Hope Williams and Glenn Anders after all, but not *tamper*."

"Did I tell you I showed it to Jed?"

"You didn't! You are quite, quite mad."

"I ran into him at Sardi's and he said he'd never speak to us unless we showed *The Goose and the Gander* to him."

I shrugged the mercurial Jed Harris off. Let him settle for hacks like Hecht and MacArthur. "Be interesting to know what he had to say, though. Tell."

"He had but one criticism," Philip said. "There were too many laughs. They come so fast that the audience won't be able to keep up with the plot. We'll have to elide every other one."

He stopped then and looked about him in embarrassment. I had run down, too, but Maureen and Esme and Daniel were applauding, and Joe Tyler cried, "Hear, hear." Lucy put her arms around me, hugged me, and whispered, "You're good for Philip. You loosen him up." Then she grabbed him and kissed him on the mouth.

The party was over. We took a cab and dropped Lucy and Cornelia at their place on Twenty-third Street. Cornelia said we made a good team, but she hoped we had our living arrangements all settled. Things like who goes to the john first when you get ready for bed, who sends out the laundry, who buys the orange juice, and suppose one of you wants to read and his light keeps the other awake?

"No problem. I have a trusty little six-shooter for emergencies," I said.

"Well," she said, "you want to have such things understood or there can be nasty repercussions. When we moved in together, Lucy and I, we decided somebody had to play the bitch about living arrangements. So I looked at Lucy, and then I looked in the mirror, and I said to myself, 'Cornelia, you're perfect casting. You don't even have to read for the part.'"

The glow persisted. Philip and I had shared in an alcoholic improvisation, and however crude it may have been, it was stimulating for me and, I guess, for Philip too, because all the way up to East Forty-fourth Street and even while we got ready for bed, the frown on his brow and the pucker of his lips were absent.

"You go first," I said, bowing dangerously low and sweeping one arm regally toward the john.

"No. Age takes precedence," Philip said.

"Very considerate of you, but you must toil in the vineyards tomorrow. I intend to sleep all day."

"Good idea. I noticed your raveled sleeve needed a little knitting."

He proceeded, unsteadily, to the bathroom and closed the door. I thought I heard the key turn in the lock, but I may have been mistaken. I pulled down the squeaking beds, adjusted the pillows, and then waited an unconscionable while for Philip to accomplish whatever ministrations he felt necessary. I was half-asleep when he finally emerged.

I was drunker than I had thought. "If you're going to take all that long," I said as I lurched toward the john, "it's every man for himself from here on in."

"You know," he said, as if he had not heard me, "I was just thinking."

"A process fraught with peril at this time of night."

"Oh, go fraught yourself," he said.

"Wait till I come out. I'm bursting."

"Okay," I said three minutes later. "You were just thinking."

Philip sat propped up in bed, his eyes beginning to glaze. "What?" he muttered.

"You were just thinking. Out with it. It took you fifteen minutes. It better be good."

He forced his eyes to open. "That silly dialogue of ours at Maureen's. You know, it wasn't half-bad for right off the top of our heads."

"Mine was serviceable," I said, getting into bed. "Yours could do with some revision, but it showed promise."

"I'm not kidding," he went on. "Let's think about writing a play. We might make some money and it could be — well, I hate the term, but it could be fun."

"What's the matter with fun? That's what we're here for, isn't it?"

"Good night," Philip said, and turned over, his back to me.

"Turn out the light," I said. "You're closest."

He reached out, snapped off the light, and then lay down again. I could not go to sleep. Ten minutes later I heard him fighting his pillow.

"Philip, you awake?"

"No. I'm talking in my sleep. One of my many talents."

"There *is* something I want to mention." It was dark. We were unable to see each other's faces. It seemed easier to bring it up this way.

"I can guess. Should the byline be by Pearson and Ewing, or by Ewing and Pearson?"

"No. Not about the play. There'll probably be occasions when you want me out of here, when you need the joint for — well — personal purposes."

"I don't know what you mean." There was that tight voice again.

"A girl. I'm pretty sure there will be times when I'd like the apartment alone for — well — an evening, maybe a weekend. Can we level with each other?"

"Oh *that!*" he said, and he sounded angry. "You can have the place any time you want it. Just let me know and I'll clear out!"

"Well, thanks. Thanks a lot, and the same to you, fella!"

I could feel the adrenalin beginning to pump, and was suddenly wide awake.

I thought about *International* and what it was going to be like to work there. It would be different living in New York as a resident instead of the pampered all-expenses-paid employee of Rupert Hughes. I thought, with a rush of affection, about my parents left behind in Inglewood, and what a tough life they had had and how comparatively easy it all was for me, and had they ever really loved each other, or was it merely custom and tolerance? Write a play? My father had never seen a play, did not read books, didn't even like movies. They were just "made-up," a waste of time, he said.

My thoughts began to skitter. My sister. I must write to her . . . Whatever happened to Gerry and what was her last name? . . . My Lyon and Healy piano . . . shall I send for it when I can afford to? Better wait till I see if the job lasts . . .

The ceaseless bass grumble of the city was finally making coherent thought impossible, and then — through my eyelids — I sensed that Philip had turned on a light. Oh, well, he probably had to go to the john — he'd drunk a hell of a lot — and didn't want to bump into anything. I waited for the sound of footsteps.

There were none.

I opened my eyes. The reading light beside Philip's bed was on. He was not reading or anything. Just lying there with his eyes closed.

After a minute or two he began to snore.

16

The Age of Mrs. Page
A Comedy in Three Acts
by
John Ewing & Philip Pearson
Based on the novel by
Adele Dalton Franklin

ACT ONE

SCENE: The drawing room of the East Hampton residence of the Harwood Pages. This is a bright, formal room that immediately establishes the Pages as persons of good, though extravagant, taste, and one would suspect that it was Mrs. Page who designed and furnished it. Everything matches, every chair is in place, the draperies are soft and feminine, the serene prints on the walls seem less important than their frames. Even the sea, glimpsed through a window at the back, is docile. TIME: The Present. A Friday morning in May. AT RISE: ELENA PAGE, a charming and beautiful woman of thirty-two or -three, but still retaining the bloom of—

"Wait a minute," I said. Philip sat at the typewriter. I was reading over his shoulder. "I read that you're never supposed to be explicit about the age of your star in a stage direction."

"Why not?"

"Well, if she's younger than it says, she won't want to play anybody that old, and if she's older people will say, 'Who does she think she's kidding?' How about 'a charming and beautiful woman of indeterminate years, but still retaining the bloom of et cetera?'"

"But the plot hinges on the age of the woman. It's right there in the title."

"That's so. Well, let it ride."

"You type," Philip said. "I just use two fingers."

I changed places with him.

—youth is discovered arranging a bowl of spring flowers.
She hums "Love, Your Magic Spell Is Everywhere." From its
decorative aviary in one corner of the room a canary begins
to sing along. This amuses Elena. She smiles. Presently the
telephone rings.

"Who's calling?" Philip asked.

"How should I know?" I said. "We've got to think that up. It's
the way you always begin a drawing room comedy. Madame is
discovered arranging flowers as the curtain rises—you know,
you've seen Jane Cowl and Francine Larrimore do it a thousand
times—and pretty soon the telephone rings, Madame answers,
and you slip across a lot of exposition while the audience gets
seated and stops coughing. It doesn't matter who's on the phone,
it's just one of the rules. I read it somewhere."

"You read too much," Philip said.

Philip had discovered *The Age of Mrs. Page,* a number of its
pages still uncut, in the editorial library at the *Unicorn.* Adele
Dalton Franklin, whose only novel it was, had autographed a
copy of the first (and sole) edition and presented it to her cousin,
Elwood Grainger. Grainger had recently departed the *Unicorn* for
a better-paying and more prestigious job as assistant to Frank
Crowninshield at *Vanity Fair,* and left behind him such intellectual chaff as *Mrs. Page* and Gertrude Atherton's *Black Oxen.* Both
books dealt with rejuvenation, but Miss Franklin's treated the
subject whimsically. Which was, possibly, why its sales did not
exhaust a first edition of four thousand, while Mrs. Atherton's
deadly serious, though sometimes unintentionally hilarious,
tome, became a runaway best-seller.

"Read this," Philip said one evening. I had stopped for a drink
and dinner at the corner speakeasy before I came home. Philip
had got there ahead of me.

I looked at the title and glanced at a paragraph or two. "I have
to read crap like this all day," I told him. "I thought I'd go over
and see *June Moon.*"

"You'll never get a ticket."

"It's snowing. There'll be some turnbacks." I closed the book. The blurb on the jacket caught my eye: "The delicious dilemma of Mrs. Page, who dreamed of being a girl once more . . . and then the dream — to the dismay of everyone — came true."

"This doesn't sound like your cup of tea," I said.

Philip cleared his throat, a mannerism, I had discovered, which forecast importance to what he was about to say. "It's not," he said. "But everything's laid out there — in three acts. And the dialogue is pretty good. Of course some of it is arch and old-fashioned, but we could fix that."

"*We?*"

"You and me, you know. The play we were going to write in our spare time. Well, this has got an idea that could work."

"You mean you were serious about the play? I thought you were kidding."

"I am only serious when I am kidding."

I had not thought about our writing a play since the night of Maureen's party. Meanwhile I had settled in at *International,* made casual friends amongst the four other junior editors and secretaries, and found that the job of reading the junk, which was what we called the unsolicited manuscripts that arrived by the bushel every day, was a breeze. Well, a depressing breeze, because one seldom came across anything worth more than a rejection slip. During the first three months I had found only four manuscripts worth passing along to the editor.

Esme Jones of the Ober office had sold the story I had written on the train to Kenneth Littauer at *Collier's* — both *International,* which demanded first look at anything I might write, and Gertrude Lane of *Woman's Home Companion* had declined it with a not-quite-up-our-alley — and I had found time during evenings and weekends to write another, which was making the rounds. Philip too had sold another — with a jump in price for him to $300 — to *Vanity Fair,* where he now had another *in* because of Elwood Grainger.

So far there was no sign of a depression for either Philip Pearson or John Ewing. We even had checking accounts.

Our life together on East Forty-fourth Street, which I guess we had both viewed in prospect with apprehension (I know I had, and Philip always viewed *everything* with apprehension), had produced no intolerable friction. We were being careful — perhaps too careful — not to impinge upon each other. I had never, since that first night, mentioned wanting the apartment to myself, nor had he. We were both usually invited to parties given by members of the Crowd, but if one of us was and the other was not, we made nothing of it.

Sometimes Philip and I had dinner together and sometimes we went on to a play or movie, but we tried to avoid making anything habitual. If we spent evenings apart, as we often did, we never asked where the other had been. (I learned my lesson on that early in the game when he came in late once and I asked him what he'd been doing, and he said, "I was out," and clammed up.)

As for household expenses, we shared and shared alike. The stories we wrote — separately — we instinctively sensed had better be kept that way. Separate. I would not have tolerated his criticism (though I admired his writing), and I am sure he would have had nothing but contempt for mine. (After all, he had been to Harvard and delighted in the use of obscurantisms. He overcame that later.) Our styles were different, his introspective and meticulously executed, his characters indulging in long streams of consciousness, very much in vogue then, cherishing secret neuroses, and pressing thorns to the bosom, while mine . . . well, what happened happened right out there in the open to people I thought I would recognize if I met them on the street, people I might even ask home for a drink or two.

Still, as well as I knew Philip, I was not at all sure that we could merge whatever burgeoning and disparate talents we might have into a play, a form neither of us had ever tried. It could tempt fate. On the other hand, maybe fate was the only thing worth tempting.

The Age of Mrs. Page concerned a moderately happy married woman who, at thirty-two or -three, sees — through her drawing room window — an extremely beautiful young man stretched out to dry on the sand after a dip in the sea. He reminds her of that exquisite marble figure of Shelley reclining forevermore in his niche at University College in Oxford. Obsessed with the kid, Mrs. Page arranges a meeting and asks him to model for her. She has not painted in years, and Mr. Page is delighted that she has decided to take it up again. It will give her something to do while he is away on those business trips, or wherever it is that he goes.

The boy, whose name is just plain Bill, is flattered by Mrs. Page's interest in his body. He can use the two dollars an hour that she pays him. But of course to him she is almost middle-aged, and while he is well-mannered and formal with her (which is charming, she thinks) and calls her "Ma'am," his attention wanders, and through the window he keeps noticing, and sometimes calls out to, giggling, silly girls passing on the beach below. They are so young, so—well—perhaps they are stupid, but the charm of youth compensates for so much. If only she could be one of them again, Mrs. Page sighs.

Well, there is, she hears, a doctor in Vienna who can do the trick with the glands from a certain extremely rare simian.

In brief, Mrs. Page goes to Vienna, has the first injection and returns home with several vials of the stuff to be administered at intervals. She begins to grow younger. And younger. Her dialogue loses its wit and sparkle, and she begins to speak in the slang of her own departed youth as she becomes a silly, giggling girl. And she can no longer paint, having had the lessons at the Art Students League when she was in her early twenties.

Her husband, a likeable, solid, and not very sensitive character, is at first amused, then bored and provoked by what he thinks is a tedious affectation. Bill? Well, Bill goes for her "in a big way" as he puts it, but now that he is being himself and not the polite young two-dollar-an-hour model, she finds him a colossal bore, and tells him so. He walks out on her.

When I had got that far in the plot I looked up and asked, "It's all a dream, isn't it? From the time she makes the wish."

"There's no other way out of that situation," Philip said. "But it's—amusing—isn't it?"

"I don't like the dream bit. Couldn't she have a counter vial and we maybe use the lady and the tiger ending? There she is as the curtain starts to fall, staring at the two vials. One will keep her young as long as she lives, the other will permit her to grow old gracefully. Which does she take, after the curtain falls?"

Philip slapped his hands together, then came over and shook my hand. "Jesus," he said, and it was the first time I had ever heard him take the name of his lord in vain, "you're not as dumb as I thought!"

"It's still got some holes in it," I said, "but—"

"Let me fix us a drink," he said. His hands were trembling with excitement. I joined him in the kitchenette as he poured what passed for scotch into two glasses.

"There's a matter of rights," I said. "You've got to pay for an option, you know."

"But not much," Philip said. "The book is five years old, it never sold well, and nobody wanted the movie rights. I've gone into that already."

"How come?"

He looked sheepish. "Well, when I first read the thing I thought I might do the play alone."

"Oh. I see. And your better self came to the rescue when you realized you couldn't lick it alone." I lifted my glass. "Cheers."

He cleared his throat. "So I asked Elwood if he thought Mrs. Franklin would give me the rights for, say, six months, and he said he was sure she would, for something—oh, minimal."

"What does he mean by minimal?"

"I don't know. Maybe two hundred and fifty dollars? She doesn't need money, he said. He said she'd be quite an experience too."

"Let's skip experience and stick to the money. You couldn't come up with the two hundred and fifty so you decided to let me in on it for half."

"My, my, we learn fast," he said.

"If I didn't think there was money in this thing I'd say take your goddamn book and stuff it."

"Let's try not to let that tone creep into our drawing room comedy dialogue," Philip laughed. "Start thinking Philip Barry, Philip Barry."

"Okay. How would Philip Barry say fuck you, Jack?"

Philip pretended intense pain. "You see what I'm up against for a collaborator? No style." He sighed wearily. "But okay. I'll ask Elwood to make an appointment with Mrs. Dalton. Are you free Saturday afternoon?"

I said . . . yes, I did say it. It was the sort of thing we indulged in during those days because we considered a straight answer out of bounds. That's what other people did, not people like us. "Well, the Hoovers were having a little do for me, but I'll plead the flu or something. Lou Henry's a lamb, but Herb is heavy weather. Understand, I'm going ahead with this project only because I'd like to see Ina Claire trail yards and yards of chiffon across the Pages' drawing room."

"And speak the incomparable dialogue of Pearson and Ewing," Philip said.

I bowed reverently, which was difficult in the kitchenette, so I went back into the living room and bowed again. "That goes without saying," I said. Philip followed me, and bent his knee.

"No, dear fellow. Where would the theatah be if our dialogue went without saying?"

"Make a note of that," I said. "We may find a spot for it."

★ ★ ★

It was obvious that Adele Dalton Franklin did not need money. She and her husband, the industrialist Judson Franklin, lived behind locked gates in what immediately impressed Philip and me as an upper-case mansion overlooking Cold Spring Harbor. We had both seen big houses, but none that quite deserved the word *mansion* before. Resthaven, for that is what it was called, looked as if it had always been there and would continue to stand when all of us were gone. Built of weathered granite, its turreted center section was three stories tall, buttressed by two-storied wings that eventually curved back and formed a U enclosing a sunken garden with greenhouse at the back.

Philip and I were met at the station by an English chauffeur named Hawes whose critical eye informed us that we were not the sort he usually transported in the tonneau of his Lancia. I remember that Philip lolled against the crushed velvet of the seat and tapped an imaginary cigarette as if to dispose of the ashes on the rug, and I picked up the speaking tube and whispered, "What would happen if I blew a raspberry in this thing?"

"Don't you dare, you clown! Remind me never to take you out in society again."

Everything that happened that day seemed almost too good to be true. The gateman coming out of the gatehouse, itself the size of an ordinary dwelling in Cottonwood, to unlock the gates. Two deer feeding on the lawn. The butler opening the door into the great hall before we could ring. (There was no sign of a door bell. "Now that's real class," Philip said. "Remember to have ours removed the instant we get home.")

"Madame is expecting you in the green study," the butler said, and Philip whispered, "I thought it was always a brown study."

"Only when Madame is depressed."

The door opened, and there stood Adele Dalton Franklin. She was moving toward us — one could not call it stepping because the motion was even and constant as if she were on wheels — she was smiling but the smile was almost audible, and extending both of her hands as if she had been waiting for us all her life. She was one of the most beautiful women I had ever seen — tall, elegant, blonde (at least she was blonde that day), and wearing a gray tea gown that even Ina Claire would have envied. She was not young, she was not old. "Indeterminate," I thought. The word was made for her.

She took each of us by a hand, and looked from one to the other as if what she saw gave her nothing but delight. "But you're so *young!*" she cried. "How naughty of you to be so young. And handsome."

The smile became a gay little laugh that tinkled about the study, the room which she had obviously translated into the drawing room described in her novel. "And dear Elwood tells me you are so talented. I really think that's unfair. *Now*. Both of you come right over here into the bay and sit down. We'll have tea, and then we'll talk—if we must—about that silly old novel of mine."

It was theater, pure theater, and I admired her for the act, as I could admire Lynn Fontanne for turning a mere entrance into an event with that throaty, knowing laugh of hers. I turned to look at Philip, and he was *gone*. His lips were slightly parted, and he was staring at Mrs. Franklin reverently, as if in the presence of a miracle at Lourdes. It was a look I was to see many times, usually when Philip was in the presence of charming, beautiful, preferably fragile and unavailable, women.

Mrs. Franklin poured tea. Neither of us liked tea, but how could one refuse a hostess who could turn "Sugar? One lump or two?" into a lyric? She chattered gaily of the Riviera, of London and Paris, of having once seen Réjane in *Zaza*. "A revival, of course, but the old wizard still had élan. Such a pity poor Gloria Swanson ever attempted it, don't you agree?"

Tea finished, she asked us why we wanted to dramatize her silly old novel. It was the second time she had applied that denigration. Obviously she wanted us to deny its pertinence. Philip glanced at me and coughed, as if to say, You take it, and I said that I did not think it silly at all, that it was charming, whimsical, and—well—"we'd like to take a crack at it."

Philip looked pained at that crass phrase, but it did not seem to ruffle Mrs. Franklin. "Maybe I say it's a silly old book so nobody else can say it first," she laughed. "Actually, I should describe it as Adele's Conceit, because she certainly is not a writer."

"Oh, but you are, she is," Philip protested.

"Well, whatever," she dismissed it. The book was merely something she had done because, "as they say, idle hands are the devil's workshop. It was that abysmally hot summer of twenty-three, and dear Judson had been called to Washington to try to help Mr. Coolidge—such an odd little man—unscramble the mess left by Warren Harding." She had been in this very room, "and I walked over to this window—it was open—to find a breath of air." She illustrated, breathing deeply and tossing back her head until the line of her porcelain throat was that of the moon at quarter. "And I stood here with my eyes closed for a long moment. Then I opened them and there — right *there* — was Bill, looking like a Greek god. Of course Bill was not the young man's name — God knows what it was, I never met him — but for some reason I began to muse, What if? What if I weren't me, but I was a lonely frustrated woman, and this young man, this boy answered a suppressed desire. And suppose I were a painter." She paused and looked from one of us to the other in the most flattering way. "Isn't that the way it sometimes is even with you professionals?"

"It happened to me coming east on the Chief not long ago," I said. "I just sold the story to *Collier's*."

"You *see?* I knew it!" she cried. "Well, enough of how Adele Dalton Franklin is inspired to create her deathless prose! Frankly, I had forgotten all about *Mrs. Page,* when Elwood telephoned the other day and told me about you two young playwrights. I cannot tell you how flattered I am to be noticed."

Philip and I looked at each other. It was the moment for us to get down to specifics. He remained mute, so it was up to me. "What we wanted to know, Mrs. Franklin, is — would you give us an option on the property for — well — a year, let's say a year. That ought to give us time to dramatize it and get a production, if we can do it at all."

"Done!" Mrs. Franklin said. "Take as much time as you need."

"You mean you'll let us do it?" Philip said breathlessly.

"It's my pleasure," she said. "And I shall be fascinated to see how you young geniuses improve upon my silly old novel."

"There's just one thing, Mrs. Franklin. How much do you want? We can't afford more than — well — how does two hundred and fifty dollars strike you?"

The moment I said it I knew I was wrong. The mention of any sum under a million dollars inside those granite walls would sound vulgar. What could $250 mean to a woman like this?

"Oh, dear boy," she said, "let's not mention money, shall we not? Take my book and do with it what you will. And — well — if it is ever produced on Broadway, then — if that is satisfactory to you, we can — 'go halvers.'" She grinned and wrinkled her perfect nose like a mischievous gamine, then extended both her hands and said, "Let's shake on it!"

Thus the Goddess stepped down off her pedestal and completed Philip's total bemusement.

"Well—well, gosh," he said. "I don't know what to say, Mrs.—"

"*Adele*," she said, and then—looking him square in the eye—"*John*."

"I'm John," I said. "He's Philip."

"Oh, how stupid of me. Adele, you may go stand in the corner." She marched stiffly toward a corner of the room and stood directly beneath her own full-length portrait. If it was not a Sargent it was a good imitation.

"Please, Mrs. Franklin—Adele—" Philip said. "It doesn't matter."

She peered over her shoulder pitifully. "Then you both forgive me?"

"Certainly," I said, "what's to forgive?"

She took us by the arms and subtly began to drift toward the door, murmuring how sorry Judson would be not to have met us, but that he was "doing something abysmally dull about a merger of something in Chicago this weekend. Or is it Pittsburgh? And now I don't mean to rush you, but if you're going to catch the five-seventeen back to the city . . ."

"I can't tell you, Mrs.—Adele—what this has meant to me—to us, I mean," Philip said, and made a fumbling gesture toward shaking hands with her, and then thought better of it.

"You are dears, both of you," she said.

"Just one more thing," I said, as the butler opened the massive door ahead of us. "About a contract. Do you want your—your lawyer or your agent to draw one up, or should I ask Harold Ober if—"

"*Contract?*" She looked stricken. "I thought we were friends."

"Yes, I know. And we are," I went on doggedly, "but they say just in case—well—suppose one of us died."

She turned pale, or perhaps it was only a trick of light. "Don't speak that word to me," she said. "I won't *hear* that word." She turned to Philip and almost whimpered. "Tell John never to mention death to me, please, Philip?"

"We'll never mention it again," Philip said staunchly.

As Elwood Grainger had forewarned us, Adele Dalton Franklin was an experience.

★ ★ ★

Each of us had seen many plays and read dozens more, but seldom until that winter had we bothered to wonder why one could be a bore while another, on the same subject, was moving and stimulating. Now, faced with constructing and writing one of the damn things—and many times it was a thing that we damned and were tempted to drop in the garbage chute at the end of the hall—we suddenly realized that we knew relatively nothing about how to crank it up and make it go. Oh there were those timeworn conventions like the ones already mentioned: Don't be exact about the heroine's age, and discover Madame on stage fixing the flowers, and then the phone rings and you get across a batch of exposition. *What* exposition?

"You might at least have gone to the 47 *Workshop* while you were right there," I chided Philip as we stared gloomily at that first blank piece of paper in the L. C. Smith.

"Baker had gone over to Yale by the time I got to Harvard," he said.

"Then you should have gone to Yale."

Rupert Hughes, who had written any number of successful comedies a decade or more earlier, had once mentioned what used to be a cardinal rule. I repeated it to Philip: Give your audience a wish in the first act. (Say, boy meets girl and audience wants them to get married.) Thwart the wish in the second act. (Boy loses girl through some misunderstanding or shenanigan of the heavy.) Grant the wish in the third act. (Boy gets girl and villain gets comeuppance.)

It was a fairly simple formula, and when we examined the current crop of Broadway plays we were surprised to discover how many playwrights had knowingly, or instinctively, used it.

But how would that formula apply to *The Age of Mrs. Page,* we wondered. Our (and Mrs. Franklin's) Mrs. Page, who, whatever her age, was old enough to know better, hankered after a very young man. Would an audience want her to get him, no matter what the consequence? Or would they want him to escape her? A problem right there. We decided, finally, that they would want (the wish) her to flirt with, and come dangerously close to, the titillating tragedy of seducing the boy, but in the end be saved from it. We were not, after all, writing heavy drama, and we must satisfy the self-righteous as well as the prurient who still felt they ought not to be. Of course, there was a small segment of the audience that would cheer a woman for doing what they themselves would not have the courage to do. The lady and the tiger ending ought to satisfy both elements, as well as generate discussion, as they waited for taxis outside the theater, about which vial the fascinating Mrs. Page swallowed after the curtain came down.

That momentous problem solved, all we had to do was begin that telephone conversation with — with *Whom?*

I have no copy of *The Age of Mrs. Page,* nor did I discover one in Philip's dreary apartment, but I remember the play's composition as being one of the happiest, most joyful, and exhilarating times of my life.

There is little joy or exhilaration in locking yourself into a room alone and staring at the blank wall above your typewriter while you wait for the words, the ideas to flow. (Flow? You're lucky to grunt them out.) You muse, when you are a young man, what the hell am I doing here? What makes you think you're a writer? What could you possibly have to say that hasn't been said a thousand times, and much better? Anyhow, suppose you force it out. It won't sell. No editor — and most of them are certified fools — no editor would be a big enough fool to be fooled by what I'm going to write. What am I doing, me, a grown man, sitting here, indulging in this mental masturbation? (Who called it that?) Better I should be mowing the lawn — or washing the car — or playing the piano.

A collaboration is an entirely different bowl of wax. It can be a purgatory sentence with two prisoners locked in a single cramped cell from which — no matter how they may despise each other — only a joint, agonized, shoulders-to-the-squeaking-wheel effort will finally set them free to go their blessed separate ways.

Or — perhaps once in a lifetime if you are lucky — it can be the way it was with Philip and me.

We had been through all the preliminaries, the endless excuses to keep from coming to grips, psychic ailments, dates that could not be broken, what's the use of starting before we see a little clear time ahead of us, etc.

We convulsed ourselves (and further delayed going to work) by quoting future reviews. "The tone of *The Age of Mrs. Page* miraculously bridges that yawning rift between the sophistication of *Candlelight* and the heartbreak of Barrie's *Mary Rose*." Benchley would write that for the *New Yorker,* of course. And Alexander Woollcott could not resist devoting one whole segment of his "Shouts and Murmurs" in the same publication to Broadway's biggest smash since *The Royal Family.* "It has been many a harvest moon since these old eyes have crinkled with laughter while dripping salty tears," he would begin. Oh, all the notices were superb, but the *Daily News* missed the point. Too subtle for a mass audience.

But finally one Saturday afternoon we were faced with a few words on paper. There was the title, the byline (whose name would come first we would fight about later), *Scene, Time, At Rise,* our leading lady discovered on stage arranging flowers, "Presently the telephone rings." The moment of truth had arrived.

If we introduced a character via the telephone we would have to bring him/her on stage later, wouldn't we? Otherwise it would be a mere convenience. So, who could it be? Somebody, Philip said, pacing and muttering to himself behind me, somebody who could be useful to us.

Preferably somebody amusing, I said. "Neither *Bill* nor *Mr. Page* can have much humor. Which, so far, leaves us with *Elena* and . . . who?"

"Another man?" Philip said. "A wise old uncle?"

I frowned. "I'm sick of wise old uncles. How about a woman friend? Somebody who knows *Elena* well, so when she's lying to people — and herself — this character sees through her so the audience will know what's going on underneath?"

"You're right," Philip said with enthusiasm.

"They went to college together."

"Radcliffe. I know that background."

"And Elena got married right out of college, but what's her name? . . . Give this dame a name," I said. "Don't just stand there."

"Ah . . . Phyllis — Evelyn — Sarah — Louella — Maxine — "

"No. We're stuck with one fancy moniker — Elena. Something plain — ordinary — salty — "

"Kate!" Philip said. "If she was good enough for Shakespeare — "

"Kate it is!" I turned to the typewriter and wrote:

ELENA (into phone): Hello? . . . Oh, it's you, Kate.

"An immortal line," Philip said, "destined to live alongside 'The son of a bitch stole my watch!' "

And so we were off, and we seldom stopped for anything but food and sleep. We would rush home from our offices every evening, and refuse weekend invitations in order to push on with *Mrs. Page,* who was more real, more demanding, far more stimulating than any of our friends. We began to respect and depend upon each other as we never had before, the way one depends upon a partner in a marriage. We were concerned, for the first time, about each other's health, about getting enough sleep, about eating properly and evacuating regularly.

Philip's night-light, his nail biting, the peculiar way he walked became endearing character traits instead of annoying habits, for he was — in a manner of speaking — a part of me, and his flaws were mine, and mine his.

Together, we both realized, I think, we were more than the sum of our individual selves. The blend of the two of us became a separate entity, a *being,* that had little to do with either of us

alone. Oh, it was not always so. There were times when we
fought over a major — or a minor — point, but those times were
rare and ended without rancor. Usually, when one of us sat at the
typewriter and the other paced, it would soon begin to happen.
We could feel it tugging at us, the way you can feel your boat
being slowly sucked out of the shallows into a strong current.
Ideas, lines, gambits would nibble at our hooks. One of us would
say, "I think she says thus and so," and the other might nod and
say "Fine," or "Yes, but wouldn't it be better — or funnier, or
more economical — if . . ." And then we would agree, or argue,
and further juggle and polish the line. And we would know —
after a certain passage of time — when the current finally left us in
the doldrums. One of us would yawn and say, "Well, that's it for
me tonight," and the other never pushed on alone, or even
wanted to.

Once, as we got ready for bed, I said, "Philip, do you think it's
as good as we think it is?" and he laughed, and said, "It couldn't
be. But who cares? I love doing it."

I never heard him use the word "love" before.

★ ★ ★

It was during this period that Philip began to skip mass. The first
time I noticed it he claimed he had forgotten until too late. But
on a Sunday morning early in May I said, "Why don't you get up
and go to early mass this morning, get yourself all holied up, and
then we'll have the rest of the day for the sinful Mrs. Page."

"I'm holy enough for today," he said.

I went into the kitchenette and poured myself a cup of black
coffee. "You want some coffee?" I called.

"Yeah, thanks."

I poured another cup and carried it over to Philip. I began to
laugh.

"What's so funny?"

"I was just thinking of something. Remember, a long time ago,
we were just kids, you asked me if we didn't have the Holy
Mother in our church, and I said, no, we have Mrs. Schilling."

"Who was Mrs. Schilling?"

"The first reader. That's when I was a Christian Scientist."

He sat up in bed. "When did you stop going to church?"

"At what I laughingly call the age of reason, I guess. Or maybe it was when I found out that the Man Upstairs was usually tied up in conference when I tried to get Him on the horn."

"Don't you believe in anything?"

"Sure. In what I see and feel and hear, and the rest of it nobody's ever going to prove, so why worry? But you're a Catholic, so you'd better go to mass or you'll go to hell."

"Are you trying to make me feel guilty?"

"I just thought if I was going to get a decent day's work out of you it would be better not to stop in the middle of it for you to go say your beads and bend the knee."

He got out of his bed and folded it into the wall without bothering to arrange the sheets or blankets. He seemed angry. "Don't worry about me," he said, starting for the bathroom. "I'll be ready to work in a minute."

"What you're saying is," I said, "it doesn't matter whether you go to mass or not. You can go to confession and be absolved of any sin. So why don't you sin more?"

"I don't think that's any of your business." He slammed the door into the bathroom, but five minute later emerged fully dressed, his unruly red hair slicked down, and said, "Okay. Where were we?"

17

The play was finished. We had rewritten it three times. Now it was typed and bound professionally (twenty-five cents a page) and we held it in our hands, a palpable thing, our creation, our brainchild. By John Ewing and Philip Pearson out of Adele Dalton Franklin. (We had tossed a coin to determine the final sequence in the byline, and I had won. "Or lost," Philip gloomed. "If you get bad notices they always blame the first name.") It was time for *Mrs. Page* to make her debut, time for the world to pass judgment, and we dreaded it. As long as we kept her to ourselves she was a creature of immaculate conception who all but glowed in the dark, but if the world said her eyes were too close together or her legs bowed, what would happen to the pride of parenthood?

Having no play agent, we asked Harold Ober if he would read it and perhaps suggest someone. "I'm really no judge of plays," Ober said after he read it. (Did that mean he did not like it? You never knew about Harold. He played his cards close to the vest.) "But it seems a professional job" (we could breathe a little deeper), "so I suspect I'd better pass the buck and send you young fellas over to Dick Madden at Century Play Company. If he likes it . . . well, I can recommend him highly, and if he doesn't he knows what he's talking about. He's a gentleman and much respected in a not very respectable field."

The offices of Century Play Company were impressive, more in the style of a book publisher than a theatrical enterprise. Badly lighted, smelling faintly of must and dust, the shelves were crammed higgledy-piggledy with published and unpublished plays, histories, biographies, and varied ancient and modern theatrical memorabilia. The fourteen-foot-high walls — those few not paved with books — were crazy quilts of photographs and caricatures, even a few paintings, of past and present reigning stars, producers, and playwrights. At a quick glance I recognized Otis Skinner as Haaj, Ethel Barrymore as a nun (that would be *The Kingdom of God*), and her brothers in *The Jest*. Up there over the receptionist's desk (she had asked us to wait a few minutes while Madden completed a long-distance call) was Eugene O'Neill wearing an eternal frown, to his right George Kaufman pretending to look saturnine, and beside him Elmer Rice, grinning. Rice's *Street Scene* was still packing them in and paying him a handsome royalty each week. He could well grin, I thought, and wondered furtively if one day our photographs would be hanging there.

I put a cigarette in my mouth, but my lighter had run dry. Philip struck a match from a flap labeled Schrafft's (which seemed anomalous in this rarefied atmosphere). I had to grab his hand to keep it from shaking out the flame.

"You may go in now," the receptionist said, and handed me another flap of matches. It was labeled Child's. I felt better.

Richard Madden was not the sort of man who would ever say anybody's play "stank." "Somewhat amateurish," perhaps, or, in extreme cases, "Lacking any discernible merit," but never "stank." One could understand why he and Harold Ober were friends. Both were gentlemen and exuded what I could only think of as quality.

Madden's voice was soft but resonant, with no regional accent. He looks like somebody I know, I thought, and then realized it was nobody I knew personally but Ronald Colman, the way Colman would probably look by the time he was old, say fifty or fifty-five.

"Harold tells me you gentlemen have a new play for me," Madden said after seating us in deep leather (slightly cracked) chairs across the desk from his own.

"We hope you like it well enough to take it on," I said, trying for just the proper tone, not arrogant, but not too humble either. After all, we thought it was good.

"It's our first play," Philip said. That was the wrong tone. It sounded like an apology.

"Apparently my friend Harold thought highly enough of it to send it along to me," Madden said. "And by the authors personally."

"He doesn't know anything about plays," Philip said. If I had been close enough I would have kicked him.

"Oh, come, come," Madden said. "Harold may not be a professional critic, thank God, but he's a competent judge of writing in any form, I should think. Wouldn't you?" He turned and addressed me alone with that last.

"I certainly would!" I agreed with emphasis.

"I assume you have a copy there in that nice, clean envelope?" He smiled and pointed at the eleven-by-thirteen manila package in my hand. I gave it to him. He opened it, and seemed to heft the manuscript. "Three acts?"

"Yes, sir," Philip said. "Present day."

"Nice title," Madden said. "I like a rhyme if you don't have to strain for it. Mrs. Page. A female star called for?"

We both nodded. "A very big part," I offered. "She — runs the gamut."

A smile tugged at the corners of his mouth. "How old?"

"In her midthirties," Philip said.

"But we don't want to be — categorical," I said. (God, where had that word come from?) "She could be in the early forties." Why was I offering to compromise before anyone even suggested it? "And only one set."

"Ah, yes. A drawing room." His voice sounded a bit weary.

His desk telephone buzzed. Madden asked to be excused, then picked it up. "Yes? . . . Oh, very well . . . of course, Miss Baker. Ask him to come in." He put down the phone and turned to us apologetically. "Sorry. Lester Force. An old friend, very old and very old friend, a dear man and a character. Perhaps the name rings a bell? No, you're of another generation. Lester dates back to the heyday of Belasco. He knew Irving and Booth. Manager-director. Had his own theater, his own stock company. Force in name and force in nature, people used to say. Nobody like him these days. Lester does not believe in appointments — those are for the common herd. He just — blows in when he's passing by."

The door opened and Lester Force blew in. It seemed more likely, from the look of him, that the wind had blown him in, for he was very small and gave the impression (an erroneous one, we discovered) of fragility. He must have been eighty—eighty-five?—and stood no taller than five feet five, a couple of those inches contributed by Adler elevator shoes, I suspect, for he tottered in a rickety manner upon occasion. He wore pearl-gray vest and spats, and carried a gold-handled cane. His hair—what little was left—made such a perfect silver halo that the bald patch remaining in its center suggested a rakish, pink yarmulke. He was immaculately clean and, in passing, wafted an odor of Aqua Velva our way. The words *jaunty* and *elf* came to mind.

He did not notice us as Madden rose and came out from behind his desk to greet him. "Richard," Lester Force said, "I was passing by, and I suddenly thinks to myself, thinks I, if my debonair old friend Madden is not—"

"I'd never forgive you if you hadn't," Madden said, shaking his hand, but his visitor did not hear him and was plunging on.

" — in the act of swindling one of my helpless competitors or perhaps tumbling some giggling doxy on yon creaking couch, I'll drop in and pass the time of day with the darlin' son of a bitch."

"As you can see, I am doing neither, Lester," Madden laughed, "but I'm afraid you're giving me a bad notice in the eyes of my new friends"—he glanced at the names on our manuscript—"John Ewing and Philip Pearson."

Force whirled and raised his stick before him, as if we might be highwaymen about to belay him, but his wrinkled old face was instantly split by a smile.

"Richard, you should have told me you had visitors."

"What difference? You'd have barged in anyhow, wouldn't you?" Madden said.

"Of course. But I'd have made a better entrance."

"You couldn't have, Mr. Force," Philip said, smothering a nervous cough.

"Ah, but you don't know me. And what brings you two innocents into this rapscallion's den, may I ask?"

Philip and I turned to Madden for a cue. He shrugged. "Lester is innately curious," he sighed. "You might as well tell him."

"We've just given Mr. Madden our new play," I said.

"What in the devil for?"

"Well, for his opinion," Philip explained.

"Ah, the follies of youth, as foolish as asking a whore if she is a virgin. The difference, the whore will tell a practical lie, while the agent, who has no opinion and deserves none, will invent one to distress you. No opinion means a damn except the producer's. So, be kind enough, dear sirs, to retrieve the play under discussion from this piss-elegant huckster and hand it to me."

Lester Force was actually standing there before us with his hand out, awaiting the play script.

"Les, old man," Madden placated, "much as we would all value your opinion, there's the element of time — and priority. I haven't read the play. These young men are anxious to have my word on it, and I have promised to read it over the weekend."

"You think I'm an old dodderer, don't you, boy?" Lester Force was, as he would probably have said himself, getting his dander up.

"That's ridiculous, Lester. You know how my wife and I both feel about you. You're — family."

"Who should be locked up on the third floor."

"Oh, Lester, let's not get into a silly squabble. Why — tell me *why* — you want to read this play and — well, we'll see."

"Because I've been looking for just the right play for the last five years. If David can produce one at his time of life, why can't Lester Force?" *David* was Belasco, of course, and at age seventy-seven had just produced *Tonight or Never,* a hit with Helen Gahagan and Melvyn Douglas.

There was, as they say, a strained silence. Finally I said, "We'll be honored to let you read our play, Mr. Force." Force's hand was still out. Reluctantly, helplessly, poor Richard Madden picked up his copy of *The Age of Mrs. Page* and handed it to him.

He had not given up completely. He laid his arm affectionately across the shoulders of the feisty little bantam, who was only now beginning to settle his feathers. "Let's be realistic, Les. Suppose you like this play — any play. What can you do about it? You'd need an organization — a star — a theater. You've been out of it all for so long that —"

"One thing you seem to forget, Dick," Lester Force said, looking down at the manuscript. "Mmm. I like the title," he murmured, almost to himself. "Five words. Five-word titles are always lucky for me. Remember my production of *The Taming of the Shrew*, and *The Man Who Stood Still*"?

"Barely," Madden said under his breath. "Now what is it that we forget?"

"Speak up, Richard." Lester Force cupped his hand to his ear. "You've been mumbling lately. Bad habit and discourteous."

Madden took a deep breath and raised his voice. "You said that there was one thing I seemed to forget."

"I did? No recollection of it. Oh, yes. You forget I have money. There's a depression on. All the play backers have lined up and jumped down into Wall Street. But I have money. My own money, made on five-word titles. Myself and the Theater Guild, we're the only people with money to produce any damn play that suits our fucking fancy. So, thank you, gentlemen. You will hear from me in the a.m."

Lester Force bowed low, steadied himself with his gold-headed walking stick, and, sweeping an invisible opera cloak over one shoulder, strolled out. It was a star exit. I half expected to hear the splatter of applause. Instead, Philip and I turned to catch Richard Madden shaking his head in total befuddlement. Then he began to laugh.

"I must apologize," he said.

"Oh, that's all right," Philip said.

"What else could we do?" I asked. "He's such a delightful old party. I almost wish he *could* produce our play. He'd be so much fun to have around."

The next morning at ten-fifteen Madden ran me down at *International*. I had just finished reading (first paragraph only) a young love story about a penniless chauffeur and a wealthy debutante written by an aspiring author from Greybull, Wyoming, who could not spell. "You'll never believe this," Madden said over the phone. "Lester Force wants an option on your play."

"Oh, my God!" My voice must have sounded as if I had just heard of a death in the family because the other four readers in the big room all looked up.

"I felt I ought to tell you," Madden went on. And waited.

"Do you think he's serious about it?"

"Oh, of that I have no doubt." Another pause.

"What do we do now?"

"I should think this calls for consultation. I suggest that you, Mr. Pearson, and I get together as quickly as possible. Naturally, Lester wants a decision yesterday. The dear, outrageous man has always been impossible. Oh, yes. And bring me another copy of the play, if you will. I'd like to read it."

★   ★   ★

The three of us were grouped again as we had been only the day before in Richard Madden's office, but the situation had altered drastically. We were no longer his supplicants. He had permitted us to be involved in an awkward predicament. (A fine fix, my father might have called it.) With our formal greetings I had handed him another copy of *The Age of Mrs. Page*. "I must read this," he said (you damn well better, I thought), laid it on his desk, and placed a paperweight on it, as if to keep it from evanescing.

"I presume you two have had a private discussion before coming here?"

"Yes, sir," Philip said. I nodded.

"And did you reach a conclusion?"

"We wanted to hear what you have to say," I said. "After all, we are — neophytes. I guess that translates as we don't know our ass from a hole in the ground in this business."

Philip's pained expression translated as disapproval of such a barnyard cliché, but Madden merely sighed. "After all these years, I can say the same thing about myself. The theater is the only profession in the world in which we are all amateurs every time we become involved in a project. It is all forever new."

"How much will Force give for an option?" I asked.

"Five hundred dollars." He lifted a corner of his desk blotter and extracted an envelope. "Here's the check. In case we decide to cash it." He placed the envelope beneath the paperweight atop the play.

"Honestly, Mr. Madden," Philip said. "Would anybody with any real judgment—a director, the actors, the staff in general—take Lester Force seriously enough to go to work for him?"

Madden cocked his head and smiled. "You'd be surprised at how sufficient of the long green can transform a scoffer into an apostle."

"But should we let it do that to us? And such a little of it," I laughed. "Five hundred dollars—two-fifty apiece. Two-twenty-five after your commission is paid, Mr. Madden."

"All I can say is, it's the best offer we've had today," he said.

"But nobody else has had a chance to see it. What about Gilbert Miller—ah—Arthur Hopkins—the Guild?" Philip wanted to know.

Madden's hands were folded atop his desk, his thumbs circling each other absently. "Mmm," he said. "They take months—years—to decide. Then a thousand to one, the answer is no."

"Herman Shumlin," I went on. "Jed Harris?"

"Not Jed," Madden said. "I wouldn't subject you to Jed. You're too young. Not that you wouldn't age fast."

"Are you saying," I asked, "that we ought to settle for Lester Force?"

"That's up to you. Let me say this for dear old Lester. He's honest. He hasn't done anything for years, but that's no proof of dementia. God knows he has compounded his eccentricities lately, but the mind, the enthusiasm still survive intact. I suspect that he does not know much about modern taste—who does? Who would have said that a black Sunday-school teacher masquerading as De Lawd would be the hit of the season? And in this instance Lester is probably motivated primarily by jealousy of David Belasco. He wants to show that he can do it too, and he's considerably older than Belasco. But maybe none of those things is important. The only thing that matters is that he's got money and he wants to do your play."

Philip and I looked at each other. After a long moment he said, "It would be for only six months."

"Just what I was going to say," I said.

"I think you've made a sensible decision. At worst it will delay us for only six months. And there's always the possibility that the old boy will — as De Lawd says — pass a miracle." He lifted the paperweight once more and picked up Lester Force's check. "I'll have Miss Baker make out checks to each of you for two hundred and twenty-five dollars while you sign the representation agreement with Century." He handed each of us a form. "No jokers. Just the standard form." He smiled. "Ten percent off the top to Shylock, the same one we have with John Galsworthy and Michael Arlen."

"Oh, by the way," Madden said as he handed us our checks. "Lester would prefer to keep all this — under the rose — until he has signed a star and a director. Then he will merit a feature story and a headline, not just a squib in Zolotow's column. Something like 'Lester Force returns to the theater. Signs Kit Cornell to star and Guthrie McClintic to direct new play.'"

We emerged from the Century Play Company building and joined the cakewalk of humanity on Madison Avenue. I glanced at my watch. It was five-thirty p.m. Five-thirty on May 14, 1930. I tried to fix that date in my head. When you are only twenty-six years old and have just signed a contract to have your play produced on Broadway (well, an option), the moment of it ought to be memorable, oughtn't it?

We were both high, slightly breathless. It seemed odd that nobody noticed and asked why, that none of these office workers and clerks and late-afternoon shoppers hurrying home, or wherever, was aware of us and our . . . well, it would be stretching things to label it good fortune, wouldn't it? But why not stretch it a little?

"I think we ought to go out on the town tonight," I said. "Live it up. Celebrate."

"We're not sure we have anything to celebrate," Philip said.

"Then maybe we'd better gather ye rosebuds before the frost hits them. I'll call Maureen, you call Lucy or whoever, and we'll play successful playwrights. You're Philip Barry and I'm Sam Behrman."

Philip seemed to be hesitating. "Madden said we weren't to talk about it yet."

"He didn't mean you couldn't tell Maureen and Lucy."

"I have another date," Philip said after a few more steps.

"Well, why didn't you say so. Who with?"

"Someone I know."

"How dull of you," I said, and waited for him to explain. We walked a full block, passed Tripler's, where a vicuña jacket in the window lured me. Well . . . if we had a smash . . . Philip remained silent. It seemed odd. The whole time we had been working on the play neither of us had separate dates.

Then something occurred to me. The play was finished. Maybe sex was thawing after the deep freeze. The drain of a protracted creative session could be as effective a libido suppressor as saltpeter, I had heard.

Well, the pressure was off now.

"Look, Philip," I said. "If you want me to clear out of the joint tonight, just say so. I understand."

"Why should I want you to clear out?"

"You said you had a date."

"So?" He was being either stupid or deliberately obtuse.

"Well — I was remembering what we said — oh, all right, what *I* said — about if one of us should . . ." For some fool reason I was finding it hard to say what I meant. You're a big boy now, I thought. Men talk to each other about their sex lives. You've known this man since you were a dirty-minded, horny adolescent. What's the matter? Get with it.

"In case you want to lay some dame, you wouldn't need a witness, would you?"

Philip's freckles turned brick red. His short, tight steps grew shorter, his tan brogans hammered the pavement. Cornelia had been right. He did walk as if his underwear pinched him. "You don't need to worry about that," he finally said.

I felt an urge to tell someone, though it did not seem quite fair of me to break our news to anyone Philip knew. Maureen would be thrilled for him—pleased for me, too—but he should share her first flush of delight. Lucy and Cornelia would be polite about it, but they might think I was showing off (they would be right) if I telephoned and said, "Say, guess what? Philip and I have sold an option on our play."

After Philip and I separated, he to keep his anonymous date, I strolled west on Forty-second Street. It was still early, not yet six. A pale sun was sinking reluctantly behind the Times flatiron into the murk of Hoboken and stirring up evening zephyrs redolent of the Jersey flats.

I crossed Fifth and paused to consider the effect of the bronze light on the gray pile of the Public Library. Behind it lay the dirty expanse of Bryant Park, dotted with papers and refuse, drabbing off toward Sixth Avenue, the habitat of trollops and tramps and playwrights who could not face Broadway after being downed for the count by the critics. I heard an apologetic, cultured voice murmur, "A dime for an apple, sir?"

I turned to confront a well-dressed, middle-aged man extending a very red McIntosh apple in my direction. He could not seem to meet my eye. A few more apples lay on a crumpled brown sack at his feet. A young woman—his daughter?—with a faded shawl dripping from her bony shoulders, gripped the fist of a big-eyed two-year-old girl. One sock was pinned to her drawers, the other sagged over an old shoe. There was a well-defined smudge of dirt across one cheek. It was somehow phony. The child could have been out of central casting, recruited from the file labeled Pathetic Tots, Ages One to Five.

Perhaps the setup was genuine. Who could tell these days? The wrong sort, as some grim wit had recently been quoted by F.P.A., was panhandling. Still, it made scant difference to a budding playwright on his way to inspect future Broadway haunts. I gave the man a fifty-cent piece. He reached for change. "Never mind, that's for the little girl," I said. He whispered, "Thank you." I moved on, feeling uneasily like operetta gentry scattering largesse amongst the forelock-tugging peasants. I heard him call,

"Here's your apple, Mister." I paused, but could not suddenly switch roles. I said, "Oh, that's all right. Keep it." The man's voice rose. It sounded strained. "Take it, please. I am not a beggar."

He handed the apple to the child. She toddled over and dropped it into my hand. Then I turned and, without daring to look back, hurried on toward the Great White Way.

I ordered a shrimp cocktail, frog legs, and iced coffee at Sardi's, where I sat alone at a table for four in the middle of the room. Nobody who was anybody was there yet. Oh, the theatrical oasis was half-full — tourists probably. The Lunts, Noel and Tallu, Kit and Bea, and Fred and Adele, the regulars who would be obsequiously ushered to favorite spots along the wall beneath their own caricatures, these were night bloomers who would wither if exposed to the setting sun.

I was almost finished eating when I noticed the maitre d' leading a very old couple past me. (I could scarcely escape noticing, because the cape of the old man swept across my head in passing.) He seated them next to me. The woman was tall and thin, wore a red wig, slightly askew, and a jeweled dog collar. She had that resistless mien, that overpowering sense of self, of an actress. Across her shoulders was carelessly slung a fawn-colored cashmere cardigan, under it a pale-blue chiffon dinner dress that had obviously been the creation of a couturier but was now out of fashion and slightly ombréd by time. The bodice was heavy with bugle beads appliquéd in a paisley design, and her long gnarled fingers were studded with costume rings, as if to hide the arthritic bumps. (Or *were* they costume?) She would be, I thought, perfect casting for Miss Havisham. Who was she? Or rather, who had she been?

She scrounged through her gold mesh reticule and presently surfaced with a yellowing ivory lorgnette. She held it to her eyes, squinted at the menu, muttered, "I can't see a fucking thing," and laid the glasses elegantly on the table beside her plate. She touched the hand of her companion.

"It's been so long since we dined out," she said. "Suggest something, Lester, old poop."

Lester Force looked up at the extraordinary old woman and smiled. "You are exquisite tonight, Belle. Suppose we raise the curtain on our celebration with a bottle of Moët and Chandon, nineteen thirteen."

"Are you joking, or do I detect the onset of senility?" she said, and giggled like a young girl. "You old goat, if you had wanted to make me tiddly in order to have your way with me later, you should have hied me to a speakeasy."

She reached across the table, slid a bejeweled hand on one of his, and squeezed hard. They stared into each other's eyes like — like adolescents in love, but far more tenderly. "Lester," she said after a long moment, "tell me I don't need to worry about you."

"You don't need to worry about me. But why do you ask?"

"Well, face it. You're not a kid. A new play at your time of life?"

"Is precisely what I need. Far more effective than monkey glands."

I had been unable to take my eyes off the couple. At last the woman became aware of me and frowned. Lester Force turned to see what was causing her discomfort and scowled, as if to say, Why can't people mind their own business? He was either very nearsighted or — humiliating thought — did not remember that he had ever met me. I asked for my check and left.

I strolled through the theatrical district — up Broadway, through Shubert Alley, down Forty-fifth to Eighth, back up Forty-sixth. Marquee lights were winking on at the Booth, the Plymouth, the Morosco, the Music Box where any world you chose would materialize at about eight-thirty. Bright, ordered worlds where insoluble problems were presented and you could count on their neat solution by eleven. Groups of ragged black boys were already jockeying for position — despite policing by New York's finest on horseback — ready to shuffle and sing and grin for whatever coins they could charm out of playgoers between the acts.

It was still barely eight o'clock. I decided to go to the Capitol and see Greta Garbo in *Anna Christie*. "Garbo talks!" screamed the ads. I knew she could talk. I had met her when we were both twenty years old at MGM, but it was nice to hear that deep voice with its Swedish accent drawl, "Give me a viskey straight, an' don' be stingy, baby."

I got back to our apartment at ten-thirty. I tried to read, but that was not the sort of communication I craved at the moment. What I needed, I supposed, was a girl, but I didn't know any girls like that in New York. I put in a long-distance call to the Hugheses. They would be interested in the news I had to tell (they wouldn't talk) and would understand my mixed emotions about it.

They were not at home. Evelyn, the maid, said they were in Santa Monica at Miss Pringle's for dinner. Did I want that number? No, I said. It wasn't that important.

I telephoned my parents. It was a bad connection. My mother, when she finally realized who it was, grew short of breath and began to pant audibly. "Something's wrong!" she gasped. "What's wrong?"

"Nothing's wrong, Mamma," I shouted. "I just wanted to tell you something. Philip and I — sold a play."

"Sold a what?"

"A play."

"What kind of a play?"

"Well, it's got three acts," I explained helplessly.

"Where did you get it?" she wanted to know.

"We — we wrote it," I said.

There was a pause. Then, "Are you sure you're not sick or anything?"

"No, Mamma. I'm fine."

"Well, it's just that — the phone rings — it's long distance. It *is* long distance, isn't it? You're sure you're not back over there in Hollywood?"

"Yes, Mamma, I'm sure. I'm in New York."

"What time is it back there?"

"It's — it's eleven o'clock."

"It's only eight o'clock here. Isn't that right, Daddy? Look and see. Doesn't that say eight o'clock?"

"Yup," I heard my father say. "It says eight o'clock. Who's that wants to know?"

"Johnny," Mamma said.

"Johnny who?"

"Johnny Ewing."

"That's our boy's name."

"Well, it *is* our boy. He's calling all the way from New York City, and he says he's not sick or anything."

"Let me talk to Papa," I said.

After a moment he came on the phone. "Hello. Who is this?"

"It's me, Papa. John."

"What's the matter?"

"Nothing, Papa. I just—just wanted to hear your voices." There was no point in going into the play with him.

"Yes. Well." A pause. "How's the weather back there?"

"Very nice," I said. "Quite warm."

"That's too bad. What did you say?"

"I—I love you," I shouted.

"Oh, that's all right," he said. "Take care of yourself." And he hung up.

I poured myself a stiff shot of gin—half water, half Daniel Mobridge grain alcohol laced with a few drops of juniper juice. Thomas Wolfe was only half-right, I thought. Not only can you not go home again, you can't even telephone. I tossed off the shot, and thanked God for Dan. Otherwise we might all be blind.

The telephone rang. It was a woman's voice, one with a slight southern accent. Pat Hughes? "Where the hell have you been all evening?" No, Pat Hughes would never say that, or if she said it, not in that tone.

"Who wants to know?" I asked.

"It's Liz, you idiot."

"Oh, God," I said, "I'm glad you called!"

"Something wrong?"

"Anything but. And I'm dying to tell somebody. Let me call you back so you won't have to pay for it."

"Go ahead. I'm flush. Just got a raise."

"Great. Now sit down, light a cigarette, and *listen*."

I told her about *The Age of Mrs. Page,* about Dick Madden and the incredible, maddening, frail Lester Force, and Sardi's this evening. I don't know how long it took or what it cost her, but all her reactions were right. She wanted to know more, how I felt, how Philip felt, what was said.

"Was Philip with you — at Sardi's, I mean?"

"No. I was there in lonely splendor."

"Aw, poor baby," she said. "I wish I'd been with you."

"So do I," I said.

"Is Philip there with you now?"

"No. He's out on a date of some kind."

"Celebrating too, I suppose."

"Something like that." And then I heard myself say, "Liz, you know something? I miss you."

She laughed. "Oh, I daresay the native women will begin to look good to you before long."

"Bad joke. Why don't you proposition Jim Quirk to bring you to New York for a few months?" (Quirk was the editor-owner of *Photoplay.*) "Tell him you need practical experience in the New York office. You know, editing, writing captions, putting the magazine to bed, putting me to bed, details like that."

"You've been reading my mind," Liz said.

"Well?"

"It might solve a personal problem for me too."

"What's that?"

"Robin."

"Who's Robin?"

"You remember Robin — the last car I was engaged to? Well, Robin is a dear, and he even likes my mother's cats, but he doesn't see why we don't get married."

"Why don't you, if I may ask?"

"Because — well — if you must know, he has the most peculiar body odor."

"I would think there'd have been some close bodily contact when you got engaged."

"Oh, darling, don't you see, that was during the winter."

"And now that it is warming up out there . . ."

"Exactly. But can a person mention a thing like that to a nice, clean young man?"

"Just say, you stink. Nice to have known you."

"Thanks. Thanks a lot. So if I can persuade Jim to bring me to New York for two or three months this summer — and he's already mentioned it a couple of times in the past but I've always said no — Robin might cool off and find himself another girl."

"With a less sensitive nose, let's hope."

"And so I was wondering, would it be too much trouble for you to scout around and see what a decent room and bath would cost, one up in the neighborhood of *Photoplay* on Fifty-seventh Street?"

★   ★   ★

I don't know what time it was when I felt my bed jostled, and woke with a start. I could just make out the silhouette of Philip standing there. He seemed to be nude, but it was hard to tell in the dark. He had bumped into my bed crossing from the bathroom to his own. Now he bent over and nursed the bruise on his leg, lost his balance, and sat down hard on my right foot. I yelped, "Jesus, Philip, watch the hell where you're going!"

"Jesus had nothing to do with it," he said. He was quite drunk and relaxed, all inhibitions dissolved in alcohol. "Nothing whatsoever. If memory serves, He was not even in the neighborhood at the time of the accident but off on a fishing trip so don't blame Him." He tried to focus on his own bed. "How far is it across to that plateau, ol' chap?"

"About a yard," I said.

"Oh, what a big yard you have, grandpa."

He staggered to his feet and started to fall. I grabbed his hand and steadied him. He collapsed onto his bed. I got up and pulled the sheet and blanket up over him.

"There is a word for people like you," he said.

"Sucker?" I suggested.

"No, but you're getting warm. Su — samaritan."

"You really tied one on, didn't you?"

He did not reply. After a very short interval he began to snore. I went to the bathroom and put the light on. His clothes were strewn across the floor, his undershirt in the washbasin and one end of his blue knit tie draped into the john. I rescued it and hung it up to dry. His pajamas were undisturbed on their own hook on the door. I scooped up his clothes, carried them out, and laid them on the old Morris chair. In the darkness it was not difficult to visualize Sam Pearson sitting in it. Knitting.

I got back into bed and tried to go to sleep again, but sleep would not come. I could not help wondering whom Philip had been with, and how he had happened to get so blotto. Did he find somebody he could tell about the play? Had Philip celebrated with him . . . her? But why be secretive about it?

The snoring ceased abruptly, then a childish whimper introduced a babble of fright noises. He was having a nightmare. The light, I thought. He usually sleeps with his light on. Well, I can't sleep anyhow . . .

I got up, walked around his bed, and turned on the light. The nocturne of distress slowly subsided. I looked down at him. His thumb was in his mouth.

★   ★   ★

I would swear that all of the above took place on May 14, 1930, and during the early hours of the fifteenth. What makes me most suspect my memory is that, in trying to check myself, I leafed through Philip's yellowing Day Book. There was no entry at all for May 14, 1930, nor any for the fifteenth. (If I am right about the date, there is little wonder about his slighting the fifteenth. He woke up with a pounding hangover and did not go to work.)

But I did find an entry for the sixteenth:

Freddie gave me a good title for a story, a play on Hemingway's definition of courage as grace under pressure. "Grace, Under Pressure." Grace would be the girl's name.

Perhaps that was the genesis of the story he finally wrote under the title "There but for Grace." He could never resist juggling words. His delight in it became almost an obsession during the later years. He might be glooming in "Philip's chair" in any one of our living rooms, but just mention a word game and he would spring to life.

But who was Freddie? I never heard of him.

18

If we agreed, Lester Force said — "we" were Philip and I — we would go into rehearsal around the middle of September, open out of town in Wilmington or Baltimore say October 12, try out for two, three weeks if necessary, and bring in the show in late October or early November.

"Sugar? Cream?" Belle Dexter Force interrupted. She was Pouring Tea and dressed for the part in a pleated, old rose Fortuny tea gown. Lester, in maroon smoking jacket, leaned against the marble fireplace in the vaulted drawing room of their house in Turtle Bay, while he favored us with a nostalgic résumé of his years in the theater. ("You may call me Lester," he had suggested earlier. "No need for formality between us bohemians.") Intermittently, he puffed on an evil-smelling cigar that kept going out and had to be relit.

The time of year that you come in, Lester opined, could make the difference. Summer, of course, was pure "Harry Carey," as he pronounced it. The theaters were sweatboxes and nobody, but nobody, would come. Early fall *they* just didn't seem to want to go to the theater, God knows why. It wasn't *the thing*. Then again between Thanksgiving and Christmas they squandered their dough on gifts for the wife, the kids, the mistress, whomever. After the first of the year there was a brief period that was okay, but again you might open in a blizzard and they'd all stay home, even the first-string critics, those high-and-mighty assassins, and send along second-stringers. April was suicide on account of income tax, and after that it was warming up again and business went to hell, even if you had a smash.

"So, if it is satisfactory with the authors," Lester said, "we shall aim for New York about November first."

Philip nodded his agreement and I said, "You know much more about things like that than we do, Lester." Privately I had gooseflesh. A real, live producer (yes, he was definitely alive, no matter that he was a relict of the nineteenth century) was actually speaking, and casually, about *opening,* about *tryouts out of town* and *bringing the show in,* and "the show" was ours!

Philip, managing to sound much less spooked than I would have, coughed and then asked, "What — ah — house do you have in mind, Mr. — that is, Lester?"

House. I wished I had said that.

"That is no problem," Lester said. "Belle my blossom, pour a tot of brandy in my tea, will you?" He held his teacup before her and his blossom carefully poured the tot of Hennessy into it. Then he set the Spode teacup on the end of the ancient nine-foot-long Steinway, dipped the oral tip of his cigar into it, and lit the thing again.

"You see, we have our own house. The Dexter." He looked at his wife, smiled and bobbed his head in her direction. "You've never heard of it? Tell them, Belle."

"Well," Mrs. Force twinkled, turning to us. "David — Mr. Belasco, that is — was a most unpredictable man. One time he begrudged lending you a quarter for the ladies'-room attendant, and another . . . well, you see, he was very much enamored of me at one time."

"Those were the days when he had all his buttons," Lester put in. "Before he sainted himself by turning his collar around."

"Tut tut, Lester. That's naughty of you. Anyhow, there came one Christmas Eve — I think it was about ninety-one — we had finished our midnight collation — champagne, pheasants, I can't remember what all — just the two of us in his apartment, the one over the Belasco — still there for all I know — and he says, 'I have a surprise for you, Beulah.' I'd better explain, I had been Beulah Blum, and I was just getting my feet wet in the Yiddish theater when David saw me and decided to bring me uptown. But of course I had to have an uptown name with no chopped chicken liver on it. Can you imagine 'David Belasco presents Beulah Blum in *To Have and to Hold'?* So I became Belle Dexter, but David always called me Beulah for some reason or another when we were alone . . ."

Mrs. Force had been staring off into space, talking almost to herself. Now she seemed confused. "Where was I? What was I supposed to tell them, old cock?"

"About David — and Christmas," Lester prompted.

"Oh, of course. Well, David said, 'I have a surprise for you, Beulah, put your duds on.' So I put on my mink coat — *that* had been for my birthday — and he took me by the hand and led me down the street to the Stanley. It was empty at the time, but he had keys. See, David sometimes used the Stanley when the Belasco was occupied. Anyhow, he led me into the joint and switched on the houselights, and we stood there and he said, 'Merry Christmas, Beulah.'

"I still didn't know what he was talking about, dumb me, so I said, 'And Happy New Year to you too, Davie poo.' And he said, 'Well, doesn't anybody know how to say thank you?' and I said, 'Thank you for what?' And he said, 'For this old house. Didn't you notice as we entered that the name was changed to the Dexter? It's yours.'"

"And that was my Blum Blossom's dowry when she talked me into marrying her," Lester said, glowing with pride.

All Philip could manage to say was, "That's very interesting," and I said, "You must have been very pleased, Mrs. Force."

"Pleased!" she said. "I was so excited that I went right out onto Forty-seventh Street and threw up my pheasant and champagne."

That was the beginning of our relationship with Lester and Belle Dexter Force. It did not last long, but while it lasted I think neither of us was ever so beglamored. They were dear and, in their singular manner, simple people who introduced us, and gave us fascinating, personally guided tours, into a private world long since dead and buried.

We were escorted through the Dexter. We were a little disappointed because the theater was, to our way of thinking, on the wrong side of Broadway, between Broadway and Sixth. But then, so were the Belasco and the Henry Miller and they seemed to be doing all right. The Dexter, for reasons unknown to us, had been dark for several years and it smelled musty. No problem, Lester said. A cleaning crew with some Lysol would take care of that.

There were eight boxes — two tiers. The lower-right stage box (its gilt peeling slightly now) had originally been reserved by Ward McAllister for his patroness, Mrs. Astor, and the one opposite had once been occupied by Mrs. Belmont and party.

Yes, the boxes needed touching up. No problem. A day's work for the paint crew. The important thing was the seats. They were in good condition, all 957 of them. They ought to be because Lester Force had installed them the same season he produced his last big hit, *The Woman Who Came Back*.

"Five words," he said. "Just like your play."

We were presented with a prospective director, a handsome old man named Edward Childs Carpenter. I had been dreaming in terms of Kaufman or Connolly, and Philip leaned toward Reginald Denham, whose suspense play *Rope's End* had impressed him the season before I came east to live. Lester Force dismissed them all, however. For him there was nobody like Eddie Carpenter, with whom he had worked a number of times in the past. After lunching with them both at the Players we reluctantly agreed that Carpenter would do. He was as charming — and in a much more literate, truly cosmopolitan manner — as Lester himself. The only thing was, he was so *old*. Sixty at least, though he didn't look it. Why, the old gentleman had been one of the founders of the Dramatists' Guild. He had been writing plays in the olden days when the poor son of a bitch of an author had to sell them outright, twenty-five dollars cash per act if he could find his producer when he was solvent. All very interesting, but could such a period piece, granted he was intelligent and well versed in the classics, appreciate and communicate the *today* humor, the Chekhovian innuendo, the understated poignance of our sensitive little piece?

"I like it," he said.

"Now then," Lester said. "Into the breach. If we could only get Laurette Taylor, and if dear Laurette were only herself."

"She's so *old*," I protested.

"I thought she was dead," Philip said.

"She's a lush," Lester explained, lowering his voice.

"Dead or alive, drunk or sober, I'd take her if I had a play. That dear woman could make me believe Ophelia," Carpenter said.

"If you say so," Lester said, and crossed himself the wrong way. "I'll take the gamble."

We sent Laurette Taylor a copy of *The Age of Mrs. Page* to the last address anybody had for her. And waited. And waited.

While we waited Philip and I made a list of other first ladies whom we considered to be possibilities. Heading it was Ina Claire, followed by Lynn Fontanne, Elsie Ferguson, Alice Brady, Jane Cowl, Francine Larrimore, and Margalo Gilmore. Ina Claire was on tour with a revival of *Our Betters*. Lynn Fontanne was already rehearsing for *Elizabeth the Queen,* and Alice Brady was ticketed for *Love, Honor, and Betray*. *Let Us Be Gay* was still keeping Francine Larrimore's nose to the footlights, Mr. Carpenter had once had a brouhaha with Jane Cowl, and our producer had no enthusiasm for the Misses Ferguson and Gilmore.

"Let's give Laurette a little more time," said Lester, crossing his fingers. "I hear she's been at one of the spas in Europe, taking the cure, let us hope." We were dining with Lester and his wife at Dinty Moore's. They had both put away healthy portions of corned beef and cabbage. "And by the way," Lester went on, as if it had just occurred to him, "have you young geniuses been thinking about the soubrette? That is, Mrs. Page's friend."

Philip and I glanced at each other. He nodded, You take the ball. "Why, yes," I said. "What would you think of Jean Dixon?"

He looked puzzled. "Who?"

"You know. Jean Dixon," Philip said. "*June Moon, Once in a Lifetime*. She's marvelous."

"I haven't caught those," Lester said. He had not, we discovered, "caught" very many plays recently. So much of the current crop was trashy and vulgar, he thought. No class. No elegance. Cheap wisecracks masquerading as dialogue. "I'm sure Miss Dixon must be a talent if you young men like her," he went on. "But I confess I was thinking in terms of—well—someone with star quality. A famous figure, a comedienne in the grand tradition."

He lit a cigar and blew a fan of smoke above our heads. "There is someone in this very room who could burn the socks off that part if we could convince her to accept a second lead."

He turned slowly and settled his gaze on his wife, then he took her hand, lifted it, turned it over, and kissed its palm. It was pure ham, and I would have loved it had our play not been involved. "For me? Just for me, Miss Dexter?"

Belle lowered her eyes, giving a star-quality rendition of "modesty."

"The boys think I'm too old," she laughed.

"Nonsense," Lester scoffed. "And if we get Laurette, she'll need a more mature friend. Otherwise it's ridiculous. Well, what think ye, merry gentlemen?"

He turned on us an elfin expression of such magic necromancy that Philip's high color turned magenta.

Lester chuckled. "You're speechless, aren't you?"

"We're — surprised," I said weakly. "It's such a — such a small part, really, it never occurred to either of us that — "

"I never count the sides, I just count what's *on* the sides." Belle spoke that line as if nobody else had ever spoken it before.

"Well," I said, "let us mull it over, will you?"

Lester bowed and made a grandiose gesture that scattered cigar ashes across Dinty Moore's white linen. "By all means, you authors mull. Plenty of time." He turned again to his wife. "Well, well, it's going to be quite a story, quite a story. Belle Dexter comes out of retirement and returns in triumph to her own theater!"

It was a sweltering night. Philip and I walked slowly across town. Both of us were thinking the same thing: What had we got ourselves into? And now, how could we hope to cope and not offend two persons we had grown very fond of? We could say no to Belle Dexter, of course. Our Dramatists' Guild contract gave us cast approval. But if we did, would Lester want to go on with the play? And if he did not, would that perhaps be a good idea? We might get the play back, and . . .

"We'll talk with Dick Madden tomorrow," Philip said.

I mumbled "Mmm." We walked another block in silence. The flies were sticky. We crossed Fifth. "Edward Carpenter will think the idea's crazy, won't he?" I offered hopefully.

"Who knows? He's their generation almost."

"But she *totters*."

We crossed Madison. "When did you say your friend Liz was coming to New York?"

"First of August. Why?"

"I just wondered."

"I found her a room up on Fifty-eighth. Off Sixth. Twenty-five a week. She'll only have two blocks to walk to *Photoplay*."

"She'll keep you pretty busy, huh?"

"Oh, I don't know. She's going to be working. It's not as if she was my guest. You'll like her."

I wondered about that. Philip usually warmed up to girls who were not quite so extroverted, girls who didn't come on quite as strong, girls who thought more of what they were going to say before they said it.

We walked through Grand Central. It was cooler in there. I picked up a bulldog of the *Herald Tribune* for the weather report. Maybe the heat would break tomorrow.

When we got up to the apartment we cranked open the windows, which had been shut with the blinds drawn in the hope of keeping the heat out. It was about the same temperature inside as out. Philip turned on the oscillating fan. We both took off ties, jackets, shirts, and pants and sprawled in our shorts in chairs before the fan, Philip in his father's, I in a canvas sling. He reached for the *Trib*.

I could read one headline from where I sat: "Unemployment Hits 15 Percent."

"Hand me the weather," I said. "After all, I paid for it."

"Here," he said grandly, and threw the whole paper across to me.

I opened it to the weather. There was no break in sight. Ninety degrees predicted for tomorrow with humidity holding at eighty and possible thundershowers, which would only make the siz-zling streets steam. I turned to the theater section. Three more closings. A couple of kids from the chorus of *Strike Up the Band* get married. A smart-aleck second-stringer who thinks he is Dorothy Parker casually crucifies a brave little turkey that has dared its first gobble during the dog days of summer.

My eye slid down the column.

"Zoë Akins, whose recent sleight-of-hand *The Greeks Had a Word for It* is still packing them in, has just returned from Switzerland where she was the guest of an old friend, Adele Dalton Franklin, wife of the industrialist Judson Franklin. Miss Akins informs us that her next play will be a dramatization of Mrs. Franklin's recent novel, *The Age of Mrs. Page.*"

Later, much, much later, I constructed our proper, civilized reactions (or what Noel Coward, if he was half the man I thought he was, would have done under the circumstances). I should have lit a cigarette, risen nonchalantly and crossed to the bar (our kitchenette, unfortunately), poured myself a jigger of scotch and tossed it down. Then I would shrug, Oh, what the hell, pour a generous slug for Philip, walk across the room again, and hand it to him. I would say, "Bottoms up." He would say, "I don't need a drink right now." And I would say, "No, but you will in a minute." Then and only then would I hand him the paper with a lightly dropped "It seems, old chap, that Belle Dexter will be no problem."

It did not happen that way, of course. Philip and I were not products of Noel Coward but, in the clutch, of Cottonwood. I simply handed him the paper and said, "Read that!"

He read it through twice and said nothing.

I said, "What have you got to say!"

He swallowed hard and finally said, "There must be a mistake."

And I said, "Yes, you're goddamn right there's been a mistake, a big goddamn mistake, and you know who made it, *you* made it!" We didn't have a contract with the bitch, I went on to point out, because he was impressed with her, he had fallen for her, he had said we didn't need a contract, if I remembered correctly, because Mrs. Judson Franklin was a lovely woman, and as everybody knew, lovely women did not need contracts, they just shook hands and you kissed their asses.

"Lovely person, not woman," Philip interrupted.

"What's the difference? And you told her you would never permit me to mention the word 'death' again. Oh, *shit!*"

"Oh, dry up."

"That's rich, that is. 'Oh, dry up.' I haven't heard that since the seventh grade."

I walked out and poured myself a drink. Sweat was running into my eyes, down my belly and legs. After a minute Philip appeared in the kitchenette, nudged me aside, and poured himself one. He was not sweating at all. "Look," he said. "We're in this together."

"You're fucking right we are, and you got us into it! You brought the book home in the first place."

"You want me to kill myself?"

"Oh, no, please. We mustn't mention death, must we?"

He did not hit me. I did not hit him, but we were close to blows, closer than we had ever been except for that time when Philip had grabbed my undershirt on the way back from Mr. Cram's gym race and we actually had come to blows. I went into the toilet to cool off, and glare at myself in the mirror.

We did not speak again. Finally we went to bed, but not to sleep. (He did not switch on his night-light.) Sometime around four, it must have been, I was aware that he was up. When I opened my eyes I could see him standing in profile before the window, smoking a cigarette.

"I'm sorry," I said.

"That makes two of us."

"We've got to do something about this first thing in the morning. Lester's going to see the item . . . Dick Madden too."

"I'll telephone Elwood Grainger at *Vanity Fair.*"

"What's the good of that?"

"She's his aunt. Mrs. Franklin, I mean. Maybe he can touch base with her and find out if it's true."

"Good idea," I said. "And let's duck telephone calls till you find out."

I sat up in bed, found a cigarette, and lighted it in the dark. "Your pal Grainger said she was quite a character. Maybe this is what he meant."

"Funny," Philip mused. "She seemed so—so . . ."

"You know, you're right," I said. "*So* just about sums it up, and we're sewed in."

"Puns," Philip sneered, but affably. "Please."

At nine-thirty in the morning he telephoned me at *International*. He had talked with Elwood Grainger who did not know where his aunt was. Philip had asked him if he thought her capable of such a double cross and he said, Why? Didn't we have a contract with the lady? No? Well, we certainly should have, especially since it took us so long to write the damn play. She hadn't heard from us, she probably thought we were just a couple of young whippersnappers who had romanced her and then disappeared. Was Zoë Akins an old friend of hers? Philip had asked. Oh, yes, bosom buddies, known each other since college. So when Zoë showed up and wanted to do her play . . . "Well, you know women," Grainger had laughed. "I'll bet Akins has a contract."

When Philip finished telling me the dismal account there was a long silence all the way from the *Unicorn* to *International*. Finally I said, "Who wants to call Richard Madden?"

"It's your turn," Philip said.

I hung up and sat staring at the phone. Walter Schmidt, a young man from Brooklyn who had recently been elevated from secretary to reader, said, "Mind if I make a quick call?"

"The longer the better."

But the phone rang as he picked it up. He answered, then said, "It's for you."

"John? This is Dick Madden," I heard him say.

I took a deep breath. His tone of voice told me that he had already seen the item in the *Herald Tribune*. "Yes, Mr. Madden. I was just about to call you."

"I'm afraid I have some very bad news for us."

"I know," I said. "I've already seen it. That's why I was going to—"

He interrupted, seemed confused. "But it hasn't been in the papers, has it? It couldn't have been yet. He was found dead only this morning about seven."

"Dead? Who? Who's dead?"

"Lester. Lester Force. Belle went in to give him his heart pill this morning. He had died sometime during the night."

★   ★   ★

I found one entry about that period in Philip's Day Book. It was dated July 18, 1930. That must have been about a week after it happened, and before Liz got there.

> Lester Force, our producer, died of cardiac arrest only a few hours after we learned that Adele Franklin had sold us out for Zoë Akins. . . . Had an interview with Frank Crowninshield about editorial job on *Vanity Fair*. Think I'd like it. Like him. Old World Gentleman. Also met Clare Boothe Brokaw. There is something about her . . .

Philip never mentioned it, but I always suspected he got that job on *Vanity Fair* because Elwood Grainger, despite his lofty unconcern about his aunt's duplicity, felt uneasy over having introduced Philip to her and — in a roundabout way — was trying to make it up to him. It was Grainger, of course, who brought Philip to Crowninshield's attention. Not that Philip did not deserve it.

Grainger was no friend of mine, so I got nothing as tangible as a job out of the experience, nothing actually but the experience itself, which I have never regretted. In the first place, there were those two people, those delightful, maddening, talented, egocentric, vivid, calculating, and generous people who suddenly swept across my sky, like decaying comets obeying no known celestial orbit, and were as suddenly gone. Irreplaceable, blurring the other stars while they blazed, haunting the memory forever. Lester and Belle. Were they real? If not real, what were they?

And there was the making of the play itself, working with Philip all those months, supplementing each other and occasionally striking a vein of gold (we thought), then the hours of torpor, of smoking cigarettes and staring at blank paper . . .

And then that rare moment of exhilaration when it would all come together and — call it inspiration, that's as good a word as any, though it sounds so pretentious, so artsy-fartsy — we would read something we had just written, maybe only a line or two, maybe a whole scene, but it was something that brought out the gooseflesh, something not to be lost, a revelation that neither of us had suspected was in us.

We would look at each other and say, because it was not good form to admit what we really felt, "That's not too bad."

Such a waste, our friends — the few who knew what we were up to — said. They were wrong. Nothing is wasted if you're a writer, unless everything is, in the end, a waste to everybody. It's all grist for that old mill, Philip. I'm sorry you never lived to grind it, as I am doing now.

19

Liz knew the ritual for *Arrival in Grand Central*. She had as models the Swansons, the Crawfords, the Shearers, and others she had enviously watched board the Chief at the Santa Fe station in Pasadena. She wore a slinky black suit and cloche hat (Swanson), a gardenia in the buttonhole (Crawford), and carried an enormous hatbox (all of them). Her suit was a superb copy of a Hattie Carnegie, by Philip's aunt Grace. She had everything but a poodle on a leash, everything including a handy, portable male she had picked up en route. Well, she had actually met him a time or two in Hollywood, but had not known he was on the train with her until they both got off in Albuquerque to stretch their legs.

His name was Norman (Norm) Conley and he was extremely — well, handsome is not the word and men are not supposed to be beautiful, but Norm was. (Black Irish, we used to call that type. Wavy black hair, perfect features, and innocent blue eyes that crinkled at the corners in a smile that said, Like me, please, and the next thing a girl knew she'd be in the hay with him.) "Look at him!" Liz said as we trailed a couple of redcaps up the ramp, "not a wrinkle in his pants. That's because he never sits down, just stands around looking gorgeous."

Norman laughed. The laugh lay in the upper register and seemed strangely humorless, more nervous defense than spontaneous reaction. He could turn it on or not as he chose, but the appealing, somehow touching, smile was always there.

"Now," Liz said. "Where are you going to put Norman up?"

"Who, me?"

"Of course. You know things like that."

"She's just kidding," Norman said.

"Why shouldn't John help? He's a New Yorker now. He found me some fleabag."

"Thanks," I said, and turned to Norman. "You'll have to tell me how much you want to shell out, how long you plan to stay, a few nonessentials like that."

Norman shrugged his beautifully tailored shoulders. The suit looked like an Eddie Schmidt to me, and Eddie Schmidt spelled money in Hollywood.

"Norman's broke," Liz said, very matter-of-fact. "He's here to find a job, and —"

"And I don't know how long that will take, so —"

"So," Liz finished, "if you've got something at about ten a week . . . can you afford that, Norm?"

Norm laughed nervously. "I might go to fifteen."

"Have you ever heard of the Allerton House?" I asked.

He had not, so I told him. It was a man's residence on Lexington, within walking distance of everything, fairly Spartan, but clean, rather like the Y, but without God.

My description curdled Norman's smile, though he was brave about it. Liz said, "We'll take it."

"Look," I said. "Norman's the one who's got to live there. In fact, women aren't permitted above the first floor."

"That won't be the end of the world, will it, Norman?" Liz asked.

"I'll try to bear up for a few days."

"Then let's get this show on the road," Liz said. By then we were at the taxi lineup. "We'll drop you off, Norman."

I tipped the porters while Norman was protesting, "Here, let me," then we piled into one taxi.

After we dropped Norman at the Allerton, I settled back and gave the cabbie an address on West Fifty-eighth Street. "I hope you're going to like it."

"Why wouldn't I?" Liz said. "It's in New York. Oh, my God," she cried. "Do you see that street sign? It says Fifth Avenue. We're on Fifth Avenue."

"You take everything so damn big," I said.

She was wiping a tear off her cheek as we passed Saks, which seemed much more an emotional catharsis for her than St.

Patrick's. "Liz Bartlett was seen shopping at Saks Fifth Avenue the other day."

I started to laugh and couldn't stop.

"If you're ashamed of me, you can get right out," she said.

"You're getting your part all mixed up," I said. "Do you think Gloria Swanson cries when she passes Cartier's?"

We turned west on Fifty-seventh Street. It was Sunday, and the temperature was already in the high eighties. There was very little traffic. "Tell me," I said, "is this — this Norman, supposed to help you short-circuit Robin?"

"Norman? No, Norman is splashed with lavender, I'm afraid. He says he wants to go straight, but I have my doubts."

There must have been thousands of studio-bed-sitting rooms in the honeycombs of Manhattan exactly like the one I had rented for Liz on the corner of Sixth and Fifty-eighth Street. It was, as I remember it, about eleven by sixteen, with a large window on the eleven-foot expanse. There was a daybed with a greenish-blue damask cover and four or five assorted pillows, two skimpy upholstered chairs slipcovered in alternate green and blue stripes, a narrow blond desk and straight-back chair. The desk could serve as a typewriter stand, but Liz would have to add the Manhattan telephone book to the chair for height. On the wall facing the bed were the inevitable prints of a Venetian gondolier and the Colosseum.

"It's perfect!" Liz said, after we had finally succeeded in lifting the window. It had been stuck fast and both of us broke out in the sweat that, in New York in August, always lurks just beneath the epidermis awaiting the slightest exertion to pop forth.

"Behold!" I said, pointing to a narrow slice of Central Park visible around the corner and up Sixth. At that moment a real-live horse could be seen clip-clopping ahead of a rickety hansom cab with an ancient, top-hatted cabbie perched precariously on top.

"Look at me! Look at Liz Bartlett — in New York!"

I looked at her. She was quite a sight. I had met nobody in New York to compare.

We did New York that day. We walked across to the Plaza for breakfast. (Liz had been too keyed up to eat this morning on the Century.) We crossed over on Fifty-seventh to Park and pretended we lived there and were out for a morning constitutional. An organ-grinder with a monkey confronted us at the corner of Fiftieth. Liz gave the monkey fifty cents. The monkey doffed his cap, jumped on her shoulder, and kissed her.

We went back over to Fifth, boarded the upper deck of the bus, and rode downtown, past the new Empire State Building, which had grown to sixty or seventy stories—it was hard to tell how many. We strolled through Washington Square where old men were bent over dominoes and checkerboards, and a few younger ones tossed horseshoes. "I thought there'd be a lot of panhandlers," Liz said. "Where are all the poor people?"

"They must have gone to Newport for the weekend," I said. "Nobody—but *nobody*—stays in town in August."

Then we rode uptown to the Met where Liz took off her shoes with their four-inch heels and carried them, padding around the marble halls in stocking feet. Nobody noticed, nobody cared. I had forgotten what beautiful legs she had.

We went to the Algonquin for tea and peeked into the quite ordinary room that housed the Round Table. It was empty today. The famous table, with no linen or silver to conceal its scars, could have been any other big round table. Liz, however, surrounded it with Dottie Parker, Bob Benchley, George Kaufman, and Alec Woollcott, who never opened their mouths except to spout imperishable good- and sometimes ill-natured insults.

We took a taxi up to Carnegie Hall and bought tickets for the Rosa Ponselle concert that evening, and then walked past the International Building where I worked and, not far from it, the *Photoplay* office where Liz would spend the next couple of months. It was cooling off, so we strolled over to Central Park and sprawled on the grass beside the lake and watched the sun sink slowly behind the massive old Dakota on Central Park West. She told me about her mother, Lulabel, and the cats, one of whom had delivered a batch of kittens that Lulabel was trying to blackmail friends into taking off her hands. She told me how she had climbed the fence surrounding Garbo's house and sneaked pictures of her.

"And what about Robin?" I asked during a lull.

"He's a dear. Much too good for me," Liz sighed. "I'm going to hate breaking his heart." (Didn't it rather please her, I wondered, doesn't it rather please any girl to be able to break a man's heart? And doesn't it disappoint her just a little when he gets over it?)

I think we dozed off for a little while. Then we got hungry and I introduced her to another Tony's, this one on West Fifty-sixth.

She had read my two published stories and said she loved them. "I cried. Why didn't you tell me you could write like that?" Then we got around to Philip, how reserved he had been till we began our collaboration and how he had emerged from his shell only to retreat into it after the collaboration was over. Now for long periods we had nothing to say to each other.

"When am I going to meet this character?"

I told her that I was giving a smallish cocktail party for her— "smallish" was *in* that year—Saturday afternoon if she would be free. I wanted her to meet the Crowd, including Philip. They were all primed for her, I said.

"What does that mean?" she wanted to know. "Do people need to be primed for me?"

"I mean I've told them a lot about you."

She eyed me suspiciously. "Okay. Let it pass. Is one of this— crowd—your girl?"

"Nothing serious," I said. "I've been squiring Maureen, Philip's sister. She's a very nice girl."

"What an awful thing to say," Liz said.

"Well, she is. I like her very much."

"I get the picture. She's crazy about you and you like her very much."

"Look. Is this an interview, Miss Bartlett?"

"Yes," Liz grinned. "What about your friend Philip? Is he shacked up with anybody?"

"Not that I know of. Sometimes he and Lucy and Maureen and I make it a foursome. You'll meet her Saturday. She's fun."

"But they're not having an affair?"

"How would I know?"

"You can tell by looking at a couple. There's something shining about them when they look at each other."

I laughed. "That's by Elizabeth Bartlett in *Photoplay*."

Liz frowned. "I suppose it is. I must get over crap like that in real life, as we laughingly call it."

"For what it's worth, my guess would be no. I've never noticed anything shining. Not that I give a damn . . . yes, actually I do. I'm fond of Philip. It would do him good to get involved, even if it all blew up later. Shake him up. And Lucy's nuts about him. Fact, lots of girls are. He seems to be a challenge to them. You know, the mountain you've got to climb just because it's there? And all the mountain talks about is somebody named Clare Boothe Brokaw, a divorcée at *Vanity Fair* who won't give him the time of day."

★　★　★

"Why don't you ask Clare to the party?" I asked Philip.

"Don't be ridiculous," he said, and winced at my irreverent use of her first name. When he spoke of her she was either Clare Boothe Brokaw or Mrs. Brokaw.

"Why? Wouldn't she like our homemade booze?"

"Mrs. Brokaw has a crowded social calendar," Philip said icily. "Besides, this room will be jammed as it is."

"You and she could stand out in the hall and discuss Kierkegaard."

Liz had already asked me if she could invite two or three of her new friends from the *Photoplay* office, which, I gathered, she had taken by storm. I had said, "Of course." Anybody she wanted to ask; it was her party. So, besides our crowd, there would be "a darling young woman" named Adelia Bird. "Dee does fashions." Her beau, Chick Ellis, was a fashion illustrator. She would have to bring him, because "they're sort of engaged." Then there was Leonard Hall, who wrote East Coast gossip — "you'll like Len" — and if she asked Len he would want to bring his wife, Alice

Hughes, who wrote a column for the *Telegram*. "I don't know her but they say she's fun."

"And," Liz went on, "what about Norman?"

"What *about* Norman?"

"Shouldn't we ask him? He'd dress up any party."

"I don't know," I said. "Philip doesn't like fairies. They seem to make him uncomfortable."

"But he wouldn't know about Norman unless you told him. You didn't, did you?"

"He doesn't know Norman exists."

"Good. Then we'll ask him. Besides, Norman may be normal by now."

I threw my arms around her and hugged her.

"Why did you do that?" Liz asked.

"Because no other person in New York would ever make a remark like that. Nobody here gets over anything without at least five years on the couch."

I have been to better, and worse, cocktail parties than the one I gave for Liz that Saturday afternoon. It had been a blazing hot day. The door into the hall was open, but it did nothing but attract a few passersby who peeked in at us before they went on. The room was jammed and there was practically no place for anyone to sit, but that did not seem to matter as long as there was enough to drink. We had plenty.

Not only were there thirteen or fourteen members of our group, plus Norman (stunning as usual, this time in a white linen suit and purple tie), but Philip had, for diplomatic reasons, also invited Elwood Grainger, who insisted upon a martini — "Five parts gin and one part vermouth, please." Then the four Liz had mentioned — Adelia and Chick and Leonard and Alice — all came, as well as Jim Quirk, *Photoplay*'s owner and editor, and his wife, May Allison.

"I didn't ask Jim," Liz whispered apologetically as soon as she could, "but he was there when I spoke to Len, and he said, 'Okay, May and I can come.'"

"It's great," I said. "But watch Philip."

It had never, in his wildest Cottonwood fantasies, occurred to Philip Pearson that he might one day entertain a movie star in his own apartment. Harvard and New York had intervened but not entirely obliterated the movie fan in him.

Philip stared. Swallowing was difficult. His hands shook worse than usual. Oh, he was polite to Liz, he welcomed her to the big city, but his eyes followed May Allison about the room. "And who is this leading man type?" May laughed, indicating Norman.

"Norman, come here," I called. "Mrs. Quirk wants to meet you."

"I think we've met," Norman said, taking her hand.

"Have we? I thought you looked familiar."

"Guy Drummond used to dress you, didn't he?"

"Why, yes, dahlin', sometimes on screen. Why? Is Guy a personal friend of yours?"

Norman blushed. "Oh, no. Not really. I—went to a party or two of his, that's all. I was studying set design."

"Oh, Ah see," May said. I was afraid she did, all too clearly. "Have you made a connection heah in New York?"

Norman said no, he was looking for something. "He's awfully good at drawing," Liz put in helpfully.

"Ah tell you what," May said. "Maybe Jim would have something for you in his art depahtment if you butter him up a little. Jim"—she turned to her husband—"come heah and meet this handsome young man. He's an artist."

I took Liz by the hand and eased her through the mob to introduce her to Lucy and Cornelia, Maureen and Joe, Esme and Daniel, Barney and Jinna. They were all polite, which was not like them, and smiled too much, saying, "How do you like New York?" and "How long do you plan to be with us?" and "I hope we see you again before you go back," creating an invisible barrier to keep the flashy intruder in her place. Hollywood. Perhaps if Liz had not brought the *Photoplay* crowd with her it would have been different, but this seemed like an invasion of their private demesne. So Liz smiled and, her duty done, stuck to her *Photoplay* friends, to Norman and me. One day before too long it would be all right, but on that first afternoon she was given the freeze and, with cause enough, felt that my new friends did not like her.

★ ★ ★

"I'm trying to convince Elizabeth that she ought to stay in New York," Jim Quirk was saying. He had invited Liz and me for dinner with him and May at Robert's after the cocktail party, which had broken up early on account of the heat.

"That's very flattering, Mr. Quirk," Liz said, "but I've got a lease on a house out there and — "

"No problem. We'll pay it off," Quirk said.

Liz laughed and went right on — "and a mother with a hundred and fifty cats and a dog and dozens of friends in California."

"Isn't a hundred and fifty just a wee bit excessive?" May asked.

"Think it over," Quirk said. "We need you here. You could find your mother a little walk-up on the West Side where they love cats."

"They do?" Liz said.

"Oh, yes, indeed. They even have cat houses. And then you and John could find yourselves something across the park."

"Me and John?" Liz said.

"Well, I figure you two are having a bit of a do do do what you have done done done before, baby," Quirk chuckled. "You ought to make it legitimate."

"Jim," May said. "May I say you're impossible?"

"Oh, what a cross-eyed bear I have for a wife," Quirk laughed. "A rude, little bitty old southern belle who just married me for my money. Why do I love her? Ah, well, us old married folks better be getting to bed. You unmarried ones have my permission to go to bed too — alone or together. I am a very broadminded Irisher, and may His Holiness forgive me for making such a carnal suggestion." He crossed himself, stood up, and turned to May. "Coming, woman?"

"Yes, Mars Jim," May said. "Good night, you two."

We walked on across Sixth and up to Fifty-eighth. A breeze had come up. Perhaps it was going to rain. "Do you mind what your elevator man will think of your taking a gentleman to your room at this time of night?" I asked as we approached her building.

"Who said you were a gentleman?"

That was no answer, but it was the only one I got.

★ ★ ★

"Are you embarrassed?" Liz asked.

"A little," I confessed.

"I am too. Maybe this is a mistake."

"No. Wait a little. It'll be all right."

And it was. All right, and natural, and wonderful.

After a while we got up and walked over to the darkened window, our arms around each other. The city outside still roared on. New York never stopped, though it had begun to rain. Lightning punctured the sky above Central Park, and the thunder sounded like the roar of one of the lions in the zoo.

"I'm glad I came to New York," Liz said.

"So am I."

"Do you feel different toward me?"

I thought about that, then said, "Yes. How do you feel?"

"Maybe we can go away for a weekend soon."

"Let's. Like next weekend."

We held each other for a little while, then I began to speak. "I —" was all I could get out before she interrupted.

"I could fall in love with you, but I'm not going to let myself. It would complicate everything."

"Yes," I agreed, "but —"

"You've got your parents to take care of, I've got Lulabel — we both have demanding jobs, which we may lose if this damned depression goes on . . ."

"It's not fair," I said, though I was actually relieved that Liz was being so practical.

"This is nineteen thirty," she said staunchly, proudly. "A woman needs a man just as much as a man needs a woman, but it's not her whole existence, as that silly Lord Byron said. What did he know? Besides this — *this* — " and she tightened her arms around me, "may not last. I've been in love before, as you well know, though right at this moment that sounds impossible. It's true though, damn it, it's true. So maybe this better be just a do do do. And when it's over we'll walk away from each other with no recrimination, no regrets, still friends."

The elevator man could not have been less interested in my sleepy exit much later. The rain had stopped. I hailed a taxi at the corner of Fifty-seventh. It must have been four a.m. when I got home. Philip's night-light was on. He was asleep and had not bothered to lower my bed. He did not waken when I let it down myself.

In the morning I was aware that the mess of the party was cleared away. "You should have let me help," I said. Philip was hidden behind the book review section of the *Times*.

"That fellow Norman whatever his name is stayed and helped," he said.

"What did you think of Liz?" I asked casually.

"Liz? Oh, you mean your friend from California. She seemed nice. I didn't talk to her much."

I would never tell Liz that. "Nice" she was not.

20

August of 1930 was the month in time when Liz and I chose to become lovers. We were our own hero and heroine, young, healthy, lusting for new experience, acting out our own love story in the most exciting city in the world. Who cared about heat or humidity? Not us. Our feet did not mire in the gummy asphalt; we floated above it. Surely, anybody taking the trouble to glance our way on Fifth, Park, Broadway, or Fifty-seventh Street could tell about us. After a few hours' separation we would glimpse each other a block away, then fly toward the wonder of that special voice, the miracle of touching, of holding, of feeling another's heartbeat against our own.

Still, knowing what we had, neither of us yet said, "I love you." This was just an affair . . .

The summer is misty except in outline. There were parties, of course. Perhaps because she was in love, she felt no need to impress anybody. She did not tell Hollywood stories unless urged to do so. Hollywood was doing a Slow Fade.

I was not doing any writing. Liz would be going home early in October; I could make up for goofing off then, I told myself. I had had two stories published already and a third was scheduled; Esme Jones had got me a raise to $600 on that one. With Wall Street in the doldrums, with big corporations going bankrupt and their late employees on breadlines, I was rolling.

Two incidental items were worth mentioning about that summer. One, Norman got a job in the art department of *Photoplay*. It did not pay very much, but it liberated him from the restrictions of the Allerton House and set him up in a walk-up on West Sixty-eighth Street. And two, Maureen and Joe Tyler unexpectedly announced their engagement. I talked to Philip about it. I said I doubted that Maureen was in love with Joe; why had she done it? Philip shrugged. It was none of his — or my — business.

"He's a Catholic," Philip went on. "Mother will be happy about that."

Joe had been given a promotion at BBD&O. No raise, though. Raises were taboo, deserved or not. It was enough to know that your job was secure for a while. "Tyler," he had been told by either Batten, Barton, Durstine, or Osborne, "we like you. We feel that you're going to be a good company man." He and Maureen could pool their resources and get by very nicely, but they were not going to be married for six months.

★ ★ ★

"I'm sorry," Liz said, "but I've got to go to Philadelphia before I go home. I promised Ann Harding."

Liz had struck up a warm friendship with Ann Harding who, at the time Liz left California, was starring in *Holiday*. Ann, a talented, beautiful, and extremely determined young woman, had threatened, "Liz, if you don't make a pilgrimage to see Susan Glaspell's *Inheritors* while you're back there, I'll never speak to you again!"

Ann had played the lead in the Glaspell play when it was introduced at Provincetown. According to her, it was a theatrical must-see. "Of course," she had laughed, "it won't be as good without me, but Jasper Deeter is a wizard as a director, and he'll be in it too."

Deeter's Hedgerow was a small prestigious summer theater on the Main Line. It would close on Labor Day. "You wouldn't want to come along, would you?" Liz asked me.

"Of course. Let's make it part of the do."

(That word was beginning to sound obnoxious to me.)

"I didn't know you could *do* anything in Philadelphia," Liz said.

I telephoned and made a reservation at the Ritz. (I remembered reading that Scott and Zelda Fitzgerald had bunked there once when they had been stuck in Philadelphia.) Pretty steep it was — seven dollars a day — but what the hell?

"For Mr. and Mrs. John Ewing?" Liz asked suspiciously.

"Who else?"

"I don't know . . . it makes me feel cheap."

"How would you have me do it? Elizabeth Roe and John Doe?"

"Why not Elizabeth Bartlett and John Ewing?"

"Then the Ritz would insist on separate rooms."

I thought I should tell Philip I would be out of town over the weekend in case of any emergency calls. My mother had had the flu and, of course, would not call a doctor. Since the flu was merely a manifestation of Mortal Error she would suffer it through without so much as an aspirin tablet.

"In case my father calls," I said, "tell him he can reach me at the Ritz in Philadelphia. Or better, you call me and I'll call him."

"I won't be here to get any calls," Philip said, and went into a paroxysm of coughing. When he finally pulled himself together, I said, "Shall I notify next of kin?"

"I'm going to Nantucket," he said and, after a long pause, added, "Lucy and I are going."

"You don't say!"

"Why not?" It was the same as saying, Two can play at that game.

"No reason. I think that's great. Congratulate Lucy."

"So you'd better send a wire to your parents or something and tell them where you're going to be."

It was one of the very few times that Philip ever voluntarily told me where he was going, or with whom. Perhaps he did so on that occasion only because he knew that sooner or later Lucy would spill. Or . . . maybe it was pride, maybe he wanted to tell me he was a man too.

If they have any alternative, only fools or lovers would choose to visit Philadelphia over Labor Day. The natives who can afford it get the hell out of town, as they say with some accuracy, leaving the town less of a hell than it ordinarily is in summer. The streets become relatively empty; you can get a cab without fighting for it, and the out-of-towners — the fools and lovers — have not been tutored in rudeness.

We gawked at the Liberty Bell in Independence Hall, we paid our respects to Betsy Ross's house and to Benjamin Franklin's grave, we inspected the lobby of the Walnut Street Theater (it was closed), where Booth, Kean, Cushing, and Rachel had trod the ancient boards, and we rented a roadster on Sunday afternoon and drove through the lazy, hazy Pennsylvania countryside to the Hedgerow. Susan Glaspell's *Inheritors* was all that Ann Harding had said it was. (I wonder if it still is? I wonder if that lovely line, which I may be misquoting, is as spine-tingling to the 1980s as it was to the 1930s? "Live your life," one of her characters says, "so that the world will be a little better because you have been.")

Monday it rained. "Mr. and Mrs. John Ewing" did not get out of bed. We slept, we made love, and we let room service take care of food and drink. I doubt that those free souls Scott and Zelda had ever had it so good in Philadelphia.

We took the eight o'clock back to New York that evening. We scarcely spoke. We were remembering, musing, savoring, reliving the last three days because the future loomed as bleak and dismal as the streets and alleys of Trenton, New Brunswick, Metuchen, and Rahway dribbling past our rain-streaked windows. Liz would be going back to California in three weeks.

We spent the night together in her room. She woke up, Liz told me, at about three-thirty and felt me still there beside her, and she knew she hadn't the will to wake me and send me out in the rain. There were only a few nights left to us; so what if eyebrows were raised at the desk downstairs? There were plenty of empty rooms in hotels and apartment houses these days. We walked out together at eight-thirty Tuesday morning. The desk clerk pretended to be reading Walter Winchell.

It had stopped raining. The streets were washed clean, the air cooled and freshened. We had breakfast at the Maple Grove across Fifty-seventh from the *Photoplay* office, but were not hungry. "Something I've been meaning to ask you," I said. Liz looked up expectantly. "Yes?"

"Have you broken your engagement to Robin's car?"

"Weeks ago. My fiancé took it rather too well."

I thought about that. "And when you go home, what are you planning to do about transportation to previews?"

"Previews," she sighed. "What are previews?"

At eleven that morning my telephone rang. It was Philip. "Are you okay?" He sounded concerned, which was not like him.

"Sure. Why wouldn't I be?"

"You didn't come home last night."

"I'm fine. Couldn't be better."

"How did you find Philadelphia?"

"You can't miss it. Right across the Delaware from Camden. We didn't come back till this morning. I went straight to the office."

"Oh . . . well okay. I just thought in case your father called."

"Thanks . . . how about you and Lucy? Did you have — fun?" I asked it quickly before he could hang up.

"Rained most of the time. Nothing much to do on Nantucket when it rains. The lobster was good though. There's a little restaurant on an old sailing ship in dock, run by some Christian Science ladies. They pull the lobster right out of the sea."

(Much later Lucy was more forthcoming about their weekend. She confided to Liz that Philip had made a reservation in an old house recently converted to an inn. Very picture-postcard, typically Nantucket, whitewashed fence, view of the sea from the window between twin beds. The beds on rolling casters: Shove them together if the mood strikes you. They were never shoved together, however, nor were there any Tarzan leaps from one to the other. "The Hays office," Lucy said, "would have given us its seal." Lucy had not gone to Nantucket merely for the lobster dinner. She had gone because she was in love with Philip and expected — and wanted — to go to bed with him.)

Liz and I had dinner that night at the Russian Tea Room and decided what we needed more than anything was a good night's sleep — alone. I delivered her at her door at eight-thirty and splurged by taking a cab down to Forty-fourth Street.

Philip was there, in shorts and undershirt, pounding away on his typewriter. He had moved the standing lamp close to illuminate the carriage. The ashtray on the coffee table was a mound of smoldering cigarette butts. He seemed grateful for an interruption. He wanted to know if it had rained in Philadelphia too, how had I liked the Ritz, what did it cost? And had Elizabeth insisted on ringing the Liberty Bell?

"Naturally," I said. "But why not call her Liz?"

"I don't know."

"You don't like Liz, do you?"

"Why wouldn't I?"

"That's not what I asked."

"I like her all right. She's — "

"Not your cup of tea."

"I wouldn't say that exactly."

"Such unbridled enthusiasm." I went on unpacking my bag, hanging up my other suit. Philip was staring at a page in his typewriter. "Fighting a new story?"

"I thought I was, but it's not going to work. Just not my kind of story."

"Corny?"

"Like life, I guess." He yanked the sheet of paper out of his machine, ripped it out, crumpled it into a ball, and tossed it at me. "Take it. It's all yours."

I picked the paper off the floor and straightened it out. On it was typed "'The End of Alma,' by Philip Pearson," then a few introductory lines, carelessly composed, the sort one sometimes feels impelled to set down in order to clarify his purpose in writing a story, then usually throws away:

How many lives does a man live, how many times the curtain rise and fall? How many changes of costume, scene, and cast? Where are Joe and Jim and Mary and Marjorie who were so vital in Act One? Now you are in Act Two and they have made their final Exits. Don't they matter anymore, or did they never matter much? Was it — is the whole thing — just a crazy accident, irrelevant incident piled on coincidence, like Ossa on Pelion?

"Pretty fancy," I said. "What triggered it?"

"Funny, the way things happen," Philip mused, then got up and disappeared in the kitchen to fix himself a drink.

"You could dispense with that first paragraph and begin 'Funny, the way things happen.' At least shovel out that shit about Ossa and Pelion."

"Oh, shut up," he said, returning. "Remember that fat kid, Kim Sumner, in Cottonwood? His mother had been overexposed to Kipling?"

"Yeah. Kim had warts and stuttered. Ku Ku Ku Kim we called him."

"I ran into him on Nantucket. There's a stock company up there this summer. The Nantucket Players. Pretty fair. They were doing *The Silver Cord*. Lucy had never seen it, so . . . well, there was something familiar about the fellow playing the son, I forget the character name. Not about his looks, his voice. I'd heard that voice somewhere. Anyhow, I looked at the program and there was his name. Kim Sumner."

"Good Lord," I said, laughing. "Kim was slated to inherit his father's feed and grain business. Whatever made him — with that figure, that stutter — think he could be an actor?"

"You don't ask anybody a question like that. Or maybe *you* do. *I* don't. At any rate, Ku Ku Ku Kim wasn't bad. He'll never be John Barrymore, but he's slimmed down and when he has lines he doesn't stutter. Maybe he was identifying with the boy in the play. Remember his mother?"

"A pretentious bitch. Get on with it. I'm fascinated. So after the play you went back and talked to him?"

Philip nodded. He and Lucy took Kim to the local greasy spoon for a bite to eat. "I never eat before a performance," Kim said with professional pride. "It takes the edge off, know what I mean?"

He and Philip exchanged reminiscences about the old days in Cottonwood, about high school, about delivering telegrams for Postal Telegraph in a Montana blizzard, and finally Kim volunteered the information that a road company playing *Seventeen* had come through Cottonwood back in '24. Kim was home on vacation from Agricultural College and he happened to go to the show. There were a number of young men in the cast; they were supposed to be adolescents but were actually older. Kim had never before seen even a second-rate stage play. Oh, he had been to high school and college shows, but they never had the effect that *Seventeen* had. He was electrified, drawn by that impalpable force that pulls actors onto a stage. Suddenly life would not be worth living unless he could be up there behind those footlights, pretending he was somebody else.

"You know," Kim explained to Philip, without any embarrassment because those days were past, "I used to look kind of funny, warts and stuff, and chubby, but I went backstage after the show — it was a one-night stand in Cottonwood, of course — and I asked to see somebody in authority and said I wanted to join the company. I'd do anything, I didn't care. It was a fool thing to do, but it paid off. I stammered — remember? I still do once in a while when I'm nervous, but not on stage. Anyhow, I guess it was the stage manager I talked to, and pretty soon everybody in the company gathered around and they were grinning and saying things like 'Listen to him.' Somebody called the company manager, and he asked how old was I, and I said I was twenty-one (well, I wasn't yet, but I would be soon), and he said, 'Well, okay.' One of the boys in the cast was getting hitched after the Butte stand. If I could be ready to leave in the morning, I could go along and they'd help me study the part. It was a small one, but . . . well, that's how it all began."

"If that's the cliché you're offering me," I said to Philip, "thanks, but no thanks. You and I would be interested in that story because it was Kim and Cottonwood, but that would leave at least a hundred and ninety million people who wouldn't give a damn."

"That's just the beginning," Philip said, "but the rest of it is just as cliché, I'm afraid."

"Okay. What's your second act?"

Well, it seemed, Philip went on, that Kim had his ups and downs, as actors do. He lost his warts, he dieted and worried and ceased being funny just because he was fat, which was his original stock-in-trade, but by that time he had become a pretty solid actor. He even came to New York a couple of times. He would try out for a few Broadway shows, never get the parts, and then settle for road companies, which did nothing for his reputation but kept him from writing home for money.

And then one night last winter he was trouping Seattle with *The Trial of Mary Dugan.* As usual he did not eat before the show—he was playing the murderer, described with unintentional humor by his accuser as "the left-handed lover of Gertrude Rice!"—and he always gave it all he had. You never knew who might be out front.

It was a relief to get to Seattle after all the one-nighters across the Dakotas, Montana, and Idaho. You could settle down there for a couple of weeks, get your clothes cleaned, find a decent barber, take out a library card, and read a new book or two. Everything but eat a good meal. Oh, there was good food in Seattle. "Don't misunderstand me," Kim had said. But it was not for him. He always had to watch his weight. So after the show he got into the habit of dropping into a joint called One for the Road, which was right at the end of the alley near the backstage entrance.

One for the Road was one of those glaring-white, depressingly antiseptic beaneries with no personality, no charm, nothing but plain and barely edible food that tempted nobody to overeat. Counters and tabletops were of imitation marble, walls and floor of white tile, which created an acoustical nightmare at rush hour. Gelatin salads and meringue pies were displayed under reflecting mirrors and looked as if they were glued to keep from sliding off the shelves onto the floor. There were never many customers right after Curtain, though a few blue-collar men might straggle in around twelve when shifts changed. Andy, the all-night waiter, was a glum, taciturn Swede who spoke only when spoken to, and Kim liked that. He had given his all and just wanted to relax over a cup of hot Ovaltine, a green salad, and a saltine.

On this particular evening it was raining. Kim folded his umbrella and hung it behind his raincoat on a hook near the cash register. He said good evening to Andy, who said, "What's good about it?" Then he ordered the usual and, while he waited, picked up the *Seattle Intelligencer* and turned to Dorothy Kilgallen's column. Though it was a hell of a long way to Broadway, you still tried to keep up on what was happening back there.

Kim was vaguely aware that another customer was seated alone at a table at the rear, but he did not know whether it was a man or a woman until he heard her voice call, "Andy. How's about another cup of Java?"

"Okay, Gerry. Keep your shirt on," Andy answered.

Kim took his time over his Spartan supper, hoping the rain would let up a little, but it did not. Finally he asked for his check, climbed down off the stool, crossed to the hook where his raincoat had made a puddle on the floor under it, put on the damp coat, grabbed his umbrella, and walked to the cash register where Andy was waiting. The bill was seventy-five cents, and Kim left a quarter for Andy. Andy said, "Thanks. Wet enough for you?"

While Kim stood there, reluctant to step out into the rain, which had momentarily turned to hail that was bouncing off the sidewalk, he was aware that the woman who had been seated at the table at the rear was moving toward him. For the first time he looked directly at her. He was about to say, "Better wait till the hail stops," or maybe even (because she had no umbrella, and was wearing only a gray cloth coat), "Let me hold my umbrella for you."

He never said it. There was something familiar about her. Kim was thrown off for a moment because she looked kind of like Blanche Sweet in *Anna Christie*. The suit, the rumpled hat, the gray coat. The blonde hair, so much of it, slightly askew. The beaten, yet defiant, pleading look, the way Anna looked when she was trying to pick up a customer. Wanting to, knowing she had to, but hating it. But then he realized that was not it. This was somebody he had once known. The woman apparently realized at the same instant that she had known him too. She suddenly turned her head and tried to brush past him.

"Hey, Gerry, dincha forget something?" Andy said.

She looked stricken, opened her bag, pawed through it, then muttered, "I had it. Somebody musta pinched it."

"Come on, Gerry," Andy said. "Don't try'n pull that one again."

"Honest," she said.

"Yeah, honest. Listen who's talkin' about honest."

"But I had plenty. I thought I did."

"You know what *thought* did," Andy said. "Peed the bed."

And then Kim heard himself say, "It's okay, Andy. This lady is my guest. We happen to be old friends."

"I can't let you do it," Gerry said. "Not you."

"Nonsense," Kim said, the way that Leslie Howard would say it, and paid her check. "My privilege."

It was still hailing outside. Kim and Gerry Malnick stood there, not meeting each other's eyes, staring at the hail through the gold lettering on the window that spelled out ONE FOR THE ROAD. Directly she made a move as if to go, and Kim said, "Take this, Gerry. One for the road."

She turned and looked at him. The umbrella was in his hand, and he was holding it out to her. She shook her head. He said "Please," and then she accepted it. "Thanks. Thanks ever so, Ku Ku Ku Kim," she said, and walked out into the hail. Kim waited until she was out of sight, then he opened the door and, careful not to slip on the icy sidewalk, hurried home to his rooming house.

"Funny, the way things happen," Philip repeated.

from Philip Pearson's Day Book

Sept. 11, 1930. Spent Labor Day weekend on Nantucket. Mostly rain. Saw *The Silver Cord*. Old-fashioned. Excellent fresh lobster. Ran across Kim Sumner. Actor now. Story idea: Young man takes girl to resort intending to lay her. She so eager for sex that he is impotent. (Comedy? Tragedy?) John spent weekend with Elizabeth Bartlett in Philadelphia.

We sat at a window table in the Maple Grove where Liz and I had met for lunch so often that she said it was becoming Our Song. She was wearing a new white linen suit. It was impractical for New York in either summer or winter, but perfect for California.

"You know something?" I said. "If it wouldn't go to your head I'd say you look on the sensational side."

"Well, I ought to. You know what this rag cost me at DePinna's? Thirty-nine dollars and ninety-five cents." She opened her compact and began to apply something labeled Red Hot to her lips. "I'm going to need as much lure as I can get to hitch rides when I go home."

"Let's not talk about that."

She put the lipstick away, dropped the compact into her new black patent leather bag, then reached across the table and laid her hand over mine. "What's bothering you, love?"

"I've been depressed ever since Philip told me about Gerry. And now—being with you—you're so much like her in some ways . . ."

"Should I know who Gerry is?"

"I never told you, did I? You're not in a hurry, are you?"

"My time is your time," she said.

And so I told her about Gerry Malnick, the country girl whom fate had conspired to lay low, how she had spent, for room and board, the $235 we had collected for our high school annual and had been expelled from school. And then the epilogue in Seattle.

Liz gave me a dirty look, opened her bag, found a hand-kerchief, and blew her nose.

"And when you write that story, leave out the hailstorm," she sniffled. "Nobody will believe that."

"But it happened."

"Sure it happened. That's the trouble with life. Life keeps pouring it on . . . Were you in love with her?"

"I don't know. I never thought about it."

"Hell," Liz cried. "Don't you know when you're in love? Maybe if you had told her—"

"We were sixteen years old."

"What's that got to do with anything?" Liz asked. She was becoming tense. "If you know somebody loves you, you can face what you've got to face a lot better than if you think you don't matter to anybody, that they'll forget you as soon as you're out of sight and, Liz Bartlett, that's one of the worst sentences ever spoken and you should be ashamed of yourself. Forget I ever said it."

I looked out of the window, my eye attracted by the approach of a very tall man and a very short, fat woman. They were waving their arms and arguing so ferociously that they finally ground to a halt directly in front of the lettering THE MAPLE GROVE, only from our angle it was EVORG ELPAM EHT. We watched them for a moment.

"I wonder if they're married?" I said.

"Only married people fight like that," Liz said.

"What's it about? Another woman? Another man?" The mere thought was ridiculous. What other woman, or other man, would look at either of them?

"I think he was supposed to meet her at Fifty-seventh and Broadway and kept her waiting."

"Would that make you mad?"

Liz laughed. "Livid! And you remember that." Then, "Well!" she said with finality. "Connie Bennett's in town. Jim Quirk wants me to run her down and find out if she's getting a divorce So . . ." She rose to her feet, looked down at her new white jacket. "Holy cow! A coffee spot on the very first day I wear the damn thing." She sat down again, wet the corner of her napkin with cold water, and went to work on the brown stain.

I watched her for a moment, then I said, "If it means anything to you — as if you didn't know already — I love you."

She stopped worrying the coffee spot for a moment. "We weren't going to say that, remember?"

"*You* weren't. I never promised."

"You think you have to say I love you because you ruined me."

She went back to work on the coffee spot. "See? Comes right out with cold water."

The quarreling couple had gone on. Jordan Bell, the editor of *International,* and Edna Ferber, whom he had taken to lunch, were passing. She was giving him hell about something, probably a cut in her last story. (I had made it; five hundred words had to come out in order to fit it to space.) I pointed Miss Ferber out to Liz. "She gets five thousand for a short," I added.

"You'll get it too some day." Then Liz continued without a pause, "Has the thought of marrying me ever occurred to you?"

"Well, yes. Frequently," I said. "But—as you said early in the do, it's impossible. We live on opposite coasts, you have Lulabel on your hands, and I've got my mother and father to support since Papa had to quit work. Besides, nobody's job is safe these days."

"Jim wants me to stay in New York," Liz said. "Look. Have you got a piece of paper?"

I found a scrap in my pocket. She glanced at it and began to laugh. What it was was a rejection slip, the kind we attached to junk manuscripts going back to hopeful, and usually hopeless, amateurs. "The editors regret that your story does not meet the needs of *International Magazine* and we are returning it herewith." Finally Liz found a pencil in her bag. "Now. I make a hundred and a quarter per week. What's your take?"

"Eighty. Just eighty."

"What do you mean *just* eighty?"

"Well, you make a lot more than I do."

"Are you so insecure that you can't face that?"

"I don't think so, but I wouldn't want you to feel that you were helping to support my parents."

"Oh, for God's sake! A hundred and twenty-five plus eighty, that's two hundred and five, isn't it? I'm lousy at arithmetic."

"It is."

"Two hundred and five times fifty-two . . ." She began to scribble on the rejection slip again. "*Plus* your short stories."

"We can't count on those."

"Okay. Strike short stories, but if we get married I'll chain you to the typewriter." She went on muttering, counting on her fingers, and finally looked up from her Einsteinian problem in awe. "Why, I don't believe it! Ten thousand, six hundred and sixty dollars a year! I must be wrong."

"No," I said, glancing at her calculations. "That's about right."

"We're richer than three-fourths of the people in New York, do you realize that?"

"But they're not supporting three households."

"We're supporting the same number of people as it is now, so what's the diff?"

"I'm trying to be practical before it's too late."

"You sound as if you're being led to the guillotine."

"I just want to recognize roadblocks before we crash into them."

"Jack Gilbert would never say that to Garbo."

And so, for the next half hour we weighed the economic pros and cons, toted up the foreseeable monthly outgo and subtracted it from our combined income. There was no time to lose. If Liz decided to stay, Jim Quirk must be notified immediately. We had to find an apartment. I had to give Philip notice.

Presently there was nothing more either of us could think of. We stared at each other. "Well," I said, "what's the verdict?"

"I'm game if you are," Liz said, a little breathless.

"Then I guess that makes us engaged."

Liz lifted the saltcellar and tossed some over her shoulder. I crossed my fingers. "Shouldn't I kiss you or something?"

We kissed as decorously as possible under the circumstances.

"Oh. And speaking of *something*," Liz said, suddenly prim. "None of *that* now until after we're married."

"Why, for God's sake?"

"I think I'd like to feel just faintly virginal on our wedding night. Oh. And another thing. Promise me! If you ever want out, tell me."

"You too," I said.

★   ★   ★

Tell Philip.

Yes. Tell Philip. It was no concern of his except for his finding somebody else to help pay the rent. Yet it seemed more — more diplomatic? — to do so in a public place. I telephoned him at *Vanity Fair* — he had got up and gone to work before I was awake — and said I would like to have lunch with him. How about the Harvard Club? We could make ourselves heard in that dining room without shouting.

And so, after our buffet trays were unloaded and we were seated, I told him that he was the first to know because it was already September and our lease would be up October first. He would have to decide whether he wanted to find a new roommate or a cheaper apartment.

"Because you're marrying Elizabeth? *Quelle* dilemma."

"Liz. I'm marrying Liz. Quote congratulations are in order unquote."

"And may I say quote about time unquote? And that all your troubles will be little ones?"

"That is humorous," I said. "That is indeed humorous."

After a moment I got off that track. "How about Norman?" I asked.

"What *about* Norman?"

"I mean as a roommate. He's intelligent, he's clean, he's good company, he's—"

"Queer," Philip said. "Forget it!"

"Okay, okay."

"No. I can swing seven-B by myself these days."

"Yes indeed. You're a big wheel now. Can afford taxis, parquet tickets, maybe find a good reconditioned mistress."

Philip snorted. "Remind me to look in the yellow pages."

"Well, your future's settled. What do I owe you?"

"Two-fifteen."

I counted out the change and handed it to him. I dropped my napkin beside my plate and was about to rise when he said something so softly that I had to ask him to repeat it: "This isn't going to make any difference between us, is it?"

"This what isn't going to make any difference?"

"Your getting married to—to Liz—and all?"

"There's no *and all* about it. I'll be living with Liz instead of you, that's the only difference."

"I mean—*between* us. That won't change, will it?"

"What's to change? We've been friends since we were kids."

"I know, I know." He sat staring at me, his hands clenched in his lap. "It's just—just—it'll keep on being the *same,* won't it? We'll still be—be—"

These were not lines he was composing. Whatever he was trying to say was wrenched uncensored from his gut. In another minute he would be crying. It was time for me to lighten it up. "If you want to know whether I'll continue to tolerate you, the answer is, how can I help it? I'm stuck with you. For some reason Liz even seems to like you."

"That's —" What he intended to say he never said. Instead he finally managed control. "That's nice . . . well, time I got back to the assembly line."

21

from Philip Pearson's Day Book

Oct. 3, 1930. John and Elizabeth were married at 4 P.M. at Little Church Around the Corner. I was best man. They drove to Quebec. Maureen left for Iowa.

It was a perfect day for a wedding. Indian summer. Liz was radiant in a tailored green suit with green orchid on the lapel, and I controlled my voice during the I-do's and I-take-thee's. Philip did not drop the ring, which was a wonder because his hand shook worse than usual.

Jim and May Quirk gave us a reception at their suite in the Buckingham, and directly we waved good-bye under a shower of rice and drove off in Jim Quirk's 1925 Buick roadster, which he had kept in case the snazzy new Stutz broke down. "You kids are welcome to it," he had said. "Don't worry. One more dent won't do it any harm."

We made the trip in three jumps: Poughkeepsie — Montreal — Quebec. Since we were already acquainted with sex we could enjoy other discoveries about each other. One thing I discovered: Liz was a shameless sightseer. The morning after we arrived at the Chateau Frontenac I awoke to find her fully dressed and staring out of our window high above the St. Lawrence.

"Look," she said. "When I go someplace, I want to see every-thing I ever read about it in the seventh grade. I want to see the Plains of Abraham, and where Wolfe died, and Dufferin Ter-race — I guess that must be it right down there, but I want to walk on it and read all the junk about it — and the cathedral and that old old church, Notre Dame des Victoires, and if you don't want to go with me, you don't have to."

It was a brisk, windy day but Liz, in four-inch heels, managed to traverse the cobblestones of Lower Town and the cement of Upper without breaking a leg. That evening — Tuesday, October

7—we went to a stock company performance of *La Page Première,* which lost something in translation, though the French audience, which had never seen *The Front Page,* seemed to like it.

Next morning it was raining, and the prediction was for rain all day. (We seemed destined to be confined to hotel rooms whenever we ventured out of New York.) After breakfast in the dining room, I bought day-old copies of the *New York Times* and the *Tribune,* and we went back to bed.

"If you see anything I ought to know, read it," I said.

"Likewise," Liz said.

"Crowds in Boston Acclaim Hoover," I read from the front page of the *Times.* "Hoover addressed the American Legion last night—"

"Spare me," Liz said. "Now this is more my speed," and read: "Nothing has been heard of Judge Crater since he disappeared on August sixth after drawing five thousand dollars from his bank account. Yesterday his safe deposit box was opened under court order and found to be empty."

"My God," I said, "we forgot all about the World Series. If we were at home we would be lynched." I found the *Times* sports section. "Athletics blank cards on Jimmy Foxx's homer in the ninth, to take a series lead three to two."

"Who's Jimmy Foxx?"

"How about Carmine Piraino, twenty-three-year-old son of 'The Clutching Hand' shot to death at nightfall yesterday in front of the Agyia Coast Apartments in Brooklyn?"

"Gangster killings don't grab me. Give me a nice, folksy minister like Dr. Hall caught in Mrs. Mills's feathers. Then tell me *all* the details." She turned back to her copy of the *Herald Trib.* "Now *this* is right up my alley. 'Small-town matron charged with contributing to delinquency of minors. Claims churchgoing widow lured teenagers with homemade chocolate candy.'"

"You're making that up," I said.

"No. Right here. How could I make up a thing like that?"

It was a sparse AP dispatch, datelined Des Moines. I read it over Liz's shoulder. "Two sets of parents in Algona, Iowa, whose names are being withheld, have charged Mrs. Samuel Parsons of that community with contributing to the delinquency of their teenage sons. According to testimony of these two couples, Mrs. Parsons, a widow, lured the youngsters into her kitchen with promise of homemade chocolate candy and then made sexual advances to them. The accused is being held in the care of her daughter from New York awaiting disposition of the charges."

"See what I mean?" Liz said. "It's got it all — sex — religion — upper-middle-class respectability. And that seduction with chocolate candy yet! Don't you love it!" And then she looked up at me. "What's the matter?"

"Don't you realize who the woman is?"

Liz shook her head. "Why should I know who Mrs. Samuel Parsons is?"

"They got it wrong," I said. "Algona, Iowa. It must be Pearson. Mrs. Sam Pearson. Philip's mother. That's why Maureen didn't come to our wedding."

"You said Philip's mother was — *interesting,*" Liz said. "Honey, it'll take me time to get used to your gift for understatement."

"It's not funny," I said.

"Maybe. But you've got to admit that a middle-aged woman out in the boondocks coaxing little boys to their sexual initiation with a plate of chocolate candy has elements of humor about it. After all, the woman didn't murder them."

"But *the woman* is obviously Philip's mother," I said. "Would it be so damn funny if she was yours?"

Liz thought about that and then laughed out loud. When she stopped to catch her breath she said, "Lulabel would have to employ another lure, though. Hates chocolate. Do you think spoonbread would bring them into the kitchen?"

Then, seeing my face, she was contrite. "Forgive me, darling. I don't know what's wrong with me, I see the funny side first, always have. I laugh, and I wonder why nobody else is laughing. Then it hits me, and I wish I was dead."

She put her arm around me and we walked to the window. Through the drab gray curtain of mist a Cunard passenger liner was drifting down the St. Lawrence on an outgoing tide.

"I wish you hadn't bought that paper," Liz murmured.

"Me too."

"What should we do about it? Pretend we never saw it? Or telephone Philip and say . . . what *do* you say?"

"Send flowers?" I said.

"You see? It's funny. You think it's funny too."

We decided to do nothing for the time being.

★ ★ ★

The one-room studio apartment that we had rented on East Fifty-seventh Street was exactly as we had last seen it before we went to Canada. There were no lights, the telephone had not been connected, paper runners crisscrossed the floor, and the walls were still a pale, sickly green. (The painters, we discovered later, had mistakenly painted an identical space on the floor below us.) There was one plus: The furniture we had ordered had been delivered, but it was stacked in the basement of the building.

"But they *promised!*" Liz said. "We'll sue."

"Fine. But not today. It's Sunday. We've got to find a place to spend the night."

"You're still paid up on Philip's apartment until the first of November, aren't you?"

I nodded. "You've seen it. There are only two single pull-down beds."

"Maybe Philip had to go out to Iowa too, if that woman is really his mother. You've still got a key, haven't you?"

I did have one, but when we got there I rang the bell. Philip came to the door with a half-eaten peanut butter sandwich in one hand and a lighted cigarette in the other. The room behind him was a stinking grotto of smoke. The portable goose-neck lamp sprayed light on his typewriter and dog-eared Roget, and the wastebasket beside it overflowed with crumpled paper, spoor of the writer-in-labor.

He looked startled, then confused, embarrassed — as if it were indecorous for persons who must have been so recently making love to appear in public — and finally pleased to see us. We had not planned how to explain our dropping in so soon after our return, but Liz was expert at extemporizing. "Our apartment is empty—no phone, no nothing—so we thought we'd come down here and make a few heartrending telephone calls. Maybe some soft-hearted soul will let us bed down in his stable for the night."

Philip laughed, nervously, then cleared his throat several times. "Well, Elizabeth," he said, with a bright smile, "you may—you *two* may—be my guests. I'll clear out."

"That's silly," I said. "If anybody goes to a hotel, we go."

"I'll go down to Maureen's. No problem," he said.

Liz and I avoided an exchange of glances. "She has only one bed, as I remember," Liz said.

"Yes, but Maureen's in Iowa."

I said, "Oh?" and Liz asked, "Is your mother still sick?" her voice managing to express only normal concern.

"She's—she's better, thank you," Philip said. "But Maureen is staying on until Aunt Grace arrives to—to be with—" he cleared his throat again, "with my—with her."

"You're lucky Miss Grace could get away," Liz said. "Half the belles in Hollywood have to forego their Chanels and Mainbochers when she leaves town."

Philip was moving jerkily about the room, picking up the debris, dumping ashtrays, the wastebasket, and crusts from his sandwich into the garbage container in the kitchenette, tying his tie, rolling down the sleeves of his shirt, and finally ripping a half-filled sheet of paper out of his typewriter.

"What are you writing, Philip?" Liz asked.

He turned as if he could not conceive of such unmitigated gall. Then, seeing that no gall was intended, that she was merely interested in knowing and knew no better than to pry, he said, "I won't know until I finish it, then you may read it. Any further questions?"

"Yes," Liz said, without missing a beat. "How would you like to go to hell?"

Since I had known Philip and his friends in New York he had been practicing—and getting away with—increasingly cavalier social behavior. On stage what he often said might have been amusing. We called it smart dialogue, when composed by Coward or Behrman or Barry. But in real life (what an odd expression) such insults were unfunny except when, upon rare occasions, I could match Philip insult for insult, rudeness for rudeness.

Stopped cold, he stood with the sheet of paper in his hand gaping at Liz, while she glared at him and then snapped her bag open to find her lipstick, which she slashed angrily across her lips. I was tempted to say, "Come on, kids, skip it," but I restrained myself and let the moment stretch to its limit, until Philip finally said, "I didn't mean anything by that, Elizabeth. I just don't like people asking me what I'm writing. It—I don't know—it's in embryo. I won't really know what I'm writing until it's written."

"Then why didn't you say so?" Liz said. "I'm not so stupid I can't understand a thing like that. But — 'Any further questions?'" She mimicked his supercilious tone and he winced. "Come *on,* Philip. That's not worthy of my husband's best friend."

More than anything Philip hated a direct confrontation. I guess he thought it was in bad taste, simply *not done,* to bring a situation out in the open and let it boil. He even avoided such scenes in his fiction, if you stop to think about it. He always chose to write *around* his characters, to see them through someone else's eyes, to hem them in with a dialectical razzle-dazzle like the Cheyennes circling a wagon train, never coming quite close enough to see their eyes, but occasionally loosing brilliant shafts of conjecture their way and, after they were decently interred, permitting old acquaintances to deliver an epilogue, speculating on what they must have been thinking, surmising what their extraordinary (or ordinary) conduct signified, what made them tick.

"I'm sorry," Philip muttered finally, staring at his feet. (What had happened to Noel Coward?)

"That makes two of us," Liz said, her sudden anger as suddenly dissipated.

He looked past her at me, and blinked several times. Then he found a crumpled handkerchief in his shirt pocket and blew his nose.

I took a deep breath. "Now that everything's hanging out," I said, "there's something I've got to tell you, Philip."

"You're getting a divorce," Philip said. "Who's the corespondent? Anyone I know?" (Noel Coward had made a comeback.)

"We saw that paragraph in the *Herald Trib* about — well, 'Mrs. Parsons' of Algona, Iowa. I'd feel like a fool to go on pretending we hadn't."

"Oh, darling," Liz sighed. "Thank God you said it."

Philip walked stiffly to the closet, put on a jacket, closed the door behind him, and crossed to the entrance of the apartment. Then he turned, smiled at both of us, said, "Help yourself to anything in the fridge," and walked out. Before we had time to speak he was back again, crossing to the closet once more. "The paper says it may rain tomorrow. Excuse me." He grabbed his umbrella, removed it from its sheath, put it up, lifted it over his head, and made quite the most absurd exit I have ever seen.

22

"I don't care what anybody says about your new digs," Philip said the first time he saw the apartment, "it's — new."

That it was. You could smell the robin's-egg-blue paint on the walls and hesitated to step on the beige carpet, lest you leave prints. From the corner windows you could see the Empire State Building way down on Thirty-fourth Street (its spire, scuttlebutt had it, would soon serve as anchor to transoceanic dirigibles), the old brewery on First Avenue, and directly across Sutton Place the windows of a townhouse currently occupied by Miss Miriam Hopkins, reigning Broadway star, who sometimes failed to draw the shades when she should.

There were but two items in the whole layout that were not straight off the floor of Macy's, Bloomingdale's, or Wanamaker's. One was my piano, the other a bergère armchair. The piano bench made the trip too, though I had told my mother not to ship it. Liz took one look and said, "Where did that monstrosity come from?" I told her it had been the gift from somebody I didn't dare offend by refusing it at the time — he had no taste whatsoever — and we would contribute it to the junk pile.

The bergère chair we had discovered in the window of an antique (secondhand) shop while walking along Fifty-seventh Street one cold morning in November. We were reluctant to ask the price; it looked authentic and beyond our means. It also looked as if it was exactly what was needed to fit into the kidney of the piano. We paused to admire it each morning and evening for a couple of weeks. Then one afternoon we steeled ourselves and went into the shop. The proprietor wanted thirty-five dollars, but we could have it for twenty-five if he did not have to deliver it. We managed to get it into a taxi.

We did not have it recovered immediately because, along with the wedding presents awaiting us when we finally had a place to put them, came news that both of us were receiving ten percent cuts in salary. Magazine circulation was holding up — the unemployed could still read and the slicks cost only twenty-five cents — but advertising was off. Even the holiday issues were lean. Whether Philip took a cut at that time I never asked and, of course, he never volunteered the information, but I suspect he did. *Vanity Fair* was losing weight too. Still we were the fortunate ones. While Liz's salary (now $112.50 per week) covered the features she wrote for *Photoplay,* Philip and I could augment ours with an occasional sale of a short story. Liz and I actually had enough stashed away in a joint account for incidental extravagances like upholstering a chair or taking an occasional taxicab instead of the bus when it was raining, but fear made us frugal. What if the next story — and the next — did not sell? What if either of us lost our jobs? What if we should get sick and have to go to the hospital? What then? The five of us — Liz and I, her poor mother, my mother, and my aging and no-longer-employable father — would be vis-à-vis the poorhouse, that's what then! So on most evenings and weekends I applied my nose to the typewriter, turning out stories that I did not particularly like, but thought might be marketable.

And then one of those slick manufactured stories sold to *Collier's.* (Hurrah, I'd fooled 'em again.) *International,* which had first look at anything I turned out, had rejected it, but Esme Jones somehow managed to jack my price up to $800, so the threat of the poorhouse receded for the time being.

"Come on," Liz said. "Let's bust out and give a housewarming."

"Well . . ."

"Nobody's seen our place, and we owe everybody. We'll have a buffet."

"How many were you thinking of?"

"Oh, I don't know. Twenty-five or thirty, around there."

"Jesus!"

"Let's make a list."

The names on our list added up to twenty-seven. And then Liz remembered Norman Conley. Liz had not wanted to worry me about Norman so she had not told me while I was working so hard, she said. Norman had confessed to her — "And he looks terrible" — that he had tried to kill himself recently because he had, well, "slipped," allowed himself to be picked up by a young man on Park Avenue one evening.

"If you're going to be picked up, you meet a tonier type there than on Broadway," I said.

"Look," Liz said, "this is no joke. He thought that sort of thing was just part of the dead-and-buried California scene, and now . . ."

"You mean if you ask Norman you have to ask this — this Park Avenue —"

"Of course not," Liz said. "I just want to help Norman get — get back to normal."

"But what we think is normal may not be normal for Norman."

"Maybe not. But whatever he is, I love Norman," Liz said. "The way you love Philip, I guess. Who's going to call *him,* by the way?"

"You."

"Gee, thanks."

It, whatever *it* was, was no longer quite the same between Philip and me despite my protests that it would be. I had tried; Liz and I had both tried. Though we had not given parties, we had called him several times and asked him to pop over and take potluck. Sometimes he had come, sometimes he had said, "No, I'm busy."

This evening Liz bubbled on over the phone about the party, how the old hermit crabs were coming out of their Fifty-seventh Street shell to celebrate my sale to *Collier's,* and how we had gone out and bought a priceless antique chair for twenty-five dollars and were going to have a bronze plaque affixed to the back with his name on it. *Philip Pearson, his chair.*

"Who else is coming?" Philip asked.

"I knew you'd ask that, and now I know what I'm going to give you for Christmas. A copy of Emily Post."

"I just wondered," Philip said.

"Well, there's one way to find out. Come about eight. And why don't you bring Lucy? She's invited too."

He cleared his throat. "Lucy knows the way."

"True," Liz said, beginning to get mad. "I merely thought, in my simple fashion, that Lucy might believe you have some manners if you pick her up."

Nobody else treated Philip quite the way Liz did. If something about his behavior bothered her, she would call him on it, while the rest of us would skip it, permit ourselves to be bullied, and, if mentioning it at all later, merely say, "Well, you know, that's Philip."

"That's Philip" was by way of becoming an accolade. If something displeased him (perhaps one of your guests did not laugh at his sallies) and he turned churlish, if he did not show up when he had promised he would, or if he did arrive and was bored (which was worse), he would retreat into his private cocoon and spend the rest of the evening sitting in silence, *in* but not *of* the group, hands folded in his lap, feet crossed and extended so that everyone had to step over him. "Well, that's Philip," his host or hostess would say in something curiously like admiration, as if honored by his surliness, as if it conferred a certain distinction and gave you membership in the club.

Or, of course, he could be a charmer. One never knew which Philip would come through the door, or when one would change—like Dr. Jekyll to Mr. Hyde—into the other.

He was not at his best the evening of our housewarming.

The party was an amalgam of Liz's friends from *Photoplay,* mine from *International,* and the crowd, those charter members of the sometimes amused, sometimes nettled, and usually forgiving "That's Philip" club.

Marriage seemed to be in the air that evening. Liz and I were smug enough to suspect that we had triggered the impulse, but more likely it was merely the proper, the psychological moment in the lives of our peers to cease shopping around and solidify relationships. Maureen and Joe Tyler had set a date. They were not ecstatic, but in all likelihood they would never know what they were missing. Ecstasy is for the privileged few. Maureen would keep on working for a while, she said, if she could find another job. (BBD&O frowned on married couples working for the firm.) Esme Jones and Dan Mobridge, after careful consideration, had concluded that it was economically absurd to continue maintaining two apartments. Besides, Esme was knocking thirty; if they were ever going to have offspring, they should get with it.

Philip had deigned to escort Lucy, but the atmosphere between them was noticeably *fraught,* as Liz observed. On arrival, Philip accepted a drink, made a beeline for Philip's chair in the kidney of the piano, and sank into self-induced quarantine. Maureen, always sensitive to her brother's moods, and hoping to put the best face on them, confided that he was distracted by a story in progress. It would not leave him alone. (Then why inflict it on us, I wanted to ask?)

Lucy meanwhile concentrated on the gaunt, handsome, eager-to-please Norman Conley. He replenished her drinks, lit her cigarettes, and seemed amused by her spirited conversation. The room being crowded, she shifted to the edge of her chair, encouraging him to share it with her. He beamed. I could not help the feeling that his behavior was tantamount to saying, Look everybody, it's girls I like. Perhaps Lucy was saying to Philip, See? I'm attractive to other men, so you can go screw.

When the hosts of a party are finally able to stand back and not distinguish a word said in eight to ten disparate, concurrent conversations, they can cease being hosts, meld with their guests, and enjoy.

I was usually semi-aware of Philip, God knows why, and felt vaguely responsible for him. I wanted him to have a good time, wanted him to be *one of us,* or at worst leave off casting a bloody pall. Conscious that I had been neglecting him, I glanced at Philip's chair, and saw it happen. I do not know whether his reclusiveness finally bored him too, whether he came to the conclusion that he was being ignored as well as ignoring, or whether one of his personal demons quietly loosed its grip. It was as if a cloud opened and the sun shot through. He straightened up, his face lost that sullen look, he got out of the damn chair, and began to integrate with the crowd. He asked Esme and Dan whether they had found an apartment. He'd keep an eye out for them. There might be something in his building. Later I heard him ask Barney Lehman, our semi-radical poet, and his noticeably pregnant housemate Jinna Dieter why they didn't get married. He listened with apparent interest while Jinna harangued him with a long and not very interesting tale about how marriage to Barney would mean she would have to take Sunday dinner with the pompous elder Lehmans in East Orange, New Jersey, which was a fate worse than labeling a kid a bastard.

Then Philip proceeded to tolerate his future brother-in-law, who warned everybody that he had the most *marvelous* story to tell and unloaded brick by brick one of his dismal shaggy dog stories. Philip even laughed, and Maureen was as amazed as she was grateful. She whispered to me, "See, he's fine now. He must have solved the problem."

Philip turned to the two of us. "Did you tell John about Mother?" he asked Maureen. Maureen started visibly. The subject of "Mother" had been taboo ever since the late scandal.

"Why no, Philip, I didn't. Just what did you want me to tell about her?"

He turned to me. "Mother's going to California to live with Aunt Grace. You remember Aunt Grace — on Genesee?"

"Of course," I said. "It was indirectly through her that I got my first job at the studio. A very cute old party."

"A good arrangement for them both. Both lonely women. Aunt Grace's friend — I forget his name — died not long ago."

Evidently several lids were off. Which one would he lift next?

"I'm sorry to hear that," I said.

Then Philip's eyes roved the room. "Where is that bright person you tricked into marrying you? I must thank her for the party before I toddle off."

"He's a dear tonight, isn't he?" Maureen said. "I'm so happy when he's — this way."

Philip found Lucy before he found Liz and offered his arm in a theatrically extravagant gesture of gallantry. "Shall we go and let John and Liz slam the door, have a nightcap, and talk about us?"

"Norman is taking me home," Lucy said with a look of defiance.

"Thank you, Norman," Philip said. "Sure it's not out of your way?"

"Not at all, not at all," Norman said nervously.

Philip turned to Liz. "Lovely party. God be with you." He gave her the benediction of a kiss on the cheek, and made his exit, the perfect guest, the perfect Man About Town.

Norman not only took Lucy home that night, he married her three weeks later. We all went into shock and kept our fingers crossed. They were both dear people who respected and liked each other. Maybe, with patience, the desire for love could be transmuted into desire itself . . .

Lucy was the first girl—so far as I know—who gave up on Philip.

PART IV

23

I have sometimes wondered what would have happened if *The Age of Mrs. Page* had been produced on Broadway. There is no point in dwelling upon its probable failure. The pain of a flop would have been more acute, the embarrassment more public than no production at all, but the result about the same. Philip and I would probably have gone our separate ways. (I doubt that I would have suggested another collaboration.) But suppose the damn thing had been a smash and the two of us lauded as another Kaufman and Connolly?

Well, first of all, we would have quit our editorial jobs — who needs a piddling seventy-two dollars, or sixty-five dollars, per week when royalties are rolling in at seven or eight hundred? The producer — hell, *producers!* — would be begging for another play and Hollywood beckoning. So we would write another. It would be best to continue living together, but we would require more room. A townhouse? No, a penthouse would be the practical solution. Of course we'd need someone to cook and clean and shop, someone who would make himself scarce when we were working. Elwood Grainger had a Philippine houseboy . . .

At that time of our lives, could we have coped with success of that sort? Could we have worked together for very long and remained on speaking terms? Could I, over the long haul, hold my temper and suppress my own ego in order to keep the pot of his talent on simmer? Could Philip do the same?

And how would Liz have adjusted to that setup? Liz was never much of an adjuster. I have a feeling that she would have taken a long look at this situation and said no thanks. The question of our marriage would never have arisen.

But, of course, that was not what happened. Our lives, Philip's and mine, no longer impinged upon each other very much. Oh, there were frequent and friendly (most of the time) contacts, but his own career and personal orbit neither attracted nor jolted me from mine. We traveled on separate, though similar and often parallel, paths, wooing and flirting with modest success for a while, managing to inform each other ("Oh, by the way, did I tell you . . .") when we hit a target, and depending upon the discretion of our mutual agent, Esme Jones (now Mrs. Dan Mobridge and twice pregnant and productive), to keep her mouth shut when we missed.

Somehow we managed to exist, during those early years of the Depression, alongside the agony and desperation of others without being much affected by it. Fortunately we did not know those others personally. They were statistics: fifteen percent, seventeen percent, twenty-one percent unemployed. Even so, mustn't we have felt a sense of shame at being happy and carefree? That isn't the way I remember it. Lucky, yes. "My God, aren't we the lucky ones? Whooo-eee!" we would say, and get dressed up and go dancing.

Roosevelt was going to straighten out everybody's problems as soon as that do-nothing Hoover vacated the White House. Oh, not *our* problems. We had none. Yes, we had all taken another ten percent cut in salary, and then a third, but my short story price continued to rise, and out of the blue John Farrar of Farrar & Rinehart called to ask me to expand one of those stories into a novel, offering me an advance of five hundred dollars.

Liz and I mulled this over—a novel would take at least six months writing nights and weekends and maybe I could not afford to ignore the short story market for that long. On the other hand, consider the prestige. A novelist! How much more impressive than short story writer! (Had anybody asked Philip to write a novel?)

But—a *novel*. The very word looked formidable. God knows the novel seas had been well charted, but, except for formula trash, I could detect on those charts no place to set sail from.

I talked to John Farrar, a charming, intelligent man who for some reason wanted the book from me. Was the writing of a novel so very different from that of a short story? No difference, Farrar said, so far as he knew. Except a novel gives you room to turn around in without scraping your fenders. Ask a silly question, you get a silly answer. Webster was not much more helpful. His dictionary quoted one Clara Reeve as stating, "The novel is a picture of real life and manners, and of the times in which it is written." Oh, is that so? Well, thanks a lot, Clara.

Meanwhile the blank page stared at me from the typewriter.

I telephoned Philip and told him that I simply wanted to warn him. We would not be upstaging him or any of our friends, but I'd be tied up for a few months on a writing assignment. A novel for Farrar & Rinehart. He would understand, wouldn't he? Maybe one day soon we could meet for lunch and I could fill him in on details.

He would appreciate that, Philip said, though he was surprised that I would be seen speaking to a mere short story hack. Had he disposed of another one of his little pastiches, I asked politely.

"Just a potboiler," he said. "A two-parter for the *Post*."

"The Newark *Post?*"

"Farther south. The *Saturday Evening Post*."

I could not find an appropriate comment on that for a moment. Then I laughed. "We all take to the streets when the weather is right, don't we? Mind telling me your price?" Philip had never got more than $350 for a story.

"Well, if you must know: four thousand dollars."

I turned to Liz and told her. She grabbed the phone out of my hand. "Philip, how awesome! What's the name of the story?"

" 'There but for Grace,' " he said.

"I didn't know you could write a popular-magazine story," she said.

"Neither did I," Philip admitted. "It's kind of embarrassing."

"Money like that is never embarrassing," Liz said. "Now I know where to look for the dough to spring me from the hospital when we have the baby . . . Oh, didn't John tell you? I'm pregnant . . ."

"Well," I said after she had hung up, "what was the reaction to that?"

"*Oh.*"

"I thought we weren't going to tell anybody about the baby until you killed the rabbit."

"I couldn't resist letting him know you could still do something he couldn't."

"That was bitchy, wasn't it?"

"Yes, it was," Liz said.

★   ★   ★

"There but for Grace" was not your typical *Post* story. Romantic tales of abnegation and renunciation might have been meat and potatoes for the late Victorians, but they were scarcely the diet for magazine readers of the 1930s. It was Philip's style—charming, gently humorous, slightly formal in texture—the word *bittersweet* comes to mind—that made it palatable. Of course it was in good taste; Philip never wrote anything that was not.

"There but for Grace" was the cornerstone of Philip Pearson's financial security; *Post* readers not only read it but gave it word-of-mouth. They cried, some admitted. Oh, there were some who scoffed and said that Grace belonged in a sequel to *Little Women,* but they talked, and that was what was important. The thing was published subsequently as a novelette, price $2.50, and sold fifty-five thousand copies.

Then MGM bought it for the movies and paid Philip twenty-five thousand dollars. (Remember Myrna Loy, in a blonde wig, as Grace? Lousy casting.)

I think Philip was stunned. I know that all of his friends were. The Depression was at its nadir (where it wallowed for a long while). Liz and I were not hurting, but we counted pennies. Philip wouldn't need to do that any longer. He could walk into Brooks Brothers and clean out the joint, if he wanted to. We were happy for him and it was—well, for Christ's sake, it was wonderful!

Wasn't it?

Not to Philip, so far as one could notice. He did not resign from his editorial job at *Vanity Fair*. He remained in the one-room apartment on Forty-fourth Street that I had shared briefly with him. Oh, he may have bought a few ties and shirts, it was hard to tell. All his ties were monochromatic, and his white-shirt collars buttoned down.

Liz said, "Philip, why don't you buy yourself a car?"

"*Car?* What would I do with a car?" She might as well have suggested that he buy an elephant.

"You could drive us all to Jones Beach. Oh, we would chip in for the gas, if that's bothering you. Or you could make a tidy sum smuggling in booze from Canada."

"Very funny."

"Well, you ought to do *something*. I'd hate to think the Pope was going to get all that green stuff eventually."

Apparently Liz struck a nerve. A few days later he telephoned. After nervously clearing his throat several times he announced portentously, "I have tickets for *Design for Living*. Will you and Elizabeth be my guests?"

In a travesty of his manner I said, "I think I can speak for Elizabeth and accept your gracious invitation."

"New Year's Eve," Philip said. "That's the only night I could get."

It was the last time Liz could get into the slinky black evening dress Philip's aunt Grace had whipped up for her from a Valentina original. All very bias cut, and you'd better be skinny as a rail to wear it.

Philip was standing alone near the box office of the Barrymore Theatre when Liz and I got out of the taxi. He looked excited and pleased with himself, as if he wanted everyone to observe that he was playing Gracious Host, a role he had by no means perfected. I suspect that he had fortified himself with a drink or two before we met him. The speakeasy across the street was now legitimately doing business as a bar.

Philip had done himself proud with seats: fourth-row center. He made a point of seeing that both Liz and I had programs, checked her coat, and asked her if she had ever seen the Lunts before. "No, I haven't," she told him. ("Why did you say that?" I asked her later. "We — you and I — saw them together in *Reunion in Vienna*." "Because he wanted me never to have seen them so he could give them to me," Liz said. "It was touching.")

The play was not, as I remember, very good. Lynn loved Alfred and Noel Coward; Alfred adored Lynn and loved Noel; Noel loved Alfred and adored Lynn; Lynn and Alfred happened to be married, so what? That was the design for living that Coward had written and the three of them were stuck with it. They were quite shameless. They flaunted every trick in their theatrical bag to make a pathological triangle amusing—and never, of course, mentioned the word *homosexuality*. They were the three most expert farceurs of their time and their charm could not be resisted.

It was snowing gently when we came out of the theater. Traffic was stalled between Sixth and Eighth avenues by the boisterous mob awaiting 1934 in Times Square. The hubbub frayed all the way over to the Barrymore. It was the first New Year's Eve since repeal and millions of Americans were overcompensating for the long dry spell. We figured we had better not try to fight our way through the drunken crowd. "It wouldn't be advisable—in your condition," Philip said to Liz.

She chuckled at that as we hurried along toward Eighth Avenue. "Philip, darling," she said, "where did you pick up *in your condition?* I'm glad Noel Coward isn't listening."

We hailed a taxi going north and piled in. I gave the driver Esme and Dan's address on West Sixty-seventh; we had told them we would join their party by midnight. Liz sat between Philip and me. The seat was never meant for three, so she put one arm around me and the other around Philip. He tensed slightly.

It was at Cornelia's that Philip passed out. When he came to—as abruptly as he had left us—he said he had an announcement to make. Very important announcement. He had had an offer from Twentieth Century-Fox, and wanted to talk to Liz about it.

"Why me?" Liz asked.

"Well, you know Hollywood. What would it cost me to live out there?"

"Depends on how you want to live," Liz said. "Would you mind telling me what you'd be making?"

That's going to do it, I thought. Liz should know better than to ask Philip a question like that. I might do it, but nobody else.

"Fifteen hundred a week," he answered without blinking. "But that's only for thirteen weeks, with an option for thirteen more at two thousand."

"Philip, are you drunk?" Cornelia asked.

"Yes, I daresay I'm drunk. Let's see if I can stand up." He tried. He just could, then crashed back into his chair. "Where was I?"

"You were earning fifteen hundred dollars a week and wondered what you could get by on in Hollywood," I said.

He frowned. "The thing is, though, I'd want to keep my apartment here just in case."

"While you're being such a blabbermouth, may I ask what you pay for that?" Cornelia asked.

"Eighty dollars. So you see . . ."

Cornelia, Liz, and I all nodded gravely. "Fifteen hundred minus eighty leaves you only fourteen hundred and twenty," Cornelia said. "That is a problem."

"How about your mother and Aunt Grace? Couldn't you shack up with them for thirteen weeks?" I somehow managed the question with a straight face.

"Mother occupies the guest room," he said, articulating each syllable, "but your suggestion is a manifest of goodwill."

"Philip," Cornelia said. "One question. Who's writing your material tonight?"

He did not hear her. His gaze had returned to Liz who told him he could probably rent a decent little furnished house in the Fox studio area for around fifty dollars a month.

"Then I could walk to work." He seemed pleased.

"I hadn't thought of that," Liz said.

"I can't tell you how relieved I am," Cornelia said. She turned up the volume of the radio, which had been featuring dance bands from across the nation. It was now 1934 at the Cocoanut Grove in Los Angeles where Freddy Martin's orchestra was playing "Auld Lang Syne." For the fourth time that night we toasted 1934 and had another drink. When Philip put his arms around Liz he said, "By the way. Something I've been meaning to tell you. Him too" — meaning me. "I love you both very much. Hap-pee New Year."

Philip drew us together, kissed us both, then kissed Cornelia.
Then he bowed to us all, put on his hat and coat, and walked out
the door. Alone.

from Philip Pearson's Day Book

Jan. 1, 1934. Overheard lines to remember. "Stupider
minds will prevail — as always . . . When priests meet in
conclave is it a celibation? . . . She was the kind of girl
who'd answer the telephone while copulating . . ." Have
monumental hangover. Will leave for Hollywood the 1st of
February.

24

Philip was back in New York when the baby was born. It was his bad luck to telephone me that morning. "I'm at the Plaza quote giving a few interviews between pictures and seeing the new plays unquote," he said. That was the sort of thing movie stars said when their options had been dropped. "And what are you up to, old man?"

"I'm glad you asked me that. I'm going to the hospital."

"You sick?"

"Not me. Liz's pains are clocking in every six minutes."

"Why is she having pains?"

"So far as we know it's a baby knocking to get out. Why don't you come by Doctors Hospital this evening? Have a preview. If the baby's train is late we can play gin or you can tell me about the love life of Shirley Temple."

Philip hesitated. I should have known hospitals were not his bag. "You sure you'd not rather be — alone?"

"I'll *be* alone. There's not much I can do to help Liz have a baby. I've done my part."

"Well," Philip said, "if you'd like me to come by for a little while . . . what time's the arrival?"

"According to Dr. Mary Halton, when the pains get down to six minutes apart you call a taxi. Then if you're lucky it shouldn't take more than four or five hours. That should make it around three or four this afternoon."

"Get off the phone," I heard Liz say. She had been hanging out the window, looking down at the street below. "The taxi's here."

"I'll bring along a bottle of champagne," Philip was saying. "We can break it over the baby's head."

Philip actually did arrive at the hospital with a bottle of Mumm's (chilled) Monday evening. Still no sign of a baby. A nurse put his champagne in a refrigerator where, for all I know, it may still be.

I kept telling him to go home but he stayed on doggedly, hating every minute of it. On Tuesday he disappeared for a while and returned with ham and cheese sandwiches, the *Times* and *Trib,* the *New Yorker, Vanity Fair, Story,* cigarettes, a safety razor, shaving cream, and a bottle of brandy. Hollywood and all that money had been good for him, I thought, and was about to thank him for his generosity when he said, "Your share comes to six dollars and forty-five cents."

"I'll write you a check." I had brought a checkbook along in case of emergencies.

"No hurry," Philip said.

No, he hadn't changed all that much. He looked stricken when I suggested that he go in and say hello to Liz. The pains had stopped for some damn reason and she was bored. Reluctantly he stepped to the door of her room and waved nervously. At that moment another constriction struck her and he withdrew hastily while I went in to hold her hands and light her a cigarette when she could relax.

Part of the time we did play gin. Philip had become addicted to the game at Fox. He had checked in upon arrival and been assigned a secretary and an office in a bungalow all his own, and informed that he belonged to the "Davis stable." He met Davis, who seemed like a decent, literate fellow, not at all the vulgar ignoramus Philip had feared he would have to deal with. Sam Davis said to call him if there was anything Philip needed. Meanwhile — get acclimated.

Then for weeks, for three months, Davis, nobody, called him. It was as if Philip were not there. He felt guilty accepting fifteen hundred dollars every Saturday noon and on several occasions attempted to see Davis, but the appointments were invariably broken at the last minute. Davis was "tied up in conference." Or, "He's with Mr. Z." (That would be Darryl Zanuck.) "Oh, he'll get back to you, Mr. Pearson." He did not.

"Funny thing," Philip said, and paused. "Nobody called me — not a soul — except . . . remember the Male Mode, in Cottonwood?"

I remembered it well, remembered the afternoon Philip and I had gone shopping for his gym clothes after his father had said he was not to buy them there. "Sure. A couple of brothers owned it. Named — what was their name?"

"Fowler," Philip said. "Everett and Chad Fowler. Well, one afternoon I was sitting in my bungalow reading. The telephone rang and it was the front gate. A Mr. Fowler was there, said he was from Montana. A place called Cottonwood. Well, I had nothing to do. I was curious, I guess, so I said send him over. I didn't remember him at all. He was about my height. Fat. He seemed a little nervous, didn't know what to say, thought I was famous, I guess. A hometown celebrity. He said it had been in the paper that I had signed a contract with Fox and he was in town overnight. 'The wife and me, we just happened to drive past the studio, and I says to myself, I guess I'll see if Phil Pearson's in there. I can tell the folks back home I saw the kid that made good.'"

He stopped speaking.

"And what else?" I prompted.

"Oh, that was all. We didn't really have anything to say to each other. I just thought it was interesting. Everett Fowler of all people from Cottonwood looking me up."

Philip haunted the sound stages and watched movies in the making; he was still a fan at heart and that heart beat a little faster when he found himself seated across from Loretta Young in the commissary. He read *Swann's Way* and *The Magic Mountain,* exercises in Required Reading for a budding author, and reread *War and Peace.* (I wondered if Philip had ever noticed his resemblance to Pierre, the observer?) He played gin with other writers basking in the same overpaid but maddening predicament, drove to the beach in a secondhand Chevy that he picked up for a hundred dollars, and wrote a couple of short stories.

Finally at the end of the first thirteen weeks Fox picked up his option. Sam Davis called him in, apologized for not getting to him sooner, "But you know how these things are," and assigned him to the rewrite of a property that had been gathering dust on the shelves ever since Sound came in.

"How'd it come out?"

Philip shrugged. "I guess they liked it—they picked me up for another six months, but there was nothing for me for a few weeks, so—here I am."

Picked up. He had learned the lingo.

Philip came to the hospital because it was the proper thing for Bachelor Friend to do. The Infant, according to that script, would be glimpsed antiseptically through glass, all pink and white. The Mother and the Father, his Old Friends, and he would make a charming and not too sentimental picture, thank you, sipping champagne and laughing it up. (Tennis, anyone?)

He remained to the agonizing end, I suspect, because during the crisis that developed I was a specimen to be filed away for future reference. He might use me sometime. The Husband of a Woman who could die giving birth to his child. The father of an infant who did not want to be born. Philip might never again have the opportunity to observe such an incident at firsthand.

I may be doing him an injustice. Whatever the reason that prompted him, I appreciated his being there.

Sometime about noon Wednesday, Dr. Halton steamed into the waiting room. Liz, she said, was still strong. "God knows where a woman's strength comes from at this period. It's a glandular storm." As soon as she showed three fingers of dilation, Mary (I had been calling her Mary for several months now) could take the baby with low forceps.

Philip, who had been dozing, staggered to his feet, took one look at Mary Halton, and sank back onto his chair.

"Your wife taking her time too?" Mary asked.

"No, no," Philip said nervously. "I'm—just a friend of *his*."

"You look as beat as John here does. But who am I to talk? I must be a sight." She hurried out. Philip took a deep breath and said that he was aware of how Liz and I felt about the lady doctor, but he had never seen Mary Halton before and—well, maybe we ought to have a second opinion. It was none of his business, of course, but he had to confess she did not look like any legitimate M.D. he had ever come across.

He had a point. Mary Halton was *sui generis*. In her sixties — or seventies? — she had begun delivering babies of mothers shocked into premature delivery on the streets of San Francisco while the earth trembled and burning buildings collapsed around them. She had dyed black hair, plastered her wrinkles with white makeup, lined her eyes with black pencil, gave her thin lips a quick slash once a day with fire-engine-red lipstick, and obviously never had time to check the result with her glasses on. She could make any practicing witch envious.

"We trust her," I said. "Sinclair Lewis trusts her." He had used her, thinly disguised, as a character in one of his less memorable novels, *Ann Vickers*.

Philip shrugged. "Well, I guess you know what you're doing."

I laid my hand on his shoulder. He got to his feet abruptly and said he thought he'd go for a walk. His legs were stiff.

"Go home," I said once more. "This is ridiculous, your sticking around."

"Don't I know."

He returned in half an hour or so with a package holding a dog's leash. "For Doc," he said, as if that explained everything.

"Who's Doc?"

"My dog."

"What breed?"

"Sort of cocker. Black."

"Is the dog in a kennel?"

"No. Mother's taking care of him."

"Doesn't that present problems with all those cats of your aunt Grace's?"

"Oh, I rented a house just a few doors north of Aunt Grace's. So they'd still be near each other."

"Look," I said, "this is the most ass backward conversation I've ever had. Okay. We'll take it a step at a time. Furnished?"

"Furnished what?"

"House."

"With a dog? You can't rent a furnished house if you have a dog."

"So you bought furniture."

"I had to."

"All right. Let's go back. Why did you buy a dog?"

"I saw him in a pet shop at Farmer's Market. Ten dollars. No papers."

I shook my head. "You never stopped to consider that a dog would change your whole way of life?"

"I don't have a way of life."

A nurse hurried into the waiting room. "Mr. Ewing?" she said. I nodded. "You have a healthy six-pound daughter."

When it came time Philip followed me, as if walking on eggs, for the "preview of our production." We could not see Amy very well through the glass but she was obviously alive. Her hands — with fingernails already! — were moving jerkily, like a tiny puppet's. She sported a black eye, the result of forceps, but had all the conventional, necessary parts and, absurdly, a lot of coarse dark hair. "Happens often with ten-month babies," a nurse explained. "It'll slough off in a week or so. Don't worry."

"I'm not worried. I'm just . . ."

Philip looked at me. "Do fathers usually cry at this time?"

"Don't you cry at miracles?" the nurse said.

"I don't know," Philip said. "I never had one."

Liz was waiting impatiently, sitting up in bed, looking not at all drawn and quartered as she had every right to be. I shall lower the curtain over the next few minutes. Anyone who has ever had a first child needs no account of that highly charged interval. But presently I told her that Philip was pacing the hall outside.

"You mean *Philip* has been here the whole damn time?"

"Except to forage for food once in a while."

"Of course I want to see him."

Philip crossed to the bed and bent to kiss her chastely on the brow. Before he could straighten up she threw her arms around him and drew him down close. He went rigid until she let him go, then straightened up and cleared his throat. He was trying to think of something that had not been said a thousand times in this situation. "I'm so happy for you"? No, Liz could repeat he'd said that. It was not worthy of him. "John looks worse than you do"? Everybody must say that to a new father. "You don't look any different"? But Liz did, somehow. More mature. What he did manage to get out was a stiff, formal "Well, congratulations, Elizabeth. Well done."

From the look on our faces he could see that we were trying not to laugh, so he lapsed into the relatively safe groove of intentional humor. "Will you accept the Oscar in person, or shall I ask them to deliver it?"

25

Nothing as sensational as a movie sale or a fifteen-hundred-dollar-a-week contract in Hollywood came my way, but I was not envious of Philip Pearson. He did not have a marriage that became more solid with each year, or a beautiful daughter. He had a ten-dollar sort of cocker, wrote what Darryl Zanuck told him to write, and played the role of Extra Man when one was needed.

No, nothing sensational happened to Liz and me. Ours was merely a step-by-step ascent into middle-class security. We had yearly medical checkups, life insurance, and a small bank account. My novel had garnered respectable reviews but nobody turned cartwheels: "A promising dip into the deep waters of fiction," Edith Walton in the *Herald Tribune*. "Ewing's Western landscapes evoke those of John Steuart Curry, his farmers Knut Hamsun figures transplanted to Montana," *New York Times*. Such quotes provoked no stampede to Brentano's or Scribner's, but they did boost my short story price another notch. I was selling almost everything I put on paper. I remember, to my shame, once saying to Liz, "I can write me no wrong these days."

There was no element of competition between Philip and me. Yet, having written that, I wonder why we both felt it necessary to itemize rather extensively our little intimations of success and upward alterations in life-style in our cross-continent exchanges?

I wrote him about our move to Connecticut where we rented — for a hundred a month — a house of post-Revolutionary vintage, with an option to buy. "Two acres on the bank of the Saugatuck . . . houseman-cook-driver named Howard . . . Liz's mother, Lulabel, living with us — she's great with Amy . . . and oh yes, Liz and I are no longer wage slaves. She has graduated from the fan mags to the slicks; sold a short story to *Redbook!* I am counting on the little woman to support me now that I'm a squire."

The screenplays Philip sweat over during this period were mostly adaptations of unsuccessful plays, dramatizations of obscure novels, or so-called polishes of other writers' aborted efforts. When completed, they seem to have been relegated, along with hundreds of others, to the files of the story department. But finally, and shortly before his second option expired, one of his screenplays actually went before the cameras with Irene Dunne and Fred MacMurray as costars. "Screenplay by Philip Pearson, from the book by I-forget-whom." It cleaned up at the box office.

Like so many screwball comedies of the thirties, this one was as suggestive (the vogue word at the time) as the Hays office would allow. The innocent — but oh, so wise — heroine lured the handsome, honorable, and not-too-aggressively horny hero right up to her bedroom door and then kept him panting, but out of her bed, until the sanctimonious I-do's made it legal for him to rush inside and close the door on the camera. Liz and I saw it again not too long ago on television. It was a terrible print and had been mangled to make way for plugs pushing depilatories, feminine hygiene, hemorrhoid cures, and jock itch remedies. Yet it still retained something beside the requisite ingredients of humor, suspense, and sexual titillation. *Class* seems as good a term as any, and something else not so rare then as now. *Charm.*

That movie was released just in time to save Philip from the ritual "vacation" in New York to give interviews and see the new shows. Fox took up his option at $2,250 per week and lent him to RKO at $3,000 for the Astaire-Rogers movie. He was hot once more.

He bought a house. Shortly after its purchase he wrote us:

. . . It's in an area called Hidden Valley, a cul-de-sac off Coldwater Canyon. Elizabeth may know where it is. Right next door to Myrna Loy. I have about an acre and, as we say here in Never-Never Land, room for a pool. Seven rooms and separate maid's quarters. My mother insists upon moving into the latter, so she will not inhibit my orgies. (Harold Grieve is my decorator. How does that strike you—my decorator? Gives you pause, doesn't it?) And it may interest you to know that my deed states I have "an easement through Miss Loy." Sorry to confess that merely means my water supply crosses her property.

When you two find the time to shake the dust of New England off your feet, do drop in. Don't wait for an engraved invitation.

                                        Still Your Old Friend Philip

PS Paramount has borrowed me to compose a Stanwyck-Mac-Murray thingamabob. Ho, as they say, hum. Still, it does discourage the wolf from creeping up on my twenty-five-thou-sand-dollar door.

Only one of us found an occasion to drop in. It was Liz. She had been approached by *Redbook* to write a profile on Mae West, who was a reigning Paramount star; Philip was temporarily at Paramount. Liz could still not drive a car. She could save the expense of a hotel, cause him no inconvenience by occupying his guest room, and accompany him to the studio each morning.

Philip, after a pregnant pause when I telephoned him, said he would be delighted. He would even meet Liz at the Santa Fe station. I told him I appreciated his Western hospitality and would remember him handsomely in my will.

Liz wrote me a couple of weeks later.

Darling:

What am I doing here with nobody I give a damn about any longer. Except Philip, of course. I'm really fond of him. He can be maddening, but he's trying hard to play Mine Host. He even took me to dinner last night at the Beverly Derby. Let me tell you about how we got there. He has a Buick sedan. (Wouldn't you know? The Brooks Brothers of automobiles, all neatly buttoned down. Black with wire wheels and white sidewalls.) There is quite a climb from the house up to Coldwater, then it's gently downhill all the way into Beverly. Philip explained how you could save gas by cutting off the ignition and coasting.

If you hit the light on Sunset just right you can make it all the way to Santa Monica Boulevard. Well, last night Philip hit the jackpot. Not only was the light on Sunset green, but so was the one on Santa Monica. He coasted all the way down to the Derby on Wilshire! I was so happy for him.

It's Sunday morning and Philip has taken his mother to mass, so I'm using his typewriter. The house itself is really quite impressive. Light and airy and a little too Harold Grieve, with wallpaper matching sofa fabrics, that sort of chichi, but — except for this rather messy spot where I'm sitting — ultracorrect, no do-jiggers, no concessions to personal taste (maybe good, maybe bad, what's the difference?) that could make it his. As it stands, it is not only not his, it's nobody's. Howard Greer calls it Bleak House.

Philip drove me over to Inglewood one evening to see your mother and father. Your father is a dear; anybody who was *your* wife would be aces with him. Your mother . . . well, she was trying but breathing heavily. Any female *her* little boy married would be named Elizabeth Mud. I'll tell you all about it when I come home to you and Amy and Lulabel — and the lilacs. Put them on hold until I get there.

Love, Love

PS Doc, the ten-dollar *soi-disant* cocker, is a love. He accompanies Philip to the studio every morning. Philip is trying to teach him a parlor trick: roll over on his back with feet in the air at the signal, "Here comes Mr. Zanuck." Doc also, without prompting, occasionally pees on the leg of the dining room table, his doggy contribution to this decorator's fantasy.

"Something I've been meaning to ask you," I said.

We were relaxing with a drink after a hard day's work. Liz had ground out a rough draft of her piece on Mae West. I had rewritten a story I was slanting at *Collier's*. Amy was in bed and Lulabel in her room listening to Fred Allen.

"Ask away," Liz said. "I'm a fount of information."

"That first letter you wrote me. You said something about Philip taking his mother to mass. Does that mean he's returned to the fold?"

"How would I know? Can you see Philip discussing that with me?"

"No, but you might have put two and two together."

"I had other things on my mind. All he ever said to me was 'I'm taking Mother to mass.' Both Sundays I was there."

"What about a girl?"

"No evidence. As a matter of fact, evidence against it. I finished my stint one afternoon and walked back to Mrs. Pearson's little bungalow for tea. She had invited me. I like it much better than the big house. Really cozy. She brought out the old family album, showed me pictures of Philip and Maureen — and one or two of you — when you were kids, and that other boy who was going to be a priest — "

"King. Killed in a motorcycle accident. With a girl."

" — and of herself and Mr. Pearson. She was a tearing beauty in those days . . ."

"Was she actually? I was too young to believe anybody over twenty could be a beauty."

"What was it you asked? Oh, yes. Philip and girls. Mrs. Pearson — she's going around the bend these days, I'm afraid, one or two buttons in the wrong holes — Mrs. Pearson said she thought it would be awfully nice if I introduced Philip to a nice girl. He didn't have many lady friends was the way she put it. He seemed shy. And he worked so hard. A young man ought to have someone to share his success with. She worried about him."

"That sounds like a normal mother's normal concern for a son. What do you mean, around the bend?"

"Wait. She's in daily communication with what's-his-name — King."

"You mean she hears voices?"

"Better. He often comes and sits with her when she's alone with the dog. She'll notice that Doc is wagging his tail and she'll look up and there's King in the chair opposite her."

"Poor Mrs. Pearson."

"Oh, I don't know. She's happier than your mother. I invited a few old chums in one evening; I didn't have much time to get around. I asked Mrs. Pearson to the little get-together. She thanked me but said, as if the two of us were putting something over on Philip, that it would be wiser for her to stay away. 'You and I know, dear, that a boy is not his own charming self with lady friends when his mother is on the scene,' she said."

"I could cry," I said.

"Wait. She came to the party. I caught a glimpse of her in the shadows on the veranda. It was something right out of *Stella Dallas*. She saw me, smiled, then faded into the darkness. That smile was my thanks for presenting her son with the Offering of Maidens."

from Philip Pearson's Day Book

June 15, 1937. Dinner at Joan Crawford's night before last. She and Franchot taking voice lessons. They sang. Not bad. Ray Milland and David Nivens there. Suspect I was invited to transport Dorothy Parker. No quotable quotes. Actually brought her knitting. Party last night at Ira and Lenore Gershwin's. George played as usual. Took Mother to doctor. No noticeable change. Slow deterioration.

A busy life, a comfortable, a productive life one would say of Philip Pearson's then. Plenty of money, work at the studio every day, parties in the evening with the rich and glamorous elite of Hollywood. No emotional involvements. Just—please pick up Dotty Parker—or Sally Benson—dress—don't dress. When did the poor devil have time to write his magazine stuff? Because he did keep plugging along with that. "You never know," he wrote me, "when the fair winds will blow foul out here."

Having mastered the Hollywood formula he could indulge himself by running more or less free with magazine fiction. There was a magazine formula too, but it was less arbitrary and a few privileged writers were permitted a long leash. Philip Pearson was one of them. His love story, "There but for Grace," had been so successful for the *Post* that Horace Lorimer probably figured his readers would tolerate an occasional "art story" from its author.

There was one, obviously inspired by the Fitzgeralds. Many modern writers have been tempted to explore their technicolored, tempestuous, syncopated sleigh ride to self-immolation. But Scott and Zelda are perhaps better left to their legend. Try to define them and they lose credibility and end up rather foolish, self-indulgent misfits. One would prefer not to have known them. Philip was more successful than most. His prose at least had style, a gloss and sheen and a jazz beat. His "Zelda" — I forget what he called her — was a smashingly beautiful but androgynous rich girl who could not be satisfied until she dominated her talented, charming, and sensitive husband. When she finally emasculated him and turned him into a helpless alcoholic, she deserted him for a younger, more talented, charming, and sensitive fellow, and thus began the pattern all over again.

There was another that I remember. "Now I Lay Me," he called it, was published in *Metropolitan*. It was a brilliantly written trifle about a girl who was terrified of sex. Though attracted to men (as they were attracted to her), she led them on and dreamed shameful, erotic dreams about them, and then finally, in desperation, made herself unattractive so that she would no longer be forced to cope with the advances she had courted. It was far from what Esme Jones would have judged to be a *Metropolitan* story, but Harvey Maynard, the editor, bought it because he wanted to lure Philip away from the *Post*. Esme did not tell Maynard that Lorimer had already thrown up his hands in horror at that one.

I wonder what it is about shocking news that makes us remember (and far too often insist upon recounting) where we were and what we were doing when we heard it?

Liz and I were in the kitchen reading a recipe for cheese soufflé in Fanny Farmer's *Cookbook* when the telephone rang. There was an extension in the dining room so, since Liz was beating egg whites, I went in and picked it up.

Esme Jones's voice sounded solemn.

"John, I realize there's nothing anybody can do, but I thought you might want to call Philip. There's been an accident. His mother is dead. I thought, since you knew her . . ."

"Oh, my God!"

Out of the corner of my eye I saw Liz step to the dining room door. The egg beater in her hand was dripping egg whites. The trivia one remembers!

"I didn't talk to him," Esme said, "Maureen called me. Philip had called her, and she said he was quite incoherent."

"But what *happened?*"

"As Maureen understands it, Philip had been driving his mother to eleven o'clock mass this morning. For some reason he had turned off the motor of his car and was coasting. At Sunset Boulevard he saw, too late, a truck bearing down on them. With the motor turned off he had no brakes. The truck rammed the door beside Mrs. Pearson, and . . . miraculously, Philip was not hurt."

I tried to call Philip. There was no answer. I telephoned his sister. (Maureen and Joe Tyler had moved out to Scarborough when Maureen found she was pregnant, but she had slipped and fallen while unpacking their possessions, and miscarried.) Joe answered. Maureen could not come to the phone. She was dressing and throwing a few things into her bag. He had called a cab — it was waiting outside — and with luck they could get to Grand Central in time to catch the Century at six. No, he was not going with her. He had an appointment with a General Motors executive at nine-thirty Monday morning. Could be a big account; keep your fingers crossed. I heard Maureen's voice call out, "Who's that?" and Joe said, "It's John. He's heard about Mother Pearson." "Then what are you doing telling him about your damned account?" "Now, Maureen, honey, I was just — "

"Is there anything I can do?" I cut in.

"What? Oh, yes, is there anything? . . . Maureen, John wants to know can he do anything?"

"No," she said. "What can anybody do? We've got to *hurry,* Joe. Oh, where the hell are my gloves?"

"Ask Maureen if she wants me to go with her," I said.

I heard Joe repeat that, and then Maureen's voice, close, as if she had taken the telephone away from Joe, as I guess she had. "Thanks, John, but I think it's better just me."

Joe, his voice distant, said, "Here are your gloves, Reenie. You want to wear them or put them in your bag?"

She did not answer him, but I could hear her taking deep breaths. I mumbled the platitudes one spouts at such a moment and repeated the idiocy about please, please to call us if there was anything, anything at all, that Liz and I could do. Then she started to cry, and I said good-bye and hung up.

I had not, of course, mentioned the one thing that had been nagging me ever since Esme had telephoned: How was Philip facing up to the guilt he must feel? He had been driving the car, coasting—for what purpose? To save money on gas when he was earning twenty-five hundred dollars a week? He had always been penurious, but that was ridiculous. But if not that, what? A childish game he played over and over? Whatever, had the motor been turning, he might have braked or stepped on the gas and avoided the truck.

"I guess you're thinking what I'm thinking," Liz said.

"How can anybody help thinking it?" I said. We walked slowly into the kitchen. Liz began to fold the beaten egg whites into the cheese mixture. From the garden outside we could hear Lulabel's soft southern voice reading, heavy on the expression—she had once taught elocution—*The Little Engine That Could,* to Amy who lay on the ground, chubby little legs crossed in the air.

"And when you add Mr. Pearson's committing suicide so that Philip might go to Harvard," Liz said quietly, "it all gets pretty damned O'Neill, doesn't it?"

"O'Neill if you know members of the cast, soap opera if they're strangers . . . I'll try Philip again. I hate to think of him alone there."

This time he answered. I thought I would know what to say but his who's-daring-to-intrude tone of voice threw me.

"Philip, this is John."

"I recognize your voice," he said, petulantly.

"Esme telephoned me and I've talked with Maureen and Joe."
Why, why did I have to go into that? What difference who told
me the grim facts, what *they* had said, what *I* said?

"Oh?"

"And I just want you to know how — how damn sorry I am."
What a weak, piddling word, *sorry*. But what other? *Devastated?*
That's for a woman whose husband has run off with another
woman. Besides, I was not devastated. It was Philip who had
every right to be.

"Gee, thanks." Was he off his rocker, or being sarcastic?

"You've been drinking — I hope?"

"Don't feel a thing. Always could hold my liquor."

"*Listen,* Philip." No reply. "Have we been cut off?"

"I'm listening. You say listen, I listen. That's why I'm so good
at Extra Man."

"Philip, can we be serious?"

"I'm not very good at that."

"I know, but — when this is over, why don't you come back
East for a while? The studio would want you to take time off.
Come and stay with us."

"I've got a dog," he said, after another pause. "I'd have to hire
someone to stay in the house with him."

"God knows you can afford that." I was growing testy under
the strain of these trivialities while the specter of his mother's
death hovered.

"And then," Philip went on, "next Saturday Claudette Colbert
and Dr. Pressman — he's her husband — are giving a big tent party.
She has asked me to bring Whizzer Wilkens, maiden lady friend
of hers, and — "

"Philip," I broke in. "Let me come out."

"You've not been invited. Very exclusive party."

"For Christ's sake, Philip," I screamed. "I'm asking do you
want me to come out and be with *you* during this time? You
stuck by me when I needed you. Maybe you'd like to talk, maybe
you'd just like to have an old friend stand by and shut up. Say the
word. I'll be there."

"Very kind of you, I'm sure, but I am unfortunately booked up. Perhaps another time?"

I pretended I had not heard that. "Philip, this is John. John from Cottonwood. I'd like to help you through a bad time. I want to—"

"Play God," Philip interrupted. "Hard for me to see you in the part. No, you there—what did you say your name was?"

"John Ewing," I repeated, "from Cottonwood. You're my oldest friend."

"Oh, *that* John. Yes, he used to come to our backdoor and beg handouts of my mother's fudge. Well, she's not *there,* she's not *here* anymore."

Strange thing, he sounded quite normal, but of course he could not have been.

"I'm coming out there, Philip. I don't care what you say."

"No," he said—obviously he had digested that last attempt to get through. "You wouldn't like it here. Stay there in your snug little house with your snug little wife—or maybe I should say your smug little house with your smug little wife and . . ." He was silent for a long interval. I thought he had hung up. Then his voice came back. "Excuse me, John. I have a guest. One Father Murphy. A man of the cloth himself," he added in an Irish accent. "He's not God but he claims to have a private line. What's the harm in giving it a try?"

Philip had the church in his emergency. He did not need me. I still think I should have gone to him.

26

It was a few days after his mother's funeral (Philip told us). In his office at the studio with Doc curled up at his feet, he was staring at his typewriter, trying to fabricate a screwball-comedy romance between Rosalind Russell and Gary Cooper. His new producer, obviously a dropout from the sixth grade, had dreamed up a premise with a "meet cute" opening. Russell, fresh out of journalism school, has blandly assured the editor of the *News-Gazette* that she has had years of experience.

Cooper, lazy, charming ne'er-do-well heir to untold millions, had been warned by his old man to cut out loafing and prove he's a man or he'll be disinherited. "Well, it just so happens," the producer said to Philip, "that there's a rodeo in town, but see, Coop knows nothing from horses. Sports cars is his game. But for some cockamamie reason — you figure that out — damned if Coop don't go out there and tell 'em he's a Montana broncobuster! I think — yeah, this is good, damn good! — the guy that runs the rodeo is a dame. He's Eve Arden! And Eve could go all out for Coop, but for him she don't warm his old cockle. This makes her goddamn sore, so she says to herself, we'll fix this crummy bastard, and she gives Coop a real motherfucker to ride." At this point the producer went into spasms of laughter that took several minutes to conquer, while Philip stared at him stony-faced. "So," he said finally, "so this mean son of a bitch tosses Coop balls over teakettle right into Roz's lap where she's making like Hildy Johnson in the press box. Ain't that a pisser?"

"The perfect word for it," Philip said.

"I knew you'd like it. Now, all you got to do is take it from there."

Philip's secretary, who had been reading *Forever Amber* for a week while Philip contemplated cutting his throat, came into his office. "It's the gate," she said. "Somebody over there would like to see you."

345

"Who?" Philip said.

"She wouldn't say, she just said she was from your hometown. Guess she wants to surprise you."

"Well, tell them to send her over," Philip sighed, pretending annoyance but grateful for any interruption of the idiocy he was stuck with, and wondering idly who this person might be. The last one from Cottonwood had been Everett Fowler.

He had gone back to staring at his typewriter and so was unaware for a moment that he was not alone. Then he heard her voice, saying, "Philip?" He looked up and frowned because he did not know who she was, but got to his feet awkwardly and put out his hand.

"I guess you don't remember me," she said. "It's been a long time. I'm — at least I used to be — Gerry Malnick."

For just a moment that meant nothing to him, then it all began to come back, my great fondness for her, the scandal of her spending the money she had collected for our *Annual*, her being expelled without graduating, and finally Kim Sumner telling us about his encounter with her in Seattle when she had tried to pick him up in that midnight beanery.

"Gerry. Of course. Forgive me."

"No wonder," she said. "I used to be kind of chunky. Guess I've lost a lot of weight."

"You look fine," Philip said. (She did not, he told us. "She looked — bedraggled — worn — years older than us.")

"Is it okay if I sit down? I walked from the bus station, and I'm kind of beat, know what I mean?"

"Of course. Please do. How about some coffee? Something stronger, maybe?" (She looked as if she needed it.)

"Just coffee. I'm off the other stuff." She sank down in a big chair. Her oversized bag kept flopping open, and she kept trying to fasten it. Philip buzzed for his secretary and asked her to bring them coffee.

"Tell me about yourself," Philip said nervously. (It was unlike Philip to find anyone else as self-conscious as himself, and the social gambit of "Tell me about yourself" must have come hard.)

She had been in Frisco, Gerry said, "Just knocking around, you know?" when she happened to pick up a dated L.A. *Times* in the Greyhound bus station, and came across the item about "Screenwriter's Mother Dead in Car Accident." Then she noticed who it was, "And I think to myself, why I used to know him. *I* know somebody kinda famous." ("The way she said it," Philip explained, "was as if it gave her some sort of—well—identity.")

Then suddenly she said, "I'm sorry, Philip."

This confused him. "Sorry about what?"

"Sorry I didn't say I was sorry right off. About your mother, I mean."

Funny thing, she finally went on. She'd been sitting there in the bus station with a ticket in her bag—a ticket to Portland, Oregon. But it was cold and raining in Frisco and it would probably be colder and more miserable in Portland. She had lived there—if you could call it living—a year or so ago. Seemed like your feet were wet most of the time. So all of a sudden, blamed if she hadn't marched right up to the ticket window and turned in the ticket to Portland and bought one for Hollywood where everybody said it was warm all year-round. "Imagine, *me* in Hollywood. Me and Greta Garbo." She smiled, a bitter smile.

"What are your plans?" Philip asked her.

"Plans?" She shrugged her shoulders and raised her hands off her lap, palms up. "I don't make plans. Oh, I'll find something to do. I like to eat."

Doc, who had not moved until then, must have noticed that pathetic movement of her hands. He got up, shook himself, walked over to her, sat up, and put his paws in her lap. Gerry stroked his head, then looked up at Philip. "No kidding, I haven't petted a dog in a thousand years. Good dog, what's your name?"

"His name's Doc," Philip said.

"Doc. Bet you never chased a coyote, did you, Doc?"

Philip watched the two of them for a long moment. Then he said, "Gerry, I hope you won't be offended, but you could do me a favor. I need somebody to sort of house- and dog-sit for a while.

I'm supposed to go to New York one of these days, and I can't on account of Doc here. Oh, I could put him in a kennel, but he'd hate it. And I don't like to leave the house with nobody in it either. It just occurred to me that — until you get your bearings in this town — you might like to — "

Philip said he stopped talking because Gerry had lowered her head so that her forehead rested on Doc's nose. After a minute or two she tried to look up, but Doc was licking her face. Philip could not tell whether she was laughing or crying.

"Well, the upshot of it is that Gerry Malnick, of all people, is staying in the maid's house," Philip said to us. "So . . . here I am."

"Philip, that just may be the nicest thing you've ever done," I said.

" 'Tis a far, far better thing than I have ever — ' " he intoned.

Philip had come out from New York on the two o'clock. Snow had begun to fall while I was driving to the Westport station to meet him. We had planned a party for him that Saturday evening — all the old gang that we could round up — but it continued to snow and blow, and the weather report sounded ominous, so we postponed it.

Sunday morning dawned bright and brisk, with just enough snow on the ground to turn Newtown Turnpike into a Christmas card. Liz and I hastily telephoned the guests and told them that the party was on again for that night. All of them accepted, provided the blizzard stayed up in Canada where it belonged. All but Joe and Maureen, who would have had to traverse secondary highways from Scarborough. Joe was afraid to drive on icy roads. He had once skidded into a Philip Morris billboard and broken a tooth.

Philip had brought a present for Amy, a very large animal coloring book. She thanked him politely and sat down on the sofa to inspect it. Amy was a serious and somewhat suspicious little girl, never enthusiastic about a gift until she had a chance to decide whether or not it was worthy of her. Philip sat beside her as she turned the pages. He did not know how to talk to a child, but was courting approval of both his gift and himself. "I'll bet you don't know what that is," he said, pointing.

She scorched him with a glance charged with a four-year-old's disdain, and sighed. "Everybody knows that's a goat." She flipped a page, and with an I'll-fix-you-mister tone, asked, "What's *that?*"

"It's a horsey," Philip said.

That was a mistake. "It is a horse," Amy said. "You should not talk baby talk to a child."

"But I don't think you're a child," he said, hoping that this would flatter her. It did not.

"If I'm not a child, why did you bring me a child's book?" she said, and proceeded to ignore him.

Philip shook his head, and turned to Liz and me. "I wonder if your daughter would sue me if I stole that dialogue?"

"I wouldn't put it past her," Liz said.

Watching him, listening to him, I thought he was maturing. The three of us got bundled up — the thermometer registered eighteen degrees at two p.m. — and went for a walk down the glistening white road toward Crooked Mile. Philip was outgoing, amusing, and not afraid to resort to a cliché when it said economically what he wanted to say. He seemed to be concerned about our news too, good and bad. The three of us enjoyed an easy, relaxed winter afternoon. The ball bounced effortlessly back and forth.

Maybe, for him, it was being with old friends again after such an exotic interlude but, whatever it was, I liked him better than I ever had, except for the months of our collaboration on *The Age of Mrs. Page.* He even related that anecdote of his encounter with the producer of the Russell-Cooper epic with tolerance. "Oh, we get along," he said. "I've met worse. Bill's scared he'll lose his job. He's got a nice wife, three kids, and a Eurasian mistress to support."

Howard, our man-of-all-work, had a fire blazing in the fireplace by the time we returned from our walk. The three of us huddled before it to warm our hands. Howard appeared from below and asked, "What's you-all's pleasure?" I asked him if he knew how to make a hot buttered rum. "Mistah John," he chuckled, lapsing into his absurd Uncle Tom act, "ole Jeff Davis taught me how to make hot buttered rum when I was one of his nigras."

"Did Davis treat you well?" Philip asked, going along with Howard's act.

"Mos' o' the time, Mistah Philip. Mos' o' the time. Cose you got whupped regular on Saturdays 'stead of gettin' paid, but money ain't everything, I always say."

Lulabel and Amy joined us, Lulabel with her knitting and Amy with her coloring book and crayons. Amy's avowed purpose was to make "Uncle" Philip look stupid. She would flash a picture at him, snap the book shut, and say — as he had said to her — "I'll bet you don't know what that is." To her delight he identified a hippo as a rhino and a giraffe as a camel.

After Howard had served drinks there occurred one of those inexplicable and protracted lulls in social conversation. Lulabel, aware of the silence, said that according to her hometown folklore they occur at either twenty minutes before or twenty minutes after the hour. I looked at the clock. It was five-thirty. Folklore took the count once more.

Another silence settled down on us. Lulabel pulled out the last row of her stitches. As she picked them up again she said, "Philip, when are you going to get married?"

Philip stiffened, cleared his throat several times. "That's a personal question, isn't it?"

"Certainly," she said. "The only kind worth asking."

"Lulabel," Liz said, "one does not ask Philip Pearson personal questions."

"Why ever not?" Lulabel asked reasonably. "He can ask me any damn thing he wants to."

Philip was on the spit, squirming, and Liz could not resist fanning the coals. "I think I know the answer, Lulabel. Philip expects to walk out into the garden some summer afternoon and find a combination of Lillian Gish and Gloria Swanson standing there under the arbor reaching for the perfect rose. She'll be wearing an enormous picture hat and trailing yards of chiffon. She'll cut the rose, turn, see her knight, and toss it to him. He'll drop to one knee and take her tiny fingers in his hand. He will lift it reverently to his lips, and then they will stroll off into the sunset together."

He was blushing, and trying hard to suppress the outrage that was piling up in him. He cleared his throat again, smiled brightly, and said, "Would you make that Colbert and Garbo? Gish and Swanson are a little long in the tooth for me. As for getting married, nobody has asked me. If anyone does, I'll be happy to take her proposal under advisement."

He looked from Liz to me to Lulabel, and took a deep breath, the athlete who has cleared the last high hurdle.

"Uncle Philip, what's this?" Amy put in, thrusting her book into his lap.

"That is a clam," Philip said, without looking.

★   ★   ★

The party that evening resembled a country playhouse revival of an old favorite. The original New York cast had been reassembled at great expense and everyone was letter perfect, but the whole thing did not quite come off. We were all a little older. The familiar lines were no longer quite as witty as they once had been. Our timing was off. All of us — except Philip and Cornelia — had had, or were about to have, offspring. Our priorities had altered. When you had answered such inane queries as "Well, what have you been up to lately?" and discovered by the glazed look on your interrogator's face that he really didn't give a damn, you found that what you needed more than anything was another drink to get you to Curtain.

We had not seen Barney Lehman and Jinna Dieter for a long while. They were now quite respectably Mr. and Mrs. Barney Lehman and son, Barney, Jr., of New Rochelle. Jinna had clung onto her identity as long as she could, but finally caved in when they either had to *be* married or pretend they were in order to sign a lease on the house after Jocko was born, and she'd be damned if she'd lie about it. And what the hell, it was only a piece of paper, wasn't it? She had had to quit her job (we had heard that she got fired) because somebody had to stay at home and care for the brat, and Barney, the poet, the Red, the world revolutionary, was now writing benevolent commercials for the "Dupont Theater of the Air." Why? Because it paid, paid more than such shit was worth, and somebody had to come up with rent and bread and formula and stuff now that Jinna was acting the domestic. But he felt guilty every time he went down to Wilmington to confer with those ignorant bastards about the copy, guilty because he didn't seize the opportunity to blow up the joint, then get on a boat, sail off to Spain, join the International Brigade, and fight Franco.

"Why don't you?" said Cornelia, taunting him.

"I knew you'd ask that," Barney answered. "Well, I'll tell you. Because I'm a coward. I'm afraid to let my wife and child starve to death. Either I'm not the man I thought I was or the establishment has got to me. One way or another, it gets all of us, doesn't it, Philip?"

"Why do you ask me?" Philip said, tight-lipped.

"Who else?" Lucy put in. She had been standing nearby, rocked back on her heels, the baby within her straining the maternity corset and plain blue dress. "You had such bright promise, Philip. And then came Hollywood."

"I have not sold my soul to the devil completely," Philip said. "I had a story in the *Journal* last month."

"Yes," Lucy said sadly. "I read it."

"And?" Philip seemed to be daring her to insult him. She obliged.

"You'd never have written that on East Forty-fourth Street."

Lucy had arrived earlier in the evening loaded for bear, as my father used to put it. Perhaps she had had a fight with Norman (though both maintained that they never had fights), or maybe seeing Philip again—rich now, successful, while Norman was still struggling—revived echoes of his rejection of her. Or—as Liz said after the party was over—it could have been merely the fact that Lucy was seven-and-a-half months pregnant and knew she looked like a blimp. Whatever it was, her blatant hostility should have made it evident to Philip that he was lucky to have escaped her. Instead it drove him to the bar for refills, while Norman stood beside Lucy smiling happily, arm possessively resting on her shoulder, as if to certify—in case anybody doubted—his contribution to her bulging belly.

At about eleven o'clock Philip poured himself another drink, progressed stiff-legged to Philip's chair in the crook of the piano, and sat down, his gaze fixed on another place, another time, his legs sprawled so that everyone had to step across them. Esme smiled fondly. It was déjà vu time.

He remained there, stoned, until everyone except Lucy and Norman had left, until I said, "Nightcap anybody?" hoping nobody, Lucy especially, would say yes.

"No thanks," Norman said. "Time we hit the road."

"You're right," Lucy said and got to her feet, puffing.

"I need one," Philip said, suddenly conscious. He peered at his empty glass as if to say, How did this happen? then struggled upright. Swaying slightly, thinking he was being funny, a drunk imitating a drunk, he extended his glass my way. "Here, boy. Fill this."

"You've had quite enough, boy," I said.

Liz shook her head. "Not that way," she whispered. "I'll give him a very weak one." She took his glass.

"Glad to encounter a little courtesy around here," he muttered.

Norman, ever polite, said, as if speaking to a deaf man, "Well, we're shoving off, Phil. Nice seeing you again. Give my regards to any old chums you run into when you go back to Hollywood."

"I doubt I come in contact with any of your old chums."

"Oh?" Norman said. "Well, just in case . . ."

"No," Philip went on, "I don't know many fags out there."

I could not quite believe what I had heard. Liz, as if pierced with a knife, dropped the glass and said, "Philip, shut up!"

I said, "Pay no mind. He doesn't know what he's saying."

"He knows damn well what he's saying," Lucy said and, ponderous as she was, lurched at Philip and slapped his face as hard as she could, sending him reeling toward the fireplace. I grabbed him with one arm to keep him from falling in, and with the other tried to restrain Lucy from continuing her attack. Thwarted, she bolted for the door, Norman following but returning to fetch her coat, which had been left in the guest room. Philip stood propped against the mantle, one hand rubbing his flaming cheek. Norman paused long enough to say, "Can you handle him?"

"He'll pass out any minute," Liz said. "Go after Lucy. Talk to you tomorrow."

And then there were just the three of us, Philip frowning, stiff-arming the mantle, Liz going about the room making a pretense of picking up glasses, emptying ashtrays.

"Howard will redd up in the morning," I told her.

"I'm doing this to keep from killing someone," Liz said.

"Gee, nobody filled my glass," Philip said, making a little moue with his mouth and pouting.

"And nobody has any intention of filling it," I said.

"What kind of talk is that? Don't you love me anymore?"

"Go to bed, you goddamn fool."

Yes, I knew that he was drunk, I knew this was not the way to handle drunks, I knew that you are supposed to be gentle, never cross them, and assure them that you love them like a brother. But I had had it.

Philip straightened up, let go the mantle, and dropped his arms stiffly to his sides, took one or two tentative steps, then moved across the room like a drunken tin soldier, opened the door on a blast of wind and sleet, turned and bowed, said "Good night," and walked out, closing the door after him with great care.

"You'll have to go after him," Liz said anxiously. "He'll freeze to death."

"Do him good," I said, and we both laughed.

We finished cleaning up. It must have taken us five or ten minutes. Philip had not returned.

I put on my overcoat and went out. Pellets of sleet stung like buckshot. There had to be a moon somewhere behind the clouds, though, because it was not very dark. Philip was nowhere in the yard so I turned up Newtown Turnpike, looking left, then

right, calling, "Philip! Philip, where the hell are you, you son of a
bitch? Answer me!" And tried to run, slipping, falling once to
my knees and bruising my hand—I had not taken the time to
find my gloves—getting up, sliding, yelling, wondering if I
mightn't wake our neighbors, the Bensons, who lived down the
road a piece. They were older people and I suspect thought we
must be bohemians or communists, anyhow the wrong sort to
infest Westport. The summer theater riff-raff were bad enough.

Then I saw him. He was lying in the middle of the road, his
body curled into the fetal position, his thumb in his mouth.

I tried to awaken him but it was no go, so I dragged him back
to the house by the arms. Liz helped lug him up the steps, across
the living room and into the guest room. Somehow we managed
to hoist him onto the bed, take off his coat and tie and shoes, and
cover him up. Finally he muttered something. I lowered my head
and tried to hear what he was saying but could not make it out.

And suddenly I was no longer angry. Poor bastard, I thought.
Poor mixed-up, talented, suspicious, charming, sensitive, insen-
sitive, irritating bastard. Why do I feel sorry for you—and I do
feel sorry for you—when whatever's wrong is your own fault? Or
is it? Are you your own victim? If not, whose?

"Where did you think you were going, Philip?" I said quietly.

"Who? Me?" he murmured, the child again.

"You, Philip. Where were you headed for in a storm like this?"

"Home," he said reasonably.

We stood there and looked down on him for a minute or two,
then Liz snapped off the light and we left him. "Will he remember any of this in the morning?" Liz wondered.

I shrugged. "I wish he would. Might do him some good."

We turned out the living room lights and Liz wearily climbed
the stairs. I made as if to follow her, but paused a moment and
went back into Philip's room. He was tossing restlessly, fighting
his pillow, muttering to himself. I laid my hand on his shoulder
and then snapped on the bedside lamp. He moaned, licked his
lips, relaxed, and lay still.

I left the light on.

★ ★ ★

When we came down in the morning Philip was gone. He had risen early and asked Howard to drive him to Westport.

"To the station?" I said.

"No, not the station. He said he'd make it down to the depot on his own. From the church."

"What church?"

"The Catholic one, I reckon. Least there's a cross on the steeple, don't that mean Catholic? He said jes' drop him off there by the steps. I told him I'd wait and carry him on down to the depot, but he say he don't know how long he'll be kep' inside, so for me to trot along. I thought it was kinda funny, it bein' Monday and all instead o' Sunday."

I agreed with Howard that it was indeed "kinda funny."

I found the note later beside the lamp in the bedroom. The lamp was still burning. He had merely written, "Dear John and Elizabeth. Thanks and sorry I had to leave before you were up. Flowers forthcoming. Philip."

from Philip Pearson's Day Book

Jan. 21, 1938. Weekend in Westport with John and Elizabeth. They had a reunion of the old group. All much married and reproducing. Serious. Main stream. Where did the fun go? Hard to revive old spirit, old sangfroid. (Sang Freud? Sing it again, Sigmund.)

The flowers arrived. A spectacular arrangement from Constance Spry. Must have cost him a pretty penny, but less than an apology.

27

Life has a way of thumbing its nose at you when you get too cocky. Good for you in the long run, perhaps. Perhaps not. Depends on who you are and what you're made of, I guess.

Everything had been going well for Liz and me. (*Poor Philip, why can't he be like us?*) There was no foreseeable reason it would not continue to do so. I was no longer a tyro in the fiction field, and Liz was beginning to catch up. We could depend, we thought, upon a comfortable income. Europe might be writhing in agony under its Francos, its Hitlers, its Stalins, but an ocean separated us from all that nonsense, and in Washington we had the godlike FDR with his fireside soothing syrup.

So the Ewings were happy and secure in their suburban idyll, their typewriters firing away in Westport and knocking over editors in New York. It was seldom necessary even to confer with those twerps any longer. Our agent delivered the product and accepted the dough.

Liz had begun a short story. Halfway through she asked my opinion. I told her it seemed too — well, too big for its britches. How could she pull together and resolve all those threads without sounding pat and synoptic? But in the middle of the night I woke up and said to myself: Play. By damn, that's a play!

Between us we had six short stories in the hands of our agent: four of mine, two of Liz's. We could live off the proceeds for six, eight months. Didn't we owe it to ourselves to stretch the creative muscles? (Of course I had had a disaster with *The Age of Mrs. Page,* but that was no fault of the play itself.) Besides, I was older now, I had experience as a writer. I had matured, hadn't I? (One is never a very good judge of oneself.)

Collaborating with Liz was fun and stimulating. It added another dimension to our marriage. She had a talent for plot and invention. I had a better grip on characterization. The blend was better than the sum of its parts.

But then, before we had brought down the curtain on Act One, my father suffered a massive stroke. I took the train to California and remained at his bedside for two weeks while he lingered in coma, his strong heart refusing to stop and let him go. After his death and funeral there was the problem of What To Do About Mamma. She did not want to come and live with us (thank God), nor with my sister, now in Tulsa and already a grandmother herself. Mamma finally agreed to move in with another Inglewood widow, a Mrs. Dole. No telling how long that setup would last.

I barely had time to see Philip, but when I did he was empathetic and supportive. Death had been one vital experience he could not escape. The day I left for home I telephoned him. "If there's anything I can do," he said. (Of course there was nothing.) "I don't mean just at this time," he went on.

"Thanks. You never know," I said. It was only afterward that I mulled over what he had said: *I don't mean just at this time*. Had he been trying to tell me something?

By the time I got home a month had passed. After a day or two of self-indulgence I forced myself to the typewriter. It would be good therapy, I thought. Short-circuit the trauma of my father's death by giving life to the characters in a play. All that pretentious, psychiatric fiddle-faddle. The fact was we would soon need money. None of those six stories, which were to have been our interim bankroll, had sold.

None did sell. Not even after the play *Birdsong* was completed and in the hands of our new agent, Audrey Wood. Audrey, a conservative little New England woman who wore "sensible" hats at the office, was not one to turn handsprings. "If I tell you I'm crazy about it and then don't come up with a producer, I'll be in the doghouse," she said.

"But do you like it?" Liz pleaded.

"Yes. That doesn't mean I can sell it. Who knows from a play?"

Our six-month, our eight-month deadline was right down the road. Something drastic had to be done. "Jim Quirk said I could always come back to *Photoplay*," Liz said.

"I can't let you do that," I said.

"Can't let you do that," she mimicked. "Are you that insecure? It would be temporary, just to tide us over. Easier for me to go back to *Photoplay* than you to *International*."

That was true, of course. *International* had folded. "Besides," Liz went on, "I'm getting bored with playing the suburban matron." *That* was not true. She had never been a "suburban matron." She had been a working woman lucky enough to live in the suburbs.

Yes, Jim Quirk would take her back on *Photoplay* — at $150 a week — but not in his New York office. That was overstaffed. What he could use was the old Elizabeth Bartlett to cover the Hollywood beat as she had nine or ten years ago.

Liz told him she would let him know.

We owned no property to borrow money on. The prospects of a young writer, unless he has had a blockbuster best-seller to his credit, don't spell collateral. I had rich friends: Rupert Hughes and Philip Pearson. Rupert Hughes would have come through had I asked him. I couldn't. Philip? He had said, "If there's anything I can do — and not just at this time." I reached for the telephone that night, but when operator said, "Number please?" I hung up.

We drove to California. We would need a car out there, and it was much cheaper to drive than pay railroad fares for three.

I had plenty of time to contemplate my own psyche during those seven long days on the road. While a writer becomes an acute observer — everything is grist for his mill: Remember this, note that, you'll use it sometime — he is his own best guinea pig. Oh, he knows his wife pretty well, but she — if she loves him — will often lie to him to bolster his ego, the ego he must rely on to write anything.

So . . . yes, I thought I was secure, I thought I would not feel diminished by staying at home (I'd be writing, wouldn't I? One of these days soon I'd click again) while the little woman set the alarm, got up every morning, and trudged off to earn our daily bread. But I had to face myself: I hated the whole idea, yet not enough to humble myself and ask my best friend for the loan of a thousand bucks instead of letting her do it. Why? Could it be that I still secretly felt in competition with Philip Pearson? Was I that *young?* Or was I afraid that if I did ask him for money he might turn me down?

I guess I merely did not want to put our long-time friendship to the test because — well — because all those years were stacked up behind us. I guess I really did love the guy. He was the closest thing to a brother I ever had.

★   ★   ★

We checked into a small, furnished, two-bedroom apartment in Hollywood, close enough for Liz to walk to work at Hollywood and Vine. I put off calling Philip that day. How to explain all this? "Tell him we're here, tell him *why* is none of his business," Liz said. "Tomorrow," I said. "I'll call him tomorrow."

Tomorrow I telephoned Esme at the Ober office. Maybe one — just one — of those six stories had sold. None had, but Audrey Wood had got in touch with Esme, trying to contact me. I was to call Miss Wood immediately.

"Where have you been?" Audrey was indignant. Here she had sold an option on *Birdsong* to Guthrie McClintic and we were irresponsibly meandering across the Bible Belt. Meanwhile, Guthrie had already shown the manuscript to MGM for financing, MGM was putting up money for its production, and — because they liked the dialogue — wanted to hire Liz and me and put us to work at fifteen hundred a week. Best she could do. Could we report at the studio Monday morning?

I telephoned Philip. Yes, we were right here in Hollywood, I told him. Six-month contract at MGM. Just checked in and were looking around for a house. A pool not necessary but would be nice. Amy should learn to swim. "If you happen to hear of anything in Beverly or Westwood . . . of course we want to see you right away."

He would check his social calendar, Philip said. It just so happened that he was free that very evening. How about Chasen's?

Somehow I was not very happy with myself when I hung up, but happier than I would have been had I telephoned him the day before and told him the embarrassing truth.

★   ★   ★

The parking boy took charge of our old Packard, still spattered with Bible Belt mud, at the entrance to Chasen's. (I could afford to tip him now.) As Liz and I approached the doorman, a woman standing near intercepted us. "John?" she said. "Mr. Ewing?"

"Yes?" I said.

She was probably about my age, though it is hard to judge a woman's years when she wears no makeup. Her gray suit was as shiny as her prominent nose, and her straight short hair was a faded no-color rather than the blonde it once must have been.

"It's Gerry Malnick," she explained. "Remember Cottonwood?"

"Oh, God. *Gerry!* I just wasn't expecting to see you—of all people."

"Yeah. Of all people. You can say that again."

I reached for her hand, seeing now the girl she had been within the woman she had become. She offered the hand tentatively, both of us acutely aware of how absurd it was for us merely to shake hands. But there was Liz watching, waiting to be introduced. "It's Gerry Malnick," I told her. "She's the first girl I ever loved."

"And I'm Elizabeth, the last—I hope," Liz laughed. "John has talked so much about you."

"I tried to get in touch with you, Gerry," I said.

"I know," she said. "Philip has told me."

Suddenly there were tears in her eyes. She brushed them away with the back of her hand, blinked and swallowed a couple of times. "This damn cold," she sniffled.

I felt tears begin to sting my eyes and then suddenly gathered her in my arms. "Gerry—Gerry," I said. "You've made me cry."

"I've made a lot of people cry," she said and pulled away from me. She turned to Liz. Philip, she explained, was held up in a story conference at the studio. He had not known how to get in touch with us so he had called her and asked her to come down and settle us at his table. He would join us as soon as he could.

Inside, I recognized Dave Chasen. Pint-sized, peripatetic, and eager to please, Chasen had been a minor Broadway comic — Liz and I had seen him in something called *Hold Your Horses* — before he settled down to a long run as a Beverly Hills restauranteur. That evening he was playing the role of host and captain of his establishment. "Mr. Pearson's table?" Gerry said. "He made a reservation for seven."

"Who?" Chasen frowned. "Sorry. I didn't catch the name."

"Pearson. Philip Pearson," Gerry repeated, but Chasen did not catch that either. He had just spotted Jimmy Stewart and his wife entering.

"Right this way, Jimmy," he beckoned.

After the Stewarts were seated Chasen returned and noted the three of us. He had never seen us before.

"Pearson," I said. "Philip Pearson."

He consulted his reservation calendar. "Oh, yes. Table for four." He looked at us, trying to place us. No, he had never seen us before. "Right *this* way."

We followed him to a table at the rear of the room, an area I was later to learn was reserved for nobodies. Nonpicture people. Civilians.

Liz and I ordered martinis, Gerry a Coca-Cola. She used to drink, she explained, but hadn't had one for a year or so. Didn't seem to want to anymore. Just as well. "I never knew when to quit."

This was treading on an area better left untrod. "Are you still living at Philip's place?" I asked.

She nodded. "Funny thing," she said. "I never knew him very well back home — not the way I knew you. I thought he was kind of stuck-up. You know — son of the banker — big house. But I was wrong. If it hadn't been for Philip Pearson . . ." She could not go on for a moment or two, then took a deep breath and continued. "He took me in when I had nowhere to turn and he didn't ask questions."

"He told me you were doing him a big favor by taking care of Doc while he was away." That was not quite what Philip had said, but it would serve.

"Yeah. That's like him. Can't admit there's anything—I don't know how to say it. Anything but just nice and like other folks." (*Folks.* What a warm, homey word that. I had lost it at Grand Central Station, I guess.)

"You want to know something else?" Gerry went on. "He's paying for me to take a course in typing. Philip's not the average-type person you meet on the street corner."

"Gerry," I said, trying to keep a straight face. "You are a master of understatement."

She did not know quite what that meant. Was I perhaps putting him down? "You like Philip, don't you?"

I nodded. "I agree with you. There's nobody like him."

"I'm glad," she went on, "because he likes you—and Mrs. Ewing. I guess you're like family, now his family is gone. He's—alone. Oh, he's got friends. They invite him out. And there's that girl, Whizzer, but it's my opinion she's out for what she can get. Me? Well, I'd do anything to make that boy happier."

"Boy? That boy is thirty-five years old. And, speaking of that boy—" I rose and took Philip's damp hand as he approached the table.

It was a pleasant evening. Philip played host to the hilt. He had brought Liz and Gerry gardenia corsages, which he pinned on them with nervous fingers. He ordered champagne. He transmitted our orders to the waiter with a hang-the-expense manner. He pointed out various celebrities and said of Fred Astaire, with pride, "I've met him." (He was still a movie fan at heart.) It pleasured him to introduce us to Lenore Gershwin, who kissed him lightly on the cheek and said, "See you Saturday eve. Be an angel and pick up June Levant, will you? Oscar can't make it." And he had gone to the trouble to call the real estate agent who had found him his house to ask her about a rental for his good friends the Ewings.

May I say this Philip was a far cry from the one I had chased down the icy road in Connecticut and found comatose, sucking his thumb?

★ ★ ★

When I began work on this book I talked to a few people who had known Philip Pearson. Not many were left, but Gerry Malnick was. She still lives in West Hollywood near the Malnick Quick-Type Service, which these days services more TV writers than screenwriters. She no longer does any of the work herself— "Look at these arthritic fingers!"—but drops into the office every few days to keep her employees on their toes. "Word processors!" she scoffs. "They'll be the death of us honest typists."

"Gerry," I told her, "I'm going to write a book about Philip, and I've been wondering if there was anything you could tell me that I don't know. He's always been an enigma to me. You lived in his little guest house for a while there just before the war. Do you remember anything that might give me a clue?"

Gerry owns the duplex that she shares with two well-behaved homosexuals. "Very nice boys who pay their rent regular," she says. "I have no complaints as long as—like the fella says—they don't do whatever it is they do in the street and frighten the horses." She rocked slowly back and forth in her bentwood rocker, thinking, frowning, cocking her head, and finally peering at me over her Franklin glasses.

"Well," she said finally, "Philip's dead now. Nothing can hurt him any longer. I guess if you want to know—"

One night Gerry was awakened by a hell of a shake. She had never experienced an earthquake. She leapt out of bed, staggered to the door, and stood there, hanging on. She had heard a doorway was the safest place. After ten or fifteen seconds the shaking stopped. Everything was quiet except dogs barking and the water in the swimming pool sloshing back and forth.

There was a full moon so she could see. Presently the door of the big house flew open and Doc came running around the pool, as if to see if she was all right. She stooped to pick him up, and then saw Philip coming toward her. "He was wearing that Sulka

robe he'd got for Christmas. Didn't you and Mrs. Ewing give it
to him?"

"Possibly," I said. "It was a long time ago."

"Well, anyway, here he comes, and he's taking those funny
little jerky steps. He marches around the pool till he stands right
in front of me — I still have Doc in my arms, he's whimpering —
and he says, Philip says, 'That was an earthquake,' and I say, 'Yes, it
sure as hell shook,' and then he asks me am I all right and I tell
him I am.

"We stand there must have been a couple of minutes, not
saying anything, just sort of waiting for another shake, and
watching the water in the pool settle down. Funny the things you
remember. I 'member finally it was quiet so I could see the moon
in the water and a cloud was passing over it like God's fingers.
Then Philip says, 'Maybe I better stay with you tonight so you
won't be scared.' No, it was 'frightened,' he said. Philip Pearson
wouldn't say 'scared.'

"I say, 'How do you mean stay? You mean sleep with me?' And
he jerks his head up and down fast two or three times. 'If it's all
the same with you,' he says.

"Well, it's probably no news to you that I went to bed with a lot
of guys I didn't know at the time, some okay, some treated me
like dirt, so what's the odds going to bed with a nice gentleman
like Philip. Besides, he's been good to me and asked nothing. So
after a minute I say, 'Come on in.' I go back into the room, get in
bed, and he comes in, takes off the robe, folds it, and lays it real
neat across the typewriter chair he had bought me, and gets in
bed beside me. He doesn't touch me, understand.

"We are both of us lying on our backs. After a little there's an
aftershock — not bad, just a jiggle — and he turns toward me and
lays one arm across me, and he says, 'You mind if I snuggle?' 'Be
my guest,' I say. 'Front or back?'

"'Back,' he says. Well, I turn my back and he comes up close
and pretty soon I feel the bed begin to shake and I think it's
another aftershock, but no. It's Philip! He's crying, for crying out
loud! So I finally say, 'Philip, it's okay, you mustn't cry, it's all
right.' And then he hangs onto me tight, but he doesn't say

anything, not a thing, and it's not long before he stops crying, and pretty soon he starts taking those long, even breaths that mean you're going to sleep.

"I don't know when it was he left, but he was gone by the time I woke up. Him and Doc both. Doc had slept on the bed with us. After that it happened several times. He wouldn't say anything, he'd just come to my little house and ask was it all right to get in bed with me. You know, I can't help wondering if what I did — which was nothing — was right. Maybe it would have made him feel better if I'd — well — responded or something. But what was there to respond to? Anyhoo, I didn't. I just let him — *sleep* with me. That's all he seemed to want, and it was kinda sweet."

28

Whizzer Wilkens had had a few haphazard shots at various professions: model, singer, dancer, actress. She was quick on the conversational draw and could relate titillating anecdotes about movies she had played in (she said; who cared?) and celebrities she had known. In a famous Bible extravaganza in which she had played a bit as Mary Magdalene, DeMille's crucified Christ was actually supported by a bicycle seat glued to the cross. Whizzer knew for a fact that a certain aging star owned three carpets for his bald head: short, medium, and long. Thus his hair "grew" naturally. One day he would announce, "Guess I need a haircut," and next morning appear in the short version. And once when she was singing at a now-defunct watering hole on Sunset Strip, Clark Gable had offered her a ride home. Well, you could have knocked her over with a feather duster when she walked out and discovered the great Gable's transportation was a Harley David- son motorcycle.

Whizzer was blonde ("It's easy to be a blonde," she said, "and gentlemen still prefer them") and had no visible means of support. She seemed to exist only at other people's parties where she was always a plus: decorative, chic, and amusing. She held her liquor like a lady and never went to bed with her hostess's husband.

There were any number of whizzers in Beverly Hills and Bel Air, but she was the only one who actually adopted the term as a name. It suited her. What her real one was nobody gave a damn. She had had a long run as a party girl and was now past thirty. "Well past" was the way Liz put it. We met her because for a time she was "Philip's girl." He brought her to dinner one evening. Just the six of us. Family. I sensed that she had expected a party with at least a couple of the caterer's waiters and a pianissimo piano player, but she adjusted to the situation and scaled down her performance. "This is *nice*," she said. "I knew there must be children out here, though I've never actually seen one before, but I didn't know they permitted mothers west of La Cienaga. It's — relaxing." Philip, proud to show off his prizewinner, was at his best, prompting her, building her up, and beaming nervously as if to say, See what I've got!

I kept wondering, what's this dame doing with the likes of Philip Pearson? Isn't he small game in her jungle? Or are the lions and tigers out of her range nowadays? Or is it just possible she's in love with him? A girl like that, it was hard to tell.

On the other hand Philip would not be such a bad catch. He had a name of sorts, though in Hollywood a writer was never a name unless he killed himself or his producer, or became involved in a scandal with a movie star. (Who knew George Kaufman until Mary Astor limned his sexual staying power in her diary?) Let's say Philip had a *reputation*. He had a good track record, having been under contract — without a break — for several years. He lived in a decorator house on the right side of the tracks with a standard, kidney-shaped swimming pool. He drove — since his mother's accident — a Lincoln Continental (he hosed it down on weekends himself — no need to go overboard) and had his hair cut at Jerry Rothchild's. All solid evidence of a bank account worth tapping into.

Perhaps, I thought, Whizzer is simply — finally — bored with living at "Loose Ends," which was how she referred to her little apartment on the wrong side of Wilshire. (Nobody she knew had ever been inside it. Philip picked her up at the curb.) The life-style must have paid few dividends, and those few only so long as she was attractive and amusing. She had seen us, Liz and me and family. Maybe it had occurred to her that marriage wasn't so bad, especially during those recurring moods marked lento, when one sees the dog days of one's forties dead ahead.

And for Philip? Why not? Whizzer Wilkens was not the girl in the picture hat that Liz had taunted him with, but she might pass as a 1940 sequel. Nothing too real, nothing disturbing. One could not envision her with a cold, slopping around in an old bathrobe. She would awaken each morning fully made up, every blonde lock in place. She and Philip could fight and make up on a high-comedy level. She would be a picture wife — sort of Irene Dunne to Cary Grant in *My Favorite Wife*. Happy ending, forever fun and games.

Well, apparently Whizzer had her own version of that ending in mind and it did not pan out. She sued Philip and turned him, briefly, into a famous writer. "Famous Writer Sued for Breach of Promise," screamed the Hearst headline we read over breakfast one morning. And "Hollywood Party Girl Demands $500,000 Heart Balm from Screenwriter Philip Pearson." The piece was illustrated with a large flattering photograph of Whizzer dabbing at her eyes and a smaller studio portrait of Philip looking somehow rakish, not at all like himself. Such a man might well promise, and then rat out on, such a girl.

The coupling of Heart Balm with Philip Pearson was patently ridiculous. Whizzer's pseudo-pathetic account of his leading her on, deceiving her, then deserting her was such a blatant rehash of the old ploy as to be laughable. Laughable if you did not know the accused. It even startled a guffaw out of me, but I sobered quickly. "That dirty little bitch," I said.

"Poor Philip," Liz said. "What'll this do to him?"

What indeed? I could picture him, shoulders hunched, eyes down, the shades drawn and doors locked, a cornered animal lurching from room to room. Go to the studio this morning? Absurd! His fellow writers would either kid him ("Well, how's our resident rogue this fine day?") or pretend they had not seen the item. Which would be just as bad. It would be up to me to break through and establish contact before he sank into trauma. I'd try to reach him by telephone, but if he would not answer — and I could understand that! — I would go over and break in.

He answered.

"Philip," I said with just the proper note of fraternal concern, "do you want to talk about it?"

"Talk about what?" he said.

"That lousy piece in the *Examiner*."

"I never read the Hearst papers," he said. "If it's that suit you're referring to, the *Times* has it too. So?"

This was not at all what I had been expecting. It was difficult to change gears. "Well, I just thought, I mean if you're not going to the studio this morning — since Liz and I are working at home — I'd come over and we could — "

"Look," he interrupted. "Are you being sympathetic?"

"What do you think I'm being? A meddler?"

"Well, thanks," he said. "But I've known about this for days."

"And you haven't — caved in?"

"The lawyer at Twentieth says Miss Wilkens tried this gambit a few years ago under another name. She got five thousand dollars that time. He says with her history we could fight the suit and win, but it would be more expensive and time consuming. So, he says, offer her five and she'll run with it."

"Well, that's fine," I said. "I'm sorry it turned out this way, Philip. Liz and I were fooled. We liked her."

"That's Hollywood," Philip said. "Mind if I call you back later? I'm due at a meeting with Zanuck in twenty minutes."

I remember thinking, little man, what now? That was Hollywood, all right, but was it Philip Pearson?

★   ★   ★

We did not really believe that we would get into the war. It was none of our business, was it? If we stood behind the British — "Give us tools and we will finish the job!" that marvelous old ham Winston Churchill had intoned from London — none of our boys would need to go over there again and get blown to hell. It was *their* fight. We would cheer lustily and safely from the bleachers.

And then suddenly it was no longer just their fight. Anybody still alive who was conscious on Sunday, December 7, 1941, remembers exactly where he was and what he was doing when the lightning struck. Most of our friends were listening to Toscanini and his NBC symphony when the radio program was interrupted with the news that the Japanese had bombed Pearl Harbor.

We missed Toscanini because Julie Hoffman, age nineteen, was reading for the lead in *Birdsong*, our play that was at last

Broadway-bound. Guthrie McClintic had long since dropped his option, but after a year or so, Audrey Wood had sold it to another, but lesser-known, producer who had been unable to cast the feminine lead in New York. Liz and I had come across a talented youngster playing a small part in a Robert Montgomery movie we had written. The star was being difficult about a scene and wanted it changed. Since we were still employed at MGM we had gone down to the set to tell him why he was wrong. Montgomery, for all his boyish charm, could be as stubborn as a country mule, so we finally compromised: We would redo the scene *his* way, but *we* would write it. He would not improvise it.

That was how we came upon Julie Hoffman. She was the fragile, fey, appealing, and slightly cloying little schemer we had written come to life. The only questions, and they were big ones because she had never been on the stage, were did she have presence, did she know how to move, could she be heard back of the fifth row? That was what we were trying to find out at lunch that Sunday — and the answer was yes to all our doubts — when Philip telephoned. *He* had been listening to Toscanini.

"Are you sure it's not another hoax of Orson Welles?" I asked.

Unfortunately, it was not. CBS confirmed it. After I told Liz and Julie and Amy and Lulabel, there was a long quivering silence. Then Julie timorously asked, "What will this — this war do to *Birdsong?*" We knew right then that we had an authentic actress on our hands. The hell with the war; what really mattered was The Play.

Since the Japanese did not follow up their initial advantage and bring the war to California, preparations for the play were scarcely interrupted. Liz and I would have to go to New York for at least six weeks — rehearsals and out-of-town tryouts. MGM gave us no trouble; Bernie Hyman, in whose unit we worked at the studio, said he'd keep his fingers crossed, to break a leg, and not let those cannibals of critics eat us alive. But there were Amy and Lulabel to consider. Lulabel was not afraid of bombs, but what about an elderly woman who could not drive and a seven-year-old child alone in the incendiary hills above Brentwood? Not good.

I thought of Gerry Malnick, and telephoned Philip. I said that
of course we would pay Gerry, and since he was working at home
at present he would not be needing a dog sitter at night.

There was a silence. Presently he said, "It's not that I need her
myself . . ."

Another pause. "Philip," I said, "it has occurred to me that you
may be just a trifle fed up with your Good Samaritan performance. This could give you a way out. When we return, I could
suggest to Gerry that she get a job—any able-bodied, able-
minded female can find a job these days, and she can type now—
and move into a place of her own. It would look better coming
from me than from you: It's a thought."

"No, no," he said quickly. "Nothing like that, nothing at all.
She's welcome here as long as—"

"If she's doing a typing job for you, she could spend the day
there and drive over here—she could use our car—and stay
overnight. Do a little shopping for Lulabel and Amy once in a
while."

"No, no," he repeated. Then he said, "What I mean to say is
had you considered Amy?"

"Of course I'd considered Amy. It's Amy that needs her most
of all. If it was Lulabel, *she* could go to a hotel."

"I meant—well—there are some people who wouldn't want
Gerry Malnick around their children."

"Why the hell not?"

"You know. What she's been."

"Oh, for Christ's sake, Philip. You sound like a character out of
Thomas Hardy."

"Very well," he snapped. "I see Gerry out there by the pool.
You can talk to her yourself."

Gerry met us in our car when we returned, exhausted but
triumphant, from New York. *Birdsong* was a hit; royalties would
be rolling in for months, there was competition for movie rights
and God was good. Amy, who had celebrated her eighth birthday
while we were away, was with Gerry. She was exploding with
news: Her third-grade teacher at Brentwood Elementary had
fractured her coccyx, a word that fractured Amy, and Tommy, the

boy who sat right behind her, had been sent to the principal's office because he said "Oh shit," and—

"Philip has some news too," Gerry said when she could get a few words in. She was looking much better than she had before we left. ("I got her to do something about her hair," Lulabel confided later.)

"Don't tell us he's going to get married," I laughed.

"No," Gerry said. "He's enlisted."

29

from Philip Pearson's Day Book

May 4, 1942. Got my commission yesterday. Lieutenant in
OSS. Ordered uniform by Eddie Schmidt. $265. Can
wear my own shoes.

As far as World War II was concerned, members of the motion
picture industry were no different from patriots involved in steel,
real estate, peanut farming, or the rag trade. Passions ran just as
high and every man champed to do his bit, but felt it only fair for
the military to employ him in his own field. What was the point
of frittering away precious talent as cannon fodder when it could
be of infinitely more value to the cause in a special capacity? And
so, before the draft could take its careless toll, there was a
stampede of movie industry patriots for the attention of con-
gressmen and military big shots who might pull strings, which
would transform a Warner Brothers producer into an instant
major in charge of training films, or a ten-thousand-dollar-
a-week star into a recruiting colonel.

There were countless channels one might tap for a commission. Darryl Zanuck, John Ford, John Huston, and plenty of
others would be filming military documentaries and propaganda
films and needing men of savvy and experience around them. It
was Zanuck, of course, who transformed my old friend into
Lieutenant Philip Pearson of the OSS.

The how-he-achieved-it and what-he-achieved were merely
incidental to the thought that plagued us: Why the hell did he do
it at all?

Philip would not have been drafted. Though he was unmarried and had no dependents, he was overage. If by chance the
draft age limit were ever stretched to encompass his knocking-
middle-age group, he could not have passed a routine army
physical. No half-assed medical examiner could have overlooked

those trembling hands, those eaten-to-the-quick fingernails, and failed to stamp him 4F.

Liz had a theory. "Whether you admit it or not, you two have always been in competition. You both chose to dig in the same lode. Sometimes he's been front-runner, sometimes you. Now you have a play running on Broadway. That may bug him. And then — big item, I suspect — you have a wife and daughter and all he's ever had in that department is a breach-of-promise suit. *But,* are you going to fight for your country? No. You are remaining safe and continuing to draw down a ridiculous salary in Hollywood. Does that make sense?"

"Too simple," I said. "Philip would never permit himself such a normal reaction."

We threw a farewell party the night before he was to embark for Destination Unknown. (Probably Fort Hollywood on Long Island, we guessed.) It could not have been more tinsel and sham, which we knew he would love — parking boys, a dance floor and tent over the lawn, food catered by Chasen's, a barman, a five-piece combo, fortune-teller, photographer, all the standard cast and paraphernalia. Philip loved movie stars? We gave him movie stars. After her hitches on *Photoplay* Liz could deliver slews of them. He danced with stars in his arms and stars in his eyes, and even made a brave attempt to revive the Charleston with Joan Crawford. Louella Parsons dropped by briefly to count the house and determine whether the shindig was worth reporting in her column. I have always thought it was the happiest single evening in Philip's life. Whatever it cost, it was worth it.

He sent Liz two dozen roses next day, along with a note to both of us: "Thanks. You must do that more often. *Ave atque vale,* Philip."

And not long behind the roses came a telephone call. "You won't believe this," Philip said, "but there's been a SNAFU. I got word this morning to stand by. They're going to try to win the war without me for a couple of months. So I just want to say, if you decide to throw another party, I'm available." He sounded happy and relaxed.

"It's Philip," I said, turning to Liz who was curling Amy's bangs. "He's stuck at home for a couple of months and doesn't know what to do with himself."

"Give me the phone," Liz said. "Listen, Philip. I've got an idea. John wants me to collaborate on another play but I'm right in the middle of a novel . . . Yes, all alone, no hands. Besides, it's not my cup of tea, so I thought if you're high and dry, why don't you two boys — and I use the word carelessly — kick it around?"

Which was how and why I found myself the following afternoon seated in Philip's study, staring out at Gerry Malnick sweeping dead bugs off his swimming pool. Gerry, once the most popular girl in high school, cheerleader and class president, then embezzler and later prostitute, now dog sitter working up to be a typist. She was going to care for Doc, the cocker who was following her around the pool, while Philip was gone. I wondered if she ever communicated with her parents? Or were they dead?

Philip interrupted my musings. "What's this Pulitzer Prize idea of yours?"

"Liz and I were driving past Pickfair," I explained. "After all these years of being the White House of Hollywood, it looks sad and lifeless. And suddenly I thought what if — yes, this is a what-if idea — what if Mary Pickford and Doug Fairbanks still own Pickfair jointly? They're divorced, but out of sentiment haven't disposed of the old relic and split the proceeds. *White Elephant.* How's that for a title?"

"Terrible," Philip said. "What the critics could do to that!"

"You're right . . . Well, anyhow Mary marries again and returns to Pickfair with her young husband for her second honeymoon. Doug marries a beautiful young babe and arrives with her an hour or so later. The estate is community property, they've always been tight with a buck, so why not take advantage of it?"

"Good premise," Philip said after a moment. "Of course it's kissin' cousin to *Private Lives.*"

"Nobody will notice if the laughs come fast enough."

"And," Philip began to smile, "they say plagiarism is no worse than a bad cold. So let's get this show on the road, shall we?"

It was different working together this time. Both of us were experienced writers now. We knew that one did not simply sit down and start to write. You talked about mood and what you were trying to say. You composed biographies of your characters so that you would know how they would talk and react, and then outlined, scene by scene, how to utilize them to the best comedic advantage for two or three acts.

We talked for a week, made dozens of pages of notes, before we wrote two words: *At Rise.* And when I finally typed that out we stared at it and decided to wait until the next day before dialogue.

"I don't know," I said to Liz a week or so later. "We don't seem to spark each other as we used to. One thing I've noticed. My instinct is for conflict and action; Philip shies away from it. He'd prefer his people to talk about such things *after* they have happened. Off stage. So I compromise a lot. If I didn't, I'd have to fight with him, and I'm not going to fight with Philip. Of course, he could be right. He's a damn good writer. It's just that we have grown and developed in different directions."

There were minutes — sometimes half hours — when we merely sat and stared at nothing, hoping that a line that could satisfy us both would sail past and one of us capture it. Or paced aimlessly about the room. Or took a swim, or went for a walk on one of the bridle paths that had been hacked through the scrub of the adjacent hills. Then — if we were still stuck — we might permit ourselves a drink, and often find ourselves too relaxed and reminiscing about the days in Cottonwood, their sometimes harsh realities now obscured by a patina of nostalgia.

We finally wrote Curtain to Act One, more in relief than with any sense of accomplishment or anticipation of coming to grips with Acts Two and Three. It had been tough sledding. But maybe that's the way writing was as you grew older and lost your amateur standing; it became a job like any other. You might not kiss your wife good-bye and go to an office, but you had to sit yourself down in front of a typewriter each day and say to your brain, here I am. Give me some idea or we don't eat. I'm waiting. Get to work, you lazy bastard.

"I think it's pretty good," I said, after reading over the manuscript that Gerry had typed.

"I like the typing," Philip said.

"Meaning you don't like the writing."

"No, I think it's pretty good."

"Had the word 'pedestrian' crossed your mind?"

Philip circled the room, absentmindedly chewing on the nail of his right forefinger, then flopped down on the sofa and swung both feet over the back. Doc, who had been trying to trip him, laid his head on Philip's chest. I strolled to the window. Heat shimmered over the mountains. A pair of angry mockingbirds were dive-bombing a turkey buzzard.

"Maybe it's the war," I mused.

"I said I thought it was pretty good. Ask Doc. He heard me." Philip's eyes were closed, his hand stroking Doc's head.

It's his fault, I was thinking. I get into this thing because Liz and I think it will be good for him, keep his mind off what he's in for, so I don't stand up for what I believe because that would spoil it for him. If I'd fought him more . . . I could not help smiling. From the expression on his face Philip might be having similar thoughts.

He sat up and yawned. "I don't know," he said. "Let's forget it over the weekend. I'm going up to Santa Barbara for a couple of days."

"Know somebody there?"

"Not a soul. That's why I'm going."

I did not comment. "Ask Elizabeth to read the first act," he went on. "See how she reacts, and don't let her con you. I'll call you Monday."

He did not telephone on Monday, nor was he at home when I called. On Tuesday there came a special delivery note:

Dear John:

Would you slit your throat if I welch out on the play? I'd hate it if you did, but I have been mulling and regretfully came to the conclusion that plays are not (a play is not?) up the Pearson alley these days. So do with it what you will. I've also come to another conclusion. I'm going to sell my house complete with easement through Myrna Loy. Who knows how long I will be gone? And when the war is over (and I have been awarded the DSC for bravery at my typewriter), I don't know that I want to return to California. I suspect I have had it with the movies. Not that they haven't been kind to me. But it's time I got back to serious writing (ahem!) if I'm ever going to. Or at least see if I can put one intelligent word after another.

Don't worry about Gerry. She is going to rent a little apartment in Westwood and hang out her shingle: Secretary-Typist for Hire. She will also take care of Doc for the duration. I'll finance her until she gets established, so if you need a part-time secretary or know of anybody who does . . .

God bless us every one,

Philip.

PART V

30

Philip had been gone for more than a year, his address an APO number in the European theater of the war. He could let us know that he was in London, but doing what, he was forbidden to say. He had written two or three short letters in which there was nothing very interesting or tempting to a censor's pencil: The London stage was superior to New York's and cheaper. The curtain went up in late afternoon so that playgoers could get home — or into a bomb shelter — by dark. The weather was miserable, the countryside green. He had met Evelyn Waugh who had not said a word all evening. If we knew of anyone who was coming across soon, would we send along some nylon stockings for a woman he knew? "She's the wife of a friend of mine and hasn't had a new pair since 1939. About your size, Elizabeth." He could live on his salary but could not save any money after paying room and board. *So he was not living in barracks or feeding in a chow line.*

(We figured that, with the sale of his house, Philip must have close to a quarter of a million socked away, so the plaint of being unable to lay anything aside out of his meager salary as a lieutenant was greeted by his friends with levity and the hopes that nobody else had heard it so they could say, "Did you hear what Philip wrote home? He can live on his salary but can't save a penny. It'll take more than V-twos to change him.")

The play we had tried to collaborate on had been all but forgotten while I wrote a number of short stories and did a stint at MGM with Liz, adapting *Birdsong*. (Hunt Stromberg had bought it for sixty thousand dollars, twenty-four of which went to our boy producer, Frank Cabbot.) We had been offered a stretch at Warner Brothers, but turned it down because of gas rationing. The Burbank studio was fifteen miles from our house in Brentwood.

Not long after the screenplay of *Birdsong* was finally okayed I woke one night to the sound of a howling Santa Ana and a temperature that had shot up to ninety-five degrees. I got out of bed, tiptoed downstairs, and walked across the living room to the kitchen and the refrigerator. It was while I was reaching for the ice water that—God knows why—the idea came to me: a totally new approach to *Double Honeymoon*. I went back into the living room, wheeled the typewriter out of the closet, and within half an hour had a rough outline. I was tempted to awaken Liz and read it to her, but decided to wait and look it over in the morning. Then I heard her steps on the stairs.

"Did I wake you?"

The door into the patio had blown open and was banging. "No. That did," she said, shutting the door.

"Well, as long as you're awake, listen to this."

When I had finished reading, Liz said, "Do you want me to work on it with you?"

"I always did. You said you didn't want to."

"This is different." She got up off the sofa and locked the patio door, which had blown open again. "What about Philip?"

"What do you mean what about Philip?"

"Well, is he going to get his nose out of joint?"

"He bowed out, remember?"

"I know, but—"

"In the first place it was my idea, and in the second we won't be using a single word that he contributed to that first version."

"You're right. But I think it would be nice if you wrote him and told him what you plan to do. I wouldn't want him to think that I was taking advantage of one of our boys while he was braving shot and shell."

"Okay. I'll tell him he can read the manuscript when it's finished. I may even offer him a percentage."

"That's going pretty far," Liz said, "but why not? He'll turn it down, of course, but it will make him feel good."

"That'll be the day," I laughed.

★ ★ ★

While Liz and I were working on *Honeymoon for Four,* which was our new title for *Double Honeymoon,* Philip's "London Bridge Is

Falling Down" was published in the *New Yorker*. It was his first
fiction in two years and it created something of a sensation. No,
that's exaggeration. A short story never "creates a sensation." The
best that can be expected of it is that it be mentioned. You would
hear people at a party say, "Did you read that thing by Philip
Pearson? Pretty good." Which is more enthusiasm than most
fiction can generate in Hollywood where only the latest preview
is talked about.

I don't remember the plot, if any, but I still recall — vividly —
one episode. It was told in the first person, the narrator a stoic
spinster of a certain age named Edna Fatheringale. Miss
Fatheringale was in Produce (harder than hen's teeth to come by
since the war) at Harrod's, and was fortunate enough to have her
own tiny flat in Kew remain intact, though bombs had dropped
uncomfortably close a number of times. At first, when sirens
moaned, she had bundled up and trotted off to the dubious
shelter of the nearby underground stop. But somehow the
blasted bombers usually managed to come over just as she was
brewing herself a cuppa, and by the time the all-clear sounded
and she could trudge back the two blocks and climb the two
flights, the water in the kettle was cold and more often than not
the gas turned off. Lately she hadn't bothered to go out at all. She
liked to think of herself as a fatalist: When your name was on a
certain bomb it would find you wherever you were hiding, and
there wasn't a blasted thing you could do about it!

Besides — and she would never tell this to a soul — she rather
enjoyed the show. It gave you something to look at instead of just
sitting there in the dark twiddling your thumbs. You had been
warned to stay away from windows on account of shards of flying
glass, but if a person chose to open her window and sit there in
the fresh air with a nice cup of Earl Grey while she watched the
performance, then it was nobody's business but her own, wasn't
it? And if she did not let herself think of bodies being mangled
and lives snuffed out a mile, three blocks, however near or far
from her — and she might as well not think about it because what
could she do about it? Not a thing! — then it was, well, stimulating. She hated to say it but that's what it was. Stimulating. A

veritable *Götterdämmerung* when the fires began to burnish the sky. Perhaps if a person had relatives or what some people called "dear ones" out there, she would feel different about it, but Miss Fatheringale had nobody.

She was an excellent character, I thought, and Philip had graphically realized her aching loneliness as well as her understated, but nonetheless implied, vindictiveness at the bombs wreaking of vengeance upon all those nameless, faceless somebodies who had passed her by, who did not even know that she was alive, who even seemed to blame her, Edna Fatheringale, for the way prices were going up at Harrod's. Philip had, perhaps unconsciously — I never asked him — written an alter ego to Miss Fatheringale in an owl she noticed one night as she was hurrying home through a bombed-out neighborhood. The face of a row of flats had been sheared neatly away and the exposed interiors reminded her of a famous dollhouse, belonging to one of the royals, on exhibition at the British Museum, which Miss Fatheringale visited periodically during her holiday. It was titillating, rather like the thrill of being a spy she supposed, to see exactly how the residents had been disposed at the instant of the fateful blast. *Those* people, whoever they were (had been?) there on the first floor right, had been slovenly; the drawers in that old commode, quite a valuable antique, she supposed, were halfopen, half-shut. And there above, would you look at that! The brass bed was a disgrace. Had they left it that way all day, or had they retired early — that particular air raid was over by tenthirty — and not bothered to make it up when they fled the room? Miss Fatheringale would certainly make *her* bed before she left her bedroom, no matter what. Always had and always would! She was about to switch her attention to an adjoining flat when her eyes were riveted by a sudden movement. It was a large barn owl, for pity's sake, perched on the foot of the brass bedstead. Miss Fatheringale had read in the *Times* that owls had migrated into the city because the bombing brought out so many rats, but she had never thought she would be fortunate enough to encounter one. As she watched, fascinated, the owl pounced on something live and flew off with it. "Good for you!" thought Miss Fatheringale. "Clean up the neighborhood."

It was that very evening that she sat once more beside her open window savoring her Earl Grey. The street outside was empty and dark. Everybody who would be going to the shelter had already gone. She could hear the ack-ack from the British batteries along the Thames and see the searchlights scissoring the clouds trying to spear the Luftwaffe bombers.

Then a bomb exploded in the very next block, the closest one had ever come. Miss Fatheringale had often wondered what it would be like, and now she was too stunned to think about it at all. She simply sat for along while in a stupor, deafened by the blast. When she finally opened her eyes and looked outside, the dust was beginning to settle and then, through it, screeching like a banshee (it was the first sound Miss Fatheringale heard) staggered a woman, naked as a jaybird. Her long hair was streaking out behind her like a fraying red banner. And back about a hundred feet or so, trying to catch her, calling "Sarah! Stop, Sarah!" stumbled a man equally nude. He caught up with her directly in front of Miss Fatheringale's flat where she had fallen to her knees, picked her up, and cradled her in his arms, whimpering, tears streaming down both their faces. Finally, instinctively, he turned and started back the way they had come, but then he must have realized that whatever house or flat they had inhabited was now on fire — Miss Fatheringale could see the flames, even hear the crackle (her hearing was returning, thank God!) — so he turned and carried his limp wife, at least Miss Fatheringale hoped she was his wife under these embarrassing circumstances, off in the other direction.

So far as Miss Fatheringale was concerned the only thing of any significance about the episode was that she had finally seen a nude man. And she found it disappointing, not nearly so — so — *decorous* as the nude males in the Elgin Marbles at the museum.

"Dear Miss Fatheringale," I wrote. "The Mrs. and I read your story in the *New Yorker* magazine and are glad you got your hearing back. Congratulations. Hearing is no joke, especially when you are deaf. I would sue the bastard, if I were in your place, which I am glad I am not because bombs leave me pretty cold. Best regards, John Ewing."

Philip and I could never compliment each other simply and directly. Why? Don't ask me. The "Miss Fatheringale" letter was a fair sample of the manner in which we acknowledged having read each other's stuff, and usually it evoked a response in kind. This one did not, though I know he received it because my envelope had conveyed another, but serious, note, which he answered immediately.

Dear John:
About the play. (*Honeymoon for Four*. Good title. Wish I'd thought of it.) When you and Elizabeth finish it, let Esme give it and the pages you and I collaborated on a quick read. I'll be satisfied with whatever percentage she feels is due to me. I don't want any credit. As the saying goes, take the cash and let the credit go. Lots of luck with it.

I had been reading his letter aloud to Liz. When I reached that point I stopped. She said, "You did tell Philip you wouldn't be using any of his material, didn't you?" I nodded.

"Maybe he was in a foul mood when my note arrived."

The remainder of his letter did not seem to bear that out.

Incidentally, would you two charming people do me a favor? Captain Rollo Woodward of the RAF is going to America shortly for some R & R. He was shot down over the Channel. If he makes it as far as California show him the town and feed him at Mike Romanoff's beanery, which he has heard about. I met Mrs. Woodward one less than blissful night in the air raid shelter. Natalie Woodward blesses you for the nylons you sent over.

Captain Woodward and his wife have taken me into their flat since mine was bombed out a few weeks ago. You don't know what you are missing, chums, but I'll let you in on what it's like: hell.
Love,
Philip

We decided to follow his suggestion: Let Esme arbitrate. Esme was fair and sensible. She could tell at a glance that Philip had contributed nothing to the final version of the damn thing.

Before we had finished the play Captain Rollo Woodward of the RAF announced his arrival. We were on the terrace working — it was a balmy winter's day — and Lulabel was monitoring the telephone. She came to the door and called excitedly, "Children, there's the cutest man on the phone. Sounds just like Leslie Howard. He's from London and Philip Pearson told him to be sure to ring us up while he was out here."

"You talk to him," I said to Liz. "Let me clean up this page before I take a break."

"You'll love him," Lulabel said as Liz passed her. "Did I say how his voice sounds just like Leslie Howard?"

"Yes, you did, Lulabel," Liz said.

Five minutes later she returned. "I can't blame Lulabel. The man is a charmer. Nice humor too. We're picking him up at the Roosevelt at seven and taking him to Romanoff's."

"Bring him out here afterward," Lulabel said.

Captain Woodward had a somewhat similar effect upon men. At first glance one was struck by the sheer perfection of his appearance, and then one began — at least I did — to search for the flaw that would humanize him and make him interesting. His features had been chiseled by that British chiseler who plagiarizes Michelangelo whenever he can get away with it. The eyes were incredibly, startlingly blue. He was six feet one, had fair hair, with just a hint of auburn in its waves, that looked as if it conveniently fell into place with a mere shake of the head after a shower that left him squeaky clean. He could not have weighed more than a hundred and fifty soaking wet, and the Bond Street tailoring of the RAF uniform (which made its U.S. counterpart look like something picked up in Macy's basement) dramatized his appealing gauntness. Besides, he carried a stick and walked with a barely noticeable limp. The effect was well-nigh irresistible.

I could not discover the flaw. Perhaps I was merely envious, but I could not help thinking to myself that the limp was unnecessary to the ensemble. That was carrying the brave hero image one step too far.

"We've got to put some meat on you," Liz said, playing the Jewish mother at dinner that night. "You don't look as if you'd had a square meal since Oxford."

"Cambridge," he corrected her gently. "The pretty one down on the Cam."

"Sorry," Liz said.

"You're forgiven. We ought to wear badges." He turned to me. "Your wife is far too sweet to be endured. I'm afraid I must kiss her before all these people. Do you mind?"

"Be my guest," I said, feeling like a fool. Captain Woodward got to his feet, looked down at Liz as if finding it difficult to forgive her for being so sweet, laid his tapered fingers against her cheeks (she was enjoying every moment of the charade), turned her face up to his, and then planted a chaste kiss on her brow.

I heard several diners at the next table applaud. One of them, I noticed, was a friend of ours, Howard Greer. With him were three somewhat younger Hollywood couturiers. Captain Woodward bowed to the group, then sat down. I was beginning not to like him very much, but Liz seemed amused.

"You've made an impression on the dressmakers," she whispered.

"Is that what they are?" Rollo turned to steal another look.

"That's how they refer to each other in private. Also sometimes known locally as the four queens. All extremely talented and famous designers on the movie landscape."

I cleared my throat. "Tell us about Philip," I said.

"Philip?" Rollo repeated the name as if about to add, "Who?" Then the questions in his eyes cleared. "Oh, you mean Phil."

"I daresay," I said, "but none of his old friends ever call him that."

"Talie and I did right from the start. *Philip* seems wrong to me. Philip is a man who can take care of himself. But a *Phil* is— well—he isn't quite whole. Something has been omitted from a Phil's psyche, and it's left him—vulnerable."

It was strange about Rollo. One moment he seemed a fatuous, silly ass. The next he was explicating something that should have seemed obvious, but had never before occurred to me.

"Maybe Philip is exposing another facet of himself over there," Liz said.

"Perhaps," Rollo said. "Anyhow, I love the fellow. Maybe because he needs love and tries so hard to make himself unworthy of it. Talie loves him too, but I understand him better. He's a child trying like the very devil to play the brave All-American who's afraid of nothing. It's — touching. Did you read that story of his about the spinster? The *New Yorker* was going to publish it over here, he told me."

We both nodded. "Damn good," I said.

"But totally false," Rollo said. "I told him that."

"I'm surprised he's still speaking to you."

"He was angry for a while, but he got over it. You see, there's no such fearless character in any language as Miss Fatheringale. Oh, the other side of her, her built-in angers at those who have slighted her, they're authentic. But, no matter what, she would have the piss scared out of her during the raids, like everyone else. Pardon me, Elizabeth."

"Shakespeare never apologized for using the word," Liz said. "Frankly I like it better than the nice-Nelly pee."

"Bless you, luv," Rollo made a grimace. "I guess what I'm trying to say is — our happy breed of men and women — condemned to this seat of Mars, this other blasted Eden — we put on a damn good show. Not for anybody else, but to save our own skins. The first scream of terror would be like yelling fire in a crowded theater. There'd be a stampede and everybody would be trampled to death. England is, in this war, a theater. We're all playing leads and no one dares let his side down. So . . ." He shrugged. "It's not so much courage as self-preservation. Nobody gets the wind up and everybody keeps the pecker up, or else." He sighed, and changed the subject. "Will it take long to drive out to Lockheed tomorrow?"

"About half an hour, and keep to the right."

"I'm supposed to take a look at their new fighter while I'm in town."

So that was how he happened to have enough cash to make the trip. The RAF had sent him.

"One thing I wanted to ask — if you can tell us," I said. "What is Philip — Phil — doing for the OSS over there?"

"Propaganda sketches, I gather. Interviews with the aviators after excursions over Berlin, things like that, then writing them up under his byline. Not his bag at all. He loathes it." Rollo paused and lit a cigarette, then looked at me. "He's very fond of you, you know that, old chap?"

"Sometimes," I said. "He expresses it in — odd ways."

"One thing I wanted to ask you. Who was that first love of his? I assume there was one, and it had to be a tremender to short-circuit everything since."

"I've often wondered," I said. "He never dropped her name."

"Are you sure it was a her?" Rollo said.

Liz and I glanced covertly at each other. "The other never occurred to me," I said.

"I keep forgetting you're an American," Rollo laughed.

"I'm an American and it has occurred to me," Liz said.

"Not that it matters," Rollo went on. "'Men have died from time to time, and worms have eaten them, but not for love.'"

"I've never held with that," Liz said. "If love isn't worth dying for, what is?"

Rollo thought about that seriously. "I almost died for England, of course, but not from choice."

"Give me a quarter for the ladies' room," Liz said.

While she was gone I turned to Rollo who seemed to be tuning in on a conversation from the next booth. "I've always thought," I said confidentially, "that Philip's neurosis or whatever it is had a very elementary basis: He can't get it up."

"Oh, but you're so wrong," Rollo said, smiling brightly.

I let the subject drop.

A little later Howard Greer and the other three dressmakers paused beside our booth on the way out. They obviously wanted to be introduced. We obliged them. Rollo stood to shake hands, and made them all look drab. They were going on to the Body Shop on the Sunset Strip for a nightcap, Guy Drummond explained. There was a new chantoosy, Tommy Williams, who was divine. "I can't seem to remember whether she's a boy trying to be a girl or a girl trying to be a boy, but he/she is gorgeous and has a voice that will haunt you," Howard Greer said.

"Looks like a young prince," Guy added. "You'll die when it sings 'I'll be seeing you.'"

"'In all the old familiar places,'" one of the others said with a leer.

"I'm afraid we've promised to be home early," Liz said, "but if you'd like to go, Captain Woodward?"

Rollo looked from one to the other of the four. Something, I would not know what, passed between them. "Well, if one of you men would chauffeur me back to the Roosevelt later . . . I'd hate to be a drag."

No one smiled at the word. "No drag at all," Guy said. "We would consider it a privilege, Captain."

"Hands across the sea and all that jazz," the fourth dressmaker said.

"Sure you wouldn't mind?" Rollo turned to Liz and me with an appealing, little boy expression on his beautiful face. "You've been too kind." He seemed to be saying, Yes, you have been kind, but I've done my duty; now I'd like to have some fun.

"Not at all," I said, "though my mother-in-law and daughter are never going to forgive me for failing to bring you back with us."

"Kiss them for me," Rollo said, "and tell them I'm not the sort that decent old ladies and innocent little children should consort with."

★   ★   ★

When we finished work on *Honeymoon for Four* we mailed a carbon, along with the first act I had written with Philip, to Esme. After she had read them both she wrote to say that, in her opinion, Philip deserved no percentage, but that she would inform him of her decision before making it final.

A few weeks later Esme telephoned me. She had heard from Philip who seemed to feel that he was entitled to a percentage.

"Why?" I asked. "Did he explain?"

"Well, he spent about a month on that first act you didn't use."

"Every writer risks his time, unless he's writing on contract. Sometimes the risk pays off, sometimes it doesn't."

"You don't have to tell me that," Esme said. She sounded embarrassed. "But under the circumstances . . ."

"You mean because he's in London playing soldier?"

"It's hard to explain."

"It sure as hell is!" I said.

At any rate, Esme went on, Philip had indicated a figure that would satisfy him: twenty-five percent. Since we were such old friends, Esme said, she proposed to draw up a memo to that effect for the three of us to sign. "After all, if you have a hit, twenty-five percent isn't going to break you. If you have a flop, what is twenty-five percent of nothing?"

"I'll call you back," I said.

There is no point in hashing over what Liz and I said to each other. What it boiled down to was the fact that if I fought for what I was convinced was fair, I ran the risk of losing a lifelong friend. If I gave in to his suggestion, I would never feel quite the same toward him.

I chose the latter.

"Funny," Liz mused. "Apparently you'd rather hang onto the friendship than continue to respect the friend."

"That's one way of looking at it," I said.

I called Esme and told her. "I think that's wise," she said. "In the end, someone always has to give in. I'll draw up the letter of agreement."

She was about to hang up when she said, "Oh, by the way, remember that friend of Philip's, Captain —"

"Rollo Woodward," I supplied.

"His plane was shot down over Cologne last week, and he's considered lost. Philip wrote me. Said to let you know."

Rollo had died for England. But then, as he had said, he had no choice.

31

"In the majority of cases," Dr. Everett was saying, "patients prefer minimal contact with relatives and former friends. We indulge them in that. They want to feel more emotionally and psychically stable before meeting with persons from the world that they prefer not yet to face. Sometimes, if too early on in recovery, they break down, for no apparent reason, and this exacerbates the basic trauma. But in Captain Pearson's situation I decided that he is in sufficient control to, well, let's say *shmoose* with an old friend, as he tells me you are."

When I had given my name at the reception desk at Walter Reed I had been informed that, before meeting with Captain Pearson (yes, he had been promoted from lieutenant), a Dr. Damon Everett would like to speak to me. This was routine procedure before contact with patients in the psychiatric wing. Everett was a sandy-haired man in his fifth decade, I should imagine. He smiled a great deal and, I suspect, had worked hard to achieve his confidential I-would-tell-this-to-no-one-else-but-I-am-positive-that-you-will-understand-and-be-so-guided manner. I had a feeling that he would drive Philip up the wall, if he was not up there already.

"You are a psychiatrist?" I asked.

"Among a few other alphabetical credentials," he said. Again that bright smile of his. "Why do you ask?"

"Philip did not say what was the matter when we spoke on the telephone yesterday."

"They seldom do." *They*. Philip was now one of *them*, whatever that meant. "A broken leg—a burst appendix—a bullet lodged in the spine—all much easier to admit and cope with than the slightest variance in brain waves. Holdover from days of being locked up in asylums."

"Can you tell me—*ought* you to tell me—what Philip's trouble is?"

"Only the collateral symptoms. The result of who knows what? Yes, he was in London during the bombing, the V-ones and V-twos. So were hundreds of thousands of others. Most of them escaped emotional damage, or the handy old portmanteau term — breakdown." Everett seemed to be loosening up. We were two men discussing a situation together. "Let's see. His condition, some evidence of which you'll observe. Trembling hands. Inability to sleep — without sedation. Night terrors. Withdrawal into self. Inability — or refusal — to communicate."

I could not help smiling. "I am tempted to say, what else is new, doctor?"

"Perhaps he is one of the ones who should never have been accepted into the service."

"That thought occurred to me at the time," I said.

"To be perfectly frank with you, Mr. Ewing," Dr. Everett said, finally breaking all the way through his professional glaze, "your friend is doing nothing to help *us* help *him*. His attitude seems to be, 'That's none of your business, doctor.'"

"You knew he was raised a Catholic?"

"Yes. But he has refused to see a priest."

"Has he mentioned the death of a friend of his? An English aviator?"

"No. Do you think that could be significant?"

"You're the doctor," I said. If Philip had chosen not to mention Rollo Woodward, that was his affair. "Is there anything I should, or should not, say to him? I assume that's why you wanted to see me."

"Actually I hoped you might be able to shed a little light, or point me at a keyhole and possibly hand me a key that would fit."

"I've been looking for that key ever since we were kids," I said, rising. "You wouldn't want to sit in?"

"That won't be necessary. As so far as what to say and what not to say — your guess is as good as mine. Perhaps better. You're his friend. I'm merely the doctor assigned to — the case of Philip Pearson. Oh, by the way. He is slightly sedated."

Philip had chosen not to meet me in his quarters so I waited in the reception room at Walter Reed where a three-day-old copy of the *New York Times* caught my eye. I wondered if Philip had seen it. It contained Brooks Atkinson's withering comment on *Honeymoon for Four,* which had taken us two years to translate from typewriter to Broadway and then closed forever after one performance. Our old New York friends had bought tickets for the opening so it seemed only hospitable for Liz and me to invite them up to our hotel room for a drink afterward. They insisted upon waiting with us for what would have to be glowing reviews. They said, "You've got a hit! . . . You're in! . . . It'll run a year!" And then came the reviews. To be present while your closest friends read such comment is worse than being photographed in flagrante delicto.

It was while we awaited our indecent exposure that Maureen told me about Philip, who had sent a telegram to the theater: DEAR PLAYWRIGHTS I AM COUNTING ON HONEY-MOON FOR FOUR TO KEEP ME IN CAVIAR DURING MY DECLINING YEARS LOVE PHILIP. I had not known he was back in the States until I noted the dateline: WASH-INGTON, D.C. Maureen explained that he was at Walter Reed Hospital for a short period before being mustered out. No, nothing seriously wrong, at least that was what he had said over the phone. Just a "condition," was the way he put it. "You know Philip."

"I'd like to see him," I said. "But I wonder if I should?"

"Oh, I wish you would," Maureen said. "I do worry about him, and for some reason he'd rather I didn't go down there."

I telephoned Philip at Walter Reed. After a considered interval he said, "Okay . . . if you want to. I'm not behind bars."

After five minutes or so I heard a door open and looked up to see Philip framed by the doorway. He was glancing about nervously, a rumpled elk that would bolt at the sound of a snapping twig. I called, "Here I am, Philip," and he saw me, smiled a twitch of a smile, looked quickly down at his slippered feet, and then let the door swing shut behind him. He wore plain white pajamas and a khaki bathrobe — he had lost weight and looked — well — *bleached.* He continued to stand there rigid, just — waiting.

I hurried over to him, grabbed his hand — it was cold and damp — and pumped it. "*Philip*. God, it's good to see you."

He cleared his throat. "You were — you were — decent to come down to see me."

"What would you have me do?" I tried for the old bantering manner, "Send you a bowl of chicken soup?"

I guess what came out of his throat was intended to be a laugh. "How is Elizabeth?"

"About as well as could be expected."

"What do you mean?" At least I had his interest.

"There's been a death in the family. Hadn't you heard?"

"Death? Who?"

"*Honeymoon for Four*."

"Oh. Your play. Yes, I read you'd closed," he said.

"And not with a whimper, but a bang. Be grateful your name was not on it."

There was a silence. He made no hostlike gesture toward chairs or sofa. I glanced out the window. The sun, which had been hidden, was breaking through the clouds. It was warm for May. "Would you like to — sit down — go for a walk outside? That is — is it against the rules — "

"You mean do they let the nuts out?"

I thought, well, all right. Let's play it straight. "If you promise not to make a break for it, I'll be responsible." He sucked in his breath and held it. I laughed. "I never could trust you, you know. I'll never forget how you always tried to get away from me and beat me back to the gym."

Something was happening to him. I watched him carefully, wondering if I had gone too far. He seemed to be trying to get the better of some cataclysm that threatened to engulf him. He took a series of quick catch-breaths. Then he began to breathe easier, even turned and smiled at me, and was at last relaxed, almost Philip-on-a-good-day. "Well, hel-*lo*, Philip Pearson," I said. "Where've you been keeping yourself?"

"Was that really you — and me — back in that gym?"

I nodded, my eyes misting. "I hadn't thought of it since — donkey's years."

"Me either." He looked puzzled. "Donkey's years," he repeated. "Father used to say that. Where did the term come from?"

"You went to Harvard, didn't they larn you a simple thing like that?"

We were communicating once more — superficially — batting words around. That was safe, always had been. I established eye contact with him briefly. We both smiled. It felt good, like the old days when we'd been fighting and then patched it up. I was glad I had not challenged him about that percentage. What the hell difference did money make? We were friends. Always would be.

"Say!" he said. *Say*. That sounded about twelve years old. "Say. I'll get me a pass. I'm sure it'll be all right. You look responsible, practically Republican."

"You take that back," I said. That was twelve-year-old lingo too. We were back in short pants.

Philip laughed, impulsively took me by the arm, and began to propel me across the room to the desk. Suddenly he realized he was touching me. He let go and thrust his hand behind his back.

We walked aimlessly about the hospital grounds for a while, vaguely aware of the sporadic off-hours traffic between us and Rock Creek Park. Philip had nothing to say — if he did, he did not say it — and I restricted my conversation to trivial queries about the quality of hospital food, did they wake him in the middle of the night to stick a thermometer up his ass, how did he get along with Dr. Everett?

"He's smarter than I thought he was."

"Why don't you like him? He's only trying to help you."

"He's such a — a nosey parker."

"Where the hell did you dredge that one up from?" I asked.

"Same old pond as donkey's years," he laughed.

The throb of an approaching plane grew insistent. I glanced at Philip. He had heard it too and was squinting up into a brilliant sky bedizened with cumulus clouds. The plane was a silver arrow aimed at the dark belly of one of them.

We sat down on a bench under a tree. "You were afraid that plane was going to shake me up, weren't you?"

"It crossed my mind."

"Mine too," he admitted after a moment. "If I were writing an incident like this I'd have me start to shake and . . ." He extended his right hand straight out before him and looked at it. It trembled slightly. "Look at that. Just about back to normal everyday tremor. I keep telling Dr. Everett that, but he'll be satisfied with nothing short of rigor mortis."

At least his humor was intact, I thought.

"How long are the bastards going to keep you in chains?" I said. Knowing Philip, I felt that such an outrageous way of putting it would be more palatable than a direct "How long do you think you'll have to stay here?"

He replied in kind. "Till I stop waking everybody up screaming, I guess. Meantime I get free room and board and laundry." His gaze followed a stray mutt that approached the tree in a businesslike manner, lifted his leg to dribble his John Henry, then trotted over to sniff at us. Philip leaned over to pet him. "You see Doc lately?" he asked.

"Just before we left for New York. Gerry brought him over. She's staying with Amy and Lulabel while we're gone. Doc's fine. He asked about you."

"Tell him I sent my love."

His eyes were closing. Dr. Everett had said something about sedation. Maybe I should walk him inside before he dozed off. "Philip," I said softly—if he was really asleep that would not wake him. "I thought—before you went away—that you were pissed off at me for not enlisting," I ventured carefully.

"A little," he said in the same half-voice. "But after I got there I wouldn't wish that on anybody I—". His eyes were still closed.

I waited. Anybody I *what?* Liked? Loved?

"I was—pissed off—at you for wanting a percentage of the play," I said. If we were going back to the old relationship, I thought, let's get that one out of the closet too.

"Were you?" He sounded amused. "You didn't say so."

"I know," I said.

"Why didn't you?"

"Because—well, you want to know the truth, Philip?"

He opened his eyes and looked at me from under heavy, drooping lids. "I guess I can take it," he said.

I wanted to say, "Because you mean too much to me." Instead, I said, "Because I figured it didn't matter much one way or the other."

We sat and stared at passing cars for a while, neither of us looking at the other. I thought, Ford and GM will be coming out with new models as soon as Japan throws in the towel. I said, "How about your writing? Got anything brewing?"

"I started a novel a few months ago. But then — things happened — I got busy — Rollo came up missing . . ."

After a minute or two I said, "Did I write you that we liked him very much?"

Philip nodded, looked away.

"He looked like Ralph Forbes. Lulabel thought his voice sounded like Leslie Howard's."

He closed his eyes again. "A little," he said. He was hearing that voice again. I ached to say, "I guessed about you and Rollo. It's all right. I understand. At least you loved another human being once in your life." Instead, I finally said, "What's his wife like?"

"Natalie?" He seemed to be rousing himself from a dream. "Oh, Talie's a nice little English sparrow." He looked at his watch. "Time for lunch," he said, rising. "Got to clamp the chains on again, take the temperature, hit the couch, and compose a few nasty anecdotes about the mater to keep Dr. Everett on his Freudian *pointes*."

For openers, how about sticking to the truth, I thought? But of course he didn't know the truth. Or all of it.

We strolled back toward the hospital. There were so many things I wanted to know. How did he feel, for one, but that's for somebody recovering from the flu or a bad back, not a patient resisting his shrink. Was he planning to come to California when he was released? Did he have any plans at all? But, though he walked beside me, he was nowhere near me. At the entrance he turned stiffly, cleared his throat a couple of times, offered a limp hand, and said, very formally, "Nice to see you again, John. Remember me to Elizabeth and the wee one."

"Amy's not so wee anymore," I said. "She's in the sixth grade."

"Think of that," he said, without thinking of it at all. Then without another word, or without waiting for one from me, he scurried into the hospital and — taking those short, jerky, mincing steps — walked down the endless hall. To what?

His island? His private hell? He had ventured off it for one brief moment. I tried to recall what had sent him scurrying back to it.

"What's his wife like?"

Was that it? Possibly. And what had been his comment? "A nice little English sparrow." An easily forgettable adjunct to that radiant, magnetic, charming creature who looked like Ralph Forbes and sounded like Leslie Howard. A mere codicil.

I did not see Philip again for several years.

32

Esme was in California on one of her periodical jaunts to jolly old clients along, prod them into occasional activity for magazine and book publishers, and hustle one or two budding young talents to compensate for the inevitable attrition in the agency list from death, creeping incompetence, or raids by rivals.

Esme was better looking than ever. Formal streaks of gray at the temples added attic elegance to her inherent style. Esme had combined career, marriage, and motherhood (two boys and two girls) with no accent on liberation. She had always been liberated. It never occurred to her that she might be permitted fewer rights or be subjected to more wrongs than a male in a comparable position.

We had finished dinner and Esme had returned from a table hop — she had seen Charlie Hoffman across the room and had a message for him from one of the *Post* editors — when Liz said, "Now. Tell us about Philip. We haven't heard from him in months. Of course we read his stuff in *World of Women*, but his fiction doesn't tell us much about him."

"Doesn't it?" Esme said. "Think about that."

We "thought about it." Presently I ventured, "Well, he tells most of his stories in the first person — like Maugham — but his first person, unlike Maugham's, is not the author himself. His has no particular identity; he's just the handy storyteller. This narrator has, quite by chance, happened upon an incident or a character that piques his interest so he delves into it, discovers its color, tragedy, resolution, whatever, and sets it down for his reader. What does that tell me?"

"Remember something you said back there," Esme said. *"The narrator has no identity*. And think about something else. Is this anonymous narrator ever actually involved in what happens?"

"No, come to think about it. The *I* seems to remain aloof from it all. He's merely the intelligent observer."

Liz got into the act. "You're right. *I* puts his characters under a microscope. *I* is a little God who dissects but never gets his hands dirty. He's amused by his humans, but never quite understands or forgives them their human antics and frailties."

"Exactly," Esme agreed. "Now I'm not one to say that is not a perfectly good way to tell a story. It can be highly effective — and in Philip's case the writing is literate, and often spellbinding, even when it is without substance. But what disturbs me is, he keeps repeating the pattern, telling *about* what happened rather than what happened, if you know what I mean."

"Can't you talk to him?" I asked.

"I tried once," Esme laughed ruefully, "and found my head rolling in the gutter. Nooo, Philip does not relish criticism from a mere agent. And — unfortunately — he's found a one-hundred-percent fan in the editor of *World of Women*. Jules Bowman loves — and buys at a top figure — anything Philip Pearson chooses to write. Philip is his Maugham, his Galsworthy, and his Edna Ferber rolled into one."

I laughed. "I don't quite understand your use of the word 'unfortunately.'"

"Because," Esme said, "no other women's magazine would publish material like that. It's dry, it does not appeal to the emotions, no one can identify with the characters. Yet it is not quite in the *Harper's* or *Atlantic* mold. So if Jules should die, or lose his job . . ."

"Meanwhile, Philip's making a bloody fortune," Liz said, "and doing it his way. Lucky Philip."

Esme shrugged. "Someday you must see that apartment of his. A residual of Jules Bowman's continuing support. When Philip rented it — and basically it's good space in a new high rise — Jules put his World of Women Academy to work decorating it. All cretonne, chintz, and hooked rugs, with roses rambling up the wallpaper. Imagine Philip, nursing a throbbing hangover, fighting his way through that rose arbor to the modern, stainless steel kitchen for a cup of black coffee and a peanut butter sandwich."

"He's drinking a lot?" Liz said.

Esme made a moue. "No more than usual, maybe. We all used to drink like that in the old days, remember? But we don't anymore, and Philip continues. The older he gets the less well he handles it."

"Does he know it's a problem?"

"Who knows? All I know is, more and more he's holing up in that rose arbor, refusing invitations from old friends like Daniel and me, and occasionally turning out a piece of exquisitely written, old-maidish memorabilia. I cross my fingers and send it over to Jules Bowman — and he buys it."

★   ★   ★

My relationship with Philip was never the same after the war. We actually saw him only two or three times, briefly, when we happened to be in New York to contact editors and catch up on old friends. We were never invited inside the "rose arbor." He would suggest that we meet him at the Drake for a drink, or we would take him to dinner, during which he drank much and talked little. Once, after a particularly trying meal, of which he had eaten almost nothing, he excused himself abruptly, mumbled something about a forgotten appointment, and walked out. Liz remarked that if it were anybody but Philip she would never speak to him again. As it was, she merely said, "Poor Philip."

He never came to California again, though Gerry received, regularly, the money for Doc's keep, until the dog finally had to be put to sleep. Gerry read me the note accompanying the check to pay for Doc's euthanasia: "Many thanks. Doc was the lucky dog."

"What's that supposed to mean?" Gerry wanted to know.

"A lot of things, I guess. Take your choice."

We "kept in touch" when, as we used to say, "stuff happened." We had all picked up and made our own that term from a delightful daytime radio program of the thirties and forties called "Vic and Sade." Just four characters, Vic and Sade, their young son Rush, and Uncle Fletcher, who sometimes came to visit. An ordinary family with no big problems, merely the daily trivia that the writer, with an acute ear for midwestern colloquialisms, made trenchant and touching. Sade kept abreast of the outside world by telephonic reports from a neighbor whom she addressed as Lady. And when Lady reported a death, a marriage, a sprained ankle, a back that went out, or a stew that boiled over, Sade's comment was inevitably "Stuff happens." Which translated as "There's nothing anybody can do about it so, let's get on with living."

When "stuff happened" to us like Christmas and birthdays and a change of address we wrote the appropriate note and Philip sometimes managed a perfectly typed, plain, no-picture postcard response. Once he remembered Amy's birthday with a souvenir necklace from Capri where he was spending two weeks. "No use trying to lie about your age, Amy," he wrote. "I was in attendance. You're seventeen. May I suggest that you stop right where you are? No point in getting older. Ask one who knows. Love from Uncle Philip and the Blue Grotto."

"If I thought I'd stay seventeen all my life I'd kill myself," Amy declared dramatically, staring at the necklace in disgust. "What does he think I am? A child?" Amy was having *man* trouble. Her most recent beau had dropped her for a sophisticated woman, practically a bedridden hag, of nineteen who drove an eggshell blue Thunderbird of her very own and smoked gold-tipped Shepherd's Hotel cigarettes.

I wrote Philip, as well as Joe Tyler, when Maureen died. "After a long illness," the obit read. Which of course meant cancer. Philip never acknowledged the note, nor did I expect him to. Joe did, however, and I was stunned by it. "Thanks so much, John. I thought you ought to know that Maureen loved you as long as she lived. I didn't mind — much. I was lucky to have her all these years." That was a secret I would rather not have known. Stuff happens.

Philip did write when he read of the death of Pat Hughes, who had swallowed too many sleeping pills. Whether it was an accident or suicide nobody ever knew. "There was a time when you were in love with her," Philip's note said. "I'm sorry. What else is there to say?" Stuff happens.

I think it was in 1955 that it occurred to me I had not come across any fiction from Philip in — well, I did not know how long. A year? Two years? The last couple of samples in *World of Women* had seemed plotless and condescending rambles through the subconscious of neurotic and not very interesting females better left undisturbed. Besides, the style seemed — well, derivative. "Philip has been reading too much John Cheever," Liz said. And, another time, "Sally Benson does this sort of thing better." No matter, Jules Bowman had bought and paid for them. But not lately. Or was Philip no longer turning them out?

During this interval a short novel had bubbled up from my own subconscious and I had indulged myself in the luxury of refusing several television assignments to write it. We were in good shape financially, and Liz got herself two or three solo shots of "Leave It to Beaver" to give her a reason to get up in the morning.

My manuscript, when it finally emerged from Malnick's Quick-Type Service (which was prospering; she had a staff of three), was too short for book publication, but, on the long chance, Esme submitted it to Jules Bowman and his *World of Women* as a three-part serial. He, in Hollywood's orthodox term, "flipped." (If a producer likes a project he "flips." If he does not, he "passes.") Esme was on the phone instantly to tell me the news. "Jules is in a Bowman buzz about you and your talent. A writer has never been discovered until *he* discovers him. You may be his new Philip Pearson."

"What's wrong with the old one?"

"Just one too many spinsters with insomnia who relive the past and wonder why Mr. Right passed them by, I suspect. Jules must have finally realized that he had read that one before."

"You haven't told Philip I've sold a piece to Bowman, have you?"

"I thought it the better part of valor not to rub his nose in it."

"Good," I said. "He may miss it when it comes out."

However, he did not. A few days after it was published (with my name in large block letters on the cover) came a card from Philip. There were typos that he had not bothered to correct and a carelessly scrawled signature: "Dear John. Congratulations. Nice storee. Make hay whil yours truely is in the Bowman doghouse. Stuff happens. Long time no see. Love to all, Philip."

I handed the card to Liz. "He's bleeding," she said.

"It happens to all of us," I said. "I'm just sorry about the timing. It makes me sort of one up. Well, thank God he doesn't need dough."

"He needs love," Liz said.

★ ★ ★

A month or so later I sat facing Jules Bowman at a poolside table in the lush gardens of the Bel Air Hotel. He had come to California to pay his respects to a few *World of Women* contributors. "Mostly yourself," he said. "I've been wanting to meet you ever since I read 'Man Without a Home.' Forgive me, I could not reconcile such a powerful, simple, genuine, creative work coming out of—all this." He made a sweeping gesture that embraced all of Southern California and the Channel Islands.

Bowman was a short, middle-aged man with ferretlike features and small black eyes under horn-rimmed glasses that he fixed on you unblinking even when he paused to permit the significance of what he said to sink in. I told him that I had never had trouble writing in the Hollywood milieu, that the widely held legend that Hollywood tarnished a writer was an unjustified cliché. "Oh, I realize that some so-called writers never write for print after exposure. But those who do usually produce work of better quality. The financial security that derives from the movies gives them more time to consider, to rewrite and polish. They don't rip a first draft out of the damn machine and airmail it off to market in order to pay last month's rent."

Bowman shook his head, not in denial but in wonder. "I'm not questioning the how of your miracle," he said. "I am merely grateful."

Miracle. Pretty fancy for my taste. But heady. A writer can absorb a little such praise without blushing. At last, he can say to himself, here is an editor who knows what I'm all about. But I kept wondering how Philip would characterize this man: Pretentious? No class?

"How about another martini?" Bowman said.

"We don't usually drink at lunchtime out here in — all this — " I imitated his former sweeping gesture, "but today? Why not?"

After two martinis, and a bottle of cabernet with lunch, I suddenly heard myself say, "Tell me, Mr. Bowman — "

"Please. It's Jules. My friends call me Julie."

I could make it to Jules, but not to Julie. Maybe after another drink . . . "Tell me, Jules, Philip Pearson has been your exclusive property for years. I haven't seen anything of his for a while. What happened?"

Bowman stiffened. He had dropped his napkin, noticed it now, and took deliberate time to recover it. "You know him?" he asked.

"We were kids together in Montana. He was best man at my wedding. He never came back to California after the war so our contacts have been — minimal lately. But I've been wondering. Is he not writing these days?"

"He may be," Bowman said, "but he's not writing for *me*. I wouldn't touch him."

"From that tone of voice I feel anything further I might have to ask would be none of my business. So let's skip Philip."

"No," Bowman said. "If you're such an old friend you ought to know."

"That may be the very reason I should not know," I said.

I could not stop him. The justification for his vindictive recital would seem to be that I, a normal man with wife and teenage daughter, should be warned about future contact with such a character.

"Understand," he began, "I have nothing against homosexuals. Mrs. B. and I even — "

"If that's all you're going to tell me," I interrupted, "I've known it about Philip for quite a while."

"That is not all," Bowman said. "As I was about to say, Mrs. Bowman and I are very modern and open-minded about such — such deviation. As for Philip Pearson, we neither knew nor cared. We have a penthouse. We — ah — took him up socially for a while." (I could imagine the "social" evenings at the Bowman penthouse, Philip looking at his watch to see how much longer he had to stay.) "He could be a plus for the evening, when he was in the mood. Or, occasionally, a minus. He sometimes drank too much and then retreated to a lone chair in the corner of the room, which might as well have had a keep out sign in front of it."

Well, he went on, that was neither here nor there. The thing was, he, Jules Bowman, thought Philip Pearson possessed an exceptional talent, and he felt privileged to be in a position to nurture it. Sometimes what Pearson wrote was inferior to his best, but whose is not? The best was so good that, as an editor, Bowman could afford to buy the not-so-good in order to keep Philip Pearson an exclusive *World of Women* property.

Until one certain evening. Bowman "and Mrs. B." — I could visualize her buzzing around him — had tickets to a performance of *Long Day's Journey into Night*. He could never understand the excitement about O'Neill. Too long, repetitious. "A real ass-acher, if you'll pardon the expression" was the way Bowman put it. After the show it was just a relief to get out of the theater. It had rained while they had been gassed by the neuroses of the Tyrones and the streets were still wet and shiny, the air "like it had been washed. I remember saying to Mrs. B. let's walk a ways and pump some of this fresh air into our lungs."

They were approaching Times Square when they noticed Philip Pearson leaning against the window of Grey's Drugstore, his head down, his fists jammed into the pockets of his old tweed jacket, which was wet and steaming. They had paused only a few feet from him and Mrs. B. was about to say, "Good evening, Philip, my, isn't this a coincidence," when he took his fists out of his pockets and had a small plastic tube of some sort in one hand. Then he removed the lid from the tube and, with his head lowered, rubbed the obscene red lipstick across his lips, clamped the top on once more, and dropped it into his pocket.

"Mrs. B. and I were absolutely stunned," Bowman went on. "Quite frankly I couldn't move for a few moments, but finally we turned up Broadway. I couldn't resist looking back. A young person — some kind of weirdo, nude to the waist, dangling chains, earrings, painted — had hold of Pearson and was directing him through the traffic of Times Square. That's the last I ever saw of Philip Pearson."

"And good riddance. Is that what you're saying?"

Bowman frowned, coughed. "Well, that's one way of putting it."

"And no more fiction from Philip Pearson, good or bad?"

"Understand, I — well — tolerate homosexuals. I find some of them amusing. Noel Coward? Discreet. Somerset Maugham? Always the perfect gentleman. But when they become openly involved in rough trade . . . Picture this: A solid, respectable slick paper magazine like *World of Women* lies on thousands of the best coffee tables in the best homes in America. A scandal involving one of its principal authors breaks wide open, or is even whispered about. Think about that . . . think about our competition out there in the Bible Belt — and that's where our readership smothers the competition, that's where they swallow our sanctity of the American home image whole. Well, our competitors, the *Journal, Good House, McCall's,* they raid our subscription list and we're left up shit creek. See my point?"

I disliked Jules Bowman heartily but, reluctantly, I had to admit he had a point. It would not be much of a point today when anything short of homicide can be interpreted (and excused) as a mere excess of high spirits, but it was different then.

"You're absolutely sure it was Philip Pearson you saw?"

"We stood not five feet from him. You can't mistake that red hair."

I asked Bowman to excuse me, and went into the men's room to throw up.

33

Liz and I were involved in a project for Dore Schary at MGM. The old czar, Louis B. Mayer, had been unseated and Schary briefly and uneasily enthroned. Schary was a civilized man who did not mind our working at home so long as we were available for occasional meetings with him and his producer at the studio.

Malnick's Quick-Type Service was doing the typing. Gerry would stop by each morning on her way to her office, deliver what had been typed and Xeroxed the day before, and pick up rough copy that Liz and I had composed. Gerry did not do this for all of her clients.

Sometimes she caught us at breakfast. When this happened we asked her to sit down and have a cup of coffee or a piece of toast. She usually said no, she had to hurry. One of the girls was out with the flu, the curse, something. But this morning she settled into a chair. "Just black coffee," she said. "Some of this flab has got to *go*."

We asked her about how the business was going, had so-and-so (a three-thousand-dollar-a-week writer and notorious pinchpenny) ever divvied up what he owed her for that last script (he had not), and — from Liz — "Do you ever hear anything from Philip? I don't think we've heard in a year."

"Funny you should bring up that name," Gerry said. "You must have been reading my mind." (Gerry was into metaphysics and thought-transference those days. They assuaged to a degree her quite understandable hunger for order and meaning, we thought.) She had not known whether to mention this to us or not, it was so — well — *eerie*. But, yes, she had heard. Sort of. Only yesterday. And she did not quite know how to acknowledge *it*. Maybe we could suggest a way. "Anyhoo . . ." She opened her voluminous, shapeless, quilted bag, scrounged through its personal debris, and brought out an envelope. "This thing here. There was no letter, no nothing but a check made out to me for ten dollars." She pulled the check out of the envelope and stared at it. "Philip used to send me ten dollars a month for dog food and any little incidentals Doc might need. But—" Gerry looked up from the check, "poor Doc's been dead for lo these many years."

She handed me the check. It was in Philip's handwriting, his signature, no doubt of that. "Of course I've got to return it," Gerry said, "but what do I say? Thanks but dog food disagrees with me? I can't just say nothing, can I?"

"Either that," Liz nodded. "Or don't send it back at all. Destroy the evidence."

"Liz is right," I said. "Returning it, no matter how tactfully, would only remind him of one more thing he had done while drunk, or in whatever condition, and then he couldn't face you again, even on paper. That would be too bad, because he is fond of you and you're fond of him, and not many people are. If you don't send back the check, he may not remember having written it."

"But if he does remember," Gerry said, still troubled, "and he writes to ask me about it. What then?"

"You never received it. It got lost in the mail," I said. "But he won't. Believe me, he won't. He might conceivably remember, but he would never mention it. It would remain another small shame to be filed—unopened—in his subconscious for some future shrink to dig for."

But where—in time—in place—where were you, Philip, when you wrote and mailed that check to Gerry?

I had to know how he was. I tried the telephone. A recording. "If you will leave your name and number, Mr. Pearson will call you when he returns." I called Esme. She did not know. A week ago he had telephoned her to report that he was going to Bermuda for a few days. He left no address, the name of no hotel. He did not want to be disturbed, he had said. "Philip is a little peeved with me for some reason," Esme said. "You know Philip. He gives no reasons. Reasons are for the common herd."

I told her about the ten-dollar check to Gerry.

"Doesn't surprise me," Esme said. "Drunk, no doubt. Frankly, John, I'm worried about him. Maybe if you were here — if he were there — you're such old friends. You might be able to talk to him and find out what's wrong."

"That will be the day," I said.

It was midnight, three a.m. New York time, when the telephone rang. Liz and I had just turned in. I reached for the phone and mumbled an angry, sleepy "Hello."

There was the tinkle of ice in a glass three thousand miles distant and, after an interval, Philip's slurred voice. "'Scuse the unavoidable delay in service. The line will be repaired as soon as our man gets a drink. Okay?"

"It's Philip," I explained to Liz. "He's plastered."

She sat up and lit a cigarette. This could be a long haul. "Give him my love," she sighed.

Finally Philip's voice said, "I'm here. Knocked over my drink. What'd you say your name was?"

"It's John," I said. "*You* called *me*, remember?"

He began to sing the old Berlin ballad, "Remember the day, the day we met, the something or something, remember?"

"Philip, would you call me back tomorrow when you sober up?"

"Never call anybody when I sober up," he said. "I write when I sober up and then I burn the evidence."

"Do you know what time it is?"

"Le'me look at my watch. For your information when you hear the signal the time will be exactly three-seven and three quarters. *Ping.*"

"And he's trying to be funny," I said to Liz. "Philip, what are you doing up at this time of night?"

"I'm singing. Remember the night, the night . . ."

"Philip, for Christ's sake! If you've got anything to tell me, tell me. Otherwise let us go to sleep."

"That's my friend, my dear friend John," Philip said, aggrieved. "Self, self, self. Never thinks of anybody but self, self, self."

I took a deep breath before continuing. "You're wrong there, Philip. I am thinking of *you*. Is there something wrong besides having too much to drink?"

"I'm glad you asked that," he said. "Yes, smart ass. There must be something wrong or I wouldn't have a low-grade temperature all the time. If it was high-grade I could hold my head up, but low grade is shy-making, so don't go spreading it around."

"Have you seen a doctor?"

"Certainly not. What do *they* know? And after we'd learned to care a lot—"

"Listen to me, Philip. I want you to call a doctor first thing in the morning."

"What for?"

"For—for *me*," I pleaded. "Then call me and tell me what he says. I—I care a lot about you, Philip."

He picked up on that with the maudlin final couplet: "You promised that you'd forget me not—and you forgot to re-memberrr."

He lapsed into silence again. I could hear what sounded like sniffles interspersed with hiccups. "Philip? Are you there? Do you hear me?"

Another sniffle, then what could have been a sob.

"Do what I tell you," I shouted, hoping to break through to him. "See a doctor tomorrow morning, then call me!"

The line went dead.

"It's bad, isn't it?" Liz asked.

"If I'm not mistaken," I told her after a moment, "that was a cry for help. But why to me?"

"Don't you know? When you're in trouble you reach for someone you love. And Philip loves you. He's always been in love with you. I spotted it the first time I ever saw you two boys together, the first time he looked at me and saw me as a threat."

"He never made a pass at me."

"Of course not. If he had he'd have lost you."

"I must have been stupid," I said.

"Or just such an unmitigated hetero that you couldn't read the stop and go signs."

"If it's true . . . what can I do now?"

"Take a couple of days — fly to New York," Liz said. "That's the least you can do."

★ ★ ★

When I got to New York I asked Esme's advice. She had seen Philip about a year ago and talked to him on the phone once after he had mailed in a muddled piece of work, a rehash about a maid of honor who stood by and watched her love marry her best friend.

"Don't call him," Esme said. "In the first place he's not answering the phone these days. And if by chance he does, he'll tell you he's about to go out, or he's working and doesn't want to be disturbed. Simply go over there and surprise him. There's no doorman, just go up to apartment 10J and ring the bell. He can't refuse to let you in."

"I feel I ought to take him something, but —"

"No booze, of course," Esme said. "This sounds silly, but — how about a barbecued chicken?"

"You're kidding," I said. "How does it look, he opens the door and there I stand and say, 'Hello, Philip, here's a nice barbecued chicken for your lunch.'"

I laughed but Esme did not. "He's not eating right. The last time I sneaked a look in his fridge there was nothing in it but vodka, two boiled eggs, and a jar of peanut butter."

"How about some Nova Scotia salmon? That's vitamins."

"Ah," Esme said. "He could accept that without losing face. But get there before noon, before he's even sniffed the cork. He's in that state where one drink and the fog moves in."

I stood outside 10J with my slab of Nova Scotia salmon neatly wrapped in oiled paper under my arm, and waited. I had thought of what to say: "Here's a little something from Liz. She always gives presents *she* likes, the hell with whether *you* like it or not." I poked the button again and could hear its chimes clang through the door. And waited. There was a one-way viewer with a magnifier in the door. I faced it so that Philip could see me if he looked out. Perhaps he was not in. Or possibly I'd made a mistake and this was not his apartment.

I finally ran down the building superintendent in the basement. He was quite deaf, but when I finally got through to him he said that 10J was the right apartment and so far as he knew Pearson was up there, all right. He probably just didn't choose to come to the door. "Management's trying to cancel his lease. There've been complaints from some of his neighbors on the tenth floor about a few of his late-night visitors. I've caught a glimpse of one or two of 'em myself. Weirdos." He gave me a look. "You a friend of his?"

"Of more than forty years . . ."

"What'd you say?"

"I've known him for more than forty years. We grew up together."

The man shook his head. "He was okay when he first come here. Wish I could help you, but if a man won't open his door . . ."

I went back up to the tenth floor and leaned on the button of 10J for a long time. Finally I thought I heard movement inside. Was Philip peering at me through the peephole? I thrust my face up close to it and said urgently, "Philip, it's John. Open the door."

Then I heard keys, two of them turning two locks, and finally the door opened a crack. I still waited because a chain held the opening to no more than three inches. "Philip," I said, "I can't come in unless you take that damn chain off."

The chain fell away at last and the door opened perhaps a foot, barely wide enough for me to sidle through with my ridiculous package of salmon. We faced each other. At first blush (and I use the word in its literal sense because I was blushing in embarrassment at having had to flush him out, and his face and nose were red, perhaps from fever or, more likely, the permanent blush of alcohol) we simply stared at each other like mutes bereft of sign language.

He looked *haunted*. He must have lost twenty pounds since last I had seen him. He wore rumpled striped pajamas and a raveling blue silk robe. I had apparently roused him from sleep; a sleep-shade was caught up in his unruly bush of hair beginning to gray. What to say? How's this for an opening: "You look great! Here's a little nothing from Liz." I put the package of salmon in my left hand and reached for his with my right. It was warm and dry. I could feel the bones.

Finally Philip spoke, angrily it sounded. "Why didn't you call me first?"

Well, why not come clean? "Because you called me."

He looked bewildered. "When?"

"Night before last. You said you were running a temperature. I think you still are. Go back to bed. We can talk in there for a little while."

"No," he said, turning uneasily toward the door that must lead into his bedroom. "The maid hasn't been here yet. It's a mess. Let's sit here where — " he glanced about the room and his voice assumed the intonation of the very young Katharine Hepburn, "where the roses are in bloom again."

I smiled. Here was at least a shadow of Philip. Now I could offer the vitamins. "The salmon happened to be running on east Sixty-fourth Street, so I bagged one. Better put it in the fridge."

He took the package and moved haltingly toward the kitchen, then turned back. "We need a little vodka to celebrate the reunion of the class of twenty-one, don't we?"

"Philip," I said reprovingly, "remember our old house rule on East Forty-fourth Street? The sun over the yardarm?"

He disappeared into the kitchen and was gone long enough to down a straight shot of vodka. When he came back he was more relaxed, less tentative. "Thanks for the salmon. I used to like it."

"Eat it all yourself," I said. "It's too good for the hoi polloi."

This was the moment to let him know why I had come, the moment to tell him how concerned I was about his health, physical and mental, but I would have to do it his way. Obliquely. He sat down and lit a cigarette. The effort to strike the match and bring the flame to the tip of the cigarette was embarrassing to watch. I looked at the ashtray beside him. It was a mound of stinking butts, the walnut tabletop beneath it scorched.

"Philip, have you seen the doctor?"

He looked up with crafty innocence. "No, I never noticed one. Where is he?"

"You promised me you would see a doctor," I said.

"Well, that was stupid of me. I wouldn't let a doctor see me like this. Got to shine my shoes, put on some weight, get a haircut." He touched his hair, discovered the sleep-shade, and took it off. "Ever try one of these? Turns day into night."

"You look as if you'd been doing just the opposite."

He was having none of that and changed the subject abruptly. Where was Elizabeth, how was Amy? I told him that Elizabeth was at home in California. Amy was fine, taking a law degree, and in love as usual. They both sent him love, and so did Gerry Malnick.

"Good old Ger," he sighed. "A friend in need is a friend . . . who said that?"

I shook my head. "Probably Anon or Ibid, I forget which."

He smiled for the first time. "You know," he said, as if it were surprising, "I'm glad to see you, John."

"I'm relieved. I thought for a while that I'd flown three thousand miles for a close-up of your door."

He squinted, trying to hold me in focus. "You don't change. Why is that?"

"No exercise, except I type fast. Not much sleep, a moderate amount of alcohol, worry over the next job or story, wondering what Amy is doing when she doesn't get home until three a.m."

Philip shook his head ruefully. Or was it enviously? "All so fucking normal. Responsibilities — mortgages — "

"Only one. Six percent."

"Wife — children. And all because Eve slept with Adam. She conceived and brought forth the fruit of her womb, which is Amy who will live long after you're dead and continue to bring forth . . ." He was not trying to be funny, I realized. This was, for his present condition, heavy stuff. I decided to play along.

"That's what I always thought was meant by God. Continuity. We're briefly passing through, links in a chain without any meaning, beginning or end."

He was staring at the smoke rising from his cigarette. "And suppose somebody chooses to break the chain—right here. Is that a sin?"

"The only sin so far as I'm concerned," I said, "is to hurt somebody else willfully." He did not comment. I pushed it, made it personal. "You've never hurt anybody else, Philip."

"I don't know, I don't know." He crushed out his cigarette. "I tell myself that. I say I believe that, and then . . ."

"Don't you ever go to confession anymore?"

"How're you getting along with Jules Bowman?" he asked with only a beat after my question.

"Our honeymoon is over. I can't stand the son of a bitch. Did you know that he and Mrs. B. 'took you up socially'?"

"Did he actually say that?"

"Scout's honor."

"I've often wondered why he dropped me."

"You probably spilled ashes on his Aubusson."

"Ah, well." Philip got to his feet, stood for a moment getting his balance. "Sure you won't have a drink? Sun must be over that yardarm by now."

"Oh, all right," I said. "A small one. Just to get me to Kennedy."

What difference? Philip was not going to stop drinking today, probably never. I followed him into the kitchen where the roaches panicked at our approach. The sink was stacked with dirty dishes. The refrigerator, when he opened it for ice, was empty except for a half-gallon of vodka, a half-loaf of bread, a stick of margarine, a jar of peanut butter, and my package of salmon. He finally scrounged a pair of clean glasses. "I take mine on the rocks," he said. "Okay with you? I forget."

"Fine," I said. We returned to the rose arbor and settled down with our drinks. Philip took a deep swig, shuddered, then sighed and sank back into the sofa. "Did I tell you," he said quietly, "that I'm glad to see you?"

"I'm glad to see you too. Something's been missing from my life. I guess it's you, Philip."

"I haven't seen anybody I give a damn about for God knows when."

"Why, Philip?"

"Why would anybody want to see me?"

He was slipping into alcoholic self-pity. "Look," I said, "I've had a thought." I told him how three years ago Liz and I had gone back to Cottonwood. "Do you want to hear about it?"

He nodded. I told him how it was almost the same as it had been when we left. I told him about Miss Main at the library and how she had bound our fiction in vellum, how he and I were sort of celebrities in Cottonwood — we were the boys who got away and they read stuff we had written while they plugged along. I told him Miss Main hoped one day he would come home for a visit.

"Why don't you and I go back together and show off a little? They'll give us a party and we can make awful speeches." I laughed. "Maybe this spring before it gets too hot. We could meet in Billings — there's no airline into Cottonwood, thank God. We'd rent a car and drive — home. How about it?"

I could tell that the concept was appealing and flattering to his ego. "Celebrity," he mused. "Just a fraud."

"Not all that much of a fraud. Who else in Cottonwood has been in the *Post* and all those other slicks?"

"Oh, we're slickers all right."

"Who else in Cottonwood has written for the movies? They think it's pretty marvelous, no matter how we feel about it."

He was smiling again. "Miss Main . . . the old gorgon of the Carnegie Library. How about that? We're on the shelves. The collected works of Philip Pearson and John Whatshisname."

"Ewing is the name."

"Never was very good at names."

"The high school is just the way it was too. The cottonwoods are a little taller, but so are we. The old Pearson house needed a coat of paint, but — "

"The old Pearson face could do with one too," Philip said. His hand rubbed the pink stubble on his chin.

"Think about it," I said. "It would do you good."

"Ho ho. You think I could do with a spot of being done good."

"A lot better than vodka, take my word."

"Where do you come by it?"

"I'm offering you a fifth. Say you'll take it."

He looked at me, still trying for the focus that kept eluding him. "You tried," he said. "Don't anybody say you didn't try."

"So build yourself up. Eat. Force yourself. Start with that salmon. Then go out and get yourself a good square meal. You'll need strength for that five-thousand-foot altitude."

"Just the two of us," he mused.

"Just the two of us," I repeated.

"John and Philip — the way it was. Nobody else."

"Nobody else," I assured him.

"We'll come in last — together."

"Ewing and Pearson — in a dead heat."

" 'At's a way."

I got him to his feet and put him to bed where he passed out immediately. There was still a half-smile on his face.

★   ★   ★

Two days after I got home to my normal family Philip choked to death on a piece of tough round steak in a short-order joint on Second Avenue. Had he been forcing himself to eat and build up strength for the homecoming that could never have been?

Who would ever know? Or care very much. Except me.

CODICIL

I mourned for Philip and grieved at last for the boy he had been and the man he never was, for the bright young promise blackened by early frost, the ignominy of impotence, the redundance of dismal days, and the doldrums of sleepless nights ravaged by shame. Esme said, "If only Philip had gone back to the church and accepted absolution . . ." But that he could not do, much as his spirit may have yearned for it. His mind recoiled at the prospect of some foggy stranger in a black cassock listening behind a dusty screen while he mumbled a recital of his illicit, gnawing hungers and the manner in which he had satisfied them, then ordering him to say fifty Hail Marys and twenty-five Our Fathers and "Go and sin no more, my son. You are forgiven." Philip had once said to me, "I don't need the cross for a crutch," but he had no other. His intellect, in persevering, had starved his spirit.

Yet he left all his money, and it was considerable for a writer, to the church. ("An anchor to windward, just in case," Liz commented sadly.)

* * *

I thought that was the end of Philip Pearson. It was not.

Liz and I had postponed a trip to Europe for various reasons: a writing assignment in the offing, Lulabel growing feeble and absentminded — she might burn the house down with a cigarette butt that she had neglected to rub out, or Amy needing help through an emotional spasm with some young man who wanted to marry her or did not, either of which was a crisis equally distressing to her at the moment.

But finally, in the spring of 1959, these impediments were lifted. Lulabel was peacefully released from the confusion that had nagged her last couple of years, and Amy had finally accepted, with enthusiasm, one of the young men, a reporter on the *San Francisco Chronicle,* who wanted to marry her. And, wonder of wonders, the script in our offing this time was one to be written for Korda in London. Transportation and all living expenses paid.

There was one minor problem: what to do about Killer. Killer was a timid, lamb-faced Bedlington terrier who had appeared, trembling with fear and hunger, on our doorstep three years before. We had coaxed him inside and fed him, then advertised in lost and found. Nobody claimed him, and it was not too difficult to understand why. He was a howling neurotic who fainted when the door bell rang, cowered before cats, and obviously thought infants were devils, for he hid under the sofa when Amy brought hers, a boy of three months, for his first visit. *Killer* seemed the only possible misnomer for him. He would never survive three months in a kennel.

"I suppose we could ask Gerry to keep him," Liz offered tentatively.

"I couldn't do that," I said.

We did not need to. A week before we were scheduled to leave Gerry came to tell us good-bye. She confessed that it was her birthday. Her fifty-fifth. I broke out a bottle of champagne. Liz and I toasted her. "To my oldest friend," I said. Tears came to her eyes.

"I suppose I am—now," she said, and then, under her breath, "I can never thank you—"

"Hush, Gerry. Old friends don't thank each other."

"—and an absent friend," she went on. "Where would I be — or would I *be* at all—without you and him?" We lifted our glasses and drank to him, and then could think of nothing to say for a moment or two. Killer lay at Gerry's feet. She noticed him for the first time. "What are you going to do with this vicious brute while you're gone?" she said, managing a laugh to break the moment.

"Well . . ." I said.

"Okay," Gerry said. "I know when I'm elected. I've done it once, I can do it again. But you two promise to come back, you hear?"

★ ★ ★

We had been at the studio for a couple of weeks when, one afternoon, we heard a knock on the door of the empty outer office. Liz and I had told Korda that we did not need a secretary, indeed did not want one, until we had something for her to do. Nobody in London knew us so we would be receiving no calls, and random notes we could type ourselves. When you collaborate on a script you are inclined to think out loud, and a third presence is inhibiting. You don't want anybody else to hear you say things like "How do you think it would be if . . ."

"Come on in," I called.

The inner office was a dark and dismal cubicle that looked out on the backs of some art director's Babylon. I sat at the typewriter and Liz sprawled on the sofa. It had been an unproductive day. She wore rumpled slacks, her shoes were off, and her feet propped on the coffee table. At sight of our visitor she swung her feet to the floor and reached for a lipstick, a normal feminine reaction, I daresay, to the sight of another, a chic, and somewhat younger, woman.

"Oh, please," the woman said, throwing up her hands, "I mustn't interrupt you. I'll come back another time."

"No, no, no. It's quite all right," I said. "You're interrupting nothing."

I don't know how old she was. Late thirties? Early forties? When you are young that seems middle-aged, when you are past fifty barely the end of adolescence. She was tall, striking-looking rather than beautiful, with that reddish-gold hair and clear, fair skin that women of the British Isles specialize in. ("To torment their American cousins with," Liz said once, grinding her teeth.)

"I heard on the studio grapevine that you two were here," she said. "I'm doing a job for Alex too. Costumes for *Judith Priest,* and I told him I wanted to meet you."

"How nice of you," Liz said, finishing her lips.

"No, not at all," the woman said. "I've been wanting to for a long while. I'm Natalie Woodward."

The name was obviously expected to ring a bell but for the moment it did not, not until she added, "Mrs. Rollo Woodward. My husband met you in California. You were very nice to him."

"It was not at all difficult to be nice to him. Captain Woodward was a charming man," Liz had the grace to say.

"Yes, he was," his widow said. "Indeed he was."

I was tongue-tied. That scene on the lawn at Walter Reed kept flashing before me. And what was it that Philip had replied when I asked him about Rollo's wife? "Oh, Talie's a nice little English sparrow." Why? What possessed him to minimize her that way? Had he been jealous? This woman was quite as charming as her husband had been, and seemed far more substantial, less a flash act.

Meanwhile Liz and Natalie had already progressed to a discussion of Philip. Natalie was saying, "We enjoyed him those months he was with us . . . such a lonely, secret man. But he could be delightful. He often spoke of you, Mr. Ewing. You'd known each other so long, he said. You were like brothers."

"Did Philip actually say that?" I asked.

She frowned. "Did he? I don't know, but he implied it."

"Did he keep in touch with you after he returned to the States?"

"There were a few letters. And I read a number of his stories when they were picked up by English magazines." She changed the subject. "Now see here. We have so much to talk about. Come to dinner one night soon, won't you?"

"We'd love to," Liz said.

"It will have to be a Saturday, so I can be on tap to whip up something edible." She laughed. "I do have a French au pair girl, but she has proved once and for all that not all French women are good cooks. And I hope I can prove to you that not every English woman is an abominable one."

"We could go out," I suggested.

"That's a cowardly attitude," Natalie said. "Besides, I'd like you to see my little digs. Meet Frank, too. Shall we say next Saturday? Sevenish? Here's the address . . . and telephone number in case you get cold feet."

Natalie's "little digs" were on Maida Avenue out toward Hampstead. "That's the street with the canal," our taxi driver informed us. And sure enough, when he turned left off the Edgeware Road the street was not only lined on both sides with trees, but sliced neatly down the middle by a canal. Fat, sightseeing barges glided sedately through the dappled, Monet shadows. Though it was seven when we arrived, the sun still rode high in the northwest. In July it would not be dark before eleven.

Frank, we had concluded, must be Natalie's beau. This being 1959 and London, she was probably living with him and making no bones about it, but the card over the call button read "Mrs. Rollo Woodward." In that event, Liz whispered, *he* would be living with *her*. Whatever their sexual arrangement, we hoped he would be one of us. When only four are locked in for an evening, one misfit can throw it all out of gear.

The buzzer unlatched the door and we opened it onto a rather steep, winding, and carpeted stairwell lined with photographs. At the first landing — the stairs proceeded to another floor — wearing a simple pale blue housecoat, stood Natalie, calling, "Up one flight. Living room's on the first floor." That was our initiation into the British code of numbering: the first floor is the ground floor, the second consequently the first. It made sense after you got used to it.

Natalie was an easy hostess, letting the conversation take its course when it would, prompting it gently when it faltered. The au pair girl had mastered the making and serving of drinks in fractured English, and the apartment, though the rooms were tiny, was light, with tall windows overlooking an enchanting garden, blazing with flowers at the back. ("One good thing about too much rain," Natalie said. "Everything burgeons.") The furnishings were comfortable, shouting neither "antique" nor high-polish new. There was a small Baldwin upright with a book of Czerny exercises on its rack.

"Do you play?" I asked.

"Oh, I used to hack it a little," Natalie said. "Frank's taking lessons. He's quite — exceptional. At least *I* think."

She wanted to know all about us, how we were getting along with Alex Korda, was London a disappointment, so much had been destroyed or damaged and still needed repair, what had we seen and still ought to see, had we been to Cambridge, we *must* go to Cambridge if for nothing but King's College Chapel! Had we found the Britishers cold and distant as some Americans claimed they were — the answer to that was a resounding no — had we been to the Ivy, it was London's answer to Sardi's only with an English cast, driven out to the Cotswolds, seen Stourhead (pronounced for no reason Starhead), and now what could she do to help make our stay more attractive? "After," she laughed, getting to her feet, "after I prod the roast. If you two can possibly think of something to say to each other for a minute or two."

"That has never been our problem," Liz said.

"May I say I envy you?" Natalie sighed, as if she meant it, and disappeared into the kitchen.

"That does not sound like a recommendation for this elusive Frank character," Liz whispered.

"Maybe he only comes by occasionally to practice his five-finger exercises," I said.

"That's a cheap crack," Liz said.

Footsteps clattering pell-mell down the stairs interrupted this silly private interchange. We heard his voice before we saw him. It was a young voice calling, "Mum, what did you do with my tickets?" And then he stood there in the doorway, eyes anticipating the sight of his mother and seeing two strangers instead. He stopped on a dime. "Oh. Terribly sorry," he apologized. "I forgot Mum was having guests."

The boy must have been fourteen or fifteen years old. He had blue eyes and wiry red hair, beetling blond brows, and full lips that seemed to be set in a perpetual pout. He bobbed his head nervously, unable to think of what to say or do next. He cleared his voice a couple of times. He was Philip to an eyelash, to a cowlick and an adolescent pimple or two, to the mannerism of clearing his throat, Philip as I had first known him forty-five years ago in Cottonwood, Montana, but Philip calling his mother Mum and affecting an absurd English accent. The hair rose on the back of my neck.

"We're Liz and John Ewing," Liz said pleasantly enough. She could speak. She had not known Philip at fourteen. She was not seeing a ghost.

"They're right there on your bed table where I told you I'd leave them," Natalie said, returning from the kitchen. "Oh, this is my son, Frank," she said. "Frank, Mr. and Mrs. Ewing. They're from California."

The boy came forward on short, stiff steps, bobbed to Liz and then offered me his hand. It was cold, a little damp, but he had a firm grip. The hair on the back of my neck began to settle once more.

"Are you all right, John?" Natalie was staring at me with some concern. So was Liz.

"I'm — all right." I managed to find my voice.

"Are you sure?" Liz said.

"Natalie, I didn't know you had a son," I said. "My surprise must have shown."

"But I thought you knew." Natalie seemed genuinely perplexed.

How could I have known, I wondered? I said, "When you mentioned 'Frank,' I thought — we thought — "

"Oh, I see. That he was a beau or something interesting. Well, I should have explained." She turned to the boy who was obviously in a hurry to be off. "We'll excuse you. I managed to come up with a couple of tickets for Judy's concert at the Palladium tonight. Frank's got to pick up whatever her name is — "

"You know what her name is," Frank said. "Christine."

" — way over in Kensington, and they'll be late unless he hurries."

"You're from California," Frank said, suddenly not in such a hurry. "You wouldn't know Judy Garland, would you?"

"Not very well," Liz said, "but we've met her. She always sings at parties. I would too if I could sing like that."

"Oh, I say!" Frank said, suddenly all dimpled charm. "You couldn't wangle me an autographed picture, could you?"

"Frank!" Natalie was shaking her head.

"I was only putting out feelers," the boy said impishly, and turned back to Liz. "You see, Mrs. Ewing, I'm making a collection. I've got Vivien Leigh — Mum knows her — and Joyce Grenfell and Noel Coward — he was a friend of my father — and — "

"And Judy will be over the rainbow without you and Christine unless you get a move on," Natalie laughed.

"I'll try for Judy when we get home," Liz said.

"Oh, that would be wizard! Thanks awfully!" He hurried out, then turned and called from the stairs, "Perhaps you'll still be here when I come home?" He wanted us to be. We were *in*. Liz and I had met Judy Garland.

The boy had Joyce Grenfell, Vivien Leigh, and Noel Coward hanging on his wall. The father had had Nazimova, Lillian Gish, May Allison. And the cross.

★　★　★

Dinner, a very good one incidentally — French, no soggy Yorkshire pudding, no bubble and squeak — was finished. We had got through it a little self-consciously, indulging in small, exceedingly small, talk. About the studio and the Korda brothers, about how Natalie broke into costume design, the London theater, an anecdote or two about our daughter Amy and our grandson, and how Rollo had charmed us on his visit to California during the war. (We skirted mention of his deserting us after dinner that evening at Romanoff's.) I suspect that each one of us had found the word *Philip* on his lips several times, and suppressed it. I know I did. The au pair girl was in and out, serving and taking away. If that subject were to be mentioned, it would not bear interruption. And, of course, Natalie herself would have to introduce it. We would not pry.

Now we sat once more in Natalie's living room, dawdling over coffee. It must have been near nine-thirty. Traffic on the Edgeware Road had quieted to a distant drone, and the sightseeing barges on the canal had tied up for the night.

"Does anyone want a lamp?" Natalie asked, in a voice that seemed to hope nobody did.

Liz shook her head. I said I thought this was the best hour of the day in London. We had no such twilight in California. A sense of time suspended. The air, barely moving, cool and redolent. An occasional male voice, the tinkle of a woman's laughter almost palpable in the gloom, drifting through the open windows. Once in a while light from a passing automobile swept across the room; briefly we could glimpse one another's faces. For some reason that exquisite, poignant melody of Puccini's counterpointing Butterfly's patient wait for Pinkerton ran through my head.

"We used to begin to hold our breath along about this time of evening," Natalie said presently. "In an hour or so it would be dark enough for the Luftwaffe. Will they come over tonight, we'd think to ourselves, never saying it aloud, of course, and if they do shall we pack up and go to the shelter or stay and dare them to hit us? If Rollo was at home he'd say, 'Who's afraid of the big bad bombers!' and we'd stay. If it was just me, or Philip and me, well, we'd usually traipse off to the shelter at the sound of the sirens. Not run, though. Nobody ran after a while. Just walk as if — as if you were out for a stroll with your beau . . . funny . . ."

There. Natalie had dropped the name.

"Were you in this flat during the war?" Liz asked.

"Oh, no. Nothing half so fancy. We had a little three-roomer in Lambeth. I thought Philip described it pretty well in the episode about Miss Fatheringale. We actually saw that nude couple staggering down Lambeth Road, you know. No, this whole building belonged to Rollo's parents at that time. It escaped damage, as you see."

She paused and got to her feet. "How about a brandy — a B and B?"

"B and B," both Liz and I said.

Natalie poured drinks into snifters for Liz and me, and brought them to us before returning to the small, portable bar for her own. Light from a passing car caught her doubling the amount in her own glass. She lifted it. "To our friend, Philip," she said.

We drank. She set down her glass, lighted a cigarette, and commenced to move aimlessly about the room. Finally she said, "I thought of course that he would be compelled to tell somebody, and that, naturally, you would be that somebody, John. I thought he would be — well, where was his male vanity, his machismo? He had sired a son, by God! Oh, a man like Philip wouldn't be passing around cigars, that would not be in good taste under the circumstances. But how could any man keep such a thing to himself all the rest of his life?"

"He knew about Frank, then?" I said.

"Of course. I wrote him. I sent him baby pictures."

"What was his comment?"

" 'He sort of looks like a Pearson.' That was in the last letter he ever wrote me. Just, well, he sort of looks like a Pearson. That was all. As if maybe the child wasn't his, as if perhaps I'd sue him for child support if he admitted to fathering it."

She stood silhouetted at the window, angrily blowing smoke into the twilight deepening to night outside. Presently I said, "Natalie, forgive me, but I assumed Philip and Rollo were — "

"Lovers?" She turned away from the window. "But of course they were. I don't think it meant much to Rollo — nothing meant very much to Rollo except his own image at the moment — but — the earth moved right out from under Philip." She returned to her chair, picked up her glass, and downed what was left in it.

Liz said, "It's none of my business, but you're a nice gal. I don't understand your part in this — well — Coward wrote something about a design for living."

"I must be drunk," Natalie said. "Or I'd better be. It's the only excuse for dredging all this up. You wonder why I married a man like Rollo? I married him because I was in love with him. Madly, isn't that the word? Oh, and I knew about him too, at least I knew his reputation. But we had been friends since we were kids. My parents were dead by then and I was having rough sledding getting started in design. The war came along, Rollo enlisted in the RAF right out of Cambridge — I suspect he could not resist those uniforms. He took me to dinner one night — God, he was beautiful — we both got a little tight and began to dilate on the evanescence of life, the intimations of our own mortality, and what the hell did it all mean anyhow? — Rollo was giving his Hamlet performance that night — and he grew maudlin in an ever so nice way, and said he was worried about me. How was I to live without a job, without someone to watch over me, from the song of the same name? And finally the solution flashed to him. Why didn't he marry me? Not, you notice, why didn't I marry him? I could live in his flat rent free, and if anything happened to him I would inherit his lares and penates as well as the Wood-ward property after his parents died. *This* house.

"What I would inherit, how I would live during the war did not mean a damn to me. What mattered was, Rollo had offered to marry me. Yes, I had heard about the boys in his life. But that's pretty much par for the course in England today. Homo — hetero — bi — nobody turns a hair unless the royal family or the Archbishop of Canterbury is involved. But I was naive. I said, just one thing I had to know. He had never said he loved me. Did he?

"He laughed and kissed me on the nose and said of course he loved me. He had always loved me, didn't I know that, silly? At that moment he probably thought he did, who knows? So I said yes, and married him before he could change his mind. I loved him so much there would be no need for boys, if there ever had been any.

"It was a little like marrying Peter Pan. Oh, we slept together a few times, but sex with Rollo was a formality to be observed on special occasions, as neatly and briefly as possible. I always rather expected him to say, when it was over, 'There, that's enough.' And off he'd fly to the lost boys.

"It seems to me, looking back," Natalie mused after a pause, "that Rollo — straight from the start — somehow regarded himself and everybody he touched as fictional characters whom he could alter, manipulate, or dispense with at will. One never quite knew who he was going to be at any given moment. Talk about infinite variety! That was one of his fascinations. He kept reinventing an image, and forever polishing a new legend, though I think he never got one quite dazzling enough to please himself. Once he said, laughing, 'If the Nazis shoot me down, I hope it's spectacular. You'll see that my name gets in the *Times,* won't you?' I did, but the size of the item would have disappointed him.

"There is an incongruous arrogance about people like Rollo. They demand reverence at their own valuation. And often — I never understood why — they receive it. If they don't then the hell with you! They'll get it from somebody else.

"He got it from me. He got it from Philip Pearson. I believe he was everything that Philip would like to have been. Superficially, at any rate. Handsome to the point of beauty, witty, charming, magnetic, roistering, the focus of any party. But — he just happened to be another thing: a homosexual. A homosexual who instantly recognized and responded to another. I've always thought that Philip did not know *he* was one — or at least had never admitted it to himself — until I brought him home with me that night after the air raid.

"I didn't know either. I thought Philip would be — safe, not another competitor for me. He had seemed to me — well — nonsexual. And a lot older than Rollo. Rolly usually liked them young. But I was wrong about Philip, and underestimated Rollo. He had never seduced an American officer, nor anyone with a mind, for that matter. I suppose that was a mountain to be climbed because it was there. So it began. I stood by and watched and waited as I had done before. The boys had come and gone, and Rolly had returned to his Cynara in his fashion. He was easily bored.

"Then, of course, he was — presumed lost. When they were presumed lost, they were dead. I knew it. Philip knew it. We sat around the flat together that evening after we had the news, and got drunk together. We both loved Rollo, but I had loved him longer. I could not cry. Philip's behavior was — well — have you ever seen subjects under sodium pentothal respond to the command of a doctor? Nothing happens on the face. They move like zombies.

"After a while I passed myself out and went to bed. In the middle of the night I came to and realized that Philip was in bed with me. He was crying. I put my arms around him . . . well . . . that's when it happened. The only time. I'm not proud.

I'm not ashamed. There it is. And Frank is a marvelous boy. IQ way up there. Astronomical. You should see some of the papers he's writing these days. I hold my breath, but maybe he's got the talent without the demons."

We sat in silence for a long, long moment.

"Say something," Natalie said.

"What's to say but—poor Philip," I said, fighting back the tears. "Stuff happens."

Liz went to Natalie and put her arms around her. I said, "Will you ever tell the boy?"

"I don't think so," Natalie said. "I suspect it would throw him." And then she imitated Frank's eager, adolescent voice, charged with pride. " 'My dad was a hero in World War II. He was shot down over Cologne.' No, I think it's better he should be a Woodward than a Pearson."

"I think so too," I agreed, finally. I did not bother to tell her that Philip was not a Pearson either. For the moment I could not remember the name of Philip's biological father. Then it came to me.

Everett Fowler . . .